A DESPERATE HUNT . . .
for a vanished man. A deadly odyssey across
thousands of miles into a strange and terrify-
ing world.

A BEAUTIFUL AMERICAN . . .
abandoned by her government in a land of an-
cient splendor and agonizing death.

A DESERTED LOVER . . .
trapped in the malevolent claws of global in-
trigue. A web of conspiracy and danger from
which there is no escape.

RED MESSAGE

"PETER ABRAHAMS HAS THE TOUCH!"
—John Saul

RED MESSAGE

PETER ABRAHAMS

AVON
PUBLISHERS OF BARD, CAMELOT, DISCUS AND FLARE BOOKS

AVON BOOKS
A division of
The Hearst Corporation
1790 Broadway
New York, New York 10019

For Jeff

I've followed the official pinyin system for rendering Chinese, except in the case of some proper nouns which may be more familiar to the reader in Wade-Giles transliteration.

Many thanks to Kelly Haggart in Beijing, Lynne Lindley in Falmouth, and X. T.-Xu in Wuxi.

To right a wrong it is necessary to exceed
the proper limits, and the wrong cannot be righted
without the proper limits being exceeded.
                    —Mao Zedong (Mao Tse-tung)

An' the dawn comes up like thunder
outer China 'crost the Bay!
                    —Rudyard Kipling

Prologue

The baby always woke up early. That was what saved his life, the morning the Green Snake men came.

The nurse felt the baby stir beside her. She sat up. He was lying on his back. In the gray, predawn light, she could not see his features very well: just his big, dark eyes, watching her. He was a beautiful baby; the nurse told her friends no baby had eyes like his.

"Good morning, little mouse," the nurse said. He batted the air with his fists. She picked him up and went outside the yellow house, walking toward the lake.

Wisps of fog hung over the water, and wrapped themselves around the plum trees like rumpled blankets. The nurse followed the gravel path around the orchard, crossed the arched footbridge over the little stream, and came to the red pavilion. It stood on a spit of land jutting into the lake, and it was there the nurse liked to give the baby his morning feeding. As she opened the door, she felt the earth shudder under her feet, and the next moment heard thunder in the north. The fighting went on.

Inside the pavilion, the nurse sat on a bench and put the baby to her breast. His lips fumbled frantically for her nipple, found it, sucked hard. There was a moment of pain; then it was gone. The nurse looked out at the water. The fog was slipping away from the shore, retreating to the middle of the lake. Her eyes closed. She dreamed about her mother.

Someone ran by, waking her with a start. The baby started too, and lost her breast. He made a little cry. "Shh," she said, offering him her nipple. Outside there were more footsteps.

Crouching, the nurse went to the latticed parapet, knelt, and peered over the edge.

She saw men running toward the Master's house; how many, she didn't know. She had never learned to count past ten. There were more than ten. They all had guns.

The men stopped in front of the house. One of them tried the door. The nurse knew he was their leader because he was the biggest, and the only one wearing shoes. The door was locked. The leader turned and made a little gesture with his hand. Two of the men flung their bodies at the door. It gave with a cracking sound and sagged on its hinges. The men went inside.

The nurse listened hard. She heard the distant booming of the war; she heard a fish splash in the lake; but from the Master's house came only silence. The nurse muttered a prayer to her ancestors. Then, in the house, a woman screamed. The nurse had never heard a scream like that. It shot an icy pulse through her body. The baby squirmed; she rocked him in her arms.

The men came out of the house. Two of them were carrying the Master of the Mountain. One held his ankles, the other his wrists. The Master's throat had been cut so deeply that the back of his head bumped between his shoulder blades as the men walked along.

The man who wore shoes was dragging the Master's wife. She was naked, and kept trying to cover her sex with her fine little hands. He jerked her upright and said something to her. She did not reply. He spoke again, more loudly. The nurse could tell it was a question, but couldn't make out the words. Again the Master's wife was silent. The man stared down at her. Then, with a movement so sudden the nurse did not understand what had happened until she heard the cracking sound, he twisted her arm behind her back and broke it. The Master's wife slumped to the ground. She moaned—a high-pitched moan like a dog having a nightmare. The nurse moaned too. When the man questioned the Master's wife again, she answered him.

The leader spoke to his men. Fanning out, they moved toward the lake. The nurse knew what the question had been. She backed quickly away from the window and looked around. There was only one place to hide: a small storage room under the pavilion. She raised the trapdoor leading down to it, saw it was filled with gardening tools, fish nets, sacks of grain. The nurse climbed down the short ladder and pulled the door shut.

Darkness. Bending to avoid the low ceiling, the nurse moved cautiously to the farthest corner. Spider webs clung to her face; her foot slid on something soft and wet. The baby stopped sucking. The nurse rubbed the back of his neck.

She felt the wall in front of her; it was damp, and crumbled at her touch. Squatting, she drew some sacks of grain into a pile around her. Then she lay down on the cold earth floor, her back to the wall. She cradled the baby in her arms.

Silence. *Go to sleep, little mouse. Go to sleep.* But the baby didn't want to sleep. He was alert. He twisted his head and tried to roll out of her arms. As she gathered him back to her breast, the nurse heard the Master's wife scream again. It sounded far away. Abruptly, the baby went very still in her arms. She put him to her other breast, and he sucked. A moment of pain. Then it was gone.

After a little while, the nurse thought she heard a faint splash in the lake. Then another. Her body began to tremble. The baby made an annoyed little grunt. *Don't be afraid,* the nurse told herself. *Fear turns milk sour, and the baby will cry.* She knew she couldn't bear to stand naked in front of those men, to have her arm twisted behind her back and broken, to have things done to her.

Footsteps sounded on the floor above. Hard, clicking footsteps, the kind shoes make. The baby grunted again. *Don't go sour, don't go sour:* She begged her breasts not to betray her.

The trapdoor opened, sending a shaft of light down into the storage room. The baby stopped sucking. The ladder creaked. The nurse huddled between the damp wall and the sacks of grain. Footsteps came closer. A hard shoe kicked one of the sacks. The baby felt it quiver, twisted, and tried once more to roll out of her arms. The nurse loved the baby, but she couldn't bear to have things done to her. She felt for his face, found it, pressed her palm over his nose and mouth.

A big hand reached over the sacks of grain. Long fingers came close to the baby's head. The baby wriggled with all his might, desperate for air. She tried to squeeze the life out of him. The hand clawed the air. The nurse saw a thick wrist with a green snake curled around it, fangs a few inches from her eyes. The hand touched the wall, felt it, and then withdrew. The ladder creaked. The trapdoor closed. Darkness.

When she could no longer hear footsteps, the nurse lifted her palm from the baby's face. For a moment, she thought she'd killed him; then he made a harsh, gasping cry, like the cry of birth. In the tight space between the sacks and the wall, she rocked him as well as she could. Soon he stopped crying. The nurse did not stop crying for a long time.

She stayed where she was. Once she heard a man shout. After that, silence. The baby slept. He woke. She fed him. He slept again. The next time he woke, she rose, mounted the ladder, and opened the trapdoor. It was very quiet. She went up. The men were gone. There was no sign of the Master of the Mountain or his wife. The nurse could not even hear the fighting in the north.

Much later, there was singing. It grew louder. Soldiers came marching up the road. They were not the soldiers in khaki she had seen many times. These were the soldiers she had only heard about, the ones with the red stars on their caps. They marched past singing. Some of them smiled at her and the baby.

The nurse did not know what the war had been about. She only knew it was over.

Part One

1

Friday, the eleventh of April, was doubly special for Beth Hunter. First, it was her wedding day. Second, the bridegroom did not appear. Among other things, that meant Beth did not learn the secret of his honeymoon plans.

Afterward, when it became crucial to remember the details of their last weeks together, Beth was able to isolate the moment she first found out Teddy had something special in mind. It had occurred two months before the wedding day, on a cool, sunny, February morning.

Beth had been up late the previous night, grading freshman essays on the Inquisition and awaiting Teddy's return from one of his Washington conferences. Grading freshman essays stole time she needed for her thesis, but, at first, it was amusing ("The Inquisition: Pros and Cons"). Then it became irritating ("Because I don't feel the Inquisition speaks very much to our times, I have chosen to write instead about food and drink in the Middle Ages."). Finally, it was drudgery ("The eight causes of the Inquisition are . . ."). Beth woke with the phrase "The Inquisition in song and story" running through her mind. She couldn't remember whether she had read it or dreamed it.

"How about an Inquisition sitcom?" she said. "Like Barney Miller, but in fancy dress." She opened her eyes. No audience. Teddy was already up. He'd left a warm depression in the sheets beside her. Getting out of bed, Beth noticed an equation written in felt pen on the floral pillowcase: $x - X(s, t)f(s, t) = u[X(s, t)t]$. The last part trailed unsteadily onto the bottom sheet. Equations like that turned up all over the apartment—on the title pages of novels, the labels of wine bottles, the wall by the bathtub. Teddy

6

wrote them down when he thought of them, with whatever came to hand.

Down on the floor. Fifty sit-ups. Twenty push-ups, from the toes; the last three or four were wobbly. Beth had a swimmer's body with the kind of long, tapering muscles that are much stronger than they look. She still swam three times a week, but her body wasn't as lean as it had been a few years ago. Gravity was at war with her, and pasta was on its side. She threw in five more push-ups, then took the pillow from the bed and went looking for Teddy.

He wasn't in the living room, where she'd expected to find him lying on the old corduroy sofa, with a cup of coffee and the *Chronicle*. Silvery morning light filled the quiet room, falling on the oil portraits of Beth and Teddy over the fireplace. The artist, recommended by a friend, was becoming well known, but Beth considered his painting of Teddy almost a failure. In the shaping of the forehead and the fine bones around the eyes, he had caught something of Teddy's intelligence, but the look of heavy, Confucian dignity which hung on the painted face was never there in life.

The artist had done better with Beth, despite some physical inaccuracy. Her hair was too light—in reality it was as dark as hair could be and still be called blonde; and her eyes weren't so blue—almost anyone with blue eyes had them bluer than Beth. But he hadn't turned her into Doris Day. The strong features were there, and the look on her face suggested she was about to say something she shouldn't: something with too much edge for polite society. She got that from her father.

Beth went out to the balcony. A north wind was blowing one or two brave sailboats across the Bay. The air was very clear. She could see white gulls soaring over the green Berkeley Hills on the other side of the water. Teddy was seated in an unraveling wicker chair, reading a letter. He wore red long underwear and a terrycloth robe.

"Are you crazy?" Beth said. "It's freezing."

Teddy looked up at her. "It's freezing because you're nude." He looked more carefully. "Naked."

"Watch your language." She held up the pillow. "Is this important?"

"Only if you don't want a stiff neck in the morning," Teddy

replied. She threw it at him. He hunched over, protecting the letter.

"What's that?"

"Just a letter."

"Who from?"

Teddy answered with his inscrutable face: eyes half closed, lips curled in a sly grin.

"Don't bother with your inscrutable face," Beth told him. "Unless you're trying to do an imitation of Warner Oland with smoke in his eyes."

Teddy Wu was not very good at being Chinese: couldn't look inscrutable, didn't know the language, and always asked for a fork in Chinese restaurants. "I'm a banana," he would say whenever Beth reminded him of these shortcomings.

Beth squeezed onto the wicker chair, put her arms around him and tried to read over his shoulder. "Subtle," Teddy said, folding the letter and pocketing it in his robe.

"Just tell me what it's about."

"That would ruin it."

"You mean it's going to be a surprise?" She wriggled her hand down under his robe.

"Not at this rate."

"Like a wedding present?"

"Nope."

"Or a trip? A honeymoon trip to somewhere far away?"

Teddy's eyes flickered, but he was only glancing at a gull flying by. "Browbeat all you like," he said. "I'm not talking."

"You don't have to talk. I'm going to look deep into your eyes and start naming names. I'll know when I've hit it." She looked deep into his eyes. "Paris. Rio. Fiji. Athens. Nairobi."

"Daly City."

"Now you die." Beth slipped her forearm under his chin. He ducked out of her grasp and went inside to perform his coffee ritual.

Beth rose and gazed out at the water. One of the sailboats, running before the wind, threw out a bright red spinnaker. It fluttered for a moment, then puffed out like a plump breast. Beth went to find Teddy. He was at the kitchen counter, pouring his special blend into the new German grinder.

"Let's go back to bed," she said.

"Can't." Again Teddy's eyes flickered; this time there was no gull. "I have to go to the office."

That was unusual. Teddy did have an office at Berkeley, where he was a professor of mathematics, but he seldom went there. It had been almost two years since he had published anything. Beth had seen his last paper: "Aspects of Mordell's Conjecture." It consisted of an introductory sentence, two pages of equations, and a concluding sentence, all incomprehensible to her. The paper had won Teddy the Crafoord Prize, the equivalent in mathematics of the Nobel. *Time* had done an article about Teddy, calling him one of the three or four most important mathematicians of the century, and then explaining the significance of his work in a way that made Teddy roll his eyes when he read it. Beth's understanding of what he did wasn't much better, but she had an idea why he did it.

"A proof is forever," he had once told her.

But then, when he tried to describe one he was working on at the time, she hadn't known the language. Teddy was used to that. "It's no shame," he'd said. "I don't know who won the Battle of Anghieri."

"Neither do I."

That had surprised him. The conversation had taken place not long after they had met (in the gallery at a Berkeley swim meet) and he wasn't yet aware of Beth's approach to history. It had little to do with wars, treaties, and power politics—or with units per hectare, surplus value, and power economics. Beth wanted to know what it would be like to open, for example, the door of a peasant cottage in the Vaucluse in 1423 and look in. What would have been cooking over the fire? How did it smell? What were the people wearing? What did they name their kids? What did they talk to the village priest about? What did they think of the seigneur on the hill? Beth's job wasn't to daydream about all this, although she sometimes did, had done since childhood. As a historian, her job was to track down the facts. Persistence counted. And so did creativity. That was the word the professionals used when they meant daydreaming.

Now, in the kitchen, Beth held out her hand. "Come on, Teddy. Back to bed. Just for five minutes."

"Five minutes!" He looked shocked. "I wouldn't dream of insulting you like that."

Beth tried another tack.

"Okay," Teddy said after a minute or two.

They went into the bedroom, leaving behind the smell of freshly ground coffee beans, and Teddy's robe. And Beth loved again the smoothness of his skin, the strength of his lean body, the glint that shone in his eyes as he grew more aroused. There was panting, hers and his, and sensations impossible to bear for long.

Afterward, they lay together on the bed. A cooling breeze drifted through the window. "It's obscene," Teddy said, "a pregnant woman wanting sex like that."

"I can't help it. Pregnancy seems to increase my . . ." She searched for a word.

"I know," he said in a weary voice.

Beth laughed and sat up. "Why should that be? What biological purpose could it possibly serve?"

"Biology?" said Teddy, who professed complete ignorance of all the other sciences.

Beth smothered him with a pillow. They wrestled for control of it. It was a good struggle. After a while, they forgot about the pillow; Teddy forgot about going to the office.

At that time, early in February, Beth was six weeks pregnant. Her pregnancy was the reason they were getting married, although Beth hadn't seen the necessity. She and Teddy had been living together for more than a year, and she was content to go on like that, without involving church or state. But Teddy had insisted.

"Why?" Beth had asked.

He'd patted her stomach. "For this little thing. To show him we're serious." He thought for a moment. "Or her."

Beth said no more about it: Teddy was an orphan.

Instead, she asked, "Have you thought of any names?"

"Adolf for a boy, of course."

"And Medusa if it's a girl?"

"Perfect."

They had booked time for the wedding at City Hall—Friday, April 11, 10:15 to 10:25. They had sent out invitations for a small reception to follow: a few friends; Beth's mother, from Arizona, who called to say she would be there; and Teddy's adoptive parents, Mildred and Arthur Merton, who wrote from Oregon to say they couldn't make it and enclosed a fifty-dollar savings bond. The Mertons had adopted Teddy after he was brought from China by missionaries; at twelve he had gone away to Andover on a scholarship, and hadn't seen them often since.

"They didn't quite fill the need," he told Beth, late one night.

Of his life in China, Teddy knew almost nothing, not even his date of birth. All he knew was written on the visa with which he'd entered the United States. It bore his name, Wu Tun-li, the date of entry—July 12, 1949—and a tiny thumbprint. In the box marked "Age" it said "One (approx.)"; under "Name of Father" and "Name of Mother": "Deceased." Teddy celebrated his birthday on July 12.

April 10, the night before the wedding, Teddy brought home a bottle of champagne. "Just one glass for you," he said, popping the cork. He'd become an expert on prenatal care.

"To the future," Teddy said. They touched glasses and drank. Beth felt the champagne slip over her tongue, cold and dry. And sudden happiness surged inside her, taking her by surprise: She was getting married in the morning. The wine, penetrating deeply, had stirred a long-buried girlhood wish.

They went out to the balcony. A full moon was rising in the east, scattering tiny broken moons all over the Bay. A liner, lights blazing, steamed toward the Golden Gate. Beth thought she could hear the ship's band playing.

"I love you, you know," Teddy said. They held each other.

There was a knock at the door. Beth kissed Teddy on the cheek. Then, glass in hand, she went through the living room, into the front hall, and opened the door.

On the landing stood a Chinese woman. She had high cheekbones and deep-set dark eyes. Her hair was glossy, streaked abundantly with gray: The gray hair and the deep-set eyes were her only signs of age. She wore green eye shadow, jade earrings, and a black silk dress with long sleeves that covered her wrists. She was very beautiful.

"Yes?" said Beth.

The Chinese woman ignored her. She looked beyond Beth, and saw Teddy watching from the living room. Tears pooled in her eyes.

"Tun-li," she said softly.

"I'm afraid you've got the wrong apartment," Beth said.

The woman seemed not to hear. She gazed at Teddy. "Tun-li," she repeated. "I—" Her voice caught. She swallowed and tried again. "I am your mother."

No one moved. Then, slowly, Teddy came forward. Beth turned to him. ''I don't understand,'' she said. He was pale; a little pulse trembled in his forehead.

''Teddy.''

He moved past her and faced the woman. She looked up at him, saying nothing. Two clear teardrops quivered at the edges of her eyelids and rolled down her smooth cheeks. Teddy stood still, a step away.

After a long moment, he took that step and embraced her. She put her arms around him. Teddy's body shook. Beth laid her hand gently on his shoulder. The woman was watching her. Her eyes were dry now. They glinted in the light of the hall lamp. Beth took her hand away.

2

Time passed. Perhaps they all became aware of its passing at the same instant. The woman backed out of Teddy's arms. He turned to Beth. His cheeks were damp, but there was a smile on his face and it was out of control. "I can't believe this is really happening," he said. "I just can't believe it." His voice broke. He inhaled deeply, as if the infusion of air might push the emotion back down his throat.

"It is happening," the woman said. "I've waited thirty-five years for this moment." She unfastened the top button of her dress, revealing a cylindrical silver amulet that hung round her neck on a chain. She unscrewed the bottom, took out a piece of paper, folded small, and handed it to Teddy.

He opened it: a faded document, written in Chinese, with a red seal at the bottom. "What's this?" Teddy asked.

The woman looked puzzled. Then she said, "Can't you read it?"

"No."

The woman's face crumpled as though she were about to burst into sobs. But none came. She quickly recomposed her features. "I should have expected that," she said. She took back the piece of paper. "This is your birth certificate. I've carried it since the day I lost you."

"How did you lose me?" asked Teddy. "How did you find me? I've got so many questions. I don't—No! Wait." He put his arm around Beth's shoulders. "This is Beth. She's—We're getting married tomorrow."

"So much good fortune at once," the woman murmured. Her English was almost perfect, marred only by a slight difficulty with the sound of *r*. Formally, like a priestess performing a ceremony, she took Beth's hand. But she didn't shake it; instead she bowed her head and kissed the backs of Beth's fingers. Her lips were smooth and cool. She smelled of mint.

The woman straightened and gazed at Beth: "She is beautiful." Then she sighed and blinked once or twice, as though coming out of a trance. The ceremony was over.

Beth looked into the deep eyes and said, "This is wonderful."

"It is." The woman turned to Teddy. Awkwardly, he held out his hand. She pressed it to her cheek. That should have looked awkward too, but somehow it didn't. "Wonderful," the woman repeated, still holding Teddy's hand.

"Well," Beth said after a few moments, "come inside."

They went into the living room. As they were sitting down, Teddy and the woman on the corduroy sofa, she on one of the love seats, Beth said, "I don't know what to call you."

The woman didn't seem to hear. She was staring at the portraits over the fireplace. Not taking her eyes off them, she spoke: "My name is Han Shih."

"Han is your surname?"

"Yes."

Beth thought for a moment. "Not Wu?"

Han Shih turned. Her mouth opened, as if to laugh, but it was just a very broad smile. "Nowadays we tend not to take the husband's name."

Beth understood that perfectly; she wasn't planning to take Teddy's name in the morning. What she didn't know was who Han Shih meant by "we." And she still didn't know what to call her. She was thinking of another way to phrase the question when Teddy spoke.

"Now," he said, "I want to hear the whole story."

"Story?"

"Yes. How did you find me? Or did I find you?"

Han Shih laid her hand on his. "I never gave up hope—that's how I found you."

Teddy leaned closer, waiting for her to continue. But Han Shih was silent, her gaze caught once more by the portraits.

Beth used the time to study Han Shih's face; then she glanced at Teddy. They both had lean faces and prominent cheekbones; beyond those, there were no obvious similarities. In the silence, she had a sudden feeling of disorientation. The sofa, the love seats, the Persian rug she got after her father died and the house was sold—nothing could be more familiar. Yet all at once, as if a spell had been cast, it was strange. Beth rose and walked around the room, snapping on lights.

Her movement broke the spell. Han Shih's eyes followed her; the woman saw that Beth noticed, and smiled. Beth smiled back. She was still smiling when she caught sight of herself in the mirror by the wall switch. The smile went away.

She heard Teddy say, "I meant to ask how you actually went about finding me."

"I kept searching for a sign," Han Shih said. "Finally it came." She took something from her purse and handed it to him. Beth walked over and saw that it was a clipping from *Time*—the two-year-old article about Teddy. It seemed longer than she remembered. She read it carefully. Was the text, too, a little different?

"What is this?" Beth asked.

Han Shih looked surprised. "*Time* magazine," she said. "Didn't you see it?" Her brow wrinkled with concern, making her face much older.

"Yes."

The wrinkles vanished as swiftly as they do in the "after" photos in a plastic surgeon's portfolio. "A woman on my street committee who works at the library saw it, too," Han Shih said. "She showed it to me."

"I'm not following you very well," Beth said.

"I'm sorry." Han Shih looked down at her hands, tugged at one of her sleeves. "I should have explained that this woman knows all about me and my history. That is one of the purposes of the street committee, you see."

"Where is this street?"

Again Han Shih's mouth opened as though she would laugh, and this time she did. It was a loud, ringing laugh that showed all her teeth: white and even. She laughed from the neck up; the rest of her was quite still. "Why, Beijing, of course. I live in Beijing."

For an instant, Beth could make no sense of the word. She pictured a bay on the California coast. Then she realized the woman was talking about Peking. She saw from Teddy's face that it wasn't clear to him. "Peking," she told him.

"That's right," said Han Shih. "Peking, under the Wade-

Giles system. But we use pinyin now." There was something faintly admonitory in her tone, and Han Shih heard it too, because she added, "It's all so bureaucratic." That seemed to Beth like a Western thought, expressed in a Western manner; the only unWestern part was the way the *r*'s slipped forward on her tongue and almost became *l*'s.

"You knew two years ago?" Teddy said. "Why didn't you write? I could have come to you."

"That wasn't part of my dream," Han Shih said. "I dreamed of finding *you*."

"How did you get here?" Beth asked.

"I waited."

"For permission?"

"Not exactly. For an opportunity. I am here officially."

"Officially?" Beth asked. "Are you with the government?"

"No, no." Han Shih raised her hand and chopped the suggestion aside. "I am not in this apartment officially. Many Chinese have relatives in America. It is of no interest to the government. But I am in San Francisco officially. I am part of a cultural exchange."

"What kind of cultural exchange?" asked Beth.

"I am a cook." Han Shih laughed ringingly; her little pink tongue danced behind her teeth.

In Beth's mind, a recent memory came into focus. She went into the kitchen and found the *Chronicle* on the breakfast table. On an inside page was the story she sought, a small article headlined "Chinese Chefs on Tour." There was an accompanying photograph of eight or nine cooks. Han Shih was in the back row, looking right into the camera.

Beth brought the paper into the living room.

"I haven't seen this yet," Han Shih said, putting on gold-framed glasses and examining the photograph with care. "I hate having my picture taken." But there was no sign on her face of displeasure with the results. She was very photogenic. She smiled at Teddy. He smiled at her.

"Would you like a drink?" he asked. "We've got champagne."

"How nice."

"And dinner," added Beth. "It's after nine."

"Let me help you," Han Shih said, following her into the kitchen.

"You must have done enough cooking already today. Why not relax?"

"Oh no. I love to cook. Besides . . ." Her eyes went to Teddy, bent over the drinks tray in the living room.

Beth was silent, a little ashamed of her insensitivity. Han Shih wanted to cook for her son.

Han Shih tied an apron over her silk dress. "May I look in your refrigerator?" she asked.

"Of course."

Han Shih selected some ingredients and placed them on a cutting block. She had taken over. With brisk, economical movements, she chopped onions, garlic, ginger. She cut a T-bone steak into thin strips, sliced carrots and mushrooms, trimmed the ends of green and yellow beans. She heated oil in a heavy pan, stirred in the onions, garlic, and ginger, then added soy sauce and salt.

"What kind of cooking do you do?" Beth asked.

"All kinds. Mandarin, Hunan, Szechuan, Cantonese, Mongolian. I can even do hamburgers and French fries."

Beth laughed. Teddy came in with three glasses of champagne. "Where do you work?" Beth asked.

"At a hotel."

"In Peking?"

"Beijing. Yes."

Han Shih turned up the heat and dropped the beef, carrots, mushrooms, and beans into the pan; she poured in all of her wine. The pan hissed. The kitchen filled with smells.

"Mmm," Teddy said. He watched Han Shih stir in the food. She didn't turn, but she knew he was watching. Beth went out to set the dining-room table.

She got out the rattan place mats, the white boneware, the stainless-steel cutlery. She stuck white candles in the holders and lit them. Then she went to the turntable, flicked on the dining-room speakers, and selected something by Jay McShann. His left hand swung boisterously through the room. Beth liked music at dinner. So had her father, although he never played anything but Broadway show tunes—except late at night, when he listened to Bach. Beth glanced at the dining-room table. She removed the cutlery and put out chopsticks instead, and a fork for Teddy.

"All set," she called.

"One more minute," answered Han Shih.

Beth walked down the hall to the study and opened the bottom drawer of her desk. Since primary school she had kept a scrapbook. Now she kept a large cardboard box full of scraps that might go into a book when she had time. She rummaged through it until she found her copy of the *Time* story. It was shorter than Han Shih's. And it omitted two details included in Han Shih's: Teddy's birthplace and his Chinese name.

When she returned to the dining room, Teddy and Han Shih were putting the food on the table. "Look at this," Beth said, showing them the clipping. Han Shih glanced at it, then took out her glasses and read it. Candlelight glinted on the lenses.

"Well?" said Han Shih.

"It's not the same as yours."

"I know," Han Shih said, taking her clipping from her purse and laying it beside Beth's. "Mine is from the Far Eastern edition. With yours, I would never have found my son."

"Why not?" Teddy asked.

"Because it doesn't mention your name," Han Shih answered in surprise. "Your real name. How else would I have known it was you?"

"But surely Wu must be a common name in China," Beth said.

"Certainly. There are millions of Wus. But only one Wu Tunli." She turned to Teddy. "You don't know about Chinese names?"

"I guess not."

Han Shih made a little clicking sound against her palate. "It's simple," she said, removing her glasses; the candlelight still glinted in her eyes. "Tun is the generational name your father chose for you and any brothers you might have. It is the twelfth word in an old poem his family had used for at least two hundred years. Your father had the eleventh word; his father, the tenth. So Tun is not a name like John or Bob. And no other Wu would have it."

"Are there any brothers?"

"No."

"Sisters?"

"No."

"What about my father?"

Han Shih looked down for a few moments. "He is dead."

They stood silently around the table, like mourners at a service. Finally Beth said gently, "What is li?"

Han Shih raised her head and smiled. "His milk name. I gave it to him myself."

Han Shih went into the kitchen and came back with three cups of tea. "Water for me," Beth said.

But Han Shih set the cup in front of her anyway. "It tastes better with tea." Then she sat down, raised her own cup, and said, "To a happy, happy marriage." They drank from their teacups.

"You'll come to the wedding, I hope," Beth said.

"I would like that very much."

"It's at ten-fifteen."

"Good. We have nothing scheduled tomorrow morning."

They ate. "Delicious," Teddy said. But he wasn't an expert. Italian food was what he really liked. Beth thought there was too much ginger in the oil.

But she only ate a bite or two. Then, almost at once, she began to feel tired. Since the beginning of pregnancy, she had been going to bed earlier. She glanced at her watch: not yet ten. By the ninth month she would be sleeping eighteen hours a day, like a newborn. She drank more tea, hoping the caffeine would keep her awake, but instead it made a yawn rise in her throat. She stifled it, and sat straighter in her chair.

Abruptly, time stopped; and everything was very clear to her: the delicacy with which Han Shih handled chopsticks; Teddy eating without tasting; the way Jay McShann was setting up a key change that would lead him back to the theme and a rousing finish; even what was wrong with the still life on the wall—the pear was off balance. It was all clear.

At the same time, she felt very tired.

Teddy turned to Han Shih. "How did we become separated?"

Han Shih did not answer right away. She stared at the still life, as if trying to see in the arrangement of the fruit a pattern that would give it deeper meaning. Or perhaps she'd noticed the problem with the pear.

"I lost you in the war," she said at last.

"What war?"

"The Revolution, of course," she said as though it were the only war there'd ever been.

"How did you . . . lose me?"

Han Shih sighed. "I don't know where to begin."

"Begin with where, then. Where did we live?"

Beth laughed. It always pleased her to catch a glimpse of Teddy's mathematical mind, or to think she had. Maybe she laughed a little too loudly. Teddy and Han Shih looked at her. The laugh became a yawn.

Han Shih laid her chopsticks on the plate. "Shanghai," she said. "But we weren't in Shanghai at the time. We had a summer house."

"Where?"

"Near Wuxi."

"Wuxi?"

Han Shih smiled. "Not far from Shanghai." She added something about turtles that Beth didn't catch. The music was very loud, booming all around her as though she were trapped under the lid of the piano. Teddy spoke; she couldn't hear him, either.

"Excuse me." Beth rose and went to the living room. She turned the volume down, but still it seemed too loud. She turned it off. A bicycle bell tinkled. Han Shih said: "the import-export business." Beth's eyelids were heavy. She walked onto the balcony.

The sky was still clear. It made the moon seem brighter, and the pink haze hovering over the cities of the East Bay seem duller. A light breeze had risen in the west. That was good; she and Teddy were taking *Pop-Up* for a sail after the reception. She smelled the sea.

Beth sat down on a chaise longue. *Just for a few minutes*, she thought. *The fresh air will wake me up*. But her neck couldn't support her head. She leaned back. *I won't put my feet up*, she told herself. She put her feet up. Far away, a telephone rang. A dog barked. A woman laughed.

Just five minutes.

When Beth woke she was in bed. Alone. She got up and opened the curtains. Daylight glared into her eyes. Her head ached. She looked for her watch. It was on the kitchen table. 9:30. Under the watch was a note.

Good morning, Sleepyhead,

    I took my mother to her hotel to change. Meet you at 10 on the front steps.

                                                    Love, T.

Beth returned to the bedroom, opened the closet, and chose a dress: gray wool with long sleeves and a mauve trim. As she bent forward to find shoes to go with it, she felt something for the first time in her life: a movement in her womb.

Maybe she'd imagined it. She was not much more than fifteen weeks' pregnant—two or three weeks early for quickening.

She stayed the way she was, very still.

It came again. A little nudge. Then another, slightly more forceful, as though the baby was taking care to eliminate any doubt. This insight, real or not, into the baby's character, sent a wave of emotion rising through Beth, making her want to laugh and cry at the same time.

"Teddy," she said aloud.

She couldn't wait to tell him.

3

Beth found the manila envelope containing the marriage license, grabbed car keys and money, and opened the door. Two men and a woman were standing in the hall. They wore tight black pants, black vests, ruffled white shirts, and rings in their earlobes.

The caterers. She had forgotten all about them. "I'm in a rush. Can you find your way around without me?"

One of the men came closer and looked deep into her eyes, with an expression in his own of measureless spiritual profundity, like a great religious leader used to easing people's pain, or like someone fresh from shock therapy. It was a look she often saw in California.

"Not to worry," he said. "We're professionals."

Beth had no doubt of that. Payment, astronomical, had been required in advance. She stepped aside. The two men came in and glanced around with keen eyes. The woman followed, pushing a trolley loaded with food and drink. "Very nice," one of the men said.

Beth went out and closed the door. As she walked down the stairs, she heard the other man say, "But can you believe the furniture?"

There were two flights, carpeted with a fading red runner. It was a reminder of the genteel days before the old mansion had been converted into three apartments. There were other reminders in the entrance hall: polished brass mailboxes, a gilt-edged mirror, cut flowers in a vase. They helped keep the rent high. Still, the landlord claimed to be losing money, and was thinking of selling. Beth and Teddy were thinking of buying. Then she could get rid of the red runner.

Outside the sky was a low, gray lid. Dampness drifted in from the Pacific, giving Beth a chill. She walked quickly around the building to the garage in back. Teddy hadn't taken his car. It was a big, anonymous-looking American model that he liked a lot but couldn't park very well; he took taxis if he had to go downtown. Beth had a little Japanese car. It bore no bumper stickers indicating where she stood on nuclear war, abortion, handguns, gay rights, or the Forty-Niners. It was just a car. She climbed into it, drove down Telegraph Hill, and turned south toward the Civic Center.

Beth found a parking space almost in front of City Hall, and approached the stone steps. The sky had darkened; the wind had died down. A fat, cold raindrop landed on the back of her hand. Another glanced off her face. The pedestrians around her began moving more quickly. .

Teddy wasn't on the steps. At their base, a man in a baseball cap was selling frozen yogurt. Two boys in blue jeans were lying on the bottom step, backpacks under their heads. A wino was sitting halfway up with a paper bag between his knees. Everyone else was walking up or down, wearing business dress. Beth looked at her watch. 10:05.

She went inside, passed through the security check, and stood under the vault of the dome. The air was damp and cold, cave air. High above, a naked man and woman, made of stone, held the state shield. He looked like Kirk Douglas. She looked bored. Beth's eyes searched the vast space for Teddy. He wasn't there.

Marriage ceremonies were performed in room 310. Beth took the elevator to the third floor. Room 310 was a courtroom, divided in half by a wooden balustrade. On one side were rows of hard benches. On the other sat the clerk's desk, the size of a Ping-Pong table; rising like a throne above it was the judge's desk. The judge's chair was empty. Behind it, the U.S. flag and the Bear flag framed a door marked PRIVATE.

It wasn't a good day for marriage. Not counting the clerk, there were six people in the courtroom, squeezed together on a front bench. They all had olive skin and shining black hair: a stout middle-aged woman wearing bright red lipstick; a thin middle-aged man with a thick graying mustache curling across his cheeks; two skinny girls whispering to each other; a young man no more than twenty-one or -two, who was staring at his shoes; and a woman of about the same age, wearing a bridal

gown and white flowers in her hair, who looked ready to give
birth at any moment.

No Teddy. Beth went through the gate in the balustrade and
handed the marriage license to the clerk. The clerk was a massive black woman with straightened hair and enormous glasses.
She took a pencil from behind her ear, ran it down the daily
schedule, found "Hunter-Wu," made a tick mark, and said,
"Be a few more minutes." She stuck the pencil behind her ear
and gazed into space. Beth looked at the clock on the wall:
10:09.

"Beth?"

She heard a familiar voice behind her and turned. A woman
was coming toward her across the room. She had fine bones in
her face and a fine silk suit on her trim body. As she approached,
other details came into focus: skin parched by the sun, metallic
red hair, watery blue eyes.

"Mother," Beth said as they embraced. Beth smelled cigarette smoke and tomato juice. Tomato juice meant Bloody
Marys.

"Am I on time? I've never been a witness before."

"You're early," Beth said. "Teddy's not here yet."

Her mother looked around the room. She saw the wedding
party and shared a brief, silent exchange with Beth: her eyes
seemed to clear, and fill with amusement. Beth remembered
many such moments in the past; but her father had died five years
ago, and her mother had moved to Arizona to parch alone in the
hot sun.

"Stay here, will you, Mother? I'll see if Teddy's waiting outside." Beth took the elevator to the lobby and looked out. It was
raining hard. The yogurt seller and the backpackers were gone;
the wino hadn't moved. His soaked shirt clung to his thin shoulders. There was no one else on the steps.

She returned to room 310. The olive-skinned people sat on
their bench. Her mother sat on another, smoking a cigarette and
flipping through a magazine. All the other benches were empty.
Behind the clerk, the door marked PRIVATE opened. Olive-
skinned people came out, set expressions on their faces. The
bride wore white. Her pregnancy wasn't as far advanced as the
other bride's. They filed out, exchanging stares with wedding
party number two. Everyone looked grim.

"Hunter-Wu," the clerk called. 10:15.

Beth approached the desk. "Wu's not here yet."

"Uh-huh."

"He didn't leave a message, did he?"

"Message?"

"Did he telephone to say he'd be late?"

"Nope."

"Then he'll probably be here any second."

"You've got until 10:25." The clerk took the pencil from behind her ear and wrote *10:25* on a pad of paper. She began drawing a picket fence around it.

Beth sat down beside her mother. "Is anything wrong?"

"He's late," Beth said.

"Brainy men are like that. Your father never got to an appointment on time in his life." She sucked on her cigarette.
Beth's father had been a gag writer.

Beth rose and again went to the lobby, this time taking the
stairs. She didn't meet Teddy coming up. Rain. Wino. She returned to room 310. The clerk was gazing into space, the picket
fence around *10:25* unfinished. "May I use your phone?"

With a sigh, the clerk brought her mind back from wherever
it was, scrutinizing first Beth, then the phone. While she was
thinking about it, the door behind her opened and a fat old man
poked his red face into the room.

"What's the holdup, Eulalia?" He had watery blue eyes like
Beth's mother.

"No hubby," the clerk said without turning to look at him,
the way a catcher talks to an umpire.

The watery blue eyes examined Beth, her mother, the olive-
skinned people. "Let's get a move on," he said. "We all know
what time is." The red face withdrew. The door closed.

"Money," the clerk explained to the olive-skinned people,
watching from their bench. "Money." She laughed; a throaty
laugh that rose in pitch until it was something only dogs could
hear.

"May I use the phone?" Beth repeated. The clerk shook her
head. "Why not?"

The clerk was taken aback. "I didn't say no. I was just laughing." She pushed the phone closer to Beth, watching her carefully. "No long distance."

The wedding party was watching her, too. Beth picked up the
phone and called home. "Hello," Teddy answered. "There's

no one here right now. If you want to leave a message, please do so after the tone." Beth hung up.

The clerk raised her eyebrows. Beth waited for her to say, "Well?" But she didn't. 10:21.

Beth crossed the room, passing the olive-skinned people, who looked away, and her mother, who said, "Well?" She went down to the lobby. The wino was flat on his back, passed out. He had rolled down a step or two. His bottle had rolled all the way down and smashed on the sidewalk. Raindrops bounced off the stone, and off the man's ruined face.

Back in the courtroom, the clock said 10:24. Beth sat down beside her mother. "What's a five-letter word for *innocent?*" her mother asked. She had found a crossword in one of the magazines.

"What's the first letter?"

"Could be *n*."

Beth was about to suggest *naive* when the clerk called, "Hernandez-Ruiz." The olive-skinned people stood up and went into the judge's room, the young man dragging his heels at the rear.

Beth got up and walked to the balustrade. "I'm sure he'll be along any minute," she said to the clerk. "Will you be able to fit us in?"

"Sorry. We're all booked up." She studied her schedule. "Through next Friday." Beth bit back an angry phrase. Perhaps the clerk noticed; her face softened and she said: "Stick around, honey. Somebody might not show. It happens all the time. Cold feet."

Beth sat down. "Men," her mother said. "Brainy ones particularly." Beth wondered what return flight she had booked.

People came in. They got married. They left. Beth and her mother completed three crossword puzzles. Beth called Teddy's office. "I'm sorry," the secretary said. "Dr. Wu is not expected today. You may reach him at home. Do you have the number?" Beth called home four times. Three times she got the recording of Teddy. The fourth time the caterer shut off the machine and answered.

"Wu-Hunter residence," he said.

"It's Beth Hunter."

"Hey! Not to worry! We're all set. And the glads are lovely. Just lovely."

"Glads?"

"I've never seen so many. We've filled everything that will hold water. It's like a painting by what's-his-name."

"Who sent them?"

"There's a card somewhere. Hang on."

"Never mind. I just wanted to know if there'd been any calls."

"Lots. But this is the first one we answered. Do you want me to check the machine?"

"Don't bother. Has my— Has Dr. Wu been there?"

"Dr. Wu?"

"Yes. My . . ."

"Oh. No. We've just had the flower man, and there was the wine man too—we were afraid the specifications in the champagne department were a bit on the mingy side. I hope you don't mind. It doesn't do to run out. I've seen it happen."

"No. That's fine."

"Good. Don't worry about a thing."

She hung up.

By noon the benches were empty. The clerk took a brown bag from one of the drawers in her desk, opened it, and started eating. The red-faced judge came out of his room. "What shall it be," he said to the clerk, "Nick's or the Oyster Bar?"

"Nick's," she replied. "You said the service was bad last time at the Oyster Bar."

"Did I?" He came through the gate, his pace slowing as he neared the bench where Beth and her mother sat. He stopped and cleared his throat. "Don't be too upset," he said briskly. "It's better to find out now than in ten years."

Beth looked up, not sure she had heard correctly.

"I know how you feel," the judge went on, trying to make his voice more soothing. "I've seen it happen a thousand times."

"What have you seen a thousand times?"

The judge glanced at Beth's mother, then at Beth. "Well, maybe not to girls like you. You're not pregnant, are you?"

None of your fucking business, she thought. But she said: "No."

"I didn't think so. You don't look like the type." Beth sat silently, thinking of the stirring she had felt in her womb, wishing she could feel it now. The judge took her silence for acquiescence. He patted her arm. "Besides," he said, "these mixed marriages aren't such a hot idea. I'm not at all biased. That's just the way it is. I know marriage. Am I right, Eulalia?''

The clerk tossed a chicken bone into the wastebasket. "You said it.''

The judge smiled. "I bet you're feeling better already. You're a good-looking girl. You'll have no trouble attracting the men. I'd be attracted myself, if I wasn't such an old geezer, and didn't have the missus to worry about.''

He laughed. The clerk laughed. Then he walked out the door, admitting for a moment the sound of lawyers going to lunch. The door closed.

"I could puke,'' Beth said.

"He was just trying to be nice,'' her mother told her.

"The hell with him,'' Beth said more fiercely than she had intended.

The clerk stopped chewing and looked up. "You said it.''

Beth and her mother went out.

It was still raining. The wino was gone. The broken glass had been washed into the gutter. Beth looked around. No Teddy.

They walked silently down the steps, along the sidewalk, and got silently into the car. There was a ticket on the windshield. "That's too bad,'' Beth's mother said. She opened a pack of cigarettes and lit one. Her hands shook. The car filled with smoke.

Beth drove home through the rain and parked behind the house. Teddy's car was still there. "I bet he's inside waiting,'' her mother said. "He probably got all involved in some mathematical problem and forgot about the time.'' Beth said nothing. They walked around to the front of the house. "Does he still write those equations all over the place?''

"Yes.''

"Your father was like that. I used to find scraps of paper with jokes scribbled on them everywhere. I found one just the other day, way back in the liquor cabinet.'' She paused. "He must have written it before he went to the *Tonight* show.''

"What was the joke?''

"I can't remember exactly. I never was much good at telling jokes. I don't think it was one of his best, though. It was a mother-in-law joke. I wish I hadn't found it, actually. I hope there aren't any more lying around.''

4

Happy sounds drifted down the stairs: corks popping, ice cubes clinking, people laughing. "Oh dear," said Beth's mother as they went up. The door to the apartment was open. Inside, the wedding reception was in full swing. No Teddy.

For a moment, Beth stood unobserved in the doorway. There were gladioli everywhere—bright red—and their friends, hers and Teddy's. It had the look of a successful party: all mouths busy—sipping, chewing, talking.

Then Marty Kesselman, one of Teddy's colleagues, spotted her and raised a jumbo shrimp in greeting. Everyone turned. Most of their friends weren't the kind who thought of marriage as a sacrament; still, everyone clapped, and one or two voices sang out "Here Comes the Bride," loud and rollicking.

Beth stepped into the room, head held high, the way the debating-team coach had taught in high school. "You're a bit premature," she said. "Teddy got cold feet." Laughter. It subsided. "In fact, he wasn't there. Has anyone seen him today?"

No one had. Their faces grew puzzled. They looked at her more closely. She couldn't think of anything to say; couldn't have said it anyway, because suddenly the muscles around her mouth were tugging down the corners of her lips. It took her by surprise. She turned, walked quickly down the hall to the bedroom, and closed the door.

There she went through a series of emotions—embarrassment, humiliation, anger. None of them stuck. They weren't real to her; they were all part of wedding business. When she came out twenty minutes later, she could have faced anyone, including the red-faced judge.

But the guests were gone. So were the caterers, the food, the

29

drink. Only her mother remained, sitting on the sofa with a Bloody Mary in her hand, and the gladioli, bright red.

"Do you want a drink?"

"No."

Beth went into the kitchen. The note lay on the table:

Good morning, Sleepyhead,

   I took my mother to her hotel to change. Meet you at 10 on the front steps.

                                                          Love, T.

Beside the note was a florist's card. Le Bouquet, it said, and gave an address on Sutter Street. In the space for a message were three Chinese characters, written in green ink. Her unease began to coalesce into an emotion that wasn't false and wouldn't fade: worry. Worry about Teddy. There were limits to his forgetfulness.

A gladiolus lay at her feet. She picked it up and held it to her nose. It had no smell. She put it on the table. She looked at the florist's card and Teddy's note.

After a while, she became aware of movement in the living room. She went there. Her mother was at the drinks tray, pouring vodka into her glass. "Just freshening my drink," she said when she realized Beth was watching. "Sure I can't make you one? It's just what the doctor ordered."

"It isn't."

Her mother took her glass and returned to the sofa. She looked older than she had a few hours before; her skin more parched: dessicated on the outside by the sun, on the inside by drink.

Beth went to the telephone and checked the answering machine. No messages. She phoned the history department at Berkeley. No one had called for her. She tried the math department again. No Teddy. She dialed room 310 at City Hall. "Hello," the judge said. Beth hung up.

She sat on one of the love seats. Her mother sat on the sofa. Her drink was already half gone. "Beth?"

"What?"

"Did you mean what you said before?"

"What did I say before?"

"That Teddy got cold feet."

"Of course not."

Beth realized that she had spoken more sharply than she'd meant to. Her mother handled it by taking a long drink and lighting another cigarette. Then she said, "What happened, then?"

"I don't know. We'll find out when he gets home."

Her mother looked at her. Beth felt the tugging at her lips. Her mother lowered her gaze. She sucked on her cigarette, blew smoke into the room. "Can I ask you something, Beth?"

No, Beth thought. But she answered, "Go ahead."

"Are you pregnant?"

"Yes."

Her mother nodded.

"What's that supposed to mean?" Beth asked.

"Nothing."

But Beth knew what it meant: Her mother and the red-faced judge thought the same way. "It was Teddy who wanted to get married because of the child, not me," Beth said. "You're thinking in worn-out clichés. They don't apply to Teddy and me."

"You needn't get angry."

"I'm sorry," Beth said. She went to the sliding door that led to the balcony and looked out. It was still raining hard. Water coursed through the gutters, ran in sheets down the pavement, carrying the dirt to a lower neighborhood.

"How many months?"

"Almost four," Beth said without turning.

"I'm very happy for you." Beth faced her mother. She didn't look happy. She looked old and tired and drunk. Then a little life flickered in her watery eyes. "I'm going to be a grandmother," she said quietly, more to herself than to Beth. She smiled a little smile. Beth hadn't seen that smile in a long time. She sat down beside her mother.

"I'm happy too," she said. "I'm just worried about Teddy, that's all."

"Don't worry, dear. He probably went somewhere for breakfast and got caught up in one of his equations."

Beth almost believed it, but something wouldn't let her; something kept tugging at the corners of her lips. She went into the kitchen. She looked at the florist's card and Teddy's note. In the living room, glass clinked against glass; her mother was in the liquor cabinet again. A few minutes later, she came to the kitchen doorway. "Mind if I have a teeny nap, dear?" she said.

"Of course not."

A little unsteadily, her mother walked off down the hall to the guest bedroom. Her drink slopped over the sides of her glass.

It was very quiet. The phone didn't ring. No one knocked at the door. Beth laid her head on the table. She studied the three Chinese characters on the florist's card. One of them reminded her of a wigwam. She wondered what Chinese typewriters were like. The thought made her sit up straight.

Beth rose and looked for yesterday's *Chronicle*. She searched every room. In the guest room her mother was sleeping on her back. Her mouth was open and her dress was hiked high up her legs; they were thin and wrinkled by the sun. Beth kept looking. Finally she opened the cupboard beneath the kitchen sink and picked through the garbage. She found half-eaten canapés, empty bottles, corks, a pound of butter, still wrapped, damp tea-bags, limp green and yellow beans. At the bottom of the plastic bag was the *Chronicle,* smeared with the brown sauce from last night's dinner. Beth opened it to the photograph on page four-teen. Han Shih's image looked back at her.

The writer of "Chinese Cooks on Tour" was R.N. Phelps. Beth called the *Chronicle* and was transferred to the city desk.

"R.N. Phelps, please," she said.

"Not here," a woman answered. Then, much more loudly, she said, "Try the Embarcadero, for Christ's sake!"

"The Embarcadero?" Beth asked.

"I wasn't talking to you," the woman snapped. "Just a min-ute." Something clicked. Beth was on hold. A few minutes later there was another click. "Sorry, baby," a man said. He lowered his voice. "That bitch is driving me crazy. I'm going to kill her."

"Mr. Phelps?" Beth said.

"What?" *Click.* On hold. Other conversations leaked into the line; tinny voices screamed at each other like cartoon characters in a cookie jar. *Click.* Another woman spoke: "Are you holding for someone?"

"R.N. Phelps."

"He's not here."

"When do you expect him?"

"I don't. He's a stringer."

"Where can I reach him?"

"Hold on." *Click.* Distant screaming. *Click.* "You still there?"

"Yes."

"Here's Mr. Phelps's home number." Beth wrote it down.

She dialed the number. After many rings, a man answered. "Phelps," he said. He had a rough, raspy voice, as though his larynx were a crude metallic contrivance.

"Hello," Beth said. "I'm interested in the article you wrote about the Chinese cooks. Can you tell me where they're staying?"

There was a pause. Then Phelps spoke. "You woke me out of a sound sleep."

"I'm sorry. It's important."

Phelps snorted. "Horseshit. Pap was all it was. For the women's page. Anyway, I don't have a clue where they're staying."

"Where did the interview take place?"

"Interview?" Phelps said. "Do you know what they paid me for that story?" He waited for her to answer. She waited for him to go on.

"No," she said at last.

"Forty-five dollars. You think I do interviews for forty-five dollars?"

She was tired of his badgering. "I wouldn't know."

He raised his voice. "I fucking well don't."

Beth swallowed her own anger. "Then how did you write the article?"

Phelps laughed a grating laugh that made her think of unoiled hinges. "From the goddamned press release," he said, a note of triumph in his voice. "How else?"

"Good work," Beth said, and hung up.

She didn't need Phelps anyway. She checked the photo credit in the *Chronicle:* Ernestine Gowers. She dialed the *Chronicle* switchboard again, and was put through to the lab.

"Ernestine Gowers, please."

"Speaking."

"I saw your photograph of the Chinese cooks in yesterday's paper. Do you know where they're staying?"

"The Beresford."

"Thank you." It was on Sutter Street.

Beth put on her raincoat. On the way out, she looked in the guest room. Her mother was still on the bed, her arm thrown over her eyes. Beth turned on the answering machine and hurried out the door.

She drove down the hill. The rain was turning to drizzle; it drifted here and there in the shifting city breezes. Fog crept onto the inside of the windshield. Beth rolled down her window; the smell of the sea was very strong.

She parked outside the Beresford. She knew it well. There was a little bar off the lobby where she and an old boyfriend had sometimes met. It was a replica of an Edinburgh pub. He had liked that sort of thing. The doorman nodded as she came under the awning.

The reception desk was on the other side of the lobby from the bar entrance. The clerk, a fine-featured black man in a tweed suit, had left a sleeve button unfastened to relieve any doubt that the suit was tailored. *Why not roll them up to the elbows?* Beth thought as he turned to her. "May I help you?" he said. He had the presence of a stage butler.

"I'm looking for one of your guests," Beth said. "Her name is Han Shih." She spelled it.

The clerk ran an elegant finger down the open page of the register. "I'm afraid there is no one registered in that name."

"I'm sure she's staying here," Beth said. "She's with the delegation of Chinese cooks."

With care and ceremony, as though it were a Gutenberg Bible, the clerk turned to the previous page in the register. His face grew solemn. "I'm afraid they checked out this morning."

"Where did they go?"

He opened a box of index cards and riffled through it; his fingers enjoyed riffling the way Segovia's liked plucking strings. "They were booked on Pan American flight four twenty-six. Departure time was eight-oh-five A.M."

"Where to?"

"Peking." He closed the box.

Beijing.

"May I see the register?" Her voice sounded distant.

He looked at her with *no* in his eyes. "Just for a moment," he said. She wanted to see if Han Shih had used Chinese characters to sign her name. They all had; there were eight names. Beside them, one hand had inscribed all the English transliterations. Han Shih was not among them.

"Thank you," Beth said.

"Not at all." He was watching her with curiosity.

Beth went into the bar. No Teddy. No Han Shih. Just hunting prints and dark beams. She asked for a glass of water.

"Anything else?"

"A brandy."

"V.S., V.S.O.P., or California?"

"It doesn't matter." She got California.

Beth sat with her drink and tried to imagine what had happened. Sometime during the night, Han Shih must have told Teddy she was leaving in the morning. That would have upset him. He would have gone to the airport to see her off. Then what? Perhaps he had gone somewhere to be alone for a while. She thought of *Pop-Up*, moored at the San Francisco Marina. She went to the telephone in the corner and called the marina. No one answered.

Beth drove up over Nob Hill and down toward Marina Boulevard. The cars ahead of her spat wet grime on her windshield; hers did the same to those behind. If he was sailing, she wished he had taken her, not so much because she thought he should come to her when he was upset—she understood wanting to be alone—but because he wasn't a very good sailor and the visibility was poor. And it was their wedding day. She tried to imagine what could have kept her from calling him if she had been in his place. She couldn't.

The marina came in sight. Masts were lined up in neat rows; looming out of the water not far to the west, the Golden Gate Bridge shrank them to matchsticks. Two sailboats moved under the bridge, one going out, one coming in; both too big. Beth parked by the harbor master's office and unlocked the gate leading to the berths. She walked along the wet dock toward their slip, 114. *Pop-Up* was gone. Teddy's sneakers lay on the dock. She picked them up. Ocean swells made sucking sounds under her feet.

5

Beth gazed out at the water. The rain was coming down hard now, flattening the crests of the waves. As Beth watched, the second sailboat came about and turned for home. Beyond the bridge, a freighter steamed north, trailing a smoky plume. There were no other boats on the water. It wasn't a good day for boating.

"Hi," someone said behind her.

Beth turned. A Tahitian ketch was berthed in the next slip: beamy and yellowed. Even in the rain, the wood seemed to glow. A man stood on the foredeck, coiling rope. His foul-weather jacket reached halfway to his knees; below it his legs were bare, stained permanently with the yellowish tan lifelong sailors get. Bleached hairs curled down to his toes; more of them grew untrimmed on his face, and long on the back of his head, to compensate for the baldness in front. He looped the rope methodically in even oblongs that just touched the deck; he wasn't in a hurry to get out of the rain.

"Hi," he repeated. "You from All-State?"

"No."

"Shit." He lost interest in her.

Beth approached him. "How long have you been docked here?"

"Couple weeks."

"I keep my boat over here," Beth said, indicating the vacant slip.

"Fiberglass sloop? Thirty-two feet?"

"Thirty-one," Beth said. "Did you see it go out this morning?"

He glanced at the water rising and falling in the empty space,

36

then at the shoes in Beth's hands. "Not exactly," he said. He raised his voice: "Hey, Blue."

Aft of the main mast, a hatch cover was raised. Music leaked out: "White Rabbit" by the Jefferson Airplane, a song that reminded Beth of seventh grade. Then Blue appeared in the opening, from her bare breasts up. She had the same tan as the man, and was about the same age; her thick hair was half black, half gray. "Yeah?" she said.

"When did that sloop go out?" the man asked her. "This chick says it's hers."

Blue screwed up her face and thought hard—as hard as if she was trying to come up with the answer to the Irish Question. "It was early," she said at last. She raised one hand through the opening; her fingers were curled around a narrow, hand-rolled cigarette. She drew on it and held it out to Beth, revealing a little clump of hair in her armpit. Beth shook her head. Blue offered it to the man; he took it. Blue let out her breath. "Just after dawn, I guess," she added.

"Who was on it?"

Before Blue could answer, the music reached up and grabbed her attention: "—and the ones that mother gives you don't do anything at all." Blue sang along to the recording, her eyes far away. She was old enough to be the mother of college kids, and she was off-key.

"Who was on it?"

Blue made the long climb out of the deep, comfortable groove the song had worn in her mind over the years, and replied: "I didn't see it. I only heard it. We'd have got up to look, except, like—"

"We were getting it on," the man said. It was a matter-of-fact statement, but he looked at Beth in a way that seemed to invite complicity, and perhaps something more. "Do you own the boat?"

"Yes."

"We've got some great dope you can have. Cheap."

"No thanks," Beth said. "When you did get up—" she began.

Blue interrupted. "We got it in Fiji. It's fantastic." She smiled encouragingly. One of her incisors was missing.

"I don't want dope." *I want Teddy.* "I want my boat. When you did get up, did you happen to notice where it was heading?"

"Is it stolen?" the man asked.

"No."

"Lost?"

"That's what I'm trying to find out," Beth said, smothering the irritation in her voice. "Did you see it?"

"Hey, don't get wired," the man said. He had caught her underlying tone and didn't like it; it wasn't laid back. He and Blue had grown up not trusting anyone over thirty; now they were long past it, while Beth was not yet there. Worse, she was not at all like them. That snarled their philosophy, and made them the harbingers of nothing.

Beth was suddenly aware of her headache, contracted now but still there, dug in behind her left eye. It surprised her: She never got headaches. "Sorry," she said. "I'm anxious about the boat, that's all."

"I can dig it," the man said, mollified. "I think I saw it when I got up. Out there." He pointed toward the freighter. "It'd tacked up toward the Marin side and was beating down to the southwest."

Beth gazed out beyond the freighter. Nothing. "Thanks," she said, and turned to go.

"Sure you don't want some of that dope?" the man asked.

"Sure," Beth said, walking away.

"We could use the bread," Blue called after her. Beth kept going, leaving them there: middle-aged Adam and Eve in their thirty-five-foot Eden.

Beth went into the marina office. The telephone was ringing. No one was there. She looked at the barometer. Falling. Then she remembered that a pair of binoculars was kept on the shelf behind the counter. She reached over and found them.

Beth went outside. The rain was lighter. She drove along the water into the Presidio and parked as close as she could to the bridge ramp. She walked the rest of the way. Joggers went by, dripping sweat and rain.

Halfway across, she stopped and looked to the west. Gray sea slanted up to meet gray sky. Beth raised the binoculars and slowly scanned the horizon from north to south. In the north she saw another freighter. In the south, hillocks of charcoal-gray sat on the edge of the sea: fog. There were no other boats.

Beth closed her eyes for a moment. Then she tried again, from south to north. This time she thought she saw something in the southwest: no more than a black dot against the gray. As she watched, it began to fade from sight.

Without taking her eyes off the black dot, Beth got a coin from her pocket and scratched a line on the railing pointing from her to it. By the time she finished it was gone. All that remained was the line, and two black dots on her retinas. Looking down at the silvery scratch on the railing, she estimated her bearing: 200 degrees, more or less. More or less could mean miles of empty water.

Beth went back to the marina. No one was in the office. But now there was a sign on the counter saying, "Back in five minutes." Beth entered the harbor master's inner office. A ship-to-shore radio was bolted to one corner of the desk. Beth switched it on, pressed the red button, and spoke into the microphone: "San Francisco Marina calling *Pop-Up*. Marina to *Pop-Up*. Come in, *Pop-Up*." She released the button. Static scratched inside the receiver. "Marina to *Pop-Up*. Come in, please. Teddy." Static. She listened to it a few more times before turning off the radio.

There was a little boatyard beside the marina. The gate was open. Beth found the manager at the wheel of a forklift; an engine block was balanced on the forks. He was soaked to the skin and smeared with grease. Seeing Beth, he shouted above the engine: "Can't do anything for you. Pablo quit."

"I want to rent the ski boat," Beth shouted back.

"Today?"

"Not for skiing."

"It'll still cost you twenty bucks an hour. Be back by seven." He roared past her, wheels spinning in the mud. She looked at her watch. 4:30. By six it would be dark.

Slipping the binoculars around her neck, Beth went down to the main dock. The ski boat was tied up at the far end. It was a nineteen-foot whaler, with a console in the middle and two big motors mounted on the transom. Beth climbed in and switched them on. They drowned out all other sound: rain falling on the water, waves slapping the pilings, her own breathing.

Beth cast off and slid the control levers into gear. The boat glided slowly away from the dock and past the open-water moorings. Beth pushed the levers forward as far as they would go. At the first surge of power, the bow rose high in the air and the compass, mounted on the console, spun wildly around. Then gravity pulled the bow back down; the compass stopped spinning. Beth sped under the bridge and turned the wheel until the compass swung round to 200.

Outside the Bay, the sea's skin roughened. The little boat bounced in the chop, making the steering sluggish and unresponsive. Beth kicked off her city shoes and planted her feet firmly on the deck. She tried to keep the compass between 190 and 210. Rain stung her face, and soaked her gray wool dress with the long sleeves and the mauve trim until it clung heavily to her body. Looking back, she saw that the marina had already shrunk to a little arrangement of boxes and poles; the boat rode a widening white V across the water.

Beth squinted into the distance. Dark-gray masses were spreading across the horizon. No black dot. From where she had stood on the bridge, the horizon might have been ten or twelve miles away; next to nothing on land, something different at sea. She pushed the levers, but they wouldn't go farther forward.

The next time she glanced back, the bridge was an Erector set construction. San Francisco was a bumpy crust on the brown hills.

After a while, Beth slowed the boat and peered ahead through the binoculars. She saw nothing but dark-gray fog, rolling in from the west. She didn't like it; she and her father had almost been cut down by a freighter in a fog bank off Catalina years before. Her father had taught her to sail. He had a graceless but tough old yawl called the *Erkjay* ("That's what I was to buy it."). His show-business friends never went on it; neither did Beth's mother, who got seasick; just Beth and her father, from the time she was four years old. At sea, he was different: no jokes, no schtick, little talk of any kind. On land he was a heart-attack man; the final one had struck him as he left the studio on the way to his boat.

The sea began to flatten. The rain turned to drizzle. The first wisps of fog crept toward her across the water. She looked back. The land had disappeared behind the earth's curve.

Fog swept over her, moist and dark. It dampened the noise of the engines. The boat sped along in a little hemisphere of visibility. Beth kept it on a course of 200 degrees, at full throttle. She didn't bother with the binoculars; she could see no farther than a hundred yards in any direction. Soon it was a hundred feet. She backed off the throttle, ready for a boat to rise up out of the fog at any moment. None did. She pulled the levers back to neutral, switched off the engines, and listened.

She heard waves lapping at her hull, and that was all. No other motor, no flapping sail, no creaking mast. The sea rose and fell beneath her, like the breathing of the earth. It could have been a peaceful moment.

"Teddy," she called. "Teddy." And once more, at the top of her voice.

No one answered. There wasn't even an echo; it was smothered by the fog.

The rain stopped. The wind died. In less than an hour, it would be dark. With no wind, Teddy would have to motor back to the marina. Beth listened for the throbbing of *Pop-Up*'s little outboard.

Fog closed around her, and darkened as evening came. Beth started the engines. She would continue on the 200-degree heading for ten minutes at half speed, head due north for ten minutes, then east, south, and west again, until she had completed a ten-minute square; she would stop every five minutes to listen.

For three minutes Beth stuck to her southwesterly course, fighting a feeling that she was already too far out. Then she stopped fighting it, and swung the wheel to the right. Two minutes later, she switched off the engines and listened.

Nothing.

She kept going. The fog thickened, misting over the bow. She throttled back, almost idling, and drifted, blind and weightless, like a dreamer in a dark cloud.

All at once, Beth thought she saw a low shadow off the port bow. She strained her eyes. It was gone. Quickly, she shut off the engines and listened. At first she heard nothing but the engines, still buzzing in her ears. Then, somewhere off the port bow, a door closed: a light, wooden door, the kind that led to the cabin on *Pop-Up*.

"Teddy!" she cried.

She heard the door open. She thought she heard bare feet moving on wood.

"Teddy! Answer me!"

But there was no time for an answer. A cone of water drilled suddenly out of the sea, a few inches from the ski boat's port side. A black metallic tube pierced the cone and rose to head level. The top of the tube was bent; there was a big glass eye at

the end. The eye swiveled around until it found Beth. It fixed its
blank gaze on her face. She froze.

The sea roiled. A dark fin burst out of the depths and loomed
streaming above her, as tall as a house. Then she and the ski boat
under her feet were rising, too, lifted high over the water. The
blank eye kept watching. For a moment, the little boat teetered
on top of a hill. Then the heavy outboards pulled it over the edge.
It slid down the side, dropped through the air, and crashed on
hard steel.

The impact knocked the breath from Beth's lungs. She skid-
ded helplessly on wet metal. Wood ripped. One of the outboards
bounced near her head and arced into the sea. The next moment
she was falling, too: a long fall into cold water. She tumbled
down, deep into blackness.

Blackness crushed her chest. She parted her lips to breathe.
Icy salt water filled her mouth. She clamped her jaws shut. In
the darkness, she sensed something darker, something enormous, moving near her; she could feel its vibration. She kicked
away from it with all her strength.

Air. Beth filled her lungs with it. She saw black. It turned to
white with trembling at the edges. A cold wave slapped her face.
She swallowed some of it and coughed. The black-edged whiteness dissolved and she saw things as they were: the gray sea
around her, the gray fog above. There was no sign of the ski
boat, *Pop-Up*, or the black fin.

Somewhere nearby, metal scraped metal. Beth heard men's
voices, muffled by the fog. She couldn't distinguish their words;
she wasn't even sure they were speaking English. She started
swimming in the direction of the sounds, from time to time raising her head out of the water to listen.

The voices came closer. Heavy chain links banged on a
wooden deck. Metal scraped metal. Then, not far away, the
ocean made a strange hissing sound, one she had never heard.
She listened for more sounds. There were none.

She swam on. The next time she raised her head, she saw a
shadowy form on the water. She knew what it was, and swam
for it as fast as she could.

Beth's hand bumped something solid. She looked up and saw
words painted in blue on a white fiberglass stern: POP-UP. SAN
FRANCISCO. Bracing herself on the rudder, she gripped the

handrail and pulled herself aboard. It was then she noticed she was wearing nothing but her underpants.

"Teddy?"

He wasn't by the wheel or on deck. The cabin door was open. Beth went in. No Teddy. A ceramic mug sat on the chart table. Coffee. She dipped her finger in it: still warm. She raised the mug to her lips: no sugar and lots of cream, the way Teddy liked it. By the sink, she found a thin oblong package tied with red ribbon. Her name was written on it, in Teddy's hand. She tore it open. Inside was the Berlitz *Chinese for Travelers*.

Beth went on deck. "Teddy?"

She began opening all the storage compartments. As she approached the bow, she noticed a heavy chain that didn't belong on the boat. Secured to the anchor cleat, it trailed across the foredeck and over the bow. She was bending for a closer look when it suddenly stretched taut. The bow began to dip. *Pop-Up* quivered. Beth felt ripping under her feet. Cupboards opened. Glasses smashed.

Slowly the bow was dragged down. It dipped under the water. Beth clutched the rail to keep her balance. For a moment, *Pop-Up* was still. Then, in a single lurch, it was yanked beneath the surface.

As Beth hit the water, the rail was torn from her grasp. Underneath, *Pop-Up* went down, very fast, down a chimney of white water. The sea tried halfheartedly to suck her down with it, but soon gave up. She struggled to the surface.

Beth treaded water, turning slowly to look in every direction. All she could see was fog, and even the fog was fading from her vision; it was almost night. And land was far away. She was a strong swimmer, but it was too far to swim in cold Pacific water. It didn't matter anyway—she didn't know where the shoreline was.

Beth treaded water. Night fell.

6

It was dark. The air was cold, the sea much colder. Beth's teeth chattered. She tried to squeeze her jaws shut, but her muscles were numb; the chattering went on. Below the surface, the Pacific was sucking the warmth from her body, doing to her what it did to all helpless creatures, not maliciously, but as a matter of course. No one lived long in the cold water—a few hours, perhaps; not from nightfall till dawn. Fear made her shiver; she heard herself cry out, a little high-pitched sound that would barely have carried across a street. Tears overflowed her eyes and rolled down her face: warm.

Stop it, she told herself. *Don't help the ocean kill you. Don't cry. Don't make that high-pitched little whimper*. She bit her lip hard to show herself she was serious. She stopped crying. The whimper in her throat subsided and sank down into her chest, where she could control it.

Beth treaded water. *Think about treading water*, she told herself. Her feet moved back and forth; her hands smoothed the surface. But it wasn't enough to occupy her mind: Soon she was thinking about her future, in the icy blackness far below. Sharks and scavengers, down in the cold-blooded world. Her blood, too, was turning cold. The whimper rose in her throat.

"Beth!" she screamed at herself in rage, expelling the whimper, unuttered, into the night. Her teeth still chattered and her body grew number, but inside she was a little calmer. Images stirred in her mind. She focused on one: the mug in *Pop-Up*'s galley, pale-brown coffee still warm inside it.

Teddy. Where are you?
Han Shih.
Tun-li.

"I love you, you know," he had said, the night the liner steamed through the Golden Gate.

Then why did you go away? Why didn't you call, at least, and say, "I'm upset, come for a sail, we'll get married another day"? Why? Where are you? Do you love me, Teddy Tun-li?

The whimper was back.

"Beth!" she screamed again. Her voice was thick. She could hardly pronounce her own name. It was a bad sign. "Coffee mug," she said, enunciating carefully. That was better.

But not much. And what was the point? He was already there, of course; he was down there on the cold black bottom. The two of them would soon be together.

The three of them.

"Beth!"

Even thicker. Just a tongueless scream beginning with *B*. "Coffee mug." *Bad tea. Killers killed him. Her. It.*

"Beth!" Then: "Tun-li!" And she heard the anger in her voice.

Tiny broken moons shone all around her. How long had they been shining like that? She looked up. The fog had vanished. The sky was clear and black. The moon was up, round and silver. Where had it risen last night? Over the Bay. In the east. Now she had no excuse for not swimming. She knew where land was.

Beth swam. Left hand up, in, pull. Right hand up, in, pull. She'd swum the four-hundred-meter freestyle for Stanford in her freshman year. Her best time had been 4:17. Good enough to make the team, but not to win. Left hand, right hand. She was at home in the water. She lifted her head; the moon was far away. That was all right: She was home, in the water. Left hand, right hand. *I'm pulling, Coach Gibbons, I'm pulling.* "You're the strongest girl I've got," Coach Gibbons had said. "All we need to do is refine your technique."

Coffee mug, bad tea. Coffee mug, bad tea.

After a while, she realized she wasn't kicking. What kind of technique was that? She kicked.

Much faster. Pull and kick. Pull and kick. She was moving now, really moving: at a 4:10 clip, maybe better, maybe good enough to win. Pull and kick, pull and kick. *No one's more at home in the water than you, Beth. No one.*

She lifted her head. No moon. She stopped swimming. Finally she found it: behind her.

"Beth!"

She turned around and began again. Pull and kick, pull and kick. *Don't go for any records this time. Just get there. Coffee mug, bad tea. Coffee mug, bad tea.*

Just swim to the moon, Beth. You can make it. She'd found her rhythm now. Pull and kick. The only problem was her left arm: It wasn't coming up out of the water. No matter. She was clipping along without it. Her right arm was the strong one. Always had been. *Swim to the moon.*

Where was it?

She stopped and looked around. It took her a while to find the moon: high overhead, at the top of the sky. That meant it was no longer in the east.

Where was east? She searched the sky, but the moon had left no trail. All she saw were the stars. The stars. Her father had taught her the stars. They would tell her where east was. She lay on her back and gazed up at them, but they refused to line up in their familiar constellations. She couldn't even find Orion, the hunter. The stars were useless to her. Light without heat. She needed heat. She was very cold.

Something hit the back of her head. She got ready to die.

She didn't die. It hit her again, not as hard, almost a tap. She turned around and saw an outboard motor, hanging from the transom of a small boat. Part of the transom had been ripped out; waves lapped through the hole, into the boat. The ski boat.

It sat very low in the water. Even the undamaged part of the transom barely cleared the surface. Beth put her hands on the edge, gripped, and pulled. She slipped back into the water. She tried again. And again. And again.

Her hands were feeble. She kept slipping back into the water. The last time, it closed over her head. She came up gasping, looking for the boat.

Don't go away, boat.

Beth stuck her fingers in her mouth, first one hand, then the other. Her fingers felt cold and soft; her left hand was bigger than her right. She kept her fingers in her mouth, licking them the way an animal licks its wounds. After a while, she again grasped the edge of the transom and pulled. Her left hand lost its grip; then her right. She slipped into the water. It closed over her head. She came up gasping.

The boat was still there.

Beth stuck her fingers in her mouth. She kept them there a long time, trying to lick them back to life. The moon slid slowly down the dome of the sky.

"Now," she said at last. No sound came out.

She grasped the edge of the transom and pulled. Her left hand lost its grip. Her right hand held. She kept pulling. Her head rose to the top of the transom. She bit it, clamping the edge between her teeth. She pulled. She kicked. Her shoulder went over the top, then her breast. It held her there. She rested, knowing that the edge of the transom was digging into the underside of her breast, but not feeling a thing.

Again she said, "Now." Silently. She pulled. She kicked. She fell into the boat.

For a long time, Beth lay shivering on the deck. It was wet. Slowly, the water crept up around her. She crawled away from it, to the bow. It wasn't wet. She shivered and watched the sky. The moon dropped out of sight. The stars faded. Milky light spilled through a hole in the east. She sat up.

The water was coming after her, rising toward the bow. The wind was up; choppy waves were breaking over the stern. The boat had a double hull, Beth knew, with an airspace in between, now full of water. She was sinking.

Beth crawled to the console, dragged herself to her feet. The keys were still in the ignition. She turned them. No response. In the storage space under the console, she found a length of nylon ski rope and a small hand pump. She knotted one end of the rope and went to the remaining engine. If she removed the cover, she could wrap the rope around the flywheel and try to start the motor manually.

The cover was held in place by two clamps. Beth couldn't force her hands to close around them. She put her fingers in her mouth. It did no good. *Unclamp the whole motor*, she thought. *Push it over. Buy time.* But she didn't even try.

The sky lightened. That made the ocean angry. It chopped at the little boat. The boat swung sluggishly in the waves, full of water. Beth got the pump. It had a handle at one end and a short hose at the other. She hung the hose over the side and sat in the water near the stern. With the palm of her right hand she worked the pump; she held it between her legs.

Water dribbled out the hose. The boat sank lower. Beth kept pumping.

Pump. Pump. Her eyes were fixed on the trickle running out of the hose. She didn't look away until the handle came off the pump. A spring sprang from its innards and flew into the sea. Beth dropped the pump and began to cry, in great heaving silent sobs.

"Beth! Beth!"

But she couldn't stop.

The transom went under. Still sobbing, she started scooping water over the side with cupped hands.

High above, the sky, too, grew angry. It made loud noises at her. She didn't look at it. She kept scooping. A man in harness came down and said: "Jesus. Christ. She's blue all over."

"I'm not Blue, I'm Beth," Beth said, but for some reason he didn't hear her, even though she was in his arms.

Together they rose in the air. The man wrapped a blanket around her. It was still very noisy. Warm liquid flowed over her tongue.

"Careful," shouted another man over the noise. "It's scalding."

"No. It's good." No one heard her.

They flew away. Far below, the city appeared. They landed on a roof. People in green lifted Beth onto a stretcher and carried her inside. They laid her on a bed. A woman in white smiled down at her.

"Let's just get you out of these wet panties," she said, tugging at them. And then: "Oh dear."

Beth looked down. She had lost the baby.

7

"That deal go through yet?"

"Deal?"

"The mall in San Mateo."

"Signed this morning. We got a bank, J. C. Penney, A and P—all long leases."

"What rate you get?"

"Prime plus one."

Whistle. "Listen—do me a favor. Next time something comes up, give me a shout."

"You bet."

Someone touched her left hand. "What do you think of this?"

"Those ungual phalanxes'll have to come off."

"No they won't," Beth said, opening her eyes. Two men were standing over her. They were about her own age, tanned, clean-cut. Except for their white coats, they could have been professional golfers. The letters on their name tags swam before her eyes.

"What have they got her on?" asked one.

The other scanned a chart. "Demerol. Ninety mills."

"Cut it down to sixty."

"Right."

"Those ungual phalanxes are staying where they are," Beth said.

They smiled at her with amusement. One had little white teeth. The other had little yellow teeth, even smaller. "Ungual phalanxes," said Whiteteeth. "And what might those be, little lady?"

"Fingertips," Beth said. "Don't they teach you anything in medical school?"

The smiles went away. "What's her name?" asked White-teeth.

Yellowteeth looked at the chart. "Elizabeth Hunter."

"Look, Liz," said Whiteteeth, "we're only trying to do what's best for you."

"Right," said Yellowteeth. "You've got to look for the silver lining in situations like this."

"Silver lining?"

"Sure. It's your left hand. You're not left-handed, are you?"

"That doesn't mean I want to give it up."

Whiteteeth glanced at his watch. Whatever he saw there irritated him. "Liz, I know you're doped up right now, but try to concentrate on what I'm telling you. We're just talking about the tips, after all, the itty-bitty ends. Half an inch, three-quarters, no more. Cross my heart."

"You're not a concert pianist, are you, Liz?" asked Yellow-teeth. "Or shortstop for the Giants?"

"Do you want to lose your whole hand?" asked Whiteteeth. "The arm, maybe?"

Their faces leaned forward. They waited for an answer.

"Don't call me Liz."

"Christ. Okay, Miss, Mrs., Ms., or whatever you like—have you looked at your goddamn hand?"

Beth looked at her left hand. The fingers were blue and puffy, the nails purple-black.

"That's better." Whiteteeth smiled. Yellowteeth smiled. They went away.

Beth stared at her hand for a while. Then she thought of her mother. She picked up the phone on the bedside table and started dialing with her right hand. She stopped, pressed the button, and began again, using her left. It wouldn't obey. After a long time, she was able to dial the first number; she finished with her right hand.

"Hello," Teddy answered. "There's no one here right now. If you want to leave a message, please do so after the tone."

Beth closed her eyes. She saw the sea. The image followed her down as she sank into sleep.

When she awoke, a man was sitting on a chair by her bed. He was thick-wristed, with a bristle of gray hair on his head and an off-the-rack assortment of big features on his face. His voice rumbled in the depths of his chest. "Good afternoon, Miss Hunter." He looked at her. "You're one tough lady."

"Afternoon?"

"My name's Gomez. Captain, USCG. I'd like to ask you a few questions, if you're feeling up to it."

"I'm okay. Except," she found herself saying, "they want to cut off my fingertips."

"Let's see." Gomez took her hand in his: big, warm, and dry, like a comfortable house. "I've seen worse. Don't let them." For a Coast Guard captain, he seemed to lack respect for authority. Beth's surprise must have shown on her face, because Gomez smiled mischievously and said, "They need to cut now and then. Otherwise they lose their mystique."

Coming out of that rough face, the word was so unexpected that Beth thought of asking to see his identification. But it wasn't necessary: Gomez wore a blue uniform with four gold stripes on the sleeves. "What do you want to know?" she asked.

"For openers, maybe you can tell me what you were doing sixteen miles off Montara in a water-ski boat." He hadn't leaned forward or changed his tone, but there was a watchfulness in his eyes that altered the atmosphere in the room.

"I was looking for *Pop-Up*. My boat. I—I think the man I live with was on it." She listened to her words. Did they make her sound vulnerable? Or just stupid?

Gomez's voice seemed sharper when he said, "What made you think that?"

Lots of things. But it was hard to make them cohere. "His sneakers were on the dock."

"Where are they now?"

"I'm not sure. I think they were in the ski boat. Where is the ski boat?"

"On the bottom."

There was a long silence. Somewhere a bell rang, and a woman called, "Dr. Perkins, Dr. Perkins." *Ring*. "Dr. Stottlemeyer, Dr. Stottlemeyer." Her hand began to hurt.

Quietly, Gomez asked, "Did you find him?"

Beth looked at him; he looked right back at her. "That's an odd question."

"Is it?" They watched each other. Then he said, "I take it back."

Ring. "Dr. Weinberg, Dr. Weinberg."

Gomez said, "Did you see your boat out there?"

"I was on it."

The squint lines deepened around Gomez's eyes. Beth told him about *Pop-Up*. The coffee mug. And how *Pop-Up* went down. The squint lines grew deeper.

Beth propped herself up, ready for questions. But Gomez didn't ask a question. He said, "I've spoken to your mother."

"Where is she?"

"On her way here." Gomez rose and went to the window. Beth watched his profile. In the sun's light it looked old and weather-beaten. He gazed outside, but Beth knew he wasn't seeing anything. At last words came, soft and deep: "Don't you want to change your story?"

"What do you mean?"

"I understand why you were so upset, Miss Hunter. But you made a lot of work for us. It wasn't right."

"What are you saying?" Her body took it in before her mind; she felt blood rushing to her head. "That I fabricated the whole thing?"

Gomez held up one of his big hands, like a traffic cop. "Not at all. It's just that sometimes, under pressure, the mind plays funny tricks. Especially at sea. And especially at night, when you're alone."

"What pressure are you talking about?" Beth got out of bed, rising without effort on a surge of anger. She took a step toward Captain Gomez. Something sucked the air out of the room. Whiteness blinded her as she fell.

A man lay prone on the ocean floor. She swam down and turned him over. Teddy. His eyes were sand pits. He put his arms around her and glued his lips to hers. His kiss was watery. A salty stream filled her mouth. She tried to get away, but he wouldn't let go. All she could do was open her eyes.

Captain Gomez was gone. Her mother had taken his place on the bedside chair. She was wearing dark glasses and smoking a cigarette. Beth felt a sliding in her stomach.

"Please put it out."

Her mother started. "I'm sorry, dear." She took a last deep drag and stubbed it out, but imperfectly. It smoldered on.

"What did you tell Gomez?"

"Gomez?"

"The Coast Guard captain. Do you have to wear those

glasses?''Her mother removed them. Beth immediately wished she hadn't—she didn't want to look at eyes that were red and drunk and begging for pity. ''I didn't tell him anything, dear. Just about the . . . wedding, and all.'' Her mother started to cry, and then, with tears rolling down her cheeks, tried to smile. ''I brought you some flowers.''

Beth looked. Bright red glads in a vase by the window. She closed her eyes.

Far away, a phone rang. Cutlery fell. A baby cried. Beth felt her mother's hand, thin and moist, on hers: her left one. It attracted touch like a relic.

''Are you all right, Beth?''

''Tired, that's all.''

''What can I do for you?''

Beth felt a storm of tears gathering behind her own eyes. Where her mother lived, that kind of weather was always threatening, and she brought it with her. ''Nothing. I'm fine. You were great at City Hall.''

''Me?'' her mother said in a scathing tone. ''What did I do? I'm useless.''

It was too much for Beth. The storm broke. She reached for her mother and pulled her down on the bed.

Beth soon stopped crying. Her mother sobbed in her arms. She smelled of smoke and tomato juice. ''What's wrong?'' Beth asked. No answer came.

The storm passed. Her mother returned to the bedside chair and put on her sunglasses. ''What are your plans?'' Beth asked.

''Whatever you want, dear.'' Her eyes moved behind the dark lenses. ''I've got to get home sometime. Paquita's been watering the plants, but she goes on holiday tomorrow.''

''Then you'd better get back, Mother. I'm okay.''

''You're sure?''

''Yes.''

''Well, if you're really sure . . .''

Beth closed her eyes and fell halfway into sleep. Dry lips brushed her cheek, footsteps went away. She dropped into the bottom half.

''Dinner,'' a woman announced loudly, banging a tray on the rolltable. Beth opened her eyes and examined the food: yellow orange juice, brown salad, gray meat, black flan. She ate every crumb.

After dinner, Beth practiced dialing the phone with her left hand. She was clumsy and slow. Her hand hurt. She kept dialing. Her hand hurt more, but it became a little less clumsy, a little less slow.

Someone knocked at the door.

"Come in."

A man walked out of a Brooks Brothers ad and into her room. He could have been an up-and-coming banker or lawyer, except for his eyes, which lacked the minimum but necessary conviviality. His irises were almost colorless, giving his eyes the appearance of black holes in white space. Beth took him for a doctor.

He came to the end of her bed and looked at her chart. Then his eyes met hers, flickered down to her hand, returned. *Maybe he's a psychiatrist*, Beth thought. The implication angered her.

"Are you a psychiatrist?"

"No. I just want to have a little talk with you."

"About what?"

"The story you told Captain Gomez. A few other things."

"Are you a doctor?"

"No."

Then why were you looking at my chart? "Are you with the Coast Guard?" He didn't have the kind of tan you got at sea. He had the kind of tan you got playing tennis three times a week and sipping gin and tonic on the clubhouse patio.

"I'm cooperating with them," the man replied. "I'm trying to find out what happened last night."

"I told him what happened."

"Gomez? I'm afraid he didn't believe you. He thinks you had hallucinations, brought on by hysteria."

"I am not hysterical."

But hearing the sound of her voice, she wasn't sure. Maybe the accusation of hysteria induced it in any woman.

"I am not hysterical," she repeated in a different tone, looking him in the eye. That sounded better. She barely stopped herself from trying it again. The drugs. She felt her face redden with embarrassment. All the while, his black-on-white eyes watched. They could have shown several reactions to her antics—amusement, annoyance, boredom. They showed nothing. She looked away.

"Don't be too hard on Gomez," the man said. "He can believe one of two things: A) you found your sailboat sixteen miles offshore in the fog and were capsized by a submarine which then dragged the sailboat under, or B) you got knocked up, jilted, went a little crazy, and acted out this drama to explain it all away. There's no precedent for A. B happens every day."

Beth hated him. At first it was the hot hatred she'd felt before in the face of rudeness or aggression, but instead of passing it turned cold, and considered—like the choice of the words *knocked up* about her dead baby. Cold hatred took up a position at her center: a cure for hysteria, not even demanding expression.

"What's your name?" she said.

"Lathrop."

She'd expected a name like that. "What do you want from me, Lathrop?"

"I want to know whose submarine it was, for starters."

Beth sat up straighter. "You mean you believe me?"

"It's not a matter of belief. It's a matter of knowing the facts. Gomez didn't. All he knew was there were no reports of any submarines, foreign or domestic, in those waters in the past forty-eight hours."

"But it was dark and foggy. And the submarine was only on the surface for a few minutes. You had to be right there to see it."

She heard a strange sound, as though a bubble of air had burst from the man's lungs, disturbing his vocal cords on the way out. It was a laugh. "We don't have to see them," he said. "SOSUS hears them for us."

"SOSUS?"

"Never heard of SOSUS?" Lathrop's tone was casual, almost offhand, but he was watching her closely.

"No."

"Dr. Wu never mentioned it?"

"No. What are you getting at?"

"SOSUS is the Sound Surveillance System. Hydrophone arrays on the ocean floor. Do you understand what I'm talking about?"

"No."

"No? The ocean is bugged, sweetie pie. We can tell what country a sub belongs to, what type it is, and often identify it by name. We can hear the fish swimming by. Is that clear enough?"

It was clear enough, but her mind recoiled from the knowledge. The subsurface dealings he was talking about dirtied the ocean for her more than any oil spill could. She forced herself to think about what he'd told her. "But you said you didn't hear anything in the past forty-eight hours."

"I also said that's just one of the facts. Others outweigh it."

"What others?"

"You tell me."

"But I don't know," Beth said, her voice rising.

His rose to match it. That surprised her. He had the kind of all-American corporate face that gave nothing away, least of all emotion. "You don't know much, do you? Do you even know what your boyfriend does?"

"Of course. He's a mathematician."

"But what does he do?"

"He works with number theory. He won a prize for his paper on Mordell's conjecture."

"Which says what?"

Beth tried to remember what Teddy had told her. Her mind was too cloudy. She tried to remember what *Time* magazine had said about it. Her mind was too cloudy even for that. "I don't know."

Lathrop snickered. "Fear of math, sweetie pie?"

"Just tell me what it says," Beth said quietly.

Lathrop looked at her for a moment before replying. "Mordell's conjecture states that there is a large class of equations which have only a finite number of solutions. Your boyfriend did two things. First, he proved that the conjecture was true. That's why he won the prize—Mordell's conjecture has been kicking around since nineteen twenty-two. The second thing he did was even more important: He figured out how to determine the exact number of solutions an equation in that class might have. That's the part that wasn't published."

"Why not?"

"It's classified material."

"Why?"

"Don't you see the implications?"

"No."

"Did you know that he sometimes went to Washington?"

"Yes. I went with him once. He has conferences there."

"About what?"

Suddenly, without her bidding, her voice rose: "Don't bait me. What are you hiding?"

Lathrop yelled back. "Stop playing dumb. Your boyfriend is a defector. He's gone over to the other side."

"What other side?"

"That's a matter of dispute," Lathrop said, nearer his normal tone. "Some of my colleagues say the Russians." He paused, watching her. "But I have a hunch," he went on, "that Wu is an ideologue of a different . . . color."

"What do you mean?"

Lathrop came closer. "I mean he's one of Mao's little yellow men."

His racism made her voice soar out of control again. "You're disgusting! And you don't even know what you're talking about. Teddy doesn't care about politics. And we were going to have a goddamned baby, for Christ's sake!" Her voice broke.

Lathrop stood over her. "I don't give a shit about your sex life. And this has nothing to do with politics, either. It has to do with treason. Wu had the highest possible security clearance, but someone got to him. I want to know how."

"What are you saying?" But even as Beth spoke, she thought of Han Shih.

"Is something wrong with you? No one can be this naive. Not even—" He cut himself off, perhaps seeing some change in the expression on her face. When he continued, his voice was more controlled. "Or are you trying to protect him? Is that it? Are you working for them, too?" He looked down at her with his colorless eyes. "Are you one of Mao's little girls?"

"If I was, why did I tell you about the submarine, you asshole?"

Lathrop's hands curled into fists. "You're the asshole, baby. What do you think's keeping you out of an interrogation cell right now?"

"Be quiet." A black nurse, very big, stood in the doorway. "This is a hospital. And visiting hours are over." She glared at Lathrop. "Long over."

Lathrop turned to her. His eyes were black pits in ice. He walked out the door.

The nurse gave Beth a pill. "You shouldn't be getting so excited, honey. Take this." Beth swallowed it. The nurse switched off the lights and went away.

For a long time, Beth watched the open doorway, waiting for Lathrop to return. She shook as though she'd just come out of the water. Someone got to Teddy, Lathrop had said. He liked facts. Han Shih was the fact he didn't know. No one knew it, except Beth. She hadn't even told her mother.

But perhaps Lathrop didn't need to know it. He spoke another language. Han Shih spoke another language. And so did Teddy.

Beth slept. Somewhere there was ringing. A woman cried, "Dr. Wu, Dr. Wu."

8

The hospital groaned in its sleep. Beth was aware of it as she drifted from dream to dream. A bat flew by, fanning her cheek. Someone shook her. "Wake up, wake up."

"What is it?"

"You've got to leave the room."

"Why?"

"There's a bat in here."

Lights flashed on. Beth blinked. A nurse was beside the bed; a massive orderly stood by her, clutching a wooden tennis racquet. Their eyes darted nervously around the room. A breeze stirred the Venetian blinds. But there couldn't be a breeze because the window was sealed shut.

"Behind the blinds," Beth said.

The orderly tiptoed over. His legs were so big they had trouble getting past each other, giving him the dainty gait of a woman in spike heels. He raised the blind. The bat was hanging on the wall, just above the top of the window. Like a player getting ready to serve, the orderly cocked the racquet; muscles puffed up under his skin.

He smashed the racquet into the wall, missing the bat by a foot. The racquet splintered. The walls trembled. The bat swept around the room in a tight circle, making the nurse scream, and veered out the door. Nurse and orderly followed. After their visit, Beth couldn't get back to sleep. Her hand didn't hurt as much and it wasn't so blue. She practiced dialing.

The shift changed. The hospital stopped groaning. Everyone made as much noise as possible. It was morning. The shopping-center magnate came in, all smiles. Whiteteeth. He was squiring a white-haired man whose black eyebrows overhung eyes as intelligent as Teddy's.

"This is Dr. McPhee," announced Whiteteeth. No one played "Hail to the Chief," but it was that kind of presentation.

Beth smiled at them. "One second." She picked up the phone. "I have to make a quick call." With her left index finger, she briskly dialed seven digits. "Hi," she said to the ringing signal.

"Hello?" a man answered.

"I'm feeling much better, thanks. Why don't you come see me? I'm in fifteen-oh-nine."

"Fifteen-oh-nine where?"

"Bye." She hung up. "Sorry," she said to the doctors. "What can I do for you?"

Dr. McPhee's eyes were on Whiteteeth, their expression balanced between puzzlement and annoyance. Whiteteeth didn't look happy. Dr. McPhee approached the bed. "May I see your hand for a moment?" Beth held it out. He took it in his. His touch was soft. He examined the front, the back, and tapped her fingernails. "Thank you, Miss Hunter." He turned and started walking to the door.

"Dr. McPhee?"

He stopped and looked back. "Yes?"

"Is it all right?"

"No. Your fingers have suffered severe exposure. There is some cell and circulatory damage and a significant impairment of nervous response, some of which will be permanent."

Something pressed against her chest. "Does that mean they have to come off?"

"Of course not." He was almost angry.

The pressure was cut off. Buoyancy took its place. "When can I leave the hospital?"

"Today, as far as I'm concerned," Dr. McPhee said. "Call my office tomorrow and arrange an appointment." He went out the door. Whiteteeth flapped after him.

The buoyancy began leaking out of Beth when she got home. A half-eaten sandwich lay on the bare dining-room table. Empty vodka bottles sprawled like tenpins on the kitchen counter. Everything that could contain cigarette butts did. The apartment was a depiction of her mother's inner state.

Beth cleaned it from top to bottom. It made her tired. It didn't bring her any closer to Teddy. She lay down on one of the love seats and closed her eyes.

Metal scraped metal, faint and far away. A door opened—her front door. Beth opened her eyes and sat up. Shadows were driving the eastern light from the room; it was early evening. Someone was walking down the hall to the kitchen. Teddy? The footsteps were slow and careful and heavier than Teddy's. Beth considered confronting the intruder. But she was weak and afraid.

The vacuum cleaner lay on the rug; she'd been too tired to heave it back into the closet. She switched it on and dropped behind the old corduroy couch.

From there she had a partial view of the front door, through the entrance to the living room. Beth listened, but heard nothing except the vacuum cleaner. Then a man came into view, moving quickly. His back was to her. He opened the front door and went out. Beth ran to it and slid the bolt into place. Footsteps hurried down the stairs.

Beth went to the balcony and crouched, peering over the railing. A man came out of the building and walked quickly down the street. He wore a navy pinstripe suit and a frown between his eyes: Lathrop.

Beth went inside and switched on all the lights. She turned off the vacuum cleaner, but that made the apartment too quiet. She put the Trout Quintet on the turntable—the first record she laid her hand on. But after only a few bars she knew it was a bad choice. Whenever Teddy heard it, he did an imitation of a hooked trout trying to dance to the music; it always made her giddy. Beth lifted the needle and put on something else.

She sat down to think. There was a lot of thinking to do. But she wasn't thinking; she was falling asleep. She went into the kitchen to make coffee. Because of Teddy's fondness for coffee, they had beans from Colombia, Java, and Brazil, and a complicated French drip-filter to go with the German grinder. Beth uncovered a jar of instant at the back of the shelf.

Waiting for the water to boil, she found a starting place for her thoughts: Teddy's coffee. He liked to try new beans, experiment with different blends. That was Teddy. A man who was a banana; who danced the dance of the hooked trout; who scribbled prize-winning equations on bedsheets; who wanted to be a father; who loved her. He was not a man who would disappear without warning on their wedding day, to defect to the Chinese, the Russians, or anyone else. So whatever he had done had not been voluntary. That meant he was in trouble.

There were two flaws with her reasoning. (She found herself thinking like Lathrop.) The first was that none of it would hold up in a court of law, to say nothing of the court of non-law where people like Lathrop came from.

The second was Han Shih.

Beth went into the living room. Over the fireplace hung the portraits that Han Shih had looked at with such interest. There was Teddy, wearing a Confucian mask. At that moment, Beth faced the third flaw, the flaw that had been widening in her mind the whole time—in Eulalia's waiting room, on the drive to the marina, in the fog, on board *Pop-Up* with the coffee mug: Maybe her reasoning was all wrong because *she* was all wrong. Maybe the artist was better than she thought. Maybe Teddy didn't love her.

Why would he stop loving her? The baby. But he had wanted the baby. He could have changed his mind: "B happens every day." That's what Gomez thought, what Lathrop thought, what everyone would think of any explanation that depended on the truth or falseness of Teddy's love for her. If that was all she cared about she would never see straight. She would see only what she wished to see, and get in shouting matches. She wouldn't find Teddy. And finding Teddy was all that mattered.

Facts.

Han Shih.

Beth returned to the kitchen. Her mind was suddenly clear for the first time in two days—since her wedding day. On the kitchen table lay Teddy's note: "Good morning, Sleepyhead." And the florist's card with the three Chinese characters. And the *Chronicle*: "Chinese Chefs on Tour."

Beth read R.N. Phelps's short article, cribbed from a press release. She stared at Ernestine Gowers's photograph, taken at the Beresford Hotel, where the chefs had stayed. She gazed at Han Shih's handsome face, which gazed directly back. None of the other chefs had looked into the lens like that. Were they better cooks than Han Shih? Han Shih had used too much ginger.

Beth reread the article, stared at the photograph. The Beresford Hotel. The elegant clerk. His elegant finger on the guest list. Han Shih's name hadn't been on it. Eight names, but not hers. Beth picked up the paper again. She knew the story by heart. "Eight cooks from the People's Republic of China are in San Francisco this week on the last leg of a mouth-watering tour of the U.S.," it began. Beth counted the faces in the picture. There were nine.

Eight chefs in the article. Eight at the Beresford. Nine in the photograph. Han Shih was the ninth: the one who couldn't cook.

Beth boiled more water and paced the kitchen until the coffee was ready. She picked up the pot with her left hand. It crashed on the floor. She looked at her hand in surprise: bluer than in the morning, almost as blue as the day before.

Forget about it.

Fact one: Han Shih.

Fact two: Lathrop. Cooperating with the Coast Guard.

Beth examined the lock on the front door. There were no signs that it had been forced. So Lathrop had some sort of key. He had let himself in. But the Hoover had made him run. He hadn't expected to find anyone home, not for days; he'd known about Whiteteeth's diagnosis from her chart, but not about Dr. McPhee's reprieve.

Lathrop had come. What for? Teddy? He was looking for Teddy, just as she was. But he thought Teddy was on a submarine in the Pacific. So he hadn't come for Teddy in the flesh, but for a sign, something that would lead to him. Beth closed the door and did what Lathrop had come to do: She searched her apartment.

That meant emptying every drawer, closet, and cupboard; looking under mattresses, cushions, and the Persian rug; going through Teddy's desk and hers. In hers, she found a postcard Teddy had sent from Washington in September. On the front was a picture of a panda chewing leaves. On the back she read:

Dear Beth,

I've had one too many. The conference is a bore. And it's hot as hell. If the locals ever push the button it'll be on a day like this.

Went to the Gallery. They've got a Giorgione. His best stuff's all in the background—distant mountains, etc. Your eyes are the color of his mountains. Now I've had two too many. See you soon.

Love, T.

Beth read over the sentence about the locals. "Teddy doesn't care about politics," she'd told Lathrop. But change of context made the sentence disturbing. Had Lathrop been after something like that? Or more?

Beth found nothing else that seemed useful. At last there was nowhere left but the plastic garbage bag under the kitchen sink. She'd already been through it once, looking for the *Chronicle* after the caterers had gone. She went through it again.

The garbage was soggier now, and reeked of something acidic. Otherwise, it was the same: half-eaten canapés, empty bottles, corks, butter seeping through its wrapper, damp tea-bags, limp green and yellow beans.

She picked out the teabags. There were three of them. "It tastes better with tea," Han Shih had said when Beth asked for water. "To a happy, happy marriage." Beth sealed the teabags in separate sandwich bags and put them on the counter.

The search had taken a long time. The coffee's power to fight fatigue had worn off, but it retained enough strength to make her nervous. She stood on the balcony. It was after midnight, cool and quiet. Millions of lights ringed the Bay, like a glittering wreath tossed on the water. She gazed at Berkeley.

Dead end. Start over.

Lathrop. Lathrop was willing to believe there was a submarine, even though they hadn't heard it, because of Teddy. There were implications to Teddy's number theory, implications obvious to Lathrop. Beth thought of Marty Kesselman in Berkeley, a mathematics professor and Teddy's friend. He'd been invited to the reception. She tried to recall if she had seen him there when she made her little speech about Teddy's cold feet. Yes. He'd been standing in the corner, chewing on a jumbo shrimp.

Beth went to the phone. Maybe he'd called sometime in the past two days, giving her an excuse to bother him now at one in the morning. She rewound the answering machine and switched it on.

"Beth. It's Maggie. Are you okay? Call me."

"Hello. I'm calling for Beth Hunter. It's Tom Simpson. I'm in your history seminar. Four-oh-four. I'm sorry, but I still haven't finished that paper, and I'd like to talk to you about another extension. I haven't been feeling too well lately. Yesterday I had a fever of a hundred and one, and the doctor—" He'd used up his thirty seconds.

"The food was great, Beth. Give Teddy a spanking and let's do it again." Jane.

"This is Ron Todd from the marina." A long pause. "Call me."

"Hi. It's Angie from Empress Travel. Your tickets are ready, Mr. Wu. You can pick them up any time."

"Mrs. Hunter? It's Paquita. Do you want me to leave the key under the mat? I go away tomorrow."

"Hello. This is Robert Means from *The New York Times*. Would Miss Hunter please call me?" He left a number.

There were no more messages. Beth rewound the tape partway and listened again. "Hi. It's Angie from Empress Travel. Your tickets are ready, Mr. Wu. You can pick them up any time."

Beth sat hunched over the answering machine, listening to Angie tell Mr. Wu about his tickets a few more times. The rhythm of her heart was fast and light, like tom-toms. Sweat popped through the skin in her armpits and trickled down her ribs. She took a deep breath, hoping it would somehow quiet her heart, and called Marty Kesselman.

He answered on the first ring. "Hello?"

"It's Beth Hunter. Did I wake you?"

"No. No. Just doing a little work." Pause. "Is Ted . . . ?"

"I don't know where he is. I think something's happened to him." Her voice almost broke. She bit her lip to control it.

There was silence on the other end. Then Marty said: "Like what?"

"I don't know."

"Have you called the police?"

"It's not that kind of thing." Or was it? "I'd like to talk to you, Marty. Can I see you in the morning?"

Pause. "Why don't you come over now?"

"You don't mind?"

"No."

Beth took a manila envelope from her desk. In it she put the *Chronicle*, the florist's card, Teddy's note, and the sealed teabags. Then she went out the door, locking it behind her. There was no one in the hall, on the stairs, or outside. She walked around to the garage. Her car wasn't there. It took her a moment to remember where it was: at the marina.

Teddy's car was in the garage. He never locked it and always left the keys under the seat. She found them and started the car. Sarah Vaughan began singing "More Than You Know." Beth switched her off and backed carefully down the lane. Teddy's car was almost too wide to go through without scraping. He scraped it regularly.

The thought made Beth smile. Then it brought tears to her eyes.

Enough of that, she told herself. *You haven't the time or energy to spare.* She drove toward the Bay Bridge, resting her left hand in her lap. Night breezed through the open window, cool and quiet. Her heartbeat slowed.

Traffic was light. A few cars went by the other way. Then one came up behind her. Its white headlights glared into her eyes, doubly reflected in the interior mirror and the one on the door. They were still glaring at her as she drove across the bridge.

9

The headlights glared steadily from the two mirrors, like vectors locking on a moving target. On the far side of the bridge, Beth turned onto the freeway to Berkeley. The other car stayed right behind her. She tried to see what kind of car it was, but all she could see was white glare.

She took the University exit. The other car came with her. When she was almost past it, Beth suddenly swung onto the Marina cutoff. The glare disappeared; then it came back, brighter and closer than before. She hadn't really expected to lose it. Proving to herself that she was being followed was enough. It was proven.

Beth slowed down, circled under the freeway, drove up Telegraph Hill, and parked in the garage behind her apartment. Locking Teddy's car, she walked around to the front door. Cars were parked on the street. No headlights glared, but cooling metal made popping sounds not far away.

Beth climbed the stairs to the apartment. Everything was as she had left it. No one lurked behind the front door, in the hall closet, behind the shower curtain. Beth sat down. Like a wave-making machine controlled by someone else, her left hand started shaking. Soon her whole body was doing it.

Start over. Much smarter. Much more carefully.

Beth went to the phone and was about to pick it up when she stopped herself. She couldn't think of it as her phone anymore. She could be followed across the bridge; she could be followed down the wires. Perhaps she had been already.

Then use that knowledge.

She called Marty. "I've changed my mind," she told him. "I'm too tired."

There was a long pause. "Okay."

"I'll call you tomorrow. Good night, Marty."

Beth hung up. She turned on the answering machine, re-wound the tape, and wiped it clean. Then the slyness of what she had done hit home, and her hand started shaking again. She went to the liquor cabinet and swallowed a mouthful of brandy from the bottle. It stopped the shaking. She switched on the radio and a few more lights, then went out the door and down the stairs to the basement. Descending, she thought of Lathrop's subsurface world.

Beth didn't touch the switch at the bottom of the stairs. The basement was damp and dark; pale orange light from the street-lamps glowed on the high slit windowpanes but didn't pene-trate. There wasn't much in the basement—an old washing machine, decaying furniture, rusty bicycles, kitty-litter smell. Beth felt her way to the washer. She climbed onto it, opened the high window, and squeezed out into the back yard. The window closed with a thump.

Beth stood still. She heard music, probably from her own ra-dio, three floors above, and a dog barking in the distance. But no one opened a car door.

Behind the garage was a low picket fence. Beth stepped over it into the moist earth of a newly turned garden. The movement, not very strenuous, was enough to make her dizzy. She realized how weak she was, and thought of going back. But when her head cleared she went on, through the garden and past a dark house. A lower window was open. Beth smelled marijuana as she walked softly by.

She came out on Lombard Street, turned right, and started quickly down the hill. Two men approached her on the side-walk. They were wearing hockey sweaters and holding hands. They didn't even see her.

At the bottom of the hill, a taxi was turning off Stockton. Beth hailed it and gave the driver Marty's address.

"Berkeley?" he whined, as though he couldn't cope with the prospect of a big fare. But he mastered himself and headed for the bridge. Beth glanced back several times. No glare followed.

The taxi climbed Shasta Road and stopped in front of Marty's house. Beth paid the driver. "That's all?" he said when he saw the size of the tip. He accelerated away, letting the rubber whine for him.

Marty Kesselman lived in a tall, terraced house backing into the hillside. He had a view of the Bay through the tops of the oaks across the street. It was a big house, with plenty of room for Marty, his wife, their three kids, and the mongrel Trotsky; but only Marty and Trotsky lived there now. Marilyn and the three kids lived with another man in Texas.

Beth went up the walk and rang the bell. No lights came on inside. No one stirred. She rang it a few more times. She tried knocking, first with her knuckles, then with the brass knocker. After a while, she turned the knob. The door opened. She was deciding whether to go in when she heard footsteps on the sidewalk.

A tall, gaunt man was running toward her. He wore running shorts, a singlet, jogging shoes. He was not a natural runner; his left heel kicked out to the side like a hitch in a batter's swing. Trotsky trotted along beside him, drooling.

"Marty."

He drew up in surprise. Trotsky growled and inflated himself to demonstrate that he was approaching condition red, but he never got beyond that to the biting stage.

"Beth?" Marty said, and Trotsky deflated with relief. "I thought you weren't coming. I went for my run." He came closer, bending once or twice to stretch his muscles. There were black depressions under his eyes and under his cheekbones. Beth smelled his sweat, sour and heavy, as though his jogging outfit wasn't washed regularly.

"Do you always run at this hour?"

"These days. It's quiet." Trotsky brushed against her. She patted him on the head. He drooled on her foot. "We'll go inside in a minute," Marty said. "Trotsky hasn't had his shit yet. Shit, Trotsky."

Trotsky sniffed at Marty's jogging shoes. He circled anxiously around the lawn a few times, then darted across the street and used the neighbor's.

"What do the neighbors say?" asked Beth.

"I don't think they've noticed yet. Marilyn always sent one of the kids out with the scooper." He peered across the street, perhaps hoping that a kid with a scooper would scamper out of the shadows, but Trotsky came back alone.

"Come in," Marty said, pushing the door open a little harder than necessary and flicking on the lights. He blinked once or twice at the state of things. "It's a bit messy."

Beth had been to Marty's once before, but it was for a barbecue and she hadn't gone inside. She saw that Marilyn had left the furniture and the plants, all dead, but had taken the pictures—empty rectangles decorated the walls. Marty followed her gaze.

"Everything's a bit messy," he said. "Why don't we go downstairs? That's the inhabited part of the house these days."

He led her to the basement. It was a big room, empty except for two couches, a coffee table furred with dust, a desk, and papers everywhere. The ceiling was black. The walls were covered with murals painted in psychedelic style. Long-haired androgynes coupled in the light of setting suns, penises became chrysanthemums, all eyes looked like Christ's would have if He'd dropped acid three times a week. The centerpiece was a crudely executed Mount Rushmore with the faces changed to those of Marx, Engels, Lenin, and Mao.

"The whole house was like this when we bought it," Marty said. "She didn't quite have time to finish the redecorating." He sat on a couch, loosened his jogging shoes, and threw one bony knee over the other. "You said you were worried something's happened to Ted."

Beth cleared space on the opposite couch and sat down. "I am." She told him why, including everything but Han Shih; she wasn't ready to put her thoughts about Han Shih into words. Marty's sea-blue eyes never left her face.

"Is that all of it?" he asked.

"What do you mean?"

Marty shrugged. "I don't know. Has Ted been acting strangely lately? Did anything unusual happen?"

Beth opened her mouth to tell him about Han Shih, but stopped herself. It wasn't just unreadiness to put her thoughts into words; it was unwillingness to face what the words might mean. "No," she said

"No?" Marty shrugged again. "Sounds like this fellow Lathrop might be your best bet, despite his unpleasantness."

Why hadn't he said "our" instead of "your"? Beth wondered; maybe an accretion of similar little detachments had finally driven Marilyn away. "No, Marty." Lathrop might have the power to get Teddy back for her, but he didn't have the will.

His will went no further than getting Teddy, period. "Lathrop's made up his mind that Teddy's defected to China."

She waited for Marty to say what a ridiculous idea that was. He was silent. Beth said: "It's your help I need, Marty."

"Mine?" His long fingers curled toward his chest.

"Tell me about Teddy's work on Mordell's conjecture."

Marty's eyebrows made V's on his forehead. "I can't. You wouldn't understand it. I have trouble understanding it myself. I don't know enough about algebraic geometry."

"And Teddy does?"

"No one in the world knows more about algebraic geometry than Ted. The Russians have had a whole roomful of guys trying for the last twenty years to do what he did."

"They have?"

Marty pointed his finger at her. "Let me ask you something: How many mathematicians in a century really advance the science of mathematics?"

"I don't know. Thousands, I guess."

"Wrong. Five. Six, maybe. All the others are just broom-boys, tidying up after that handful. And believe me"—his eyes had developed an inward look—"they know it. They know it early. That doesn't mean they admit it to themselves. In some cases, by the time they admit it to themselves, it's too late."

"Too late for what?"

"Too late for living, that's what." Marty got up and walked stiffly to the desk in the corner. He shuffled through the papers on it, selected one, scanned it, let go. It wafted to the floor. He looked up at Beth. Behind him two naked hippies lay in a bed of purple roses. "Do you know how much of my life I've wasted just thinking?"

"I'm sure it hasn't been wasted, Marty. Teddy always speaks highly of your work."

"I don't want his fucking praise," Marty said. Then he pinched the bridge of his nose, hard. "I'm sorry, Beth. That's very nice of him." He turned to the couch and sat opposite her. "Ted and I go back a long way, back to MIT. We've never been close, exactly, but we go back a long way. That must mean something in this world." He looked off into some space far beyond Mount Rushmore.

After a few moments, Beth said: "Why is Teddy's work on Mordell's conjecture so important?"

Marty shrugged his thin shoulders. When he replied, his voice had lost its intensity. "You never know in mathematics. One solution leads to another."

There had to be more to it than that. "What are the implications of Teddy's work?"

"Implications?"

Beth stifled a sigh of frustration and tried another approach. Marty's mention of the Russians had reminded her of something Lathrop had said. "Did you know that Teddy's paper was incomplete? They didn't let him publish the rest of it."

"How do you know that?" He didn't seem surprised.

"Lathrop. How did *you* find out?"

Marty barked an abrupt little laugh. "I didn't know. I guessed."

"How?"

"The equations seemed to be leading off into new territory. It's hard to express, but I couldn't believe Ted would stop there. Besides, he said something about it, the day the paper came out."

"What did he say?"

" 'That was the easy part.' "

"Didn't you ask him to tell you the rest of it?"

The V's rose again on his forehead. "Of course not. It was no business of mine."

"But aren't you interested? As a mathematician, I mean."

Marty shrugged. "I'm not doing that kind of work."

"Don't you do number theory?"

"No."

"What kind of math do you do?"

He barked his little laugh. "It's hard to explain to a non-mathematician."

Beth tried a nonmathematical approach. "Who is 'they,' Marty?"

" 'They'?"

"The 'they' who wouldn't let Teddy publish the whole thing."

"Some sort of security people, I suppose."

"Why are they involved? What are those Washington conferences about?"

"I don't know exactly. I don't do that kind of work."

"What kind of work?"

"I told you." He was becoming irritated. "Number theory. I also don't touch any secret research for the government."

"Are you saying Teddy does secret research for the government?"

"Well, he does research they want kept secret. It comes to the same thing, doesn't it?"

Beth didn't answer his question. Instead she asked one of her own: "What are the security implications of Teddy's work?"

Marty rose. His knees cracked. He began walking back and forth, stepping on scattered newspapers, magazines, record jackets, paper plates. Trotsky walked beside him. Marty put his hands together in the attitude of prayer and touched them to his lips. "If there is a large class of equations with only a finite number of solutions, it would be very important to people who wanted to know how many answers there are to a given problem, and what those answers might be. Without that knowledge, you could put all the computers on earth to work on one of these problems from now till the end of the universe and they still wouldn't have run through all the variables." He stopped pacing and faced her. "Do you follow?"

"What people are you talking about?"

"Cryptographers and cryptoanalysts, of course. People who make and break codes."

"Teddy makes and breaks codes?"

Marty shook his head. "They've got broomboys to do that. But it's one of the ramifications of his work. He's given them the key."

"What key?"

Marty sat down and looked at her. "For breaking other people's codes. And making our own unbreakable." Excitement crept into his voice, and into his eyes.

"Are codes so vital?"

"Absolutely. Everyone listens in on everyone else."

"The whole goddamned world is bugged, isn't it, Marty?"

Marty decided she'd made a joke, and laughed. "You're right. That's why all important communications are coded—military, diplomatic, business. They've got electronic pulse codes, laser codes, substitution codes, transposition codes, all seeded with radicals and random numbers. They've probably still got invisible ink."

"Teddy never said a word about any of this."

''It's classified.'' Marty saw something in her eyes and added, ''Besides, I doubt he was very interested in the applied end of it. It's like the way the Chinese invented gunpowder, but only used it for fireworks displays.''

The Chinese. Lathrop's hunch. It would be much more than a hunch if he knew about Han Shih. ''What country would want to . . . have Teddy?''

''Any country.''

''The Russians?''

''Sure.''

''The Chinese?''

''Even more. They're farther behind. But you have to realize something. Nobody goes around kidnapping another country's scientists. There's an understanding about that kind of thing.''

''But I saw that submarine.''

''That doesn't mean he was on it.''

''Then where is he?''

Marty was silent.

''I'm tired, Marty.'' The words came out by themselves.

''Stay here if you like.''

''Thanks.''

Marty fetched a blanket. She lay down on the couch. He shut off the lights. Communist Mount Rushmore and all the stoned Christs vanished back to 1968. In the darkness, Beth heard Marty settling on the other couch. ''I bunk down here myself these nights,'' he said.

Beth slept until she heard knees crack. Then Marty was beside her, his hand on her stomach. ''It's funny how Marilyn's gone and Ted's gone and we're here,'' he said.

''No it's not.''

His hand went away. His knees cracked. He settled on the other couch. Soon he was snoring softly; he groaned once or twice in his sleep.

A few hours later, Beth heard him getting up. Grainy light seeped in through a dirty window by the stairs. Beth watched Marty through her lashes. He was still wearing shorts and singlet. He put on his jogging shoes and went off for another run, Trotsky behind him.

As soon as she heard the front door close, Beth got up and went upstairs to the kitchen. Every dish in the house was dirty.

She found a phone book. Empress Travel Consultants was on Shattuck Avenue in Berkeley.

Beth took the sealed teabags from her manila envelope and wrote a note for Marty: "Thanks for everything. Please ask someone at one of the labs to analyze these for any non-tea contents. Will call later." She taped the note and teabags to the refrigerator, and was on her way out when the phone rang.

She picked it up. "Hello?"

The line went dead.

Ten minutes later she was at Empress Travel. A young Japanese girl was bent over a computer keyboard, wings of hair closed like glossy curtains over her face.

"Good morning," Beth said. "I'm looking for Angie."

"I'm Angie," the girl said with a smile.

"I'm here to pick up some tickets."

"In what name?"

"Wu."

The girl opened a drawer and handed her an envelope. There were two tickets inside, one in Teddy's name, one in hers. They were round-trip bookings from San Francisco to Shanghai. The departure time was 10:30 A.M., Tuesday, April 15. Tomorrow.

The return flight was open.

"Have a nice trip," Angie said.

10

Beth stood on the sidewalk in front of Empress Travel, unseeing, unhearing, unfeeling. After a while, she became aware of the sun, an inch or two above the hilltop, warming her face. Slowly, she walked up Durant, passed through Sather Gate, and entered the campus.

High above, a few pockets of fog still clung to the hillside, but the sun was burning them away. Soft breezes carried the scent of eucalyptus trees. Crossing the Plaza, Beth took off her sweater and tied it round her waist; she was dressed for the climate on the other side of the Bay.

On the steps of the Student Union, where once members of the FSM had dared to utter dirty words, changing the course of history, or at least the way men wore their hair, a blond man now stood shirtless, reading from a Bible. He read haltingly and with no sign of comprehension—he was not much past the sounding-it-out stage. His audience was a toothless old man with a bottle in a brown bag, who shouted "Amen!" from time to time.

"For we wrestle not against flesh and blood—"

"Amen!"

"But—"

"Amen!"

"Against principalities, against—"

"Amen!"

The blond man lost his place and started over. Beth passed out of range.

Students were stretched out on the grass. Some read, some dozed, some shared joints. A young man on roller skates glided by shouldering a tuba. A woman juggled oranges. Springtime.

The campus was spread out across the lower slopes of the hill.

76

There were many grand buildings in Greek, Roman, Renaissance, and robber baron styles. Evans Hall wasn't one of them. It was a ten-story gray cube, utilitarian as a crew cut. The mathematics department was on the top three floors. Beth entered the elevator and pushed number ten.

A slight, bearded man got on at two. He had a carton of floppy disks under one arm and a record album under the other—*Stars of the Doo-Wop Sound.* He got off at five. Computer science.

Ten. Beth walked down the hall. Offices lined both sides. By each door was a card stating the occupant's name and visiting hours. 1082 had no card—Teddy's office. It was locked. Beth took Teddy's keys from her pocket and examined them: car keys, apartment keys, and two she couldn't identify. The first of these unlocked the door. She went in.

A folded sheet of paper lay on the floor. Beth locked the door behind her and picked it up. It was a mimeographed note, dated two days before, announcing a seminar on the impact of Sturm-Liouville problems on noncompact manifolds. "This should be a humdinger" was written in felt pen at the bottom.

Beth looked around. Nothing had changed. Teddy had a desk, bookshelves, a blackboard, and a panoramic view of San Francisco, buried at that moment under ruffled white clouds. The blackboard was unmarked; the desktop was bare; the bookshelves held nothing but Teddy's P.G. Wodehouse collection. Beth tried the drawers. Locked. The last key on Teddy's ring opened them.

In the top drawer, Beth found a black-and-white photograph, not quite in focus, of her laughing self at the wheel of *Pop-Up.* The middle drawer contained a box of paper clips and a *B.C.* cartoon strip, torn from a newspaper.

Frame one: The fat woman and snake look at each other. Frame two: She takes him by the tail, pounds him against a rock, and sneers, "How did you like that?" Frame three: The flattened snake thinks. Frame four: He says, "It had a good beat and you can dance to it—I'll give it eighty-five."

In the bottom drawer were two passports, hers and Teddy's. Both were stamped with visas for China. Under the passports was an envelope addressed to Teddy at the apartment and postmarked January 31. The return address was "Merton, 48 Maple Lane, Salem, Oregon." The Mertons were Teddy's adoptive parents.

Beth took the letter from the envelope. Tidy handwriting clung to the ruled lines on the page, so small it was hard to read:

Dear Son,
   It's me writing this instead of Mother, on account of her arthritis. Aside from that (her arthritis) no complaints.
   Old Miss Barbizon, do you remember her she taught you sixth grade, told Mother you won a prize for your math. Good work son! Miss Barbizon says you were the best math student she ever had bar none.
   We got your letter last week. The reason we didn't answer right away is because we aren't of the same mind about what to do. Myself, I can't see any good could come from going into all these past things. On the other hand, Mother holds that you have the right to know. And I always go along with her when it comes to

The door to Teddy's office clicked open and Beth looked up. A young, long-haired Chinese man stood in the doorway. He had a Giants cap on his head and an American Express card in his hand. "Oops," he said. "Maintenance. Just checking the air conditioning." He backed out and closed the door.
Beth returned to the letter:

                                And I always go along with her when it comes to emotional considerations, because she understands the "ways of the heart" a lot better than

Beth stopped reading. There was no air conditioning in Evans Hall. It had been disconnected the year before—"Bothers the computers," Teddy had told her. No air conditioning. The door had clicked open. And the maintenance man hadn't been holding keys, he'd had an American Express card.
Beth jumped up, jammed the letter and passports into her pocket, and ran down the hall. The elevator doors were shut. It was on the way down. Nine. Eight. Seven.
Beth raced down the stairs taking them two, three, four at a time, and grabbing the rail to whip herself around the turns. At the bottom, she burst through the stairwell door into the lobby. The elevator was there ahead of her, doors open, empty. Beth ran outside.

The maintenance man was walking quickly down the path that led past the campanile. As though he felt her eyes on him, he turned, saw her, and started running. In a moment, he had disappeared around a bend. Beth ran after him.

Beyond the campanile the path divided, one part leading up to the stadium, the other down to the Plaza. Beth didn't see him in either direction. She ran down toward the Plaza.

As she came in sight of it, she saw him, halfway across. He was very fast. With every smooth stride he was stretching the distance between them. Beth kicked off her sandals and ran harder.

Again he looked back and saw her. In that moment, he bumped into the juggler. Her oranges fell out of orbit and she fell with them. Beth gained a few yards.

The man seemed to feel the gap closing. Shortening stride, he pumped his legs like a sprinter, shooting through the Gate and onto Telegraph Avenue.

Don't lose him in the crowd, Beth told herself. Her sweater flew off; her skirt twisted around her waist. Free of restraint, her strong legs pumped too. She ran across the Plaza.

"—'against the rulers'—"

"Amen!"

She ran through the Gate and across the street. A car honked. The sidewalks were full of people, strolling, eating ice cream cones, staring in the windows of comic-book stores. He could have lost her by slowing down and melting into the crowd, but he hadn't. He was running on the side of the road, forty or fifty yards ahead.

Soon it was fifty or sixty. Beth willed her legs to go faster, but they wouldn't do it. She wasn't panting, she didn't have a stitch in her side, but her legs were weakening; she still hadn't recovered from her night in the water. She ran as hard as she could. He was going to get away.

"Stop him!" she shouted. "Stop that man!"

People looked at her. They looked at him. They did nothing. He ran. She ran after him.

"Stop him! Stop him!" Far ahead, a policeman writing a parking ticket glanced up. He raised his hand and said something as the long-haired man came abreast of him. Without breaking stride, the long-haired man launched himself in the air, twisted, and caught the policeman in the face with a whipping kick. The policeman went down. The long-haired man landed on his feet, took a step, and then sprawled forward on the pavement. He got up quickly and kept going, but his smooth stride was gone. He was favoring his right foot. His kicking foot.

The policeman was trying to push himself up from the sidewalk. Blood poured from his nose. Beth ran by him. Forty yards. Thirty. Twenty.

The long-haired man looked over his shoulder. His eyes were scared. He tried to run faster. His Giants cap fell off and his long hair bobbed after him like a parody of his limping run. Fifteen yards. Ten. She could hear his harsh, sucking breaths.

He reached an intersection. Ashby. Red light. Heavy traffic. *He'll have to slow down*, Beth thought. But he didn't.

A black car was parked at the curb. The rear door swung open. The long-haired man fell inside. Beth dove after him and grabbed him around the legs. The car surged forward. The long-haired man kicked her in the stomach. He was slipping away, her left hand had no strength. He kicked her again, lower. She reached down for his injured foot and twisted it. He screamed. The scream made her feel sick. She fell onto the road.

He fell with her. Two hands reached out of the open door, trying to catch him. All they caught was air. Beth glimpsed the interior of the car. The driver was an enormous Chinese man whose shaved, lumpy head seemed to sprout directly from his massive shoulders. The reaching passenger in the back was also Chinese. She wore big sunglasses and a black scarf around her head, but that didn't keep Beth from recognizing her: Han Shih.

"Halt!" a man shouted.

Beth heard a sound like an exploding firecracker, then the shriek of rubber on pavement as the black car sped away.

The long-haired man tried to get up. Beth tackled him around the chest and brought him down. She felt his heart beating wildly. He twisted and dug his fingernails into her back. They were long and sharp. She lay on top of him and hung on.

"You're dead, you son of a bitch." The policeman was standing over them, revolver pointed at the long-haired man's face. The policeman's nose was still dripping blood. His eyes were round and very small—as small and round as the opening in the barrel of his gun. He was going to shoot.

"Don't!" Beth cried. "He's an important witness."

The three little eyes swiveled toward her. "Witness to what?"

She couldn't think of a reply. People approached. A siren wailed. Louder and louder. The metal eye slowly turned away, over to the long-haired man, then toward the ground. The other two eyes grew bigger and more human. The killing fever had passed.

"A conspiracy," Beth said at last. "A horrible conspiracy." She got up, rehearsing an explanation in her mind. The long-haired man was watching her. He looked more scared now than when the gun had been pointed at his face.

"Yeah?" the policeman said. He wiped his bleeding nose on his sleeve and examined the results. "Shit." He reached down to the long-haired man, snapped handcuffs on his wrists, and jerked him to his feet. The right leg buckled and the man screamed. Beth bent over and vomited in the gutter.

A policewoman put her hand on Beth's back. "You all right?"

"Yes."

"Better do something about your skirt. "

Everyone was looking at her: the policewoman, the policeman, the crowd. Beth pulled her skirt down over her thighs.

She got into the back of a squad car with the bloody-nosed policeman. On the way to the station, she asked, "Did you get the license number of that car?"

"Car?"

"The black car on Ashby."

"I didn't see a car." His eyes got small again. "All I saw was you wrestling with that Chink."

They rode the rest of the way in silence.

Beth waited alone in a windowless green room: green walls, green filing cabinets, green metal desks. The second hand on the old-fashioned clock counted off each minute in sixty spasms. 11:27. Beth studied her left hand. It looked all right: the same color as her other hand. The nails were still black, but pink crescents of new growth bordered the cuticles. The hand wasn't good for gripping yet, that was all. She stretched it a few times. 11:51.

A tall black sergeant came in. His posture was perfect, his uniform immaculate, his skin smooth as mocha icing. He might have been fighting crime by setting a good example.

"Sorry to keep you waiting like this." He leaned against a desk and looked at her. "I understand you subdued the suspect after he knocked down one of my officers. Is that right?"

"I guess so."

He looked at her a moment more. His eyes were cool and intelligent; thoughts moved in their depths, too far down to read. "Thank you," he said.

He opened a notebook and started asking questions. Beth told him about the break-in at the office.

"Had you ever seen this man before?"

"No."

The sergeant tapped his pen on his muscular thigh. "So you have no idea who he is?"

"No."

"That's too bad."

"Why?"

"Because he's not talking. Not even his name. And he's got no ID. We had to book him on a John Doe."

"What about the American Express card?"

"The name on it is Altobelli. It was reported stolen a month ago."

"He'll have to talk eventually, won't he?" Beth asked. The sergeant tapped the pen on his thigh and said nothing. "Are you going to try again?"

"After they finish with him at the clinic. He broke his foot. He also broke Menendez's nose, and his jaw in two places." The sergeant's eyes shifted over to her for another look. "We get a lot of break-ins, Ms. Hunter. We hardly ever get a victim running down a suspect. We never get a victim running down a suspect when nothing's been taken. What made you so persistent?"

"I don't know."

They watched each other. The sergeant stopped tapping his pen and stuck it in the side of his Afro. The gesture seemed to open a gap between them, like the ocean separating America and Africa. He stood up. "You can go. We'll call you if anything comes up."

Beth went outside. There was a phone booth on the sidewalk. She called the Coast Guard and after a long wait was put through to Captain Gomez.

"How's the hand?"

"Fine. Thanks. I need to talk to Mr. Lathrop. It's very important."

Pause. "He doesn't work here, exactly."

"But he cooperates with you."

"Yes."

"Then please cooperate with him. He'll want to talk to me."
She read him the number off the phone and hung up. Then she
stepped out of the booth and looked at notices tacked to a tree.
They advertised phone-in sex, an oldies record store, Krishna's
Golden Path, and a baby-food boycott. She hadn't finished
reading them before the phone rang.

"Hello," she said.

"What is it?"

She told him.

"I'll be there in twenty minutes. Good-bye."

"Wait. Do you see what this means? Teddy's not a defector.
He was kidnapped."

"Is that what it means?" *Click*.

It had to, Beth thought, slowly replacing the receiver. Teddy
was kidnapped. The long-haired man must have come to steal
the passports. Why? Was it part of a cover-up? At least it meant
she could now tell Lathrop about Han Shih. She needed him.
The long-haired man wasn't talking. Lathrop would know how
to get him to talk. He had to talk. The long-haired man could
lead her to Han Shih. Han Shih could lead her to Teddy.

Beth watched the time. She reread the notices on the tree.
Nineteen minutes passed. A car pulled out of traffic and parked
by the phone booth. Lathrop was at the wheel, running an electric razor over his chin. He glanced in the mirror, put the razor
in the glove compartment, and got out.

Lathrop was dressed almost as she had seen him before; his
tie indicated a change of regiments. He wore dark glasses.

Beth stepped forward. "I have something to tell you, but first
I want to ask you a question."

"Ask."

"Do you work for the CIA?"

"I cooperate with them. What did you want to tell me?"

"Did you follow me last night?"

"That's another question." His dark glasses hid the expression in his eyes. He was good at hiding expression: except for
anger. His voice, his clothing, his neatly barbered hair all hid
it. He could have been the successful result of an experiment in
artificial intelligence. He infuriated her, and made her want to
infuriate him.

"Why did you break into our apartment?"

"It's just yours, now."

They were on the threshold of another one of their shouting matches. Like an old, bitterly married couple, they could get there easily, in three or four sentences. Beth took a step backward into a cooler zone. "There isn't time for fighting, Mr. Lathrop. Teddy's been kidnapped."

"So you said."

"I can prove it."

"Go ahead."

"First you should know something I held back before."

She told him about Han Shih, the photograph in the *Chronicle*, the register at the Beresford, and the black car on Ashby Avenue. On the lenses of Lathrop's dark glasses, two convex little Beths mimicked every move she made.

"It doesn't prove a thing," Lathrop said when she finished. The little Beths had carried the day.

"But Han Shih's an imposter."

"Of course. That should have been obvious from the word go."

"Not to an orphan."

"Are you an orphan, Ms. Hunter?"

"I meant Teddy. You know that."

Lathrop shook his head. Little Beths slid off the edges of his lenses and disappeared. "It won't add up, no matter what you do. The man is a genius. He isn't going to leap into the arms of the first middle-aged woman who walks in off the street and says she's his mother."

"He's not a genius about things like that."

"That's what you say. You didn't even know he was . . ." Lathrop stopped himself.

"A genius about codes? Is that what you were going to say?"

"Who told you that?"

"A friend."

Lathrop came closer. The little Beths grew. "Who do you think you're protecting now?" Beth was silent. He went on: "Face it: That night in your apartment was a little play performed for your benefit. It was a set-up. The picture in the paper, the timing of the wedding, everything."

"I don't believe it."

"Sure you do. You've already proved half of it yourself. All you have to do is say the rest out loud: Your prospective hubby knocked you up and walked out, just like Gomez says. But he did it all deliberately, to cover his tracks."

With all her strength, Beth threw a punch at his head. Lathrop parried it easily with his left hand and slapped her hard across the face with his right. The little Beths went very still. Beth felt the blood rush to her stinging face. The color in Lathrop's face had risen, too; the blow had had the same effect on the striker as the struck.

Lathrop smiled—a smile that was far too wide. "Don't be angry at me. I'm just the messenger."

"And you love it."

He kept smiling. "I like to help people. I'll help you understand the rest of it. You deserve to know: If you hadn't seen the sub he would have disappeared without a trace." Lathrop paused. "He left you for dead out there. You know that, don't you?"

"No."

"I can't hear you."

"No!"

"You'll come around. You'll have to. Because you saw what you saw, they won't be able to keep it secret. Not," he added, "that it will ever be public knowledge." The smile wouldn't go away. "SOSUS got a fix on your sub, by the way. At eight this morning it was four hundred miles northeast of Midway, heading due west at forty knots. Very fast, very deep. If it's Chinese—and I don't see why we have to say 'if' anymore; the cooks' tour was clearly a cover for getting their agent in place— it has to be one of their new Han-class subs. First time out of their coastal waters, as far as we know. A bright Navy boy even ran a computer simulation of how they could have come in undetected. The way the currents are at this time of year, they could have angled in from the north, shut off the power plant, and drifted down the coast. Slow, but smart."

"You don't have to prove to me that there was a submarine. I saw it. That doesn't mean Teddy went on it voluntarily. If he left voluntarily, why was there a break-in at his office?"

"Maybe he left something behind."

Beth stopped herself from reaching into her pocket. She felt the weight of its contents against her leg: plane tickets, passports with China visas, the letter from the Mertons.

Lathrop turned to the police station. "Let's find out."

Inside, he opened his wallet and showed something to the sergeant. The sergeant led them downstairs. They walked along a cement hallway, lined with cells. Faces loomed between the bars.

Someone whistled.

A hand reached for her.

She hurried by.

The long-haired man was alone in the last cell. He lay face-down on a steel cot, his freshly plastered foot hanging between the bars.

"Hey, Kung fu," the sergeant said. "Wakie-wakie."

Then he rushed forward. Beth saw the big red pool on the floor. The sergeant flipped the long-haired man on his back. There was a jagged gash in his throat, no longer bleeding. All the blood was on the floor.

A doctor came. They moved the long-haired man into the hall. The faces between the bars watched in silence. The sergeant searched the cell without success for a sharp object. The doctor knelt over the long-haired man. The long-haired man's eyes gazed blindly at the naked ceiling bulb. They didn't seem to bother anyone: The sergeant was talking on his walkie-talkie, Lathrop was watching the doctor from behind his dark glasses. Beth stared at the red pool on the floor.

"Aha," the doctor said after a while. He was examining the long-haired man's right hand. The nails were long and sharp. "Lookie here, " the doctor said. Little bits of pink pulp were caught under the nails.

"You're kidding," the sergeant said.

"Nope. The son of a bitch ripped open his own throat. Right at the jugular."

The sergeant sighed. "We take away their belts, we take away their shoelaces, and still the bastards find ways to kill themselves."

"Man the inventor," said the doctor. He pulled back the long-haired man's sleeve.

"Tracks?" the sergeant asked.

"Nope. Nice tattoo, though."

Beth looked. A green snake was tattooed around the long-haired man's wrist. It had red fangs and a split red tongue. The colors were vivid against the long-haired man's bloodless skin.

11

"It doesn't mean a thing," Lathrop said when they were back on the street. His cheeks were still rosy. "He was just a low-level operative."

"For whom?" Beth asked.

He looked at her but didn't reply. Because of his dark glasses, she couldn't tell whether he didn't know the answer or thought it was obvious. Lathrop unlocked his car and took a folder from the glove compartment. "Have a look at these."

In the folder were eight-by-ten glossy photographs of submarines, numbered one to fifty-three. Some were stamped CIA; others, DOD. Beth examined them one by one.

"Well?" Lathrop said.

She went through the photographs again. They were all slightly different, all much the same. "I didn't realize there were so many kinds of submarines."

"That's nothing."

Beth separated three photographs from the group—numbers seventeen, twenty-three, and forty-nine—and laid them on the roof of Lathrop's car. "And of those?" Lathrop asked, barely glancing at them.

"I'm not sure." She tried to match the pictures with the memory of the black fin surging from the sea. "Maybe this one," she said, pointing to number seventeen. It had square portholes along the side, and a long, low fin.

Lathrop picked it up. "Alfa class," he said. "It'll make forty-two knots submerged, and can dive to two thousand feet, maybe more. Titanium-alloy hull, anti-echoic coating, state of the art. You're close, but no prize."

"What do you mean?"

"Alfa class is Soviet. This isn't a Soviet operation."

"What makes you so sure?"

"We've been through that." Lathrop tapped number forty-nine. "The reason you're close is that this is the Chinese version of the same thing. Han class."

Beth looked at it. The Han-class submarine had round ports and a fin that seemed shorter than the Alfa's. "The fin seemed longer than that," she said.

"We call it a sail."

"And the ports . . ."

"Yes?"

But she couldn't remember whether they'd been square or round. Lathrop slipped the pictures back in the envelope and got into the car.

"What happens now?" Beth asked. The sergeant had come out on the station steps and was watching them.

"Damage control," Lathrop said, sticking the key into the ignition. "Nothing that involves you."

He turned the key. Beth rocked back on her heels and punched the side of his face as hard as she could. His dark glasses flew across the seat. He reached for the door handle, eyes full of hate. Then he saw the sergeant, now coming toward them, and stopped. Beth leaned through the window, her face close to his. "Anything that involves Teddy involves me," she said. They stared into each other's eyes. Beth started to shake.

"Anything wrong?" the sergeant asked.

"Get lost," Lathrop snarled. He aimed his stare at the black man's eyes. Muscles swelled under the sergeant's tunic, but he backed away and disappeared inside the station. When Lathrop turned to her again, the hatred in his eyes was gone. They were thoughtful instead. "Find anything at hubby's office, by the way?"

"No." She came up with a thought of her own. "Was the long-haired man working for you?"

Lathrop laughed and put on his dark glasses. "Now you're getting half-smart," he said. He turned the key and looked at her. "At first, I thought you might be part of this little scheme. Now I know you're not. You're only half-smart." He stepped on the accelerator and roared away.

"Tell that to your face!" Beth yelled after him. People stared at her. She burst into tears.

Beth went home. It wasn't home. It had been home when Teddy was there. When he had still been Teddy. Now he was a defector. Or a captive. Or a hooked trout.

She locked the door, slid the bolt into place. She turned on all the lights and looked in all the closets. She pulled the corduroy sofa through the living room, into the front hall, and jammed it against the door.

She sat on it and opened a bottle of brandy. Later the phone rang. "Hello?"

"Ms. Hunter?"

"Yes."

"My name's Means. I'm a reporter for *The New York Times*. I'd like to talk to you."

"What about?"

"Dr. Theodore Wu."

Beth hung up. The phone rang again. She switched on the answering machine. Teddy's voice took the message.

Beth went to the window and looked down at the cars parked on Chestnut Street, front wheels angled into the curb in proper San Francisco style. They were all empty. There was no reason for Lathrop to be there now. She wasn't looking for him. She was looking for the Chinese man with the shaved head and the wrestler's body. Han Shih knew that she knew.

But *what?*

Taking her drink, Beth walked out onto the balcony. The west wind was blowing a low white cloud through the Golden Gate; it flowed across the Bay like a glacier. Little sailboats were racing past the eastern end of Alcatraz. Lasers. The first boat rounded a marker. Something went wrong. The sail luffed; the boat slid wide. The second boat tacked in front and took the lead, beating upwind. The Lasers tacked back and forth. One by one they disappeared beneath the white cloud. The sun sank in the sky, first gilding the cloud, then setting it on fire. Underneath, where the Lasers were, she knew it was turning black. How would it feel to soar through the fire, down into the black? She turned away from the rail. The movement made her aware of the weight in the pocket of her skirt. The letter. She took it out and finished reading it.

                                                                she
understands the "ways of the heart" a lot better than I, Mother

does. I probably don't have to tell you that, but maybe I do. You went away a long time ago. On that scholarship. Anyway, here I am running my mouth like an old man, and I'm not so old yet—caught four trout yesterday in Pudding Creek! (Remember you caught a salmon there once? No salmon now.)

So I'll get to the point. You want to find out about your past, about the circumstances of your adoption, etc. Mother says there's lots that do these days. But in your case I don't know it makes much sense, seeing as you were an orphan. In any case, back in 1949, it was, Mother found out she couldn't have children in the normal way. Rev. Luckinbill, he died that summer, put us in touch with some missionaries not long out of China. They'd brought twenty or thirty orphan kids with them. Mother and I went down to L.A. in the fall and picked you out. The couple's name was Heidemann. They had a kind of church in Santa Monica. The Pacific Church of the Holy Spirit. The address was 12880 Montana. I'm afraid that's all the information we've got, and it's pretty old at that, but I hope it does you some good.

I'm glad to hear you've got such a nice girlfriend. Any thoughts of marriage? Let us know. We'd want to send you a little present.

All the best,
Dad
(Arthur Merton)

Beth went into the front hall and sat on the couch, her back to the bolted door. She had to think. But she couldn't, not clearly. She'd drunk half a bottle of brandy.

In the kitchen she made instant coffee. *Think. Think about Teddy sitting in the unraveling wicker chair, reading a letter.* It was early February. Arthur Merton's letter was postmarked January 31.

Teddy had folded the letter and put it in his robe pocket. A honeymoon surprise. A trip. Had *he* said that, or had she? *Think.* Beth sipped coffee. It made her nervous instead of sober. All she could think was the word *think.*

She spread her exhibits on the kitchen table. Teddy's note: "Good morning, Sleepyhead." The florist's card. The *Chronicle.* The tickets to Shanghai. The passports with the China visas. Arthur Merton's letter. It was all evidence, but of what? A defection? A kidnapping? Or a crime of a more personal nature?

Think about the trip. A surprise trip. Teddy knew she had no more teaching work until the fall. She'd planned to spend the summer finishing her dissertation, before the baby came. So there was time for a trip. With an open return. She looked at the tickets. Pan Am flight 830, San Francisco to Shanghai. The departure time was less than fourteen hours away.

At that moment, she remembered the Berlitz *Chinese for Travelers* she'd found in *Pop-Up*'s galley, with her name written on the gift wrapping in Teddy's hand. She thought about that for a while. It didn't lead to another thought.

Beth went through her exhibits again. Then she packed them away in a file folder. She looked down at the cars on Chestnut Street, checked the front door, swallowed a sleeping pill, and went to bed. She heard a boat whistle, traffic, an electric bass. The city quietened. Beth sank close to sleep, but not into it. She tried her side of the bed; she tried Teddy's. She thought of Han Shih. And her driver. She got up and checked the front door. Then she went into the study. In the household filing cabinet she found the phone bill for February. On February 3 at 9:43 A.M. there had been a six-minute call to a number in Santa Monica, costing $2.05. The number was (213) 634-2926. Beth dialed it. No answer. She called L.A. information and asked if there was a listing for the Pacific Church of the Holy Spirit on Montana.

"Six three four two nine two six."

Beth swallowed another sleeping pill and lay on the couch by the front door. At first the city was quiet. Then it grew noisier. Beth drifted toward sleep.

Something thumped outside the door. She jerked up, heart pounding. Footsteps moved off down the hall. The paper boy.

Beth got up and went to the bathroom. She looked at herself in the mirror. On the top shelf of the cabinet were a few jars of make-up, which she never used. Today was the day.

Showered, dressed, made up, she drove down the Peninsula to the airport. Wasn't there a chance Teddy had left the passports in his office knowing she would find them and realize he wanted to meet her at the airport? There was no chance. She went anyway.

The sky was low and gray. As she drove south it turned to brown. Rain began to fall. She parked and entered the terminal.

On the closed-circuit screen she saw that Pan Am flight 830 was departing on time from gate 36. There was a long line at the ticket counter. No Teddy. Forty minutes to take-off.

Beth stood in line and showed her ticket to the agent.

"Smoking or non?"

"It doesn't matter." She only wanted a boarding card so she could pass through security to gate 36.

"Aisle or window?"

"It doesn't matter."

"You're no trouble," said the agent, handing her ticket and boarding card.

That's because I'm half-smart.

Beth went to gate 36. Every seat was taken. No Teddy. People held carry-ons, attaché cases, plastic bags full of booze. One man had golf clubs. He was going to lose balls in the Chinese rough and brag about it to his pals.

"This is the first boarding call for flight eight thirty, nonstop from San Francisco to Shanghai. We'll be boarding by rows, so please wait till yours is called."

Everyone got up at once and formed a long line. Very slowly the line squeezed through a door, down a covered ramp, and out of sight. Then there were three people left in the lounge—an agent at the counter, an agent by the door, and Beth. The agent at the counter looked at Beth, picked up her phone, and said: "This is the final call for flight eight thirty, nonstop from San Francisco to Shanghai. Would all those who have not yet boarded please do so at this time."

Beth rose, and started walking toward the ramp. Maybe Teddy was waiting for her at the other end. Sure. Maybe it was part of some goddamned treasure hunt. She stopped. *Fuck it. Just fuck it.*

She turned and ran out of the terminal.

Beth drove home under the soggy sky. No one was sitting in any of the cars parked on Chestnut Street. She parked behind her building, climbed the stairs, went into her apartment. She locked the door, shot the bolt, turned on all the lights, looked in all the rooms.

Beth took down the portrait of Teddy—not Teddy, but someone else wearing his face—and put it in a closet. Then she pushed the old corduroy sofa against the front door.

She lay down on it and fell asleep.

12

A bag of oranges hung from the ceiling. They never stopped swaying, back and forth. At first, he had reached up from his bunk to steady them, but as soon as he let go they started swaying again. Back and forth. They had a nice beat. You could dance to it, if you had the strength.

The bag was made of plastic string, loosely woven. A label was glued on at a haphazard angle. On it was a picture of an orange tree and some writing. The writing was in Chinese, so he didn't know what it said. He studied the characters. There were four of them. The one on the left looked like a grasshopper doffing a top hat.

He pointed to it when the silvery-haired man came in through the steel door. "Does that one mean oranges, Father?"

The silvery-haired man came to the bunk. He was big. The edge of the bunk was level with his shoulders. The other man, the one in the sailor suit who brought the food, had to stand on tiptoes to see over. The silvery-haired man looked at the bag of oranges. His face was very close. He had smooth, immaculate skin.

"It means farm," he said. "And I'm not your father."

"Then where is he?"

The silvery-haired man patted his arm. He had long fingers. They felt cold. "He's very busy right now. He's a very important man."

"What does he do?"

"He'll tell you all about it."

"I hope he comes soon."

"He will."

"Because I'm getting married."

93

"Marriage is a fine institution."

"What a funny expression!" He laughed and laughed. The silvery-haired man laughed, too. Not his eyes, though. They watched. After a while he didn't hear any more laughter, not his, not the silvery-haired man's. He glanced at his watch. It was gone. "Where's my watch?"

"You must have lost it when you fell."

"It's at ten-fifteen. I'm not going to be late, am I?"

The silvery-haired man looked at his watch. "Plenty of time."

"What time is it?"

The silvery-haired man turned his wrist so he could see it for himself. The watch was all gold; it glittered the time at him. 2:37.

"That says two-thirty-seven."

"Different time zone."

"That's a relief. Can't be late to my own institution."

He thought of her, and suddenly the little steel chamber was watery. The silvery-haired man watched from the other side of the blur. What was going on? He made the water go away. "If you're not my father, who are you?"

"Call me Jimmy."

"That watch of yours doesn't strike me as a People's watch, Jimmy."

"People's?" Jimmy didn't get it. "It's a Rolex." He turned his thick wrist again to show it. "Guaranteed to a depth of three hundred meters."

"That'll impress the fish."

Jimmy didn't get that, either. And he didn't like it. Just for a second. No. Much less than a second. Then he smiled. His teeth were big and white and even. So big and white and even they couldn't be real. He was on the verge of mentioning it when he stopped himself. *What's wrong with you?* He felt like blabbing everything.

Long cold fingers. Pat, pat. "Everything all right?" Jimmy asked.

"My head hurts."

"You banged it in the fall."

"Fall?"

"You fell off the sail."

What a silly thing to call it. Worse than silly. The oranges swung back and forth. *Hum, hum*, sang the steel walls. No windows.

"My head hurts."

"That's too bad. I was hoping you'd help me write a letter. I have trouble writing in English."

"No problem. But who's going to mail it? A porpoise?" He laughed and laughed. Jimmy laughed too. Not his eyes. After a while, he couldn't hear the laughter anymore. "My head hurts."

"It will get better soon."

"Have you got any aspirin?"

"I've got something better than aspirin." Jimmy had a hypodermic needle in his hand.

"Be gentler this time."

"I'm always gentle. Hold out your arm."

Bite. Sting.

They looked at each other. "My head still hurts."

"Give it time to take effect."

"Okay. But I haven't got much time. I've got to be on the steps at ten-fifteen. You'd better tell my father to hurry."

"I will. But he's very busy."

"Doing what?"

"Important things."

"I want to see him. That's the whole point of the exercise."

Cold pats. "Try to sleep."

"That never works."

"Don't try."

"That works."

Laughter. Cold pats. Jimmy went out through the steel door. It was very thick, but swung open with a hydraulic sigh at Jimmy's lightest touch. It made a clicking sound when it closed, very faint. Was it locked? He'd better check.

But he couldn't get up. He could raise his head. That was it.

He felt warm and rosy. Sleep was coming. It always did when you didn't try; Jimmy was right. Just a nap. Then the headache would be gone.

The oranges swung back and forth. *Hum, hum*, sang the steel walls.

Part Two

13

She went down through the warm into the cold. A yellowtail jack swam by. She pointed her speargun at it and pulled the trigger. The spear shot through the water and into the side of the fish's head, a little too far back. The fish jerked and tried frantically to wriggle off the spear. The barbs held him in place. She started up; Daddy was waiting in the galley, ready to cook. Already he was getting impatient—she could hear him knocking on the hull. She looked down. The fish, no longer wriggling, was looking up at her. It had Teddy's eyes.

Knock knock.

Beth awoke on the old corduroy sofa.

Knock knock.

She got to her feet, lost for a moment in her own apartment. Then it all came back. The dance of the hooked trout.

Knock knock.

"Who is it?"

"Marty Kesselman."

Beth pulled the sofa out of the way and opened the door. Marty stepped in and looked at her, and at the sofa. "Jesus. What's going on?"

"Nothing."

He squeezed around the sofa. "You look terrible."

He looked terrible too, gaunt and pale, with bruised pits under his eyes. He moved past her, into the living room. She locked the door and bolted it. His blue eyes took that in, too.

"I've been trying to reach you," he said, sitting on one of the love seats. "Where have you been?"

Through the sliding door, Beth saw that the setting sun had turned the East Bay orange. "What time is it?"

"After six."

Orange slowly changed to red. The city's shadows stretched onto the Bay. "Is it Tuesday, Marty?"

"Wednesday." He rose, came over, and took her hand. "What's going on, Beth?"

"Teddy's disappeared. Isn't that enough?" She drew away, not fully trusting his touch after the night in his basement.

He didn't seem to notice her qualms. "Of course. But there's more to it than that."

"Like what?"

"I heard you chased a man down Telegraph Avenue. And he killed himself in a holding cell."

"Who told you that?"

"It's all over the place."

"But who, specifically?"

"A student in the cafeteria. The lady at the bookstore. A campus is like a small town. You know that. But that's not what I wanted to talk to you about. A friend of mine ran an analysis on those teabags. 'For any non-tea contents,' as you put it. Two of them contained no non-tea material. The third was saturated with C-two, H-three, Cl-three, O-two. Chloral hydrate."

"Which does what?"

"Anesthetizes. Puts you to sleep. Or, in enough quantity, kills."

"Was there enough quantity?"

"In the teabag itself, no." Marty waited for her to speak. When she didn't, he said: "Where did you get the teabag, Beth?"

She wasn't listening. She was staring into the darkening sky, trying to see where the teabag put Teddy.

Marty said, "Did Teddy slip you the chloral hydrate?"

"No."

"Don't be angry at me. Shit. I'm only trying to help."

"I'm sorry, Marty."

"It's okay," he said, still sounding irritated. "What was the chase on Telegraph Avenue all about?"

"I really don't know."

"No?" His eyes locked on hers. "Didn't the guy say anything before he died?"

"No."

Marty sighed. He stood up. "Don't you think you'd be better

off at my place? There won't be any . . .'' He left the thought unfinished.

"I've got to stay here. Just in case." She left hers the same way.

Marty went away. A messenger. Like Lathrop. From the window, she watched him jog off into the shadows on Chestnut Street. She noticed then that he was dressed in jogging gear, and realized he had run all the way from Berkeley and was now running back. Marty was one of those old-fashioned people, still living Thoreau's life of quiet desperation. Most others had advanced to noisy desperation instead.

Including her. She was out of control. People stared at her—in room 310, on Telegraph Avenue, in the Pan Am departure lounge. All at once, she was aware she'd been taking nothing but shallow breaths for days. She forced herself to breathe normally. Then she went into the kitchen and sat at the table. Her file folder of exhibits lay on it. After a while she opened it and reexamined them one by one. She couldn't stop herself. Much later, she shoved the sofa against the front door and lay down. Everything was quiet. The quiet went on and on. She fought off urges for brandy, for sleeping pills. After a long time she fell asleep.

When she woke in the morning, Beth felt heavy and tired. She caught herself breathing shallow breaths. Sleep hovered in her mind like a dark cloud. It wouldn't go away; it wouldn't take over. She got up and stood under a cold shower, letting it drum her to life. The manic phase was over. Now she had to fight depression.

She dressed and drove down Sutter Street, looking for Le Bouquet. No one followed her. The florist's shop was on the ground floor of a small office building, a few blocks past the Beresford. Beth parked beyond it and walked back. The morning was soft and warm, a trailer for summer. The sidewalk was crowded with loose-gaited pedestrians on their way to work, muscles relaxed by the sun. They looked content.

Beth opened the door of the shop and went in. It smelled like the Pacific forest after a rain. A little pink-cheeked man stood behind the counter, snipping rose stems. He wore a burgundy ascot at his neck and a matching apron. "May I help you?" he asked, peering up at her over rimless half-glasses. "Lovely roses this morning. And tulips, first of the year."

"Not today, thanks. Someone sent me flowers from your store last Friday. I'd like to thank whoever it was." She showed him the card. "Maybe you remember."

"Glads," he said at once. "Five dozen. Bright red. I hope you liked them?"

"Very much."

The little man looked at her closely. "I bet your favorite color is red."

"Yes."

"I've always been partial to burgundy, myself. With pink a close second." He finished trimming the roses and began wrapping them. His little fingers were quick and sure. "Don't care much for glads, though. Never did anything for me."

"Me either."

"No? Then why did she order them for you?"

"I'm not sure. Maybe she doesn't know me very well. That's why I'd like to find out who she was. It must have cost a lot of money, and I feel a bit guilty about it."

"One hundred and twenty-four dollars and ninety-two cents," the little man said. "But you should never feel guilty about receiving a gift. It spoils everything." He consulted the accounts book, lying open by the cash register. "Here we go. Five dozen glads, red. Ordered and paid for Wednesday last, for Friday delivery to two eighteen Chestnut Street, apartment three. One hundred and twenty-four dollars and ninety-two cents."

"And her name?"

"It doesn't say. She paid cash."

"Do you remember what she looked like?"

"Perfectly. A Chinese lady, about fifty. Rather chic, despite the glads. Lovely jade necklace. Do you know her?"

"Yes. Thanks."

"I hope she won't mind my telling you." He glanced over the top of his half-glasses. "Some customers prefer to remain secret admirers, although I shouldn't think that's the situation in this case." His mouth opened to say more, but he stopped himself.

"Go on."

He leaned across the counter conspiratorially and lowered his voice. "But you never can tell in this city, can you?" He cackled. "Not in this city." His face was close to hers; skin small-pored and very clean. But his breath carried the odor of decay.

It ruined the image of him that had been forming in Beth's mind: elf in his forest glade. She said good-bye and left him behind the counter, smoothing his ascot.

Outside, Beth leaned against the car, letting the sun warm her face. Han Shih had ordered the flowers on Wednesday. That meant she had known where they lived a day and a half before her visit. a day and a half before she stood in the doorway with tears in her eyes and softly called, "Tun-li."

She had also paid $124.92 for the red glads. Beth was beginning to accept that China might send a submarine across the ocean to carry Teddy away. She couldn't accept that it would pay $124.92 to send her flowers. It was unnecessary. She took the florist's card from her folder and again examined the three Chinese characters; and she knew what she needed.

Beth found a phone book and looked in the yellow pages under *I*. The page she wanted had been torn out. She went into another booth. Eight Chinese names were listed under *Investigations*. She chose Y.K. Ling Private Investigation and Consultation because it was the only one that said nothing about discretion, absolute or assured. She hoped that was because Y.K. Ling thought it was understood. The address was 417 Grant Avenue. Beth left her car where it was and walked toward Chinatown.

It was Chinatown on a sunny morning and the tourists were already there. They saw busboys polishing restaurant floors, barbecued ducks glistening behind steamy windows, baskets of fruit and vegetables that had no English names. They bought ivory chopsticks they would never learn to use and trinkets made in Korea and Singapore. They paid bent old women who sat behind cash registers and made no effort to be charming, and were careful that no bills were stuck together when they counted out the change. It could have been a movie set packed with bit players, but Beth proved it wasn't when she opened the glass door marked 417 and entered a real building on the other side.

On the first floor was a store selling giant stuffed pandas and peasant footwear. Beth climbed dusty linoleum stairs. Fatt and Co. Imports was on the second floor. The door was open. Although it was dark inside, Beth could see pandas stacked floor to ceiling along the back wall. She went up to the top floor. A small watercolor was tacked to the door. It showed two people rowing a small boat in the shadow of a mountain. Beth lifted one corner of the painting and saw the card underneath: Y.K. LING: PRIVATE INVESTIGATION AND CONSULTATION. Someone had added in pencil: *Come in.*

Beth opened the door and went into a small office. No one was in it. A cactus shaped like a giant fire hydrant filled one corner. There were wooden filing cabinets, wooden chairs, and two wooden desks, all of which might have been bought at a school-board sale in 1959. On one of the desks was a word processor; on the other, a framed photograph of seven smiling children, arranged in ascending order like symbols on a graph in boom time.

The office had three inner doors. Beth was debating which to try when the middle one opened and a girl walked in with a handful of letters. She was listening to earphones and chewing gum.

"I'm looking for Y.K. Ling," Beth said.

"You don't have to shout. I speak English."

"I'm sorry. I just thought that the earphones . . ."

"What?"

"Nothing."

The girl dropped the letters on a desk and went out, cracking her gum. A minute later, Beth heard a high-pitched purring and an old man rode through the middle doorway in a motorized wheelchair. Except for his vehicle, he could have been a Ming dynasty sage, with his blue silk robe and straggly beard. He circled the room and stopped in front of her.

"I'm looking for Y.K. Ling," Beth said again.

"Your search is over." There were accents in the old man's speech, lying in strata: Californian, British, Chinese, and one or two more she couldn't identify. If she placed them all and got them in the right order, she would know his history.

But she didn't have time. She needed a younger man, and regretted she hadn't copied the names of the other investigators from the phone book. As she tried to think of a polite way to say good-bye, Y.K. Ling reached for one of the wooden chairs and drew it closer with surprising ease.

"Please sit down."

She did.

Y.K. Ling's eyes had been half closed, almost inert, but as she was sitting down they opened wider and swept over her like radar; then they resumed their inertia.

"Do you want to hire a private investigator?"

"Yes."

"I retired last month, I'm afraid." He thought for a moment. "I hung them up. Fifty years in the business." Beth started to rise. "Twenty as a detective-sergeant in Hong Kong," he continued, "five with the San Francisco police, twenty-five on my own. Fifty all together." Y.K. Ling backed the wheelchair in a tight circle and spun it around, like a hockey player waiting for the puck to drop. He liked riding it.

"Thank you anyway," said Beth, moving toward the door.

He shifted a lever and purred up beside her. "But I still do consulting work. That's why we added consultation on the sign." He looked up at her and let his radar loose for another scan. "But it's active investigation you want, isn't it?"

"Yes."

"Albert takes care of that end now."

"Albert?"

"My son. Ten years on the San Pedro force, eighteen with me. Twenty-eight all together." He didn't trust her to do the arithmetic. "I'll take you to him." Y.K. Ling pivoted and zipped out the middle door. Beth followed.

He was far ahead, speeding down a long bare corridor. She hurried after him. The corridor met another. Y.K. Ling took the turn without slowing down, scraped the outside wall, bobbed over a ramp into a sunny rectangle, and disappeared.

She found him on a rooftop terrace, fenced on all sides by vine-covered bamboo. There were potted plants the size of small trees, a herb garden neatly laid out in a patchwork of different greens, and a bronze Buddha that didn't look like it came from one of the stores on Grant Avenue. In the center of the terrace was a round table big enough for Arthur and his knights, and on it sat two enormous bowls of steaming noodles. Everyone was digging in: the girl with the earphones, eight or nine other children, two old women, a middle-aged woman, and a large middle-aged man resting a baby on the shelf of his protruding stomach.

Y.K. Ling parked beside the man. "This is my son, Albert Ling," he said.

"Beth Hunter."

"A pleasure," Albert said, patting the baby. "Have some breakfast. We don't usually eat this late, but it's a T.D. day and the kids slept in."

"T.D., Albert?" said Y.K. Ling.

"Teacher development. The teachers spend the day developing, the kids regress. It all balances out."

"Oh Daddy," said a girl beside him, rolling her eyes.

"Don't *oh Daddy*," Albert told her. "And where are your manners?" The girl stood up, put clean bowl and chopsticks at her place, and found another chair. "That's more like it. Please sit down, Miss Hunter."

She did.

"This is my family," said Albert. "You've already met my father. This is my wife. That's my mother. My mother-in-law. My nephew Li. My niece Xu. And my kids—Jamie, Carol, Angela, Tony, Danny, Tom, and Linda."

They all stopped eating and smiled, except Linda, the girl with the earphones. "My name's not Linda, Daddy. You know that."

"I forgot. What is it this week?"

"Jade."

"Jade Ling. Not bad. And this is the baby. He hasn't got a name yet." Albert ran his fingers through the silky hair at the nape of the baby's neck. The baby slept. Beth had trouble taking her eyes off him.

Albert's mother filled Beth's bowl with noodles.

"How about Charlie?" Albert said. "Doesn't he look like a Charlie?"

"Yuck," said the children.

The noodles were good. Beth realized how hungry she was. She had seconds. Beyond the bamboo fence was another rooftop terrace. Chickens strutted across it. A woman went after one with a knife. It squawked. Then it was silent. Beth put down her chopsticks.

"What are we going to do with those pandas, Albert?" asked his wife.

"Are they all defective?"

"Yes."

"Then ship them back."

His wife rose and took the baby. "Let's go," she said. They filed out, leaving Beth alone with Y.K. Ling and Albert.

"Is Fatt and Company yours?" Beth asked.

Albert nodded. "Fatt is my mother-in-law's surname."

"The store is ours, too," Y.K. Ling added. "And the building. And the buildings on either side." He smiled happily.

"I don't think Miss Hunter's interested in all that, Dad."

"Of course she is," Y.K. Ling replied immediately. "She asked, didn't she?"

For a moment Beth thought Albert was about to roll his eyes at his father, as one of his daughters had at him, but instead he turned to her and said: "What can we do for you, Miss Hunter?"

Y.K. Ling answered for her. "She wants a private investigator."

"To do what?" asked Albert.

"Find someone," Beth replied.

"Who?" Y.K. Ling asked.

She didn't know where to begin. Opening her folder, she took out the florist's card and handed it to Albert. "What does this mean?"

Y.K. Ling dodged around a chair and peered over Albert's shoulder. "The Chinese writing?" asked Albert.

"Yes."

"Grass style," muttered Y.K. Ling with disapproval.

"I don't understand."

"Grass-style calligraphy," Albert explained. "There are three styles—block, running, and grass. This wispy kind is grass."

"I don't like it," said Y.K. Ling.

"But what does it say?" Beth asked.

"*Fu, lu, shou.*"

"Meaning?"

"It's a toast," said Albert: "Happiness, wealth, and a long life."

"No charge for that," laughed Y.K. Ling, wheeling around to his former place.

One of the boys came out on the terrace. "Telephone, Grandfather."

"Who is it?"

"Mr. Chen."

"Tell him I haven't got time today. I'm working on a case." He waved the boy away.

Albert tapped the card with his fingernail. "What does this have to do with the person you're looking for?"

"I want to find the woman who sent it."

"How do you know it was a woman?"

"I've met her."

"And it's obvious from the writing," Y.K. Ling said to Albert.

Albert ignored him. "What's her name?"

"Han Shih," Beth said.

The old man laughed.

"What's so funny?" Beth asked.

Looking at his father with disapproval, Albert said, "Han Shih is not a name, exactly. It just means a woman of the Han family. It's a big family. There are probably forty million Hans on the mainland alone."

"Twenty million Han women," the old man said, trying to smother his laughter. He wouldn't let her do her own arithmetic.

One of the old women came out. Albert's mother. She said something in Chinese to her husband. It made Albert smile and the old man sigh. She turned and went away. Y.K. Ling rolled slowly after her.

Albert watched him go. "He's not taking well to retirement."

"It's only been a month."

"A month? It's almost eight years now. Every day he plays Mah-Jongg with Mr. Chen. It gets him down."

"Maybe he should come out of retirement."

Albert leaned toward her and lowered his voice. "He can't do the job anymore. Not since he got shot. And he knows it."

"How did he get shot?"

Albert gazed at Buddha, shining in the sunlight. "Get him to tell you sometime. He makes it into a funny story. Kind of." He was silent for a few moments. Then he turned to Beth and said: "Why do you want to find this woman?"

Beth told him about everything except the baby. She watched him carefully for any signs of belief or disbelief. There were none. His face, fuller than his father's, had the same capacity for looking inert; if he had his father's radar, he didn't let it show. Only once did he interrupt, asking for a fuller description of the long-haired man's tattoo. When she finished, he rose and walked to the other side of the terrace. He was much bigger than she had supposed; his bulky shoulders and chest kept his stomach in proportion. He looked almost as powerful as Han Shih's driver.

The woman on the next roof went after another chicken. She

saw Albert and waved her knife at him. He waved back and rejoined Beth. The chicken squawked.

"Miss Hunter—"

"Beth."

"Beth. Call me Albert. My father named me after Einstein. He's a Taoist, and he thinks relativity is good Taoist doctrine." Albert smiled. Then he looked at her and his smile faded. "Have you ever heard of triads?" he asked.

"Chinese secret societies? Tongs?"

He nodded. "The Red Band, the Little Spears, the Boxers, the Chee Kung Tong. There were dozens of them in China at one time, some very old. At first they were political—they opposed the Ching dynasty, the Manchus. 'Restore the Ming and exterminate the Ching.' That was their slogan. When the Manchus finally fell, most of the triads turned to crime—opium, prostitution, gambling, extortion. A few got involved in the Revolution—some on one side, some on the other, a few on both. After the Communists won, Mao tried to stamp them out, except for one or two which had helped him. The Ko Lao Hui—Society of Elder Brothers—is still a legal party in China. The surviving triads ran away—to Hong Kong, Macao, Taiwan, Singapore. They've done very well. They're like the Mafia: They thrive in a free-market economy."

"What are you telling me?"

Albert stood up. "Come inside."

She followed him down the long corridor, into another corridor, and through a doorway. They were in a small room. Unframed watercolors covered the walls. Y.K. Ling and another old man were seated at a card table. There were cards on it, but they weren't using them: Mr. Chen was asleep, and Y.K. Ling was painting a picture of rowboats in the shadow of a mountain. Daffy Duck was jumping up and down on a TV screen in the corner, but the sound was off.

Y.K. Ling mixed blue and green in a teacup and dabbed at the paper. The dabs became a lake, peaceful and still.

"Dad?" The old man looked up; his eyes were far away. "Miss Hunter saw a man with a green snake tattoo on his wrist."

The old man's eyes brightened. "Like this?" he asked, making a few quick strokes on the paper: green snake, split red tongue, red fangs.

"Yes," Beth said.

"The Brotherhood of the Green Snake," Y.K. Ling murmured, touching up the tail.

"What's that?"

"One of the triads I was telling you about," Albert said. "A secret society."

The old man mixed blue and green with his brush and made the snake disappear in the quiet water.

"What do you remember about them, Dad?"

"Everything I knew," Y.K. Ling answered with annoyance. Daffy Duck caught his attention; they all watched Daffy jump up and down. When Y.K. Ling spoke again there was no annoyance in his tone.

"Everything I knew about them wasn't much. They were based in Taiwan. They expanded to Hong Kong. This was about nineteen fifty-two. They got involved in smuggling. Gambling. Took over most of the waterfront. We did what we could, but it wasn't a lot. No one would talk. The brothers threatened traitors with the Death of a Thousand Cuts. They had a lot of hocus-pocus like that."

Y.K. Ling picked up the teacup and held it with his middle finger touching the bottom and his thumb and forefinger around the edge. "This was one of their recognition signals. More hocus-pocus, but it scares some people."

His voice trailed off. *Hocus-pocus*, thought Beth, *like sending five dozen bright red glads*. On the TV, Daffy Duck beat his fists against a tree.

The old man looked at Albert. "I once saw a corpse that had died the Death of a Thousand Cuts. Once was all they had to do. The thousand cuts come one at a time, you see, maybe over a few months. That kind of thing scares some people."

Like the long-haired man, Beth thought.

Y.K. Ling turned to her. "There's an old Chinese saying— 'Kill the chicken to scare the monkey.' " She waited for him to continue. Instead he picked up his brush and ruffled the surface of the lake.

Beth and Albert returned to the terrace. "Well?" Beth said.

"Well what?"

"Are you going to help me?"

He switched on his radar. It wasn't quite as powerful as his father's. "I charge one hundred and fifty dollars a day. Plus expenses. And I need a five-hundred-dollar retainer."

"You'll have a certified check this afternoon."

Albert turned away and looked at the bronze Buddha. "Don't waste your money," he said quietly.

She ran to face him and gripped his arm. "You don't believe me? You think it's all some hysterical invention?"

"No. I believe you." He drew his arm away. "That's why I'm telling you not to waste your money."

"Are you saying Teddy's dead?"

"He might be. He might not." Albert paused. When he continued, his voice was gentler. "The Brotherhood of the Green Snake is involved. And a foreign government—triads don't have submarines. They've gone to a lot of trouble to take your friend away. I don't think you'll see him again."

Beth reached up and took Albert by his massive shoulders. "Yes I will. Even if I have to dig him up out of the goddamned ground."

They stared into each other's eyes. Albert looked away. "All right," he said.

Beth let go. "I'll bring you a check this afternoon."

"Just put it in the mail." Albert smiled. "And it doesn't have to be certified."

14

The plane dipped down out of the blue and into the brown. Underneath, the city shimmered like dull brass at the bottom of a muddy river. The tall buildings of the new downtown were invisible. Perhaps they had already been eaten away by the air.

"That's just fog," said the man sitting next to Beth; and she knew he must live somewhere down there. Los Angeles. Its citizens had forgotten what fog looks like, or else they were just refusing to grant smog diplomatic recognition.

Until that morning, Beth had owned a small stake in the fortunes of the city: Her father had given her five hundred shares of MGM common stock as a graduation present. But after leaving Albert Ling, she had called the broker and told him to sell.

"Do you know something I don't?" he'd asked her.

"Maybe," she'd replied. But all she knew was that she needed the money to pay her detective bills.

"I've got some MGM in my own account," the broker had confessed worriedly before she hung up. He sounded very young.

Inside the terminal, Beth rented the smallest and cheapest car available. It easily held its own with the Mercedes-Benzes and Jaguars in the traffic jam on Lincoln Boulevard. Everyone drove with the windows up, sealed in individual micro-climates, mouthing the words to soft-rock cassettes. Beth turned onto Ocean Boulevard and drove along with the grassy promenade on her left. It was packed with sleepers: retired Americans on lawn chairs, illegal aliens flopped on the grass.

Beth left the ocean at Montana and drove inland until she came to 12880. The Pacific Church of the Holy Spirit was a barn made of smoked glass and steel, crowded between Seamus's Irish Pub, advertising 136 different beers, and Fabrice's Figure Salon,

promising a new body in sixty days. Beth found a parking space
and walked to the church. It was hot and still. She was the only
walker around.

A signboard at the foot of the stairs leading to the church read:
REV. DR. RORY BROCK. SUNDAY SERMON: HOOKED ON VALIUM?
TRY CHRIST INSTEAD. Beth opened the tall glass door and reentered
machine-controlled air. It was almost as cold as a meat locker.

On the far wall hung a big gold cross, roomy enough for the
crucifixion of three or four Jews at once. In front of the cross
was a raised dais, carpeted in gold shag. From there, rows of
blond maple pews stretched all the way to the entrance. They
were empty. It wasn't the kind of church where people came in
off the street and sat for a while. It was hard to imagine any god
who would want to be there, either.

A crossing aisle led from the front of the dais to a closed door
on one side of the church. Beth knocked.

"Come right in," called a man. He had the kind of baritone
used for the voice-overs in insurance commercials, when they
want you to know you're in good hands.

The door opened into a large office. It had thick wall-to-wall
gold broadloom, red leather couches and chairs, a big glass-and-
steel desk. A man sat behind the desk, watching a television
mounted on one of its corners. He had a full head of well-cut
light-brown hair that had probably been blond when he was
younger, and a tanned face with a few lines but no weak features. He glanced up at Beth, smiled a big smile with no weak
teeth, and swiveled the TV so she could see the screen.

A lone man was on TV. He had well-cut light-brown hair and
a tanned face with no weak features and enough make-up to hide
the lines. He was standing on a gold dais, before a gold cross.

"Hell is real; it's as real," he was saying, "as sin." Something
had been done with the treble to make his baritone more penetrating. The camera moved in. The man looked it right in the eye and
repeated what he'd just said, but in a menacing whisper. He
paused, turned his back, walked slowly to the rear of the dais, then
quickly spun around and shouted: "And you all know sin, don't
you?" Murmurs of assent rose from an unseen audience. "Sure
you do. And hell is every bit as real. So you should all be in mortal
fear of hell. But are you? No! So you just keep right on sinnin'."
Down to a whisper: "And if you're not shaking with the fear of
hellfire in your heart, Jesus can't save you. Jesus can't—"

The man behind the desk punched a button, freezing the image on the screen. "Look at that," he said, shaking his head. He took a cassette recorder from his pocket and spoke into it: "Page eight, line fourteen. Bad shadows under eyes and chin. Get in with a follow spot at the pause and keep it there till the second break."

He clicked off the recorder. "Worst bunch of amateurs I ever saw," he said to Beth. "I'd fire every darn one of them if it wasn't for the union." He glanced at his white-suited image trembling on the screen and switched it off. "What can I do for you, young lady?" He held out his hand and gave hers a hard squeeze. "Reverend Doctor Brock."

"Doctor Hunter," said Beth; it would be true in a few months.

His hand went tentative and slipped away. He started to speak, then stopped himself. Beth knew he wanted to ask what sort of doctor she was, but couldn't think of a way to do it without exposing himself to the same question. Instead he smiled and said: "Call me Rory." He waited for her to reveal her first name. When she didn't, the lines on his forehead deepened. He made a steeple with his fingers and pointed it at her. "What brings you to our church? I provide spiritual counseling, but only by appointment."

"I'm looking for a married couple who were involved at one time with your church, and may still be. Their name is Heidemann."

He leaned back in his chair and fit the point of the steeple into the dimple in his chin. "May I ask what you want of them?"

Beth had no desire to explain everything to the Reverend Doctor Brock. "I'm a historian at Cal. I'm doing research for a possible book on Protestant evangelism in China before the revolution. I understand the Heidemanns were there."

"How do you know?"

"It's public knowledge. I've checked the consular records."

"I see." Brock rose and walked silently across the broadloom to the floor-to-ceiling smoked-glass window. Outside, the stucco side wall of Fabrice's Figure Salon was a white glare.

"Can you tell me where I can reach the Heidemanns?"

Brock turned from the window and looked at her closely. His alert eyes had that strong but narrowly focused power for sizing up people: the eyes of a good salesman.

"Before I do, I'd like to know something of your attitude."

"Toward what?"

"The missionaries in China. Missionaries in general."

Beth thought: *Shouldn't that be the Heidemanns' concern?*

She smiled and said, "Oh, it's not that kind of research. My area's statistics: how many missionaries, where they went, what they built, how many converts they made, how much money they spent—that kind of thing. Very dry."

"Bless you."

The door opened. A big-boned woman in a leotard looked in. "Hi, Ro," she said. She saw Beth. "Oops. You're busy."

"I'm afraid we'll have to move your appointment back half an hour, Fabrice."

Her eyes on Beth, the woman backed out and closed the door. Brock sighed. "Poor woman. I do what I can." He stared out the window at the stucco and lost himself in thought. "She is one of those people who believe in keeping themselves in wonderful physical shape," he said in the kind of tone people reserve for musing to themselves; but Beth knew he was a professional talker and never gave it away. He sighed again. "If only they cared as much about their spiritual shape." He snapped a little too visibly out of his reverie and turned to Beth: "You seem to be in good physical shape."

She was beginning to form an understanding of his methodology with women. "You were going to tell me about the Heidemanns."

The lines in his forehead deepened. He sighed once more. This one might have been real. "I can't tell you about Reverend Heidemann," he said. "But Mrs. Heidemann is now Mrs. Brock. We've been married for twenty-five years. She should be at home. I'll call and tell her you're coming." He gave Beth an address in Beverly Hills.

Beth went outside. The heat tried to punish her for the time spent in cooled air; the smog tried to corrode her lungs. She got into the rented car and drove east. She gave up trying to understand Brock's methodology with women: The data were incomplete.

The Brocks' house was a Spanish pile surrounded by a wall. The wall was Spanish, too—topped with orange tiles. Beth pressed the buzzer at the gate. A thin female voice crackled in the speaker: "Who is it?"

"Beth Hunter."

The gate clicked. Beth pushed it open and walked toward the house. Big stone flowerpots stood on both sides of the door, but all they had in them was gravel. The heavy wooden door had a round beveled window, protected by a steel grille. Through the glass Beth saw darkness, then a pale face. The door opened.

"Dr. Hunter?" the woman said, squinting into the brightness.

She was a few inches shorter than Beth, and much too thin. And perhaps twenty years older than the Reverend Doctor Brock.

"Call me Beth."

"Helen Brock." She held out her hand. It was hot and dry. "Did you see Rory at the church?"

"I just came from there."

"Was he alone?"

"Yes." Fabrice had just popped in for a second.

The woman peered up at her. "You're so young to be an author."

"I'm not."

"But Rory said—"

"Not yet," Beth interrupted. "I've still got a lot of work to do." For her convenience, she had told Rory Brock a little lie. Now it was getting in the way. She had no reason to lie to Helen Brock, no reason to distrust either of them. All she had to ask were two simple questions: "Have you spoken to Teddy? What did he say?"

Ask them.

She looked down at Helen Brock and started to speak. The woman was watching her carefully; the whites of her eyes were yellow. Beth couldn't utter the words. Teddy had telephoned Brock's church. Now he was gone. She had no reason to trust them, either.

"Praise the Lord for your modesty," Helen Brock said. "Anyone working on a book is an author to me. Come in."

Beth followed her into the dark house. They passed a living room and dining room, both looking unused, and went into a small sitting room. Heavy curtains were drawn against the day; the room was lit by two table lamps and a soundless game show on TV.

They sat facing each other across a low coffee table, in soft old chairs with worn chintz arms and uncoiling springs. "You want to find out about our mission in China," Helen Brock said.

"That's right."

The woman leaned forward. Beth noticed she wore a prosthesis where her left breast should have been. It stood out pertly, like the breast of a high-school girl; her right one drooped on her chest. "I'm glad to talk about it. Partly because I think it's important. But mostly, Lord forgive me, because it was the happiest time in my life."

On TV a huge dial spun to a stop and began flashing. A woman jumped up and down; now it was the happiest time in *her* life. Helen noticed the commotion and switched off the set. "Where would you like to begin?" she asked Beth. "You must have a system for this sort of research."

She didn't even have a pencil and a note pad. "Just tell me from the beginning. How was it you went to China?"

Helen sat back in her chair, bust half pert, half withered. Her dark eyes looked inward. "My father sent me. He founded the Pacific Church of the Holy Spirit, back in the twenties."

"It doesn't look that old."

Helen frowned. "It's been rebuilt. The original was an exact replica of the old Congregational Church in Cornwall, Connecticut, where my father was born. The new building was Rory's idea. What do you think of it?"

"I don't know much about church architecture."

"Very diplomatic," Helen said with a faint smile. "You needn't be: Rory's church is a cold, awful place. I should never have let him talk me into it."

"Are you involved with the church, too?"

Helen blinked. "I own it. I'm my father's only child. He left it to me in his will."

"Are you talking about the building itself?"

"The building itself. The land it's on. The ministry. The mailing lists. Everything."

Beth had never thought of a church as someone's personal property. "When did your father die?" she asked.

"In the winter of nineteen fifty. Not long after Rex and I came back from China. At first I wanted to take over the preaching myself. But I get scared talking in front of lots of people." She closed her eyes. "I prayed every night that God would take my nervousness away. But He had something else in mind for me."

She dabbed at her eyes. "So Rex did the preaching. He was a good preacher, although not as good as Rory. Men don't seem to get nervous in front of a crowd. They seem to thrive on it. My men, anyway." Helen smiled a lopsided, embarrassed smile that pulled her face out of shape. She was turning into a kinetic piece of cubist sculpture: Her breasts didn't match, and neither did the halves of her face.

"Who is Rex?"

"Rex Heidemann. My first husband. He was a missionary too. We met and married in China, about a year before the Communists took over.'' Helen closed her eyes again, and screwed up her face, as though to squeeze her thoughts to death. Beth had a question in mind, but she didn't want to ask it. The answer came anyway: ''We were divorced in nineteen fifty-two. Rex lost his faith.''

Helen opened her eyes. ''It's dark in here.'' But she made no move to open the curtains; instead she switched one of the table lamps up to 150 watts. ''That's better.'' She turned her dark, lusterless eyes on Beth. ''I never lost my faith, Dr. Hunter. Not my faith in Jesus Christ. Faith in myself, yes. I lost that forever when Rex left—when we were divorced. I tried to run the church by myself for six years. And I didn't do a bad job. The Lord has seen fit to bless me with administrative skills. But my preaching got worse and worse. I was too nervous to sleep on Saturday nights. Then Friday nights too. Finally all nights.'' Her lower lip trembled. She mauled it with her hand. It kept trembling. ''Do you get nervous in front of an audience, Dr. Hunter?''

''Everyone does.''

''Not like me.'' Helen sighed. It seemed to Beth that a minute passed before she drew her next breath. It gave her a little spurt of energy, and she went on more briskly. ''So when Rory came along—he was just a seminary student then—I married him. He really isn't that much younger than I am, you know, despite what people think. How old do you think I am?''

''I'm terrible at guessing people's ages.''

''Go ahead; I won't be upset.''

''Fifty-nine,'' Beth said, pushing her underestimate as low as she thought she could without making her flattery obvious.

''Fifty-six,'' said Helen in a small voice. ''And Rory's forty-seven. Nine years. That's not much these days, is it?'' But no feeling backed up her words. Beth's guess had flattened her rising spirits.

''No,'' Beth said. ''Not at all.'' But Rory could pass for thirty-five. And Helen looked seventy.

''Of course, Rory's very boyish looking,'' Helen said, reading her thoughts. ''How long were you with him?''

''Just a few minutes.''

''What was he doing?''

''I think he was preparing a sermon.''

''Was he alone?''

''Yes.''

Silence. "It's hot in here," Helen said, pushing up the sleeves of her dress. She had a hospital identification bracelet around one wrist. "Do you find it hot?"

"A little."

"I'll squeeze some orange juice." Helen got up.

"Don't go to the trouble."

"No trouble. Besides, I need the vitamin C. In the meantime, you can look at my China album." She unlocked the top drawer of a heavy armoire and removed a leather-bound volume. "It might give you some ideas," she said, handing it to Beth and leaving the room.

Beth opened the album. It was full of black-and-white photographs, pasted on black paper. The photographs were turning brown. A caption was inked in white beside each one.

Most of them meant nothing to Beth. Some showed white people she didn't know; a few were Chinese people she didn't know; several were shots of a small brick building with a cross on the roof—in one of these, a bare-chested rickshaw boy pulled a white man across the foreground.

Three photographs interested Beth:

"Rex and Me, April 8, 1948." Rex had been better-looking than Rory—blonder, with bigger teeth and a deeper dent in his chin. He was wearing a morning coat, Helen a bridal gown. She was thin, but not gaunt. The smile on her face was straight. Rex had his arm around her.

"Rex, Me, and J. Han, Lake Tai, 1948." Rex, Helen, and a Chinese man were sitting around a picnic hamper; the fuzzy gray background might have been the lake. Helen wore a sleeveless dress and a kerchief; Rex, white pants and an open-neck shirt; the Chinese man, a long robe. The Chinese man looked much bigger than Rex; he had thick black hair and a broad face. He was looking right into the camera; Rex was saying something to him; Helen was watching Rex, her eyes wide and adoring.

"The Children, Shanghai, Spring 1949." Two rows of Chinese children, small ones in front, bigger ones in the rear, posed for a group picture in a small courtyard. The building with the cross on the roof was in the background. Helen was in the center of the second row, a crying baby in her arms. At the bottom of the photograph were two matching rows of handprinted names, identifying the children. The baby was the seventh child in the second row. The seventh entry in the top row of names was *Wu Tun-li*.

"Those are the orphans," Helen said. Beth hadn't heard her come in. "Twenty-six orphan children. A drop in the ocean, really," Helen said, handing her a glass of orange juice. Beth took one sip and didn't want any more.

Helen sat down on the other side of the coffee table. "We got them out of China a few months before the Communists took Shanghai. Getting them out was the easy part. It was getting them into the States that was hard. That's when I learned the Lord had blessed me with administrative skills." She raised her glass of juice to her lips and drank it down. "I'm so thirsty."

Beth gazed down at the unhappy Teddy.

"That was the best thing I ever did in my life," Helen said. "No matter what my father thought. They were all adopted by good Christian families within a year."

"What did your father think?"

Helen tried an ironic smile, but it twisted out of shape. "He believed we should have stayed in China and carried on. There were missionaries who did. They got shot."

"Maybe your father didn't realize the danger."

"He knew. That's what made him sure we were using the orphans as an excuse to come home. He and Rex had a big fight about it. He told Rex he would never let him be the preacher in his church. That's about the time Rex lost his faith. And went away."

"What became of him?" Beth asked as gently as she could.

Helen's smile twisted a little more. "He got rich. Quick. Later, I wrote to Rex asking him to come back—not to me, to the church. But it was already too late."

"How did he get rich?"

"In the wine business. Rex grew up on a farm. I guess it came easy to him."

"What did he do in the wine business?"

"He started Berryessa Wines. He still owns it, as far as I know. Have you ever had any of their wine?"

"Yes."

"Is it good? I don't touch alcohol myself."

Beth remembered a bottle at a restaurant. Too sweet for her; Teddy had liked the drawing on the label—a cart overloaded with grapes in front of a setting sun. "Not bad," Beth said. "But I'm not an expert."

There was a long silence. Beth looked at Teddy, crying long ago. A few ideas shifted in her mind, forming a new pattern. She began to understand why her instincts had led her to be careful with Helen Brock. It had to do with something Teddy had said to Han Shih, words that hadn't registered at the time: "Or did I find you?"

"Don't you like your juice?"

"It's very good." Beth forced herself to take another sip.

"They say large amounts of vitamin C can cure cancer."

It was a question. Beth didn't know the answer. She wanted to get out of the dark, airless room. She put the album on the coffee table, turning it so Helen could see the picture of the orphans. "In terms of my research, it might help to know what happened to these children."

Helen looked at her admiringly. "What a good idea! I have records of the names of all the adopting parents. That might give you a start."

Beth nodded. "The children must all be grown up. Do you ever see any of them?"

"No. The parents of two or three belonged to the church at one time, but I lost track of them long ago."

"None of the children has ever come to visit you?"

"No." Helen's face began to twist. "Why would they?"

"Maybe out of gratitude. Look at this little boy. Wu Tun-li. Here you are holding him. Wouldn't it be natural for him to want to thank you?"

Helen glanced down at the photograph. Then she closed the album and held it on her lap. She looked at Beth, looked away. "I don't know. I'm a little tired. Not thinking too clearly. The fact is I haven't been well lately."

"I'm sorry to hear that."

"I think I'd like to rest."

Beth rose. "Of course. I can find my way out."

Helen licked her lips. Her tongue was cracked and yellow. "I can't remember where Rory said you taught. Is it UCLA or USC?"

"Cal."

"Cal? Is that Berkeley?"

"Yes."

Helen reached for her glass, saw it was empty, and took Beth's. It rattled against her teeth.

Beth left her. Outside the air was hot and full of smog. Beth inhaled a big lungful. It felt good.

15

"May I speak frankly?" asked Albert Ling.

"Of course."

"You have an Oriental mind."

"What do you mean?"

"Like Anna May Wong. You should have been a forthright round-eye, like Gary Cooper. All you had to do was tell her you knew she spoke to him, and ask her what was said."

Beth stifled an angry reply. "You're right." Something about the way she said it made him laugh. She laughed too.

Albert refilled their glasses. On the jukebox a bitter young millionaire was singing that he'd love to love you baby but right now his mind was full of zombie. "That's not music," Albert said before Beth had a chance to hear what rhymed with *zombie*. "Smokey is music. Aretha is music." He dipped his big shoulders once or twice to silent Motown rhythms, slight movements but enough for Beth to see he would be a good dancer.

"Should I fly back down and try her again?"

"Not worth it."

"But I should still get in touch with her first husband, shouldn't I?"

Albert looked at her for a long moment. Then he smiled. "Why not? It can't hurt. Meanwhile I'll follow up on one or two other things."

"What things?"

"Too soon to say. I'll be in touch."

"Are they the kind of things that might get my hopes up?"

"I already told you not to get your hopes up."

Albert reached into his back pocket and unfolded some papers.

"What's that?"

"I went to the Chinese-American library this morning and looked up the Crafoord Prize article in the Far Eastern edition of *Time*." He placed a copy of it on the table. Beside it he laid a copy of the story from the U.S. edition.

"They're identical."

"Right. No mention of his Chinese name or mainland origin. He couldn't possibly have been traced from that article. The clipping you saw was a fake."

Albert paid the bill. They went outside. It was early evening. Planes dipped down from the glowing sky and glided toward the airport, not far away. Beth got into her car.

"One more thing," Albert said. "If you've got time tomorrow, maybe you should find a new place to live. Temporarily."

"Why?"

"So you don't wear yourself out pushing the sofa back and forth."

Beth drove home and parked on Chestnut Street. The windows of her apartment were dark. She sat in the car and thought of calling Albert: "Escort me into my own house." She couldn't. Instead she drove to Verdi's Pizza Bar in North Beach and ordered a pizza for delivery to her address. She drove back to Chestnut Street and parked in the same space. The windows in her apartment were darker. She sat in the car.

A small van with the words *Verdi's Pizza* on the side roared up the hill and came to a noisy stop beside her. The delivery boy got out, holding the pizza in an insulating bag. He might have played tackle on his high-school football team, except he had three or four rings in each ear and purple hair.

Beth opened the door. "Do you mind bringing it up? My wallet's inside."

They climbed the stairs together, smells of onion and garlic mounting with them. The boy was heavy on his feet; he hummed a tune that sounded like the song about the lover with a mind full of zombie.

Beth felt safe.

She unlocked the door and pushed it open. The refrigerator buzzed to life.

"Caught napping," the boy said.

Beth turned on the lights and glanced around. No one was there.

"Thank you," she said, paying the boy and adding a tip. He

took it and started out down the stairs. "What rhymes with *zombie*?" she called after him.

"*Tschombe*," the boy replied over his shoulder. "The song's called 'Katanga.' " He went down the stairs humming it.

Beth was about to close the door when she heard lighter footsteps coming up. A man appeared at the top of the stairs. He didn't look at all like Han Shih's driver; he was short and white with thick glasses and a weight problem. Beth slammed the door anyway.

"Wait!" he cried.

Running footsteps. She slid the bolt into place and pushed the sofa against the door.

He knocked on it. Beth didn't answer.

"Please, Ms. Hunter. I want to talk to you. My name's Robert Means. I'm a reporter from *The New York Times*. I've been trying to reach you." Beth said nothing. "We can talk off the record, if you like." She could feel how hard he was listening on the other side. "I have information you might want to know," he added. He wasn't going to give up.

That didn't mean he was who he said he was. "Who writes the humor column for your paper?" Beth asked.

He laughed. "Russ Baker. Craig Claiborne does the cooking, Murray Chass follows the Yankees, and Al Hirschfeld draws the Broadway caricatures. Do I pass?"

Beth let him in.

"And here's my press card," he said, handing it to her. His face looked better in the photograph, tanned and thinner. In life it was pale, pouchy, tired, and darkened with five o'clock shadow.

She gave it back. "You said you have information."

Means looked around, sniffing. "Something smells good."

"Pizza."

"What's on it?"

She couldn't remember. She hadn't considered eating it. "Help yourself."

"Thanks. I will if you join me."

Beth put the pizza on the kitchen table and opened two bottles of beer. "Lovely," said Means. "I haven't had a bite since breakfast."

Neither had Beth. She opened the cardboard box. "Perfect," Means said, taking off his jacket and draping it over the back of his chair; the armpits of his blue shirt were a deeper blue.

"Garlic, onion, tomato, pepperoni. Just the way I like it." He bit off half a piece.

Beth tried it. She realized how hungry she was. They finished the pizza in five minutes, neither saying a word or feeling the strain of silence. They had hunger in common.

Means unstuck the last morsel of crust from the box and popped it in his mouth. "God, I was hungry." He sat back and sipped his beer. "My name's not really Means, you know. I mean, it is, but my grandfather's name was Menalini. I'm Means in everything except eating. When I eat I revert to Menalini."

The refrigerator clicked off. They both glanced at it, but it did nothing to help them. They were out of pizza and small talk.

"You mentioned information," Beth said.

Means put his beer bottle onto the table before speaking, as if to mark the postprandial exit of Menalini the eater. He even looked different: more detached. On the other side of his thick lenses, his eyes seemed small and far away, as though seen through the wrong end of a telescope.

"Do you know a lot about the Central Intelligence Agency, Ms. Hunter?"

"No."

"That's the way they like it. Not so much because they're the organization in charge of secrets, which is the reason they always give, but because they're an organization, period. Secrecy gives them the excuse to act out the fantasies of all the bureaucracies. That's the most important thing to understand about the CIA, Ms. Hunter. It's office work. If you look at it that way, it begins to make sense. The main occupation of any office is the struggle for dominance. The work it does is a by-product, useful as a kind of text where those in the know can read who's in and who's out."

"That's very interesting, Mr. Means, but it's not the information I had in mind."

"You sound like my editor." Means reached for beer, then changed his mind. "The point is, Ms. Hunter, the text the CIA is now attempting to read is the story of the defection of Theodore Wu."

"He didn't defect."

"No?" Means said, pulling out a notebook and pen. "What happened to him?" The pen hovered over the blank page.

Suddenly, without knowing why, Beth was sure that if Teddy's disappearance became public knowledge she would never see him again. Means's goal was to explain what had happened to Teddy in terms of geopolitics; Lathrop's goal was to use it against enemies, internal and external; hers was to find Teddy and bring him back. "What does *off the record* mean, exactly?"

"That I won't print anything you say. It's for my background only."

"Then put your notebook away."

"I still have to take notes."

"Then I don't have to talk."

Means put the notebook away. "What happened to Theodore Wu?"

"How do you know anything has happened to him?"

Means sighed. "I tried to explain that already. There are factions inside the CIA. And in the State Department and the White House. They fight over things. Right now, they're fighting over Theodore Wu. Sometimes, if one side thinks it's losing, it goes outside for reinforcements. That's where freedom of the press comes in. They leak things. To me."

"What were you told?"

Means put his hands behind his head and leaned back in his chair. He didn't seem at all impatient, or annoyed that she was asking questions. He had none of the intense edginess of a movie reporter; they were just sitting around the kitchen table, having a chat. But the dark-blue stains kept spreading under his arms.

"I was told that Theodore Wu is one of the leading experts on the mathematics of codes in the Western world. Friday the eleventh, the day he was to marry you, he defected to the People's Republic of China. No one seems to dispute that part. They are now attempting to track a submarine across the Pacific, something they're not as good at as they think they are. There is also additional evidence of defection, which I haven't been told. I was able to establish independently that Dr. Wu is a mathematical genius and has contributed on a theoretical level to U.S. cryptography; also that no one has seen him since Friday the eleventh. Other than that, all I have are gaps. I was hoping you could help fill them in."

"You said there was an internal disagreement about Teddy. You didn't explain."

Behind the thick lenses Means's little eyes studied her. "Have you ever thought of becoming a reporter, Ms. Hunter?"

His flattery was resistible. "I'm happy doing what I'm doing."

He laid it on a little thicker. "You're writing a dissertation on an episode in the Inquisition that took place on a galleon, and what it reveals about the lives of sixteenth-century Spanish sailors. Your department head thinks it's a brilliant concept.''

"It is. I stole it from Le Roy Ladurie.''

Means gave up. ''The disagreement is between the right-wingers and the moderates. There are no left-wingers in Washington these days, and the moderates are where the right wing used to be. The right-wingers have never been happy about the rapprochement with China. In their hearts, they're still pro-Taiwan. They're going to use Dr. Wu's defection as a demonstration that the Chinese can't be trusted and we've got to return to the days when we treated them the same way we treat the Russians—as eternal enemies. Dr. Wu is the best thing that's happened to them since brainwashing in the Korean War. The moderates don't like the Chinese, either, but find them useful. They want to keep the Russians isolated, and at the same time sell the Chinese a billion dishwashers. They'd like to keep everything quiet if they can, and let the Chinese know that we see the defection of Dr. Wu as an unfortunate but not very important blip on a rising graph of good relations.''

"What if he was kidnapped?''

"That would wipe the moderates out,'' Means said. He leaned closer. ''Was he?''

"I don't know.'' Beth was realizing with a shock that Lathrop was on the side of the moderates.

"I think you have an opinion, at least. What were you doing on the morning of the twelfth, twenty miles off the coast in a dinghy?''

"I thought your sources hadn't told you the other evidence.''

"They didn't. I traced your movements on my own.'' And he was proud that he had. ''Did you take Dr. Wu out in that dinghy and rendezvous with a Chinese sub?''

"No.''

"I believe you. If the CIA thought you'd done that, you'd be in an interrogation cell right now. You don't seem to be a suspect. So what were you doing in that dinghy?''

She looked at him. He was only a few feet from her, but his eyes were as distant as the editor's desk in New York. He could see the patterns more clearly from there, the better to fit her in. ''Have you written anything about this yet?''

"Ah. I begin to understand you. You don't want to look foolish in the papers. Don't worry. I haven't written anything yet. I don't have the facts. But there's nothing you can do to keep this story from coming out."

Beth rose. "What kind of fool will I look like in the papers, Mr. Means?" His eyes weren't so distant now. "A fool in love? Knocked up? Jilted? Is that the kind of story you want to write?"

"Of course not."

"I don't care if you do. Teddy and I were way beyond all that. We *are* way beyond all that. And no amount of legwork you do will ever prove anything different."

"I'm not your enemy, Ms. Hunter."

"You're just a messenger."

"I'm married myself and I've got a kid—"

"Lucky you."

"—but there are more important things in the world than me and my family. What happened on Friday the eleventh is more important than you and Teddy."

Beth thought about it. She decided he was wrong. "I have no more to say to you, Mr. Means."

"No more? You haven't said anything yet. Don't you want to find out the truth?"

"That depends what it is."

"Or do you already know it?"

"You know the answer to that."

"Do I?" But he did. He stood up and put on his jacket. The dark-blue stains had spread down the sides of his shirt. "I don't understand what you want."

Beth said nothing. Means could have helped her, but he wasn't going to: She was only a sidebar, and reputations were made with headline stories.

"Thanks for the pizza," he said, handing her his card. "Call me if you want to talk sometime. This isn't the kind of thing a person can handle alone."

Beth let him out. She locked the door, bolted it, pushed the sofa into place. She wasn't alone: She had Y.K. Ling Private Investigation and Consultation on her side, for 150 dollars a day.

That reminded her she had to find a new place to live. It could wait until morning. She switched off the lights and lay down.

16

Night turned to fog. Wind blew the fog away. Rain pelted down. The elements chased each other across the sky like slapstick acts in a vaudeville show.

Beth packed a suitcase and drove into the Mission District. Everyone said the Mission had a better climate than the rest of the city; a few palm trees grew there to prove it. Rain dripped from their waxy leaves.

The Hotel Dolores was a shabby four-story cube depressing real-estate values on a street of gentrified Victorian houses. A dusty sign in the window advertised rooms by the day, week, or month. The clerk showed Beth one on the top floor. It had a lumpy bed and a velvet divan of the kind favored by Madame Récamier, worn enough to date from her era. There were two doors: One led to a tiny bathroom with white fixtures, all except the toilet seat, which was red; the other opened on a closet full of mothball smell.

It was a dismal room. Beth confirmed that impression in the clerk's sad eyes. She surprised him by saying, "I'll take it," and exchanged eighty-six dollars for one week's possession of the key. When the clerk had gone she hung her clothes in the closet and made a closer inspection of the room. It would do. It wasn't a home, or even a refuge; it was her war room: a place to plan the campaign that would lead her to Teddy.

She called Albert Ling to tell him where she was.

"Not on the phone," he said. "Come by later today. And don't tell anyone else."

Beth began to worry that he was more concerned with protecting her than finding Teddy. "Aren't you exaggerating the danger?"

"No one ever got sued for that."

"But the boy who cried wolf got eaten."

"That's not a Chinese story."

"Does that make it false?"

Albert laughed. "That's a very old question in China. There's still no agreement on the answer."

Beth went to the library and looked up Berryessa Wines in the business catalog. It was a limited company, owned by the Berryessa Corporation. The president and chief executive officer of the Berryessa Corporation was Rex Heidemann. The corporation was owned by the Gladd Group, which had an address in Nassau, Bahamas. There was no other information on the Gladd Group.

Berryessa Wines had an office in the financial district. Beth dialed the number. "Berryessa Wines," a woman said.

"Mr. Heidemann's office, please."

"One moment." *Buzz. Buzz.*

"Mr. Heidemann's office," said an older woman.

"Rex Heidemann, please," Beth said.

"Mr. Heidemann is not in right now. May I tell him who called?"

"Is there somewhere else I can reach him?"

"If you give me your name and number, I can have him return your call."

"The problem is I'm getting on a plane in five minutes. I promised I'd pass a message on to Mr. Heidemann."

"I'll be happy to do that for you."

"I'm afraid it's personal," Beth said. "It's from Helen Heidemann Brock."

There was a long pause. "In that case, Miss—I'm sorry, I didn't get your name . . ." She waited.

"Dolores. Liz Dolores."

"In that case, Miss Dolores, you can reach him at the winery. It's a Napa number—seven six eight, four three one one."

Beth didn't write it down. She got in her car and drove to the wine country.

The rainfall lightened on the east side of the Bay. Here and there the sun found holes in the clouds and sent down golden probes. The brassy air over Vallejo shut them out, but on the road to Napa the sky turned postcard-blue. Beth glided through fields of yellow mustard, glittering in the breeze. She rolled down the window and felt the sun on her arm.

Beth reached Napa at lunchtime. The tour buses were double-parked. The tourists had a choice of cuisine: western, nouvelle, health, or junk. Beth stopped for gas and asked directions to the Berryessa Winery. It was off Route 121, halfway to Lake Berryessa.

Route 121 ran northeast from Napa and soon began climbing out of the valley. Beth smelled eucalyptus; then oak and pine. The air grew hotter and drier. It made her thirsty. In Wooden Valley, three pickups and a horse waited outside Reno's Bar: BUD ON DRAUGHT —50 CENTS. Beth didn't stop.

The road wound along the eastern edge of the valley. There was no traffic. A barbed-wire fence began on her right. An arrow pointed to Berryessa Wines. Beth turned onto a narrow road that curved to the top of the ridge. She parked in a roadside clearing and got out of the car.

A green valley lay to the east. A few low hills rose up in the middle, sheltering some buildings. In the distance, a second set of hills marked the horizon. At the foot of one of those hills, a little milky patch reflected the sunshine: possibly another building, but she couldn't be sure. Barbed wire glinted around the valley as far as she could see. Within it the green vines mustered in orderly rows, across the valley floor, up the side of the low hills, and beyond. Too far away to be heard, a tractor moved along the rows, spraying pink clouds. A circling hawk watched it, high above. There wasn't a sound.

Beth got into her car and followed the road down the ridge until she came to a gate. There was a guardhouse; a hand emerged from its open doorway to wave her through. BER-RYESSA WINES—VISITORS WELCOME said a wooden sign arching over the road; it showed a picture of a grape-laden cart before a setting sun. Beth drove under it.

She crossed the valley floor. Green shoots softened the profiles of the stubby vine stocks. Between two rows a brown rabbit sat still on its haunches, long ears stiffened to the sky. The hawk drifted lazily across the blue.

The road ended in a broad parking lot in front of the buildings by the first set of hills. The buildings were mission style, made of stone: an office, equipment sheds, and the winery—as big as a church and much resembling one, lacking only a tower. A black Rolls-Royce was parked in front of the office, a few humbler cars by the winery. To one side of the lot was a grove of olive trees; the leaves flashed their tarnished undersides in the occasional breeze. A family picnicked in the shade: bread, cheese, and *vin* of the *pays* they sat on.

As Beth parked in front of the office, the door opened and two men came out. One was a big Chinese man with silvery hair that grew very thickly for someone his age. He glanced around, taking in without a pause the picnickers and Beth at the wheel of her car, and said: "Ah, what a beautiful day."

The remark seemed to irritate the second man. "I suppose," he said, not bothering to look. He was a fat man of medium height, but he seemed shorter beside the Chinese man.

The Chinese man looked at the big gold watch on his wrist, then opened the driver's door of the Rolls-Royce and got in. The window slid smoothly down.

"Keep in touch, Rex," he said.

"You'll be the first to know," the fat man replied. Again Beth caught the annoyance in his tone.

The Chinese man looked at him, a look that made the fat man turn away. Even at some distance, Beth felt its power. Quietly, the big car backed, circled, and drove off. The men didn't wave good-bye.

Beth got out of her car. The fat man heard the door close and turned to her. His face went public. Beth saw in it the remains of the handsome features in the thirty-five-year-old photographs, now almost all swallowed up by fat. "Parking for tours and tasting is over there, by the winery building," he said with a smile. "Just go right in and they'll take care of you."

"I'm not here for a tour, Mr. Heidemann. I came to talk to you."

The fat man abandoned his smile; it faded quickly without his support. "Do I know you?" he asked, looking at Beth more closely.

"No." She had made up her mind to follow Albert's advice and try the direct approach. "I'm a friend of Theodore Wu. His Chinese name was Wu Tun-li."

"I don't believe I know him, either," Heidemann said with a puzzled frown.

"Wu Tun-li was one of the orphans you and Helen brought back from China in nineteen forty-nine."

Puzzlement vanished. The frown remained. "You've been talking to my ex-wife?"

"Yes. Theodore Wu was interested in tracing his roots. That's why he contacted her."

"Is that what she said?"

Beth nodded. "You seem annoyed."

"I am."

He let it show, or manufactured more of it. Beth wondered whether he had an actor's control of his face, dating from his preaching days. "I'm very annoyed," he continued, "for the simple reason that no good can come of digging up the past like that. And it's very irresponsible to encourage it. Helen knows that—or at least she knew it once. I can't imagine what she's thinking." He looked up, as if hoping for a clue from above, but there was nothing to see but the hawk in the sky.

Heidemann sighed. "Now that you've given me a few more details, I think I remember your friend. But he didn't call himself Theodore. He said his name was Ted. That's what threw me off."

"When did you see him?" Hope stirred inside her, not the baseless hope she'd been living on since Friday the eleventh, but something more tangible. She felt closer to Teddy than at any moment since she'd held the warm coffee mug in her hands.

"I didn't see him," Heidemann replied. "He telephoned me at the office in San Francisco."

"When?"

Heidemann raised his hand like a traffic cop. "Just a second. You haven't explained your interest in this man."

"I told you—we're friends." Heidemann's pale eyebrows went up like quotation marks. "He's disappeared. Like you, I don't think much good can come from digging up the past. That's why I'm worried about him. I'd like to know what you and he talked about."

Heidemann looked at his watch. "I can't right now. I'm way behind schedule as it is."

Beth reached out and touched his arm. "This is important," she said quietly.

"I'm sure it is," Heidemann said, stepping back. "Why not let the police handle it? They can reach me in the city."

"I don't like their approach. Besides, they don't know about Teddy's interest in his past. I've just learned about it myself."

The puzzled frown appeared again. "Let me get this straight. This man Wu talks to my ex-wife about his past. She puts him on to me. Now he's disappeared. Is that it?"

"Yes."

"Are you suggesting I was involved in his disappearance?"

"Not at all. But I think he may have learned something from you that led him to go somewhere. If I knew what it was I could find him."

"I see." In the olive grove, the picnickers were packing their hamper. Heidemann watched them for a moment. "Is that your own theory?" he asked, eyes still on the picnickers.

"I don't understand."

He shrugged. "I can't believe the police aren't doing more, that's all. Don't they even know you're looking into this?"

"No."

"What about your friends and family?"

"No."

"You sound like a very determined young lady." He regarded her with admiration. "How did you find out that your friend had contacted Helen?" Beth told him about the phone bill. "Determined and resourceful," Heidemann said.

On the other side of the parking lot, the picnickers loaded their hamper into a car and drove away. Heidemann looked at his watch again. "Tell you what. I've got some new grafts to check, not far from here. We can have our talk at the same time."

They crossed the parking lot and entered the olive grove. Something shone in the mown grass: a corkscrew, forgotten by the picnickers. Beth picked it up.

"Keep it," Heidemann said. "You should see this place in the fall, when the hordes arrive. They turn it into a garbage dump."

It was a waiter's corkscrew, the kind Teddy liked. Beth put it in her pocket.

They walked through the olive grove into the vineyard. There were no hordes now, no people at all. Through an opening in the first set of hills, Beth could see the tractor spraying pink smoke, but she couldn't hear its motor. In the distance, the little milky patch at the base of the farther hills resolved itself into geometric shapes.

"What's that?" Beth asked.

He followed her pointing finger. "Barracks. They're only oc-
cupied during the harvest."

"You own a lot of land."

"The company does."

"And who owns the company? Another company?"

Heidemann smiled. "You have a good sense of humor. But
I thought you wanted to discuss your friend Wu."

"That's right. I do."

Heidemann knelt in the soft earth and examined a vine.
"Grenache," he explained. "We've grafted a new California
strain onto the European stock. More prolific." A rubber band
still helped bind the new branch in place, but the graft had taken:
Soft green buds poked through the bark.

Heidemann rose and dusted off his knees. They walked a little
farther into the vineyard. "Your friend called me at the beginning of February, if I remember right," Heidemann said. "He
wanted to know about his past in China—where he'd come from,
who his parents were, if there was any family left behind. I had
to tell him that we never had much information about the orphans, and now, so long after . . ." He bent over a vine. "I assured him that the parents of all the children were dead. In one
or two cases we'd found other relatives still living. Those children were left behind, at my insistence."

"Did someone object?"

Heidemann plucked a caterpillar off a leaf, dropped it on the
ground, and pressed it under his heel. "Helen. She was much
keener on the orphan project than I was."

"Was that because she had more faith?" The words were out
before she could stop them—her mind seemed to insist on fitting
pieces together, even if they had nothing to do with Teddy's disappearance.

"Helen's a fountain of information, isn't she?" Heidemann
said, walking ahead. Then he added more quietly: "It was a long
time ago. None of it matters anymore."

"It matters to me," Beth said, following him.

"I wish I could help you, but I've already told you everything
your friend and I talked about. We only spoke for two or three
minutes."

"That was all?"

Heidemann nodded.

"What was his reaction to what you told him?"

"No particular reaction."

"He didn't seem disappointed?"

"Not that I noticed. I didn't get the impression he cared all that much. More like a mild curiosity."

"Mild curiosity?"

"That's right."

Beth's energy drained out of her, all at once. She couldn't take another step. Arthur Merton's letter, Helen Brock, Heidemann, all added up to nothing more than mild curiosity. "I guess I've taken enough of your time," she said at last. "Thank you."

"You're welcome."

A brown rabbit hopped out from behind a vine and landed a few feet away, maybe the same rabbit she'd seen before. It saw her and froze.

"Oh, he did mention one other thing," Heidemann said, turning to face her. "But I don't see how it could be very helpful, now."

"What did he say?"

"That he was going to China on his honeymoon."

"Does that mean he hoped to look for relatives while he was there?"

"Who knows?"

Did it mean he really had planned a honeymoon, or was it part of a set-up? Did he really care about his past, or was getting to China all that mattered? Heidemann wouldn't know the answers to those questions, either. There was nothing more to say. Dead end. Time to go.

The rabbit's ears twitched. The movement caught Heidemann's eye. He looked down and saw the rabbit. Then he reached into the pocket of his tweed jacket and pulled out a gun.

"Don't," Beth said.

"Don't what?"

"Don't shoot the rabbit."

Heidemann laughed. He had a high-pitched laugh that jiggled the fat under his chin. He laughed his high-pitched laugh, but looked Beth in the eye at the same time.

A woman appeared at the edge of the olive grove. Heidemann stopped laughing. "Hello there," she called. "Did either of you notice our corkscrew?"

"I have it," Beth called back.

"I'll come get it."

"No, I'll bring it. I was just going." She turned to Heidemann. He blinked. "Good-bye," she said.

"Yes," Heidemann said. "Sorry I couldn't be more help. Good-bye." Then he pulled the trigger. There was a crack, not very loud, and the rabbit flipped over and lay still.

"Was that necessary?"

"Don't tell me what is necessary on my own property. They gnaw the vines." He put the gun in his pocket and moved off along the row.

Beth walked to the olive grove and handed the woman her corkscrew. "Sentimental value," the woman explained with a smile.

High above the hawk caught an updraft and soared out of sight.

17

Beth climbed the dusty linoleum stairs. The door to Fatt and Co. was open and the lights were on. Giant stuffed pandas lay sprawled in a disorderly heap like bodies flung in a mass grave. Defective pandas, Beth remembered. It was easy to see what was wrong with them: They all had both eyes squeezed together on the same side of their noses, as though the machine that made them had fallen under Picasso's spell—rendering them, like Helen Brock, undesirable in the real world.

"Machines?" snorted Y.K. Ling after Beth had been brought into his painting room. "Machines had nothing to do with it. That's the whole point of Singapore—cheap labor." He sat in his wheelchair, before an easel. Beth walked around to see what he was painting: another lake, with a blue mountain in the distance. A man was rowing a woman across the water. She sat in the stern, skirt raised and legs spread so the rower could see her vagina. Her eyes were boldly fixed on her companion's face, which was without expression, without feature of any kind, since Y.K. Ling hadn't yet filled in the oval blank. Now, as Beth watched, he dipped a pointed brush in a black pot and stroked in an avid eye.

Beth moved away from the easel. The painting had awakened feelings inside her that had been dormant since the evening *Pop-Up* went under.

She wrote down her address at the Hotel Dolores and the number of the phone in her room. "Please give this to Albert," she said.

Y.K. Ling looked up. "What?" His eyes were far away. Beth repeated what she'd said. The old man's eyes made the long journey from the quiet lake to her request. Abruptly, he pointed the brush at her. "Albert wants to see you."

"Where is he?"

"The Ta-Tang Café."

"Where's that?"

"You don't know it?"

"No."

"Then you'll never find it. Get one of the kids to take you." He had hardly finished speaking before his eyes swung back to the painting, as if some magnetic principle were at work.

Beth walked down one long corridor, turned into another, and came to the kitchen. There was enough equipment to outfit a restaurant. Steam rose from a big copper pot on the stove. It mesmerized the baby, who was sitting on the floor with a pacifier in his mouth. The girl who called herself Jade sat on the counter painting her toenails blue. They both looked at Beth.

"Your father's meeting me at the Ta-Tang Café. Can you tell me how to get there?"

"You'll never find it."

"That's what your grandfather said. He doesn't think I can add, either."

Jade seemed displeased. "Did you see his dirty picture?"

"I didn't think it was dirty."

"He just does it to shock people."

"If that's true it's not an uncommon desire."

Jade glanced down at her blue toenails. "I can take you to the Ta-Tang if you like."

Jade wrapped the baby in a backpack, swung it onto her shoulders, clipped her Walkman on her belt, and led Beth down the linoleum stairs. One of her grandmothers was coming slowly up, arms full of groceries. Jade plucked an apple from one of the bags as it went by. The old woman spoke sharply in Chinese. Jade took a noisy bite of the apple and went out the front door.

It was late afternoon. The morning rain was now just a faint drizzle, visible against dark buildings. "Which grandmother was that?" Beth asked.

But Jade had already donned earphones and passed out of aural range. As they walked, she took sunglasses from the pocket of her camouflage jacket and put them on, too, warding off probes in the visible spectrum. The baby peered over her shoulder with his big, dark eyes.

They turned off Grant Avenue, walked west for a few blocks, entered an unmarked cul-de-sac. It was lined with vegetable stalls, greens glistening in the moist air. Clotheslines drooped overhead; on one of them a school of fish was hung out to dry. There were no tourists in the cul-de-sac, only Chinese, less prosperous-looking than those on Grant Avenue.

At the end of the cul-de-sac stood two tall, neglected buildings. One was boarded up. The door to the other was open; inside, rows of women bent over sewing machines. Jade led Beth through a narrow passage between the buildings. It was full of smells: rancid oil, rotting fish, urine.

On the other side, the passage grew into a little alley. The buildings on both sides were peeling and shabby, mostly small warehouses and garages. In the distance, Beth could see that the alley met a busy street. Clay? Washington? She wasn't sure. About a third of the way to it was a small café, with two Chinese characters painted in red on the window.

"Here it is," Jade said

They went in. The Ta-Tang Café was cramped and comfortless. It had a low tin ceiling, bare wooden floor, a few rickety tables, mismatched chairs. Over the bar at the back was the sole decoration: a garishly tinted photo portrait of Chiang Kai-shek.

There was no one in the café but an old woman in black. She was standing behind the bar with a flyswatter in her hand. A fly landed by her teacup. She took a big backswing and lashed out, with surprising force but not enough speed. The fly darted away as the the swatter smacked the bar. It performed a series of aerial maneuvers. The woman followed its flight with hatred in her eyes. "Excuse me," Beth said.

Without looking at her, the woman answered in Chinese.

"What did she say?" Beth asked Jade.

"What?" Jade raised an earphone.

"Ask her if your father's been here."

Jade asked. The old woman replied with annoyance.

"What did she say?"

"I'm not sure. She speaks some kind of dialect."

"Let's wait a few minutes," Beth said. "Would you like a cup of tea?"

"Thanks."

They sat at the table by the window. Jade held the baby. The old woman brought two chipped cups and a pot of tea: oolong, hot and clear. They each drank a cup. The old woman stalked the fly. The baby grew restless.

"Do you want me to hold him?" Beth asked. "I don't mind."

"It's okay." Jade adjusted the earphones and placed them on the baby's head. His dark eyes assumed a faraway look that reminded Beth of his grandfather in front of the easel. He was quiet now, but she still wanted to hold him.

Across the street was a pockmarked brick building with a sign over the door. "What does that say?" Beth asked.

"Taipei Social Club," Jade told her. It was getting dark. The characters on the sign were already fading. Jade went to the pay phone in the corner and called home. "He's not there," she said, returning to the table. "And I've got to go. You're invited to dinner."

"I'll stay here a little longer."

Jade shifted the baby onto her back. "I wish he did something else for a living."

"Why?"

"I don't know." Jade busied herself with the earphones, readjusting them to fit her head. "My grandfather got shot."

"I heard."

"Who told you?"

"Your father."

"Did he tell you what happened after that?"

"No."

"Daddy killed the man who did it. He chopped him in the throat. The man died. Right on Grant Avenue. I saw the whole thing."

Jade put on the earphones, turned up the volume, and left the café. The baby looked back at Beth as he was carried out the door.

Shadows fell across the alley. The Taipei Social Club sign disappeared in the darkness. Beth paid for the tea and asked for more. The exchange of money seemed to relax the old woman. After bringing the second pot, she laid her head on the bar and dozed off.

Slowly the alley came to life. A man, walking from the direction of the busy street, stopped in front of the Taipei Social Club and knocked on the door. It opened at once and he went inside. Beth glimpsed another man and beyond him a second door, but it was hard to distinguish anything; the only light came from the café.

Two more men came, knocked, were admitted. A taxi nosed down the alley and let off a few others, who also went inside. It wasn't long before Beth had seen twenty or thirty men, and a few women, enter the Taipei Social Club. After a while she stopped paying attention.

She called the Lings. Albert hadn't returned. There was nothing for her to do but go back to her dismal room at the Hotel Dolores. She drank the tea remaining in her cup and was about to leave, when it struck her that although all those people had gone into the Taipei Social Club, no lights showed inside the building. The windows were completely dark.

The old woman snored softly, her head on the bar. A fly landed on her hand. Beth sat at the table by the window, watching the Taipei Social Club.

Suddenly a light shone on the second floor. A shadow flitted through it and was gone. A minute or two later, more shadows followed. On the top floor, another light went on. A shadow blotted it out for a moment; then more shadows. They danced madly. The lights went out.

Time passed. No more lights shone. The building was dark and still. After a while the door opened. A man came out. He was very big. For an instant he was caught in the yellow beam that slanted across the alley from the café: a Chinese man with a wrestler's body and a shaved skull. Then he ran into darkness.

Almost before she realized it, Beth was running too: out of the café and down the alley. The man's footsteps echoed through the narrow space; his running form was silhouetted against the light of the busy street in the distance. He ran with quick, scuttling movements, very fast for a big man. Reaching the street, he darted to the left and disappeared.

Beth raced to the end of the alley and turned left on the street. Clay. It was full of traffic. A group of tourists went by, following a guide on a nighttime tour of Chinatown. There was no sign of the bald man.

She stood at the entrance to the alley, wondering what to do. All at once, a black van pulled out of traffic and swung into the alley, almost hitting her. As she jumped out of the way, the van passed under a streetlight; it glared on the driver's hairless skull.

The van went down the alley and stopped in front of the Taipei

Social Club. Beth heard the metallic thump of the closing door. She didn't know anything about the Taipei Social Club, or why Albert Ling wanted to meet her at the Ta-Tang Café; all she knew was that the bald man had been in the car with Han Shih in Berkeley, and she must not lose him now.

Her car was in a parking lot off Grant Avenue, a few blocks away. She looked around for a taxi. There were none. She started running, as hard as she could. Clay to Grant. Grant to the parking lot. She jumped in the car, sped from the lot, through a red light on Sacramento, and squealed to a stop on Clay, a few yards from the entrance to the alley. The whole trip had taken less than ten minutes—but the van was gone. She hadn't even noticed its license number.

"Beth!" she said with fury. A passing couple glanced at her and hurried on.

She entered the alley and walked toward the Taipei Social Club. It was dark. So was the Ta-Tang Café, on the other side. She went past them, halting by the narrow passage at the end of the alley. There she waited, her back to the boarded-up building, hidden in its shadow.

The sky overhead was a fuzzy pink band, no wider than the alley. Sometimes a plane flew over, flashing its lights. There was no moon or star, only dampness that coalesced into drizzle and grew to rain. It wet Beth's hair, her face, her shoulders, and slowly spread through her clothes.

At the far end of the alley, headlights gleamed through the rain. Beth crouched in a corner. The beams touched the wall above her, sharpening their focus as the sound of a motor approached. The motor died; the lights went out. Beth looked up, but her pupils hadn't adjusted to the darkness. She heard a metal door open and close. Footsteps. Knocking. A wooden door opened and closed. Her pupils widened, letting in what light there was. The black van was parked in front of the Taipei Social Club. There was no one in the cab.

Beth walked quietly to the van. It had a California plate. She memorized the number as she continued down the alley. She got into her car and waited.

A few minutes later, Beth saw a red glow in the alley. The van backed out, turned, and drove down Clay. Han Shih's driver was at the wheel. Beth started her car and followed.

Traffic was light now, and it was easy to keep the van in view.

It went south, crossed the Bay Bridge, and entered the north-bound lane of the freeway. Beth stayed a few hundred feet behind, closing the gap whenever an exit came in sight. But Han Shih's driver wasn't interested in any of the exits. He followed the freeway, at a steady sixty miles an hour, past Berkeley, Richmond, San Pablo. Beth wondered whether he was going all the way to Sacramento. Or Reno. Or across the country. She followed the van's little red eyes, a few hundred feet ahead.

At Vallejo, the van left the freeway and took the Napa road. Beth dropped a little farther back, feeling conspicuous without the cover of freeway traffic. But Han Shih's driver gave no indication of being aware of her. He drove on at sixty miles an hour, slowing down to thirty as he came into Napa.

The town was dark and silent. The tour buses were gone. The wine tasters were sleeping it off. The van rolled past the empty restaurants—Western, nouvelle, health, junk—and turned onto Route 121. Beth followed.

The road began climbing out of the valley. The sky was clear; a half-moon shone in the west. Beth rolled down the window, letting the breeze dry her clothes. She smelled eucalyptus, then oak and pine.

There was no traffic at all. The van passed through Wooden Valley. As soon as the red eyes disappeared around a bend, Beth switched off her lights, hoping that if Han Shih's driver had noticed her at all, he would now suppose her destination had been Wooden Valley. She drove on by the light of the moon. On her right, barbed wire gleamed in the silvery rays.

Beth saw the arrow pointing to Berryessa Wines. Ahead, the red lights bobbed onto the narrow entrance road, mounted the ridge, and dipped out of sight. When Beth reached the top, she pulled into the same clearing where she'd parked that morning, shut off the engine, and got out of the car, softly closing the door.

On the far side of the ridge, the van came to the gate and stopped. The gate was closed. The van's headlights shone on the guardhouse. A man came out. He had a big dog on a leash and a rifle in his hand. The dog's bark carried all the way up the ridge to Beth.

The man opened the gate. The dog pulled him forward, trying to attack the van. It drove through, passing under the wooden sign: "BERRYESSA WINES—VISITORS WELCOME." The dog strained at the leash, barking furiously. The guard locked the gate, tugged the dog back to the guardhouse, and went inside.

Two red lights moved across the valley floor. They went by the winery and the office, through the notch in the low hills and out of sight. A few minutes later, Beth saw them again, much dimmer now, still receding on the far side of the valley. The second set of hills was a black band at the edge of the night sky. Beth could not make out the milky patch she had seen earlier—barracks, Rex Heidemann had said.

The red light flickered weakly on the border of her vision. They did not fade completely or grow brighter. The van had stopped.

An owl hooted. The moon slowly slipped away.

Suddenly the red lights were gone.

But in the next moment, white ones took their place, and brightened. The van had turned and was coming back. The headlights shone across the valley floor, vanished behind the central hills, then poked through the notch. The van went by the winery and the office and came toward the gate. Beth could hear its motor.

Less than a hundred feet from the gate, the van stopped. Inside the guardhouse, the dog began to rage. The van turned and drove the other way—past the winery and the office, through the notch, across the far side of the valley; the red eyes diminished from a glare to a twinkle. At the edge of sight, they stopped, disappeared, turned white. Headlights.

The headlights brightened. The van came back. Near the gate it stopped again. The dog howled. The van turned and drove away: to the edge of vision. And all the way back. It didn't move fast or slowly, but kept a steady pace, as though on a long journey. Back and forth it went across the dark valley.

After a while the dog stopped barking.

Later, orange and purple spread across the eastern sky. The two red eyes twinkled out of sight on the far side of the valley. Beth waited for the headlights. This time they didn't come.

18

The baby sat in Y.K. Ling's lap. The old man held him with one hand; his other was busy with a fine-tipped brush, strewing a few flowering lily pads on the lake where the lovers rowed. Grandson and grandfather followed the brushwork with unwavering eyes: dark, intense eyes which looked identical to Beth.

She sagged in a chair, more tired than she should have been from missing a night's sleep; her left hand hurt. She still hadn't regained all the strength lost during her night in the sea. Stirring coffee, she thought about what Y.K. Ling had just told her: Albert had not returned last night, nor had he called.

Y.K. Ling dipped his brush in a paint pot. "Don't worry about Albert. He can take care of himself."

"Doesn't he normally call if he's not coming home?"

"What?" the old man asked; she had lost his attention to a lily pad. Beth repeated her words. "He wouldn't call," Y.K. Ling said. "Not when he's on a case." He raised the brush to make a point. "You have to let the facts of the case flow around you. Avoid interruptions. That's Albert's MO. He learned it from me. I learned it from Lao-tze."

The baby touched the brush and sucked the yellow-green paint from his fingertip. The old man didn't notice. "MO," he said. "*Modus operandi*. Latin for *method of operation*. Did you know that?"

"Yes."

The old man frowned. "When Julius Caesar crossed the Rubicon, the Great Wall was already two hundred and fifty years old."

He switched on his radar to see if she grasped the implication. The Great Wall was still there, of course, while the Romans were gone—or had become Italians. The Chinese were still the Chinese. Was that it?

She wondered whether the baby had radar, too.

Her silence seemed to satisfy the old man. He dabbed a yellow flower on a lily pad. It didn't interest the couple in the rowboat. The man's eyes were forever fixed on the plumpness between the woman's legs; her eyes were glued to his. *Forever wilt thou love, and she be fair!* Y.K. Ling's imagination was a little gamier than Keats's, that was all.

Lust and lily pads. Perhaps she was looking for ironies that weren't there, looking through Western eyes. She tried to see the painting whole: blue mountain, still water, lily pads, the couple in the rowboat. The irony vanished. That didn't mean the lust became more tender; it meant irony wasn't required to make it art. Was that Albert's MO applied to art? Had she let the facts of the painting flow around her?

"I like the painting you're doing," Beth said.

"You've got good taste," Y.K. Ling responded. "It dates from the most refined era of Chinese art." He gestured to a book lying open on his worktable. Beth hadn't noticed it before. Now she looked, and saw a full-page color reproduction of a painting identical to the one on the easel. "Blue Mountain," read the caption. "Tang Yin (1470–1523)." Y.K. Ling's painting was a copy. Next time she would be sure she knew all the facts before letting them flow around her.

Facts. She had been swimming in a cold sea of them since Teddy disappeared. But she had no better understanding of their meaning than a mackerel had of the Humboldt current. Where was the current that led to Teddy? She let her eyes close, but opened them almost immediately. *Don't sleep. Keep going.*

The old man had stopped painting to look at her. "Why don't you go home to bed? Albert will call you as soon as he gets back."

Beth shook her head. "Did he tell you what he wanted to talk to me about?"

"No."

"Is that unusual?"

"Why would it be unusual?"

"You're his father. You work in the same business."

Y.K. Ling considered her words. Then he turned to the easel and began touching up a bullfrog. "If you speak too soon," he said, "understanding never ripens."

"It depends who you talk to, doesn't it?"

His radar swept over her. "I don't understand you."

Facts. "Did Albert often go to the Ta-Tang Café?"

"Not that he mentioned. It's not much of a place, is it?"

"No. It's across from the Taipei Social Club. Would that have interested him?"

"Maybe. Chinatown is full of social clubs. Old people go to them to pass the time. Albert might have been meeting someone there."

"Someone from Taipei?"

"Maybe. More likely a descendant of someone from Taipei. That's the way most of those social clubs are nowadays."

"You said the Brotherhood of the Green Snake was based in Taiwan."

"That was a long time ago." He put down his brush. "There's no use speculating. Why not go home to bed?"

Because home is the Hotel Dolores and the bed is empty, Beth thought. *Because I want to talk to Albert about last night.* But she rose and started for the door. The baby was chewing the paintbrush. Y.K. Ling took it from his chubby hand and swirled it in a glass of water.

Beth made her way along the corridors. She met Mr. Chen hobbling in carpet slippers, a deck of cards in his hand. He smiled warmly, showing the three or four brown teeth he still had.

Beth went outside, but didn't return to her car. Instead, she found herself retracing her steps of the afternoon before, into the lane with the vegetable stalls, through the narrow passage between the boarded-up building and the sweatshop, to the Ta-Tang Café. It was closed. Across the alley, two old women were knocking at the door of the Taipei Social Club. It opened and they went inside. Beth walked on to the end of the alley.

On Clay Street she bought a clipboard, pad of paper, pen, and a jar of instant coffee. Then she returned to the Taipei Social Club and knocked on the door.

It was opened by a trim middle-aged woman with her hair in a kerchief and a broom in her hand. Beyond her, the second door was open, allowing Beth to see a large, drab room furnished with card tables, Ping-Pong tables, and a six-foot TV screen at the far end; there, a few old people sat on folding chairs, feet on the bare hardwood, backs to the door.

Beth smiled and held out the jar of coffee. "Hi," she said. "I represent Aztec Instant Coffee. We're giving away free jars of

Aztec Instant Coffee this week so you can see for yourself how good it tastes.''

Wordlessly, the woman accepted the offering, gazing without expression at the Central American sun god sipping from a Rosenthal cup on the label.

Beth pushed her smile to its anatomical limit. ''In return,'' she went on, poising pen over paper, ''we'd like to ask you a few questions about coffee consumption habits here at the—'' She stepped back so she could read the sign over the door. ''I'm sorry, what does that say?''

''Taipei Social Club,'' the woman said. Her English wasn't very good, and Beth wondered how much of her spiel was getting across.

''Thank you,'' she said, writing it down. ''Now, a few questions about coffee consumption habits at the Taipei Social Club.''

''I don't know,'' the woman said, looking dubious.

''Perhaps the manager can help me.''

''I don't know.'' The woman's hand moved as though she would return the jar of coffee.

''Would you mind getting him for me? I'm sure he'd want to know about our other special offers.''

The woman's eyes shifted from Beth to the sun god. ''You wait,'' she said, closing the door.

Beth stuck out her foot as it shut. Metal slid on metal, but there was no click of brass tumblers falling into place. Quickly Beth wrote, ''Be back later—Aztec Coffee,'' on a sheet of paper and pushed the door open.

The trim middle-aged woman wasn't in sight. There were only the old people sitting with their backs to her by the six-foot screen; on it, a heavily made-up man drifted in a sampan, singing a song.

Beth closed the door, placed the sheet of paper on the floor as though it had been shoved underneath, and walked in.

On one side of the room were vending machines, pictures of a few old Chinese men in business suits, and the same portrait of Chiang Kai-shek that hung in the Ta-Tang Café. On the other side rose a wooden staircase, bleached and worn. At the bottom of the stairs was a closed door. Beth had her foot on the first step when she heard voices at the top. She grabbed the doorknob and turned. The door opened. Inside was a narrow landing, then steep stairs leading down into darkness. Beth moved onto the landing and closed the door.

Blackness.

Outside, feet trod down the wooden stairs. The voices came closer. A woman asked a question in Chinese; Beth recognized the voice of the trim middle-aged woman. A man replied. Beth thought she knew his voice also, but couldn't place it. The footsteps and the voices faded. Then, for a moment, the voices rose: female surprise, male annoyance. After that they ceased. One set of footsteps remounted the stairs; a broom made brisk sweeping sounds on the hardwood floor.

Beth stood on the landing, listening. The sweeping sound became fainter and died away. The singing from the sampan on the six-foot screen was reduced to a tinny quaver. One of the old people started coughing. It spread to the others. The contagion passed. Then there was nothing to hear but the tinny singing. Beth turned and slowly felt her way down the stairs.

They were bare, and worn at the edges. One creaked, then another. Beth kept to the side where they were firmer, leaning her weight against the wall. The staircase seemed very long. At the bottom, she saw a dim circle of light in the distance, and moved toward it.

She was in a long hallway. Without raising her arms very much, she could touch the walls on either side. Her hand bumped against a doorknob. She stopped, listened. No sound came from the other side. Very slowly, she rotated the knob and pushed. The door swung smoothly open into a darkness deeper than that in the hall. Without making a sound, she closed it and listened again. She heard nothing but water running in a pipe somewhere overhead.

Motionless, Beth waited in the darkness. The water stopped running. It began again. She felt along the nearest wall. It was strangely soft. Her fingertips brushed a light switch, rested on it. She paused, listening. But there was only the high-pitched sound of water flowing in a steel pipe. Beth flicked the switch.

Light from countless crystal facets dazzled her unready eyes. Squinting into it, she saw an enormous chandelier hanging from a high ceiling. As her pupils narrowed, the chandelier assumed a teardrop shape, graceless and bottom-heavy. The floor was polished parquet. The walls were gray suede. There were no windows. That was convenient: The huge room was outfitted with roulette wheels, slot machines, and dice and card tables, baized in green. There was a small opening in one wall, guarded by a brass grille.

Walking to it on the balls of her feet, Beth peered through. Inside was a small room with table, chair, adding machine, and wall safe.

Beth switched off the chandelier and let her eyes adjust to the darkness. Then she went into the hall and softly moved toward the circle of light.

At its end, the hallway joined another, forming a T. To the right was darkness; the light came from the other end. From there too came a faint clinking sound, like a giant rattling change. One slow step at a time, Beth walked toward the end of the hall.

She passed two doors, both on the left, both closed. Now she saw where the light was coming from: a large oblong opening in the right-hand wall, as wide as a squash court. The clinking grew louder. Dropping to her hands and knees, Beth crawled to the opening and peered over the edge.

The room below was quite like a squash court—similar in size, shape, and lighting, but filled with weight-lifting equipment. A mirror was mounted across the lower half of the far wall. The image of a naked man stood in the mirror; the man himself must have been too close to the near wall to be in her field of vision. The man in the mirror had an enormous barbell across his shoulders, bent in the middle by the weight it carried. Slowly the man in the mirror bent his knees, lowered himself to a half-squat, and straightened. Down and up, down and up; sweat ran down his huge body; veins popped; muscles inflated like balloons under his skin. The eyes of the man in the mirror were glazed with effort and concentration, and something else. They rested unwaveringly on the man she couldn't see, like a lover's. The man in the mirror had a shaved, lumpy skull. He was Han Shih's driver.

Down and up, down and up. Afraid he might see her in the mirror, Beth crouched lower, so her eyes barely topped the ledge. But the image only had eyes for the man. Down and up, down and up.

Slowly his penis, like his muscles, began to inflate. The glaze on the image's eyes thickened. The image came forward, bearing the great weight without difficulty. Han Shih's driver appeared, his back to Beth. He tore his eyes from the image in the mirror, lowered the barbell onto a rack, then looked himself over, up and down. His massive hand trailed over the ridges of his stomach, touched his penis, rubbed its end. Suddenly he turned and barked a word that Beth didn't catch. She ducked out of sight.

A door opened in the room below. After a few moments, Beth looked over the ledge. Han Shih's driver lay prone on the carpeted floor. A naked young girl straddled him, massaging oil into his back muscles: a very young girl, with no more than the beginnings of breasts and hips. She was no older than Jade Ling.

Han Shih's driver muttered something. The girl rose; he rolled over. She began rubbing the oil on his chest. His hand moved around hers, down to his penis. She saw, and slipped her hand there as well. He knocked it away, and muttered something else.

"No, Baldy," the girl said.

Baldy sat up and pushed her onto her back. Then, watching it all in the mirror, he lowered his heavy buttocks onto the girl's face; he took care of his penis himself. The girl was a pale, headless form on the weight-room floor.

Beth backed away. Y.K. Ling's painting had aroused her; this made her sick. And careless. She lost her balance and tumbled backward with a thump.

Silence.

Then Beth heard two bounding footsteps; a door was flung open. She scrambled up and looked around frantically. Two doors. She opened the nearest and darted inside. It was completely dark. Beth stepped forward and fell down a flight of stairs.

She landed on cold cement and jumped up, unaware of any pain, conscious only of her fluttering heart and the taste of blood in her mouth. Rushing on into the blackness, she banged into something big and metallic: a furnace, a boiler. She felt her way around and tripped sideways over a low, solid form. A steamer trunk. She shoved it across the floor until it bumped bound paper—magazines? newspapers?—piled against a wall.

The steamer trunk was big and heavy, but Beth didn't even feel the weight as she grabbed the handles and jerked it up onto the pile of papers.

At the top of the stairs, the door crashed open. Beth jumped around the barrier formed by the papers and the trunk, squeezing sideways into the space behind them, her back to the wall.

A bright light flashed on. Bare feet came down the stairs. They padded across the cement floor. Heavy objects were shifted back and forth. Something tinny fell and made noise like a rolling hubcap. As it died away, the footsteps came closer.

Beth felt pressure against the trunk, and gave into it, squeezing even closer to the wall. A huge arm, corded with thick muscle, reached over the top of the trunk. A green snake was tattooed around the wrist, a green snake with bloody fangs and a bloody split tongue.

Splayed fingers groped the air inches from her face. She shrank back, holding her breath so he wouldn't feel it on his skin.

The hand withdrew.

Footsteps padded away across the cement floor. And mounted the stairs. The light went out. The door closed.

Beth stayed where she was, not moving a muscle, bathed in her own sweat, mouth full of blood. Blackness surrounded her. Water ran in a pipe, far away. There was no other sound.

Time went by, unmeasured. Beth let the blood trickle from her mouth. No more blood came. Aches throbbed, here and there. They would turn to bruises, nothing more. Her fluttering heart resumed its normal beat.

Much later, she began to feel sleepy. She fought it as long as she could, but the room was dark and quiet and she was very tired. She fell asleep.

Beth awoke with a start, cramped and chilled in the little space behind the trunk. Memory spoke instantly, like an electric prod. She listened: silence; and crawled out from her hiding place.

Cautiously she crossed the cold floor and climbed the shadowy stairs, rising in the darkness. At the top, she put her ear to the door. She heard the sound, very faint, of a giant rattling change. It made her pause, there at the top of the stairs with her hand on the doorknob and Baldy on the other side: a long pause.

She let go of the doorknob.

Somewhere high up on the wall there must be a window, she reasoned, blacked out but still glass, and breakable. She calculated the risk, small but awful, then found the light switch and flicked it on.

There was no window. She was in a furnace room, full of basement clutter: dingy mattresses, cardboard boxes, rubber tires. At head level in the wall behind the furnace was a blackened steel door, no bigger than a porthole. A coal chute, probably long unused. But coal chutes led to the street. Beth shut off the light and descended the stairs.

The steel door opened with a squeak. Without pausing, Beth pulled herself up. She got her shoulders into the coal chute, her chest, her hips. Something was in front of her: a man's shoe. And another. They were big. Beyond the shoes was a pile of clothing, damp and sticky. Beth inched past it.

The chute rose at a steep angle, slippery with dust. Beth could see nothing. She pushed herself up in the peristaltic style of a mountaineer in an Alpine chimney.

Her head bumped something hard. She explored it with her hands: rough wooden planks, nailed together to form a square. She pushed. It gave—a trapdoor. Gripping the edge of the floor above, she pulled herself up. She was in a small kitchen. Blue light shone weakly from the control panel of a stove in the corner. There was a door. Beth went through it and found herself behind a bar in a dim room. On the other side were a few tables and chairs. The Ta-Tang Café. Through the window she saw night, and the dark shadow of the Taipei Social Club across the alley.

Beth went out the door and ran to the lights of Clay Street. There were people. They were out on dates, doing some late shopping, on the way to work the midnight shift. She was a creature who had crawled up from some underground world they wanted no part of; she could tell that from the looks they gave her. She was an alien in her own city.

That was why she got in her car and drove home—not to the Hotel Dolores, but the apartment on Chestnut Street. Home.

She parked her car in the garage, behind Teddy's, and went inside. Newspapers lay on the red runner outside the door. Gathering them up, she unlocked the door, entered, and turned on the lights.

The apartment was undisturbed. Normal. She might have been coming home from a late evening at the library. Teddy might have been in his study scribbling equations, or soaking in the bath with a glass of cognac.

Beth listened to the answering machine. No message from Albert, but Helen Brock had called, leaving her number in Beverly Hills. Beth tried it. No answer.

She went into the bathroom and saw herself in the full-length mirror. She was blackened with coal dust; her hands and arms were caked with blood. Where had it come from? Stripping off her clothes, she turned the shower on hot and hard and stood under it for a long time. Then she scrubbed clean, and dried herself with a thick towel.

In the medicine cabinet was her dental floss, unwaxed, beside Teddy's, waxed and mint-flavored. She went into her nightly routine: flossing teeth, brushing them, brushing her hair. She had slept, for how long she didn't know, but she was very tired. One last bit of business—urinating—and then to bed.

Beth raised the toilet-seat cover.

In the bowl was the head of Albert Ling, floating in a pool of blood. His eyes were open.

She spun off into blackness.

19

Beth came to on the bathroom floor.

Looking at nothing, she got up and ran to her bedroom. She threw on clothes, rushed out, down the stairs, outside.

Early morning. Paper boy coming up the walk.

"Good morning," he said.

Beth pushed past him and kept running.

She ran all the way to Chinatown: to 417 Grant Avenue. Pushing open the glass door, she ran up the linoleum stairs, past Fatt and Co., and stopped outside the door on the third floor, chest heaving. A new watercolor was tacked to the door, just above the sign , Y.K. LING: PRIVATE INVESTIGATION AND CONSULTATION. A mountain, a still lake; no rowboats, no people.

Beth knocked.

Jade Ling opened the door, cracking gum. Baldy's girl was younger. "Hi," she said with a smile. "I've been thinking—you're right. It's not a dirty painting. What's dirty is that Grandpa's still interested in that stuff." She laughed.

Beth couldn't laugh. She couldn't talk. Her chest heaved.

Jade looked at her more closely. "I didn't know you were a jogger," she said. "Come out on the terrace. We're having breakfast. Daddy's not home, but you can talk to Grandpa."

It was a Chinese-American breakfast: Rice Krispies and dim sum. They sat around the big table—Albert's wife with the baby in her lap, the children, Y.K. Ling, the two grandmothers. They all looked up as Beth came onto the terrace. Y.K. Ling frowned.

The sun was shining over the rooftops. The physical world melted under its rays; the faces of the Lings swam before Beth's eyes. Her mind reeled, so dizzyingly it might spin her off the terrace into the sky.

She said to the old man: "Can I talk to you for a minute?" The sound came from deep in her chest, baritone and alien.

"Talk." Y.K. Ling didn't like fretful clients. She was getting on his nerves.

"Privately."

Y.K. Ling made a little clicking sound to show his annoyance, backed his wheelchair out from the table, and shot across the terrace. "Come on."

She followed him through the corridors to his painting room. He pivoted the wheelchair in a tight circle and said, "Well, what is it?"

Beth told him in her baritone voice.

The old man flinched and looked away.

When he turned his face back to hers, it was unreadable. His eyes were hard and dry. His tone was professional. He asked a few questions. He told Beth he would handle it.

"How?"

The hard eyes bored through her, deep into a violent future. "You'll know." Y.K. Ling switched on the motor of his wheelchair. "Now please leave. I have things to do."

He rolled slowly down the corridor to do them. Beth left the apartment. She was out the door and on the sidewalk when she heard a woman scream, high above. It went on and on, like a siren wailing in the sky.

Beth walked through a full-scale putty model of the city. Buildings grew and shrank under the sun. The pavement rose and fell beneath her feet.

She walked and kept walking, not going anywhere, not wanting to stop. After a long time, she found herself standing before a pleasantly proportioned three-story stone building on Chestnut Street. Her body had taken her home.

But not inside. Never again. Beth went around to the garage. Lathrop was leaning against her car, arms folded across his chest. "We've got a little problem," he said.

"What do you want?"

Lathrop raised his eyes to heaven, a caricature of Patience tried. "Look," he said. "I'm sorry if we got off on the wrong foot. You were upset. Naturally. It was a critical situation for all of us."

"It still is."

Lathrop smiled. "Maybe not."

Beth moved toward him, hope swelling inside her. "Do you mean—?"

"What?" Lathrop retreated, puzzled.

"That you've found Teddy?"

"Oh, nothing like that. Just the opposite, in fact. That's what I wanted to talk to you about."

Hope died. She waited for the next blow. "Go on."

"Not here. The Colonel wants to meet you."

"What Colonel?"

"My boss."

The Colonel had a suite at the Stanford Court. Lathrop drove Beth there in his black car. The doorman's eyes fawned and sized them up at the same time. They took the elevator to the top floor and walked soundlessly on a thick floral carpet to a door at the end. Lathrop opened it with a key.

"There you are," the Colonel said, glancing sharply at Lathrop. The Colonel wore a pinstripe suit much like Lathrop's, a white shirt with a ruffled neck, and a single string of pearls. She'd been standing by the window, gazing down at the city; her view took in the park, the Golden Gate, the Bay.

"What a ludicrous place," she said. She sat down at a table that bore the remains of breakfast. "Get room service up here."

Lathrop picked up the phone. The Colonel lit a cigarette and squinted at Beth through the smoke. A decade or more separated them. Those years showed in the wrinkles around the Colonel's eyes and the softness of her jawline. There was nothing else soft about her. She didn't ask Beth to sit down. "So you're the plucky little sub chaser," she said, blowing smoke. Beth said nothing. The Colonel went on staring at her. "Christ," she said, finally turning away.

A waiter came. He cleared the table. Lathrop covered it with the glossy submarine photos. "Have a look at these."

"I've already seen them."

"Try again," Lathrop said.

"Pretend it's an IQ test," the Colonel added. "Something academic."

"Why should I?"

The Colonel stiffened.

"Ms. Hunter likes explanations," Lathrop explained.

"I don't give a shit what she likes."

"Of course not, Colonel. But it can't hurt in this case, can it?"

"It wastes time." But the Colonel waved her hand in a gesture that gave permission.

Lathrop turned to Beth. "We tracked your submarine across the Pacific. At first it followed a course that would have taken it to China. Then, a few hundred miles past Midway, it veered north. Two days ago it surfaced at Petropavlovsk Naval Base on Kamchatka. It was a Russian submarine, Alfa class, the *Timoshenko*. Now, as I told you before, we never ruled the Russians out."

"You did," the Colonel interrupted.

Lathrop's face flushed, but he went on. "The problem is Wu wasn't on the sub."

"How do you know that?"

"We know."

"Did you have someone watching?"

"Not exactly. It doesn't matter. The point is—"

"It matters to me."

Lathrop looked at the Colonel.

"Show her the fucking pictures," the Colonel said.

Lathrop unfastened a briefcase and withdrew a stack of black-and-white photographs. "These are pictures of everyone who disembarked from the *Timoshenko*," he said, handing them to her. "They were shot from a satellite."

Each photograph showed two or three men in dark uniforms walking on a pier. They could have been taken from the top of a tall tree: not quite good enough to identify individual faces, but more than good enough to classify the faces by race. There were no Chinese faces.

"Couldn't that mean he's still on board?" Beth asked.

"Hardly. The *Timoshenko*'s in dry dock, swarming with maintenance men. They wouldn't leave Wu in such an insecure situation. He'd be on a jet to Moscow two minutes after they tied up."

"Then he must have got off somewhere else."

"You guessed it, sweetie," the Colonel said. "In Atlantis."

She knew how to make words sting. Beth couldn't think of a way to sting back before Lathrop slipped the photographs into the briefcase and said: "The point is we may have picked up the wrong boat. We want you to have another look at the sub pictures.''

Beth went through them again. With no more certainty than before, she picked out number seventeen. The Colonel leaned across the table to look.

"The Alfa?" she asked. Lathrop nodded. "Christ," the Colonel said.

Lathrop held up one of the other photographs. "What about this one?"

Number forty-nine. Beth remembered it from the first photo viewing. Han-class sub. Chinese. "No. I'm almost positive." She thought for a moment. "Have you got a picture of the *Timoshenko* itself?"

"It's an Alfa. They all look the same."

"Have you got one?"

Lathrop had one in his briefcase. The *Timoshenko*, shot from orbit, lay beside the pier. Because of the lens's power, the overhead view wasn't much different from what Beth had seen as the fin lifted her out of the water. "Yes," she said, "I think that could be it."

"I just explained why that's not possible," Lathrop said, taking the photograph.

"She's not remembering very well," the Colonel said.

"Do you think you'd remember better if you were a bit more relaxed?" Lathrop asked.

"I've remembered as well as I can. It's not my fault if you don't like the results."

Lathrop looked at the Colonel. The Colonel looked at Beth. "Try it," she said.

Lathrop went into the bathroom. He came back with a hypodermic needle in his hand. "Just a little relaxant," he said. "It helps the memory."

"Forget it." Beth backed toward the door.

Lathrop's other hand slipped into his jacket pocket and pulled out a small silver gun. "Let's not have a scene."

Beth whirled and wrenched the door open. She was two steps into the hall when Lathrop brought her down. She'd forgotten how quick he was, how his hand had once flashed across her cheek. Now they wrestled on the thick carpet. He was stronger and heavier. He used his weight to force her onto her back; she tried to twist away; he dug his forearm into her throat.

"Help!" she screamed, but it wasn't very loud.

"Shut her up," said the Colonel from the doorway.

"Help!"

Lathrop raised the gun and brought the butt down against the side of her head—just hard enough to push her down, sickened, to the edge of blackness.

Bump, bump along the thick carpet: wreaths of bluebells against a gray background. As the doorjamb went by, Beth tried to grab it; it slipped away. The door closed. The bolt snicked into place. A hand raised her skirt.

"Any muscle will do," Lathrop said.

"This is better," replied the Colonel through gritted teeth.

The needle sank hard and deep into Beth's flesh. She cried out, a cry that faded to a faint whine at the top of her throat. Then a warm wave rolled through her and the room grew still.

"Put her in a chair," said the Colonel.

Lathrop lifted her with a grunt and sat her down. *What a sound a grunt is*, Beth thought. *It proves we're descended from the apes.*

Lathrop and the Colonel stood before the chair, looking down at her. She could see the pores in their faces. The Colonel's were partly hidden under a light dusting of powder, not enough to keep Beth from noticing that they were larger than Lathrop's. She also saw that one of his ginger sideburns was slightly longer than the other, and that a spot of wax was stuck in the bowl of his ear.

"Too bad you're not as perfect as your suits," she said.

"Was the solution too strong?" asked the Colonel.

"No," Lathrop said. "That's the way she is."

"Christ." The word was like a nervous tic.

"Is either of you religious?" Beth asked.

Leaning forward, the Colonel peered into her eyes. Beth smelled apple deodorant—and, very faintly, sour sweat. She began to laugh.

"I think the solution was too strong," the Colonel said.

"I followed the directions on the package."

Beth kept laughing. "Sweaty Apples," she said. "The deodorant that keeps them guessing. My father could have made something of that."

The Colonel's eyes narrowed; a split second later, so did Lathrop's. They both had narrow eyes to begin with, Beth saw; and they were both wearing contact lenses: tiny plastic shields they lurked behind. In prehistoric times they would have been left to mope myopically around the cave, while Beth went out into the world.

"Where's your father?" asked the Colonel.

"Out of town."

"Where?"

"You can't reach him. The number's unlisted." Beth smiled. This was humor. Teddy's kind of humor. Her smile started to crack.

"Christ. Make a note to check on the father."

"I want Teddy," Beth said. She started to cry.

"Where is he?"

"In the toilet. In the toilet with the green snakes."

"What the hell are you talking about?"

Tears streamed out of her eyes. "Don't you know?"

"Stop playing games."

"It's no game. You've got ears in the ocean and eyes in the sky, but you still don't know about the green snakes." The Colonel and Lathrop watched from the other side of her tears. "You're both very tough. Much tougher than me. But that's all you are."

"Damn you, Lathrop. You've fucked up the solution. I've sat through dozens of these things and never seen this."

Lathrop fumbled with a cardboard package. "Look, it says right here—three cc's for an adult weighing one hundred and fifty pounds."

The Colonel batted the package out of his hand. "Asshole. She doesn't weigh anything like one fifty."

"She must. She's a big strong girl."

"Christ."

Beth cried and cried. She slid off the chair and curled up on the floor. The rug grew damp under her face. She felt another deep, sharp pain in her buttock.

Then another warm wave.

And nothing.

20

Beth opened her eyes. She saw little tile squares, black and white, and beside her head, the pedestal of a toilet. Fright shot through her; but in the next moment she realized it was not her bathroom where she lay, not her toilet by her head.

Her body was weak, her mind slow. She dragged herself to her feet and went into a large bedroom. The king-sized bed was unmade, the bedding on one side rumpled into a nest for a single body. Soft and warm. Beth fought the desire to sink into the big bed and walked through an open doorway, into the living room of the Colonel's suite at the Stanford Court.

The Colonel and Lathrop were gone. There was nothing to show they were ever coming back.

Beth went down to the lobby. A different doorman was on duty, busy directing a line of Mercedes-Benzes through the narrow drive, but when he saw Beth hailing a taxi he hurried forward to open the door for her and collect a tip.

"Where to, madam?" he asked, so he could pass the information onto the driver and perhaps pocket a little more.

"Hotel Dolores." His face was a blank. "In the Mission," she added.

Blankness turned to distaste; his expectations shrank. It was the kind of neighborhood where he himself might have lived. Guests sometimes left the Stanford Court for another hotel, but never, in his experience, for the Dolores. Another taxi pulled up behind Beth's and an old woman, bent under the weight of her jewelry, struggled out. The doorman gave up on Beth and trotted to her.

Beth closed the door herself. "Hotel Dolores."

The driver nodded matter-of-factly: Taxi drivers were paid to get people from A to B; doormen, to destabilize the self-confidence of the middle class.

Inside her eighty-six-dollar-a-week room, Beth sat on the lumpy bed and dialed Helen Brock's number in Beverly Hills. It rang a dozen times. Beth pictured Helen in her darkened sitting room, gazing at the phone, and let it ring a dozen more before hanging up.

She stretched out, covering herself with the worn bedspread. Her body, except for a deep ache in her left buttock, went numb. Sunshine flowed in through the dusty window. *Clean Me*, someone had written in the dust, instead of doing it. Beth's eyes closed.

"We'll see about that, bitch," a man snarled.

Beth sat up with a jerk. She was alone in her shabby room. On the other side of the wall, a woman said: "You make me sick."

"Not anymore, babe," the man said. "You'll have to get by with this from now on."

A door slammed. "Pig!" the woman yelled. A hard object struck the wall. Heavy feet went by Beth's door, down the hall. The woman began to sob, loudly at first, then in a muffled way. After a while there was no sound at all. Then snoring.

Beth had a vision of the Hotel Dolores with all its exterior walls removed, and in every dingy room a lone woman. "Enough of that," she said aloud, rising from the bed. There were already too many candidates for pity—the Lings, Helen, Marty, her mother—without including her.

Going home was out of the question. But how could she stay at the Hotel Dolores?

Quite suddenly, she knew what she needed. She needed what others seemed to have: a weapon. The Colonel had a needle; Lathrop had a gun, Rex Heidemann too, she remembered, had a gun for shooting rabbits. And Baldy had muscles that blew up like balloons under his skin.

But Beth had never fired a gun, never even held one in her hands. The only weapon she knew how to use was a speargun. And that had been long ago, when she and her father would anchor for the night, and Beth would dive for their dinner. It had taken all her strength to pull the thick rubber band back to the notch in the spear; jack or snapper in view, she would flick off the safety with her thumb, sight along the metal tube of the gun, and pull the trigger, sending the steel spear flashing through the water. It was effective underwater. On land it would be much more powerful, but not very accurate.

Dive shops were listed in the yellow pages. There was one within walking distance. Beth went there and selected a spear-gun, much like the one she'd used years before, but longer. It had a three-quarter-inch rubber band.

"That's a pretty big gun for a lady," said the man behind the counter. "Sure you can load it?"

Beth nodded.

But back in her room, she found she couldn't. With the butt of the gun pressed against her stomach, she pulled the rubber band with all her might. The steel catch came within an inch of the notch in the spear. The next time it was two inches. Then three. Finally, Beth lay on the floor with the point of the spear wedged under the bathroom door. Then, sitting with the butt of the gun against her feet, she leaned forward and drew the rubber band toward her, using all her muscles. The catch slipped into place. Making sure the safety was on, she laid the loaded gun under the bed.

On the other side of the wall, the woman was crying again.

Beth telephoned Helen Brock. No answer. She tried the church in Santa Monica. Rory Brock answered.

"She wants to talk to you," he told Beth.

"I've called her three times. There's no answer."

"She's not at home." Pause. "Can you come down here?"

"Where is she?"

"The hospital. She went in yesterday."

"What happened?"

"Nothing happened, exactly. Helen's sick."

Beth remembered the hospital bracelet on Helen's wrist. "Is it serious?"

"Only God knows the answer to that."

"What do the doctors think?"

"Helen's had cancer for a long time. It's spreading."

Beth flew to L.A. Inside the terminal, the taxi, and the hospital, the air was cold; outside, it was hot and harsh.

At the front desk, Beth was given Helen Brock's room number. She rode up in an unpainted elevator with other visitors, nurses, interns, residents, and a little Chinese boy in a wheel-chair.

Helen's room was in an old wing. The hall smelled strongly of disinfectant, but no matter how much they used, they couldn't get rid of disease: Through every open door Beth saw gray-skinned people flat on their backs, all of them hooked to IV solutions, a few to respirators as well.

Helen Brock was one of those. She had a private room at the end of the hall. When Beth walked in, Helen's eyes were closed. Her chest rose and fell heavily, as though every breath was a deep one.

The air came from a metal box rolled up beside the bed. The box pumped it through a hose and into a white plastic tube stuck into her nose and taped in place. Helen's gown had slipped open; every pumping of the box stretched her ribs apart. They were easy to see because she wasn't wearing her prosthesis; there was just a long white scar where her breast had been.

A nurse came in. She didn't look at Helen or at Beth. Her only interest was the metal box. She read its dial, jotted figures on a clipboard, and turned to go.

"Do you think it's pumping a little too strongly?" Beth asked quietly, so Helen's sleep would be undisturbed.

"Are you a doctor?" responded the nurse in a louder-than-normal tone, compensating for Beth's quiet in a world of her own where a fixed amount of noise was required.

"No."

The nurse left without another word.

Helen's eyes opened. They darted around in fright. Then it all came back to her, and her eyes were still: two dark, listless smudges on yellow whites.

"Helen."

Helen turned her head and saw Beth. Her lips parted slightly; her eyes spoke complex, pleading speech Beth couldn't understand. She realized that the tube in Helen's nose reached down into her throat. She couldn't talk.

Helen raised her hand to her throat and turned her head once from side to side, very slowly. Her fingers touched the bare skin at her neck, fumbled for the edges of her gown. Beth drew it closed for her. Helen's hand found hers, grabbed it, held hard: cold, damp, trembling. Her eyes pleaded.

"Is the machine pumping too hard? Is it hurting you?"

Helen's head moved once from side to side.

"Is there something I can do for you?"

Helen nodded. She had forgotten about the obstruction in her throat. Her brow rose in furrows of agony. She dug her nails into Beth's hand, and Beth felt her pulse, faint and rapid as a bird's. After a minute or two it slowed, but remained faint.

"Do you want to see the doctor?"

Again Helen nodded, this time almost imperceptibly.

Beth started for the doctor. "You'll have to let go of my hand." Helen let go.

Beth went to the nurses' station. "Mrs. Brock in seven eighty-three wants to see her doctor."

The nurse on duty stopped filling in a chart and looked up; the same nurse who had checked the respirator. "What about?" she asked.

"I don't know. She can't talk because of the respirator."

From the expression on the nurse's face, Beth thought she was about to say: "Then how do you know she wants her doctor?" But the nurse wasn't up to that standard of repartee. She said, "Dr. Mills will be back for rounds at five-thirty. Unless it's an emergency, she'll have to wait."

"I don't know if it's an emergency or not. She seems frantic."

"Frantic is normal behavior around here." The nurse returned to her chart.

Beth went back to Helen's room. The dark, anxious eyes were waiting. "The doctor will be here soon." Beth looked at her watch. 3:45.

Helen reached for her hand. Beth took it and felt the bird pulse. Helen's eyes were full of communication, exaggeratedly expressive, like parent to child in some telepathic species.

"You wanted to talk to me. Was it about Teddy?"

The dark eyes clouded in confusion.

"Wu Tun-li."

Helen nodded, very slightly.

"He's disappeared. I'm looking for him."

Nod.

"Do you know where he is?"

Helen turned her head once from side to side.

"But you know something. Teddy came to see you."

Confusion.

"Or spoke to you on the phone."

Nod.

"What did he say?"

Pleading eyes. Helen raised her other hand, the one with the IV needle sticking into it, and made a little writing motion.

Beth went to the nurses' station. No one was there. She found a pad and a pencil and brought them back to Helen's room. The nurse was by the bed, taking Helen's blood pressure. When she finished, she produced a hypodermic and injected it in Helen's arm.

"What's that?"

"For pain." The nurse left the room, not wasting the name of the drug on a civilian.

Beth approached the bed with the pencil and paper. Helen's eyes were closed. Her chest rose and fell like a miler's after the finishing kick. Beth pulled up a chair.

Later, there were voices in the hall. A doctor came in, trailed by a couple of interns and the nurse.

The doctor's face tensed into a smile. Then he saw that Helen was asleep and let it fade; his face drooped with fatigue. "I'm Mills," he said to Beth. "The resident. Are you a relative of the patient?"

"A friend."

Dr. Mills inspected Helen's chart, felt her pulse. "Nurse," he said, "draw up two vials of atropine." The interns exchanged a glance. The nurse left the room.

"What's that?" Beth asked.

"A stimulant," Mills replied, writing on the chart. "Her heart's not doing the job it should."

"Is that what's wrong with her, Doctor? Her heart?"

"That's part of it."

"Is that why she's on the respirator?"

He shook his head. "That's because of her pneumonia. She doesn't have the strength to do her own breathing right now."

"It makes her uncomfortable. Do you think it's pumping too strongly?"

Mills glanced at the dials on the metal box. "No." He didn't look at Helen's chest, where the ribs stretched wide apart with every mechanical breath.

"How long will she have to be on it?"

Mills put down the chart. "Do you know the patient well?"

"Not very."

"Two years ago she had breast cancer. It was caught too late.

It's since spread to her liver—her bones too, we think. She's''—he searched for a phrase—''not very well.''

The nurse returned and gave Helen another injection. The doctor felt her pulse; the expression on his face didn't change, but his eyes shifted slightly. He lowered Helen's arm to the bed. Then he, the interns, and the nurse filed out. At the door, Mills turned and said: ''Does she have any relatives?''

''A husband.''

''You'd better call and ask him to come.''

''Why?''

The question annoyed him; he didn't like being forced out from behind his euphemisms. His tired eyes looked sharply at Beth, taking her in for the first time. ''Because she may not last the night.''

From a pay-phone in the hall, Beth called the church in Santa Monica. No answer. She tried Helen's house in Beverly Hills.

''Hello,'' said a woman.

''Rory Brock, please.''

''Ro,'' the woman called, ''it's for you.''

''Find out who it is, Fabrice,'' said Brock in the background.

Beth explained. Brock came to the phone. Beth relayed what the doctor had said.

''Oh dear, dear God.'' There was a long pause, full of unspoken emotion—or else he was lighting a cigarette. ''I'll be right over.''

Beth went back to Helen's room and sat by the bed. Helen's chest rose and fell, parting her gown, exposing her ribs and her scar. Beth straightened the gown several times; then she gave up.

Helen's eyes opened. They filled with panic, and her hand jerked up as though to ward off a blow. Beth took it in hers.

Helen turned to her. The pleading, telepathic look came into her eyes. Helen made a writing motion. Propping her into a half-sitting position, Beth gave her the pad and pencil. She couldn't manage both. Beth held the pad. Clutching the pencil in her trembling hand, Helen pressed the point against the paper and, in the shaky letters of a young child, printed: *Take it out.*

''No, Helen. Can't you write what you want to tell me?''

Helen shook her head once, carefully, from side to side. On the pad, even more slowly and shakily than before, she printed: *Too much.*

Helen looked at her. She pointed to the words on the pad: *Take it out*. Pleading eyes. Tears soaked them, flowed out, ran down her gray cheeks. *Take it out*.

Beth reached over and pulled off the tape. Then she took the tube between her fingers and drew it gently out of Helen's nose. Not gently enough: Furrows of pain appeared again on her brow. But they faded immediately. Whatever the nurse had given her for pain was strong.

Helen sighed with relief, a small sound almost beyond hearing. She closed her eyes. The exaggerated rise and fall of her chest ceased. It didn't seem to be moving at all. Beth bent forward, her cheek touching Helen's. A faint exhalation from Helen's nostrils brushed her skin.

"Helen?"

Helen's eyes opened. They had lost the pleading look, but nothing had come to take its place; they were dull and flat. Helen parted her lips. Her tongue was cracked and yellow.

"You're so far away," Helen said. Her voice was a low rasp in her throat, barely audible.

"I'm right here."

"Yes. You're very good. You lied to me, but I understand."

Not many words, but they left Helen gasping for breath. A whooping sound came from her gaping mouth. Beth grabbed the respirator tube, although she had no idea how to reinsert it. Gasping turned to coughing, coughing far too weak to clear the blockage inside. Sputum dribbled onto Helen's chin. Her breathing quieted, weak and irregular.

"Do you want this?" Beth asked, holding the tube.

Helen shook her head. "I heard what the doctor said. I just didn't want to open my eyes." She closed them. Gasps came, but no whooping. They faded away. "I'm dying."

"No."

"Yes." Helen opened her eyes, flatter and duller than before. "I'm not afraid. I believe in Jesus Christ. I believe in the immortal life of the soul." Her dark eyes burned brighter. They stared into Beth's. "Do you?"

"No."

"Yes, you do. I can feel it." Her hand, colder now, reached for Beth's and took it. "You're the last human being I'll—" Gasps choked off the rest of her thought. When they went away she said: "I want to do it right, no matter what Rex says."

"What does Rex say?"

"Not to talk. But it was already too late. I'd told Tun-li. Besides, Rex was wrong. He lost his faith. He got involved with evil men. He slept with other women." Her eyes closed. She said something Beth couldn't hear.

Beth bent closer. "What?"

Helen's lips moved and sound came in a whisper: "He thought I was sexless." Tears leaked from her closed eyes. "But I wasn't. I swear to Jesus Christ. Rex was too rough. I was young. He never gave me a chance." Her eyes opened. They gazed unseeing at the ceiling. "You know something? Rory was too rough also. But I tried my best for him, and he knew it. That's why he never slept with other women." Helen looked at Beth. Beth looked down at the respirator tube in her hand. "Do you think Rory loves me?"

"Yes."

Helen glanced around. "He insisted on this private room, you know. Wasn't that the sweetest thing?"

"Yes."

Helen squeezed her hand, but very weakly; the fire in her eyes had gone out. They stared emptily at the ceiling. She breathed.

Hard shoes went clicking down the hall outside. Beth said: "What evil men did Rex get involved with?"

Helen was silent for such a long time that Beth thought she hadn't heard. Finally she spoke, very quietly.

"I didn't hear you," Beth said, tilting her ear down to Helen's lips.

Helen spoke again, no louder, but this time Beth heard: "Jimmy Han."

"Who is Jimmy Han?"

Helen's eyes closed. "I don't want to talk about evil." Her hand let go of Beth's and wandered to her throat. She began to gasp, then whoop, then cough, a weaker cough than before, not strong enough to bring up anything. Beth stood up to go for the nurse. Helen reached out and stopped her. The spasm passed. Helen lay still on the bed.

Beth asked: "What did Tun-li want?"

Helen gazed at her. "You're so far away."

"I'm right beside you." Beth squeezed her hand. "What did Tun-li want?"

"His amah."

"His amah?"

"Pei Ming. She didn't believe." Helen's eyes moved to the ceiling, and beyond; their whites were yellow, rimmed in red. "But she was a good woman. She saved his life at the lake house." Her voice rose slightly: "And I helped. I disobeyed Rory."

"Rory?"

But Helen couldn't answer. Her body was shaken with whoops and coughs; the tendons in her thin neck stood out like buttresses made of tissue paper. She fought for air.

"I'm getting the nurse," Beth said.

But Helen's hand squeezed hers with sudden strength—strength that quickly ebbed. Her body grew still. "I believe in the immortal life of the soul," she said; after a long silence: "Do you?"

"No." Helen's hand was colder now, and dry. "Did you disobey Rory?"

"Rory?"

"Or Rex?"

Helen nodded. "He got involved with evil men." Her voice was less than a whisper. Beth's ear was a few inches from her cracked, colorless lips.

"What did they do?"

"Follow orders."

"Whose?"

"The government's." Helen's words were so soft now, Beth felt them on the skin of her ear more than she heard them.

"What government?"

Helen spoke. Beth didn't hear. She leaned still closer. Helen's crusty lips brushed her ear: "Why don't you believe in the immortal life of the soul?"

The pleading look rose briefly in Helen's eyes, then sank away. Beth wasn't even sure about the mortal life of the soul. But she didn't say that. She said: "How did Teddy know about his amah?"

Roughened lips moved against her ear: "He didn't. I told him. But it was what he wanted to know." There was more, but it was inaudible.

"Why?"

They looked at each other, eyes as close as lovers'. Helen said nothing. Beth felt faint puffs of breath on her skin.

"Are you sure Teddy is an orphan?" she asked.

Helen closed her eyes. She nodded.

"Did you tell him that?"

Helen shook her head.

"Why not?"

Helen's eyes opened. In a few seconds they had grown much duller. "I got scared," Helen said. "Isn't that funny?"

"Scared of what?"

Helen's lips were still; so were her eyes. Gently, Beth released her hand. She was going to get the nurse. But first there was one question she had to ask: "Was it the Brotherhood of the Green Snake?"

Helen's eyes suddenly widened and filled with fear. For a moment, Beth thought she was reacting to her question. But it wasn't that. Helen tried to sit up, sank feebly back on the pillows. She gasped; she whooped. Then she stopped. Her eyes were unafraid. Beth put her face to Helen's and felt no puffs of breath.

She jumped up and grabbed the respirator tube.

"What the hell's going on in here?" The nurse was at the door. She ran in, snatched the tube from Beth, and began working it into Helen's nose.

Helen's chest began to rise and fall, swelling like an athlete's, stretching her ribs apart. Up and down. The nurse felt for a pulse. Then she put her hands over Helen's heart and pushed hard. One, two, three, four, five. Helen's chest continued to rise and fall, taking in air from the machine and letting it out. But she was dead.

The nurse straightened up from the bed and turned to Beth. "I'm going to see that you're charged for this."

Beth felt rage building inside her. It didn't really have anything to do with the nurse, and she tried to keep it out of her voice. "Try it," Beth said; her voice started to rise anyway. "The only charge you'll be able to bring is committing suicide. Helen took the tube out herself."

The nurse stepped back. "I don't believe you," she said. But there was doubt in her tone. Beth had none: Killing wasn't taking the tube from Helen's nose at her request; it was what had been done to Albert Ling.

Beth went into the hall. Rory Brock was coming the other way, a box of candy in his hand. He saw Beth.

"How is she?"

"Helen died a few minutes ago."

"Jesus." Rory hurried past her into the room. Beth followed. The nurse was writing on the chart. "What are you talking about?" Rory said. "She's still breathing."

"Turn off that fucking machine." Beth shouted.

Later, they went outside. Fabrice waited at the wheel of a BMW. She wore a sweatband, singlet, jogging shorts. Her body was tanned and sleek.

Rory said, "She passed away."

Fabrice looked sad. Rory looked sad.

Rory said to Beth: "Thank you for coming. Did you find out why she wanted to see you?"

Beth nodded. "She wanted me to have her photo album of China."

Rory looked puzzled, but he said, "I can give it to you now, if you like."

They rode in silence to the house in Beverly Hills. Rory led the way into the darkened sitting room. He threw open the heavy curtains, filling the room with hard light. The photo album lay on the coffee table. Rory picked it up and handed it to Beth.

"A drink, anybody?" asked Fabrice from the doorway.

21

The coffin, an overwrought box of mountain ash with polished brass handles on the sides, was the largest available, suitable for someone the size of Albert Ling. But only Albert's head was inside; his body had not been found.

The coffin was lowered into a freshly dug hole. A shovelful of gravelly earth rattled down on the varnished wood. Albert's mother winced, but the rest of the family watched still and dry-eyed from the far side of the grave.

On the near side stood a few dozen people, of whom Beth, at the outer edge, recognized only Mr. Chen. Everyone gazed unwaveringly at the hole in the ground, except for a bent old woman in dark glasses who twice turned to look at Beth.

The single shovelful of earth meant the end of the ceremony. A man climbed into a bulldozer to finish the job, but no one stayed to watch. The mourners filed along a flower-lined path to the parking lot. On the way, Beth felt a hand on her arm. Jade Ling. Her hand maintained contact only as long as it had to; her eyes were empty of expression.

"My grandfather wants a word with you."

Y.K. Ling waited in his wheelchair, a grandson on either side. Beth started to say something she hoped would sound right, but he cut her off. "Have you seen this?" he asked, handing her a copy of yesterday's *New York Times*, opened to page twelve.

Under the headline "China–U.S. Rift Seen," was a half-column article by Robert Means:

> The U.S. Ambassador to the People's Republic of China, his family, and several top aides left Peking last night aboard a commercial airliner on an unannounced trip to the U.S.

The unscheduled visit has given rise to speculation in the diplomatic community of the Chinese capital concerning a possible sudden rift between the two powers. One source who asked to remain anonymous said the cause of the alleged dispute may have been a recent incident of espionage involving Chinese intelligence agents in the U.S. A State Department spokesman had no comment.

"Does this have something to do with Albert?" Beth asked.
"Nothing. That's the point. Albert was barking up the wrong tree."

But how could that be? Beth thought. Albert had told her to meet him at the Ta-Tang Café; the café was connected to the Taipei Social Club; Baldy had run out of the club on the night Albert disappeared; and Baldy had been in the car with Han Shih, who was a Chinese agent, according to Lathrop. So she said: "I don't think so."

"Don't be stupid," snapped Y.K. Ling. "The PRC would never deal with those Taipei people." His voice had lost all trace of elderly reediness, as though Albert's death had made him younger, rather than broken him. He touched the wheelchair controls and rolled up to Beth. When he spoke, his tone was soft, so no one else could hear—and murderous: "I've got a case of dynamite. And I know how to use it. Have you ever seen what a case of dynamite can do?" His eyes glowed with the imagined pleasure of revenge.

"You're talking about the coal chute, aren't you?"
The glow went out of his eyes. "You're a smart woman," he said. "Smart enough to cause a lot of grief for me and my family."

Beth turned and walked away. The bent woman in the dark glasses watched her from the driver's seat of a rusty Volkswagen.

Beth got in her car. For a while she just sat there, empty. Then she began to think about Berryessa Wines. There was still time to make the drive before dark. But first she had to speak to Robert Means.

She drove to the Hotel Dolores, called *The New York Times*, and was put through to him. "Thanks for returning my call," he said. "You should have reversed the charges."

Beth tried to recall the last recording on her machine. Helen.

Had there been a message from Means as well? "I read your article," she began.

"That was written before I saw the letter, of course," Means said. "In fact, I still haven't seen it, exactly. That's one of the things I wanted to discuss with you."

"What letter?"

There was a long pause, filled with the buzz of tiny conversations across the country. "Are you telling me you don't know about the letter?" asked Means at last.

"No." The echo of her voice in the wire was sharp and scared.

Means took a deep breath; it sounded like distant surf. "Dr. Wu sent you a letter from China. Explaining his defection. That's why the ambassador was recalled. Their ambassador's on a plane back to China right now. Everyone's trying to keep it quiet, but it's caused an uproar on both sides. The administration's angry because the Chinese have gone public. I haven't figured out yet why the Chinese are angry. But they are. The new reactor agreement is already down the drain, and the oil leases are next."

Beth's heart raced; she was pressing the receiver so hard against her ear that it hurt. "But I haven't received a letter from Teddy."

"They must have intercepted it. Just a—" A muffled voice in the background spoke to Means. His voice, also muffled, responded: "For Christ's sake, give me two more minutes—this is a new angle." The other voice spoke again. "Jesus H.," Means said, coming back on the line: "Are you still there? Sorry. I've got a few questions to ask you so I can wrap this up before deadline. Then I'll call you back and we can go over the whole schmear." He was talking fast and frantically, like someone with a full bladder.

"Good-bye," said Beth.

"No, wait! Where are you? Don't hang up!"

But she did.

She hurried down to the street and called Captain Gomez of the Coast Guard from a phone booth: Gomez because he was her only link to Lathrop; the phone booth because she didn't want Lathrop to know her number at the Dolores. Last time it had taken five minutes. Now forty went by before the phone rang.

Beth grabbed it. "Lathrop?"

"Hello tristesse," he said cheerfully, his voice rising over a background of tinkling ice cubes, loud talk, and laughter. "What's up?"

"I want my letter, you bastard."

"Ah, so the news is out. That's democracy for you."

"I want my letter."

"And you shall have it. Will you be home tomorrow? And where would that be, by the way?"

"I want it now. It's mine. You've stolen it."

"That's where you're wrong, sweetheart." His voice came cutting through the wire, riding the sharp edge where triumph and hatred meet; to her he could say what he only dreamed of saying to the Colonel. "I've got a judge's order authorizing interception and opening of all your mail. But I won't need it much longer. Our role is just about over. Now it's time for the politicians to fuck it up."

Lathrop agreed to meet her in Union Square in an hour. He was late. Beth sat on a bench. It was early evening; downtown glowed brick-red in the setting sun. A Navy band was on a stage at the western end, playing show tunes. Tourists and shoppers had stopped to watch. A shirtless man who hadn't bathed since the Summer of Love danced in front of the trumpets; his curled lip and jutting pelvis were meant to demonstrate the innate rhythmic sense of sixties man, but he wasn't coming close to the beat. A clown appeared, red-nosed and floppy-footed, collecting for lesbian mothers. Then Hare Krishna, their tinny cymbals silenced by the blare of the Navy brass. And so on. The tourists snapped pictures and pretended they thought it was all outrageous.

Lathrop arrived. He wasn't wearing a pinstripe suit. Instead he had on a madras jacket and red pants, like a country-club bumpkin. "I've been to a party," he said, sitting on the bench and stretching his legs.

She smelled it on his breath. "What's the occasion?"

If he heard the anger in her tone, he didn't care. "I'm celebrating."

"What?"

"Don't make me toot my own horn." But after a short silence he tooted it anyway: "I hit the two key points of this business right off the bat. It was China, not Russia; and a defection, not a kidnapping. The powers that be don't overlook things like that."

Beth searched for words to hurt him, but found none. She was a new angle to Means, a note in Lathrop's horn, grist for their career mills. It had nothing to do with Teddy. He was just a text wherein they read who was in and who was out, as Means had said in his discourse on the CIA. He hadn't applied that analysis to himself, but *The New York Times* was a bureaucracy, too.

"I want my letter."

"Relax. I've got it. It came the other night. The night of our little meeting at the Stanford Court." As though about to confide a secret, Lathrop leaned closer, breathing whiskey: "If we'd had it a few hours earlier, that whole shindig wouldn't have been necessary. But when that sub came up Russian and empty we had to go over the facts with you again. I hope you didn't take it personally."

Beth didn't answer. The setting sun turned Lathrop's face brick-red and struck sparks in his ginger hair. He reached into the pocket of his madras jacket. "Here's the letter. Absolutely authentic. Had his fingertips all over it. We also ran a computer comparison of the handwriting with other samples we had. Bang on."

Beth took the envelope. On the stamp was a red and brown picture of a quiet lake, much like Y.K. Ling's, except for the radio antenna in the foreground. Her name and address were written on the envelope in blue ink. She didn't need a computer to tell her that the writing was Teddy's. There was no return address.

"That's a Shanghai postmark, by the way," Lathrop said.

Beth opened the letter: a single sheet of white paper bearing more blue words in Teddy's hand. Beth knew something was wrong from the first one.

Dearest Beth,

Writing this letter is not an easy task, but I feel you are entitled to some explanation. Our relationship was strong and agreeable—mutually, I hope!—and I did not end it without a lot of thought.

But, finally, there are some aspects of this world that are more important than the lives of any individuals, including you or me. My destiny is with my people and I have rejoined them at last. My goal, inseparable from theirs, is total victory over the forces of capitalist imperialism. It is to this cause that I dedicate my life!

I trust this letter will provide you with some understanding of recent events. Please do not try to contact me. No such attempts will be successful.

> With all best wishes for the future,
> Ted

Beth laughed—a strange harsh sound that took her by surprise and had nothing to do with amusement.

"What's so funny?" asked Lathrop.

Beth was silent for a moment, recovering her self-control. When she spoke her voice was quiet. "Teddy didn't write this tripe."

"Please don't start. I've already explained there isn't a particle of doubt that he did."

"Forget your computer, Lathrop. This isn't Teddy. He would never write 'dearest.' He would only use 'relationship' sarcastically. And he was Teddy to me, never Ted." And there was more: the mincing little joke ("mutually, I hope!"), the political clichés, the stiff closing. It wasn't Teddy; it wasn't even the work of someone whose first language was English—but Lathrop wasn't listening.

"You get everything backwards," he said. "The whole point is that the Teddy you knew was false. This"—he flicked the letter with his fingernail—"is the real Teddy. You'll just have to accept it."

"Why? Your theory's full of holes. You don't even know how he got to China."

"That's simple. In a sub. We tracked the wrong one, that's all."

"But the one I saw wasn't Chinese. It was Russian."

"You're still stuck in that groove? Look, it was dark and foggy, just like you said. Even a professional couldn't be positive in those circumstances." He smiled. "Stop fighting it."

"Thanks for listening," the bandleader said. "Hope you had as much fun as we did." The band swung into "Anchors Aweigh."

"What about the two men who died?" Beth asked. "The long-haired man and —"

"—your detective pal?" Lathrop shrugged. "He got you involved in some Chinatown gang warfare. What did you expect? That's the only beat he knew. But it had nothing to do with Teddy-boy. Nothing at all."

With a shock, Beth realized that Lathrop and Y.K. Ling were on the same side of that question. What had the old man said? "Albert was barking up the wrong tree."

And so was she, in Lathrop's eyes. But she couldn't stop: "This letter doesn't rule out kidnapping. It might have been written under duress. That's probably what Teddy's trying to tell me."

"By calling you 'dearest'?" Lathrop's lips curled up. "Are you going to base the rest of your life on what you learned in freshman literary analysis? Forget kidnapping. Kidnapping means compulsion, force, violence. There was none of that. A Chinese agent contacted Wu at your apartment. She went through a song and dance about being his mother that a soap-opera audience wouldn't have swallowed. But you did. That allowed them to slip away for their rendezvous with the sub. Defection, pure and simple."

"No violence? Two men have died."

"None of that happened until you stuck your nose in."

For a moment, Beth wanted to hit him; but there was some truth in his words, and it stopped her. She lowered her head and reread the letter. *How can you know the way a man would say good-bye until he says it?*

Until we meet again
Here's wishing you a happy voyage home.

"Anchors Aweigh" rose to its climax. Lathrop looked at his watch. "If I were you, I'd take a little trip. Try to get your mind on other things." He stood up. The last cymbal clash echoed across the square. Beth felt his eyes on her. Looking up, she saw they held a new expression. "If you're interested, you could come back with me to this little party. It might be a good way to start."

He was inviting her to his victory celebration. "Go away," she said, and waited for his anger.

But he didn't get angry. He said: "Or we could have dinner, just the two of us. I know a nice little place on Polk. Kind of a bistro."

"Go away."

"All right."

Nothing she said could upset him now. He was probably due for a quick promotion, if it hadn't come already—perhaps right over the Colonel's head. He reached down and took the letter from her hand.

"I want that," Beth said, grabbing at it.

"I've brought you a copy." He took it from his pocket; he'd xeroxed the envelope, too. "The original is for our records."

Lathrop went away. The band packed up its instruments, loaded them in a truck, and drove off. Day people left. Night people came. The only holdover was the aging hippie; he stood at the foot of the bandstand, fingering an imaginary guitar.

Beth sat on the bench, the copy of Teddy's letter in her lap. The handwriting was his. And perhaps he could have written those words. Maybe he would have thought Ted more appropriate than Teddy in a good-bye letter. But what about the part that was unwritten?

He hadn't mentioned the baby.

Could she have been that wrong about him?

She read the letter over and over, until the very shapes of the letters grew strange and full of secret messages. Ted. She began to hate Ted. She didn't know what she would do if Ted turned out to be real. That was the whole point, of course; had been from the beginning. It was time to stop fooling herself.

"Hey!"

The silent musician had noticed her. He came forward, slinging the invisible guitar on his back. Beth got up and walked away.

"Hey!" he called, adding, "Baby!" after some thought.

Beth walked on, across the square, south toward Market and the Hotel Dolores. This would be her last night there. Lathrop had recommended a trip. He was right. She had a few hundred dollars in cash, credit cards, an unused airplane ticket, and a visa valid for one visit to China: all she needed.

If Teddy had defected, she wanted to see him say to her face what he'd written in the letter. If he'd been kidnapped, the letter was a call for help. Either way, her next move was the same. Shanghai wasn't on the moon. It was waiting at the end of a long plane ride.

From her room, Beth telephoned the airline and reserved a seat on the morning flight to Shanghai. After that, she opened the dark, mothball-smelling closet, felt for her clothes, folded them into the suitcase. She added her file folder and Helen's album. In the lobby, she settled her bill, bought toothpaste, soap, and Tampax. Then she returned to her room, undressed, and went to bed.

On the other side of the wall, the man had come back. He and the woman began to argue. Then they tried to make love. It didn't work. They fought again. A bottle gurgled. Later it rolled across the floor.

After a long time, sleep came. It took Beth down a coal chute

that never seemed to end. At last she came to a round black door.
She opened it. And smelled mothballs.

Beth sat up. A shadow moved. She turned on the bedside light.

Baldy stood naked by the open closet door, a long knife in his
hand.

"Oh God."

Baldy smiled a big sick smile and stepped forward.

Beth reached under the bed and found the speargun. She
pointed it at Baldy's head. "Don't move."

The long gun wobbled in her shaking hand. Baldy moved.
Beth pulled the trigger. Nothing happened. Baldy smiled. His
penis started to grow.

The safety. Beth flicked it with her thumb. "Don't move."
Her voice shook. Her hand shook.

Baldy kept moving. Without hurry, he extended his bulging
arm to knock the speargun aside.

Beth pulled the trigger.

The gun flew backward, striking her head and knocking her
down. She scrambled to her feet. Baldy was backed against the
closet door. The spear was stuck deep in his shoulder, at a down-
ward angle. His knife lay on the floor. There was a puzzled look
in his eyes. It turned to rage. He went for Beth. But he couldn't
move. The spear had gone all the way through, burying its barbs
in the closet door.

Beth ran past him. Her suitcase lay by the door to the hall.
She grabbed it, threw open the door, and raced out.

Baldy roared. There was a tremendous ripping sound. Beth
looked back. Baldy was coming after her with his short scuttling
stride; the closet door, torn from its hinges, was stuck to his back.

He lunged through the open doorway. But no farther. The closet
door caught against the frame. Baldy strained to free himself, muscles surging, veins popping; a trickle of blood ran down his chest
from the plugged hole in his shoulder. He couldn't move.

Beth ran down the stairs. At the bottom she opened her suitcase and hurried into some clothes. High above she heard Baldy
roar. She went into the lobby. No one was there.

On the street, she saw a rusty Volkswagen parked near the
hotel. The bent old woman slept behind the wheel, waiting for
Baldy to finish raping and murdering.

A taxi came by. Beth raised her hand. It took her to the airport.

22

The steel walls stopped humming. The bag of oranges stopped swaying.

Just like that. It frightened him. He felt cold. He shook.

He tried to sit up. Couldn't. Tried to raise his head. Couldn't do that either.

He could feel. Weak. He needed food. Solid food. The IV wasn't enough. The plastic bag dangled over his head, half-filled with clear liquid. There was writing on the bag, but it was in Chinese, so he didn't know what he was getting. He had banged his head on the sail. They were treating him. But did they know what they were doing?

"You'd better take me to the University Hospital," he'd said. When?

"It's not that serious," Jimmy had told him. "Besides, you haven't seen your father yet."

"When will I?"

"Soon."

"Is it ten-fifteen yet?"

But it was past 10:15. Long past.

Oh Beth.

But the letter. It would help. He'd done something very clever about that letter. What was it?

That was long ago when he was smart. Now he was stupid. He couldn't remember.

The thick steel door swung open with a hydraulic sigh. Footsteps. Then Jimmy stood over him, big, smooth-skinned, silver-haired.

"What's wrong with the oranges, Father?"

"I'm not your father.

''What's wrong with the oranges?''

Jimmy studied them. ''They look fine to me.''

''They're not swaying. To and fro.''

Jimmy smiled one of his mouth smiles. ''That's because we've docked. We're there.''

''Where?''

''Shanghai Naval Base.''

''Is my father on the dock?''

''He was too busy.''

''He was supposed to be there.'' Wasn't he? ''He was supposed to be on the submarine, too.''

''He was too busy. He's going to meet us at a rest house in the country. Your mother's already there.''

''Is Pei Ming with her?''

''You're talking nonsense again.''

China. He could smell it. Chinese air. It smelled of oak and pine. Especially pine. He took a few deep breaths. It made him dizzy. He closed his eyes. Then he felt a sudden bite in his arm.

''No! Why do you keep biting me?''

No answer.

Blackness.

He smelled ginger.

Bump bump bump. Roads were bad in China. He was alone in the back of a truck, strapped into a stretcher. No windows. No light leaked in. It must be night. He could feel its coolness. He could feel the IV needle in his hand. His head didn't hurt. But he'd done something to it, all right.

Bump bump bump. Bad roads in China. But they had dogs—he heard barking now and then. Why shouldn't they have dogs? They'd bred the Pekinese, hadn't they?

Bump bump bump. The road went on and on. Slivers of light poked through the crack between the doors. The interior of the truck became visible. There was nothing in it but the IV apparatus, the stretcher, and him.

The truck stopped. The motor cut off. The fan kept whirring.

The doors opened. He was lifted out. He saw Chinese faces against a blue sky. The faces weren't interesting. The sky was. A blue dome, light blue at the edges, darker blue on top. You could soar into it forever. That's what a hawk was doing. They had hawks in China. Why not?

They carried him beneath the blue dome. *Bump bump bump*.

They wore white outfits like hospital orderlies. Out of the corners of his eyes he saw the tops of a few pines, and in the distance a green hillside. He tried to make out if it was terraced for rice paddies, but lying on his back he couldn't tell. He'd always wanted to see that.

He passed under a white stone arch. There were two Chinese characters on it, written in gold, and a poster of Mao Zedong. Above the arch rose a three-tiered pagoda roof, each level borne on the heads of squat stone gargoyles. The tiles were green, the edges of the tiers decorated with red knobs.

The stretcher bearers' feet clicked across stone. He heard a fountain splashing, smelled blossoming fruit trees. The stretcher bearers halted at an ornate green door, encrusted with carved butterflies, painted red. The door opened. They carried him into a white room and laid him on a bed. Then they went away.

It was a simple room, walls white, ceiling white, windows trimmed with red. Through them he saw a blossoming plum tree, and in the distance a high white wall. Beyond it rose a green hillside.

Two scroll paintings hung on the walls. Landscapes. Clouds at the top; mountains in the middle; lakes at the bottom. In one corner of the room were a bamboo desk and chair. A goldfish bowl sat on the desk and two fish hovered inside it, one gold, one red.

The bed was bamboo also. It was soft and comfortable. He was tired.

The door opened. A woman came in. Han Shih. His mother. He started to cry. She came to him. "Hold me," he said.

She patted his head. Cold pats. "How do you feel?"

"Something's wrong with me."

"You look fine."

"Bring me a mirror."

"There are none. You look fine."

"I need solid food."

"The doctor knows best."

"Hold me."

She leaned down and held him for a minute. He cried. She let go, straightened.

"Where's Father?"

"He'll be here as soon as he can. He's very busy."

"He's always busy. Doesn't he want to see me?"

"Of course."

"You have trouble with your *r*'s, Mother. I hope you don't mind my saying that."

"No." But her eyes showed she did.

"I'm worried, Mother."

"There's nothing to worry about."

"Hold me."

She held him, longer this time. He relaxed and fell asleep.

When he awoke, she was sitting by the bed in the bamboo chair. She had a notebook in her lap.

"Is Father here yet?"

"Not yet. How do you feel?"

She had trouble with her *l*'s too, but he didn't say it. Instead he said: "Better."

"Good." She opened the notebook. The pages were covered with Chinese writing and Arabic numerals. "Then perhaps we can talk a little about Mordell's conjecture."

Behind her, a hole opened in the ornate door: a butterfly-shaped hole. A blue eye watched on the other side.

Part Three

23

The fat man in the aisle seat looked up angrily from his newspaper. "You know what this is all about, don't you?"

"No," Beth said, turning from the window, where there was nothing to see but ice-blue. Six hours gone. Six to go. "I don't."

"Our goddamn government," said the man, smacking the paper with the backs of his hairy fingers. "They've got this compulsion to sell arms to Taiwan. For a lousy five, six hundred million a year, they're going to screw us out of the biggest potential market in the history of human business. We are talking one billion consumers."

The stewardess came by with steaming white towels; the drinks cart, dinner cart, and after-dinner drinks cart would soon be blocking the aisle. The man laid a towel on his fat face and moaned. Beth stepped over his knees and went to the toilet.

She looked at herself in the mirror. There were two vertical thought lines between her eyes, but she had no thoughts. She smoothed her forehead; the lines didn't go away.

Beth walked back to her seat. The air in the plane had dried out. Smokers were filling it with fumes. Drinkers were swallowing Bloody Marys, Scotch, or champagne, depending on what time of day they thought it was. Skin was gritty; eyes were red. Hairs grew out of noses; blackheads dotted cheeks. The jet age.

The fat man was cleaning his big, soft ears with the towel. He resumed their conversation in a calmer tone: "The Chinese are very patient, but they're proud, too. Never ever forget what Mao said. First of October. Nineteen hundred and forty-nine."

"What was that?"

He folded the towel into a neat rectangle, but not before she saw

188

a smear of earwax in one corner, and leaned closer. He didn't look like an expert on Sino-American relations. He looked like Mark Fishbein, Beth's dentist. "The single most important declaration of the twentieth century: 'The Chinese people have stood up.' " He allowed time for the quotation to sink in before adding, "If there's one thing I know, it's the Chinese people. I've been doing business with them for twelve years, and that's the only way to really get to know anybody—haggle over money."

"How long did it take you to learn the language?"

He blinked. "I don't speak a word of it. You don't have to. They provide interpreters, at their own expense."

"What kind of business are you in?"

"Curios." The man pulled a handful of ivory figurines from his pocket and held them out. It took a few moment before Beth saw that the tiny yellowed forms were coupled in various sexual attitudes. "Cute, huh?" said the man. "Take one. With my compliments."

"No thanks."

"Go on. They won't bite."

"Really, I . . ."

"Here's a nice one," he said, selecting it for her: a grinning ivory man mounting a grinning ivory woman from behind. He placed it in her hand and pressed her fingers around it. "There we go," he said, sliding the rest of them back into the darkness of his pocket.

"Actually, these don't come from the PRC as such. I get them in Hong Kong. But I'm trying to persuade the Chinese to make them for me. They could do it for a fifth the price I'm paying now, and still make a nice profit. I'd supply the material and handle the marketing. I've already got a warehouseful of ivory in Mombasa and a contract with a chain of German sex shops for two years' entire production." The curio man sighed. "I should be on cloud nine."

"You're not?"

"There's a hitch. The Chinese don't like them. The figurines themselves, I'm talking about, not the terms of the deal."

"Why not?" asked Beth, wondering whether the Chinese objected to their puerility, the poor craftsmanship, or the elephant slaughter.

"Listen, " the curio man said, lowering his voice, "I love the Chinese people. One of the all-time great peoples. I mean it. They got rid of their flies. Sparrows too. Did you know that? It was all part of the Great Leap Forward. Wonderful people. But one thing really bugs me: They're prudes.'' He glanced at the figurine in Beth's hand, then, a little longer, at Beth. "Is this you first trip to China?"

"Yes."

"Then be prepared for nineteen fifty-six. That's what China is. Nineteen fifty-six."

"I was born in nineteen fifty-six."

"Jesus."

Food came. The curio man talked with his mouth full. "I can cope with prudery, of course. It's not the worst thing in the world. What I can't cope with is this." He gave the newspaper another smack. "Sino–U.S. Split" read the headline. "It's a hell of a way to do business."

They flew into night. The curio man watched the movie and sucked candies. Beth slept.

When she awoke lights were shining below, sparse and dim.

"Shanghai," said the curio man.

Beth stared down. The reticent display, for a city of twelve million, unsettled her. It left plenty of darkness to conceal Teddy Wu and, if still alive, Pei Ming, his amah of long ago.

Pei Ming was all she knew of Teddy's roots, roots Teddy had wanted to trace—suddenly, recently, and without telling her, although none of that necessarily made the desire suspect. It could have sprung logically from his background, their impending marriage, the baby.

But he hadn't appeared at the wedding. And she'd lost the baby. Han Shih had come with her song and dance. That made Teddy a defector, in Lathrop's eyes. But why would someone about to defect bother with visas?

Or, why would someone bothering with visas defect? Was that the way to phrase the question? Had the long-haired man come to steal the passports before anyone started asking it? Maybe she'd been wrong not to tell Lathrop about the passports. At the time she'd thought they bolstered the case for defection. Now she hoped they undermined it.

But it was too late to tell Lathrop. He had a confession, written in Teddy's hand. He wouldn't be interested in stories about passports or Pei Ming. The case was closed.

It lived on only in Beth's mind. As the plane descended, she opened the curio man's guidebook for a last look at the lines on religion in China:

> Organized western religions, while making something of a comeback in China, still occupy a very minor corner of Chinese life. The spiritual aspect of China is to be looked for in the behavior of the people: their decency, courtesy, and the tenderness of their family life. Nevertheless, visitors who insist on seeing places of Christian worship in China should be aware that some churches have reopened since the Cultural Revolution: for example, the former Moore Memorial Methodist Church *(Mu En Tang)*, 316 Xicangzhonglu, Shanghai.

It was the only church mentioned by name.

The plane bumped down on the runway and taxied toward the terminal, poorly lit and no bigger than the terminal in Madison, Wisconsin, or Albany, New York. "Where are you staying?" asked the curio man.

"I don't know yet."

"The Peace Hotel's the best, if you want the flavor of old Shanghai. Noel Coward wrote *Private Lives* there. We could share a cab. If we can find one."

"Okay." She had to stay somewhere.

The designers of the terminal had made no attempt to fool anyone into thinking air travel was fun. No one had told them about indirect lighting, bucket chairs, or accent-colored indoor-outdoor carpeting. The lighting was naked and direct; there were only a few old wooden benches to sit on and no rugs of any kind. Slow bluebottles, ignorant of the Great Leap Forward, waited for someone to open the door to the men's room.

A young woman in a green uniform examined Beth's passport. She had chapped lips and thick glossy hair, half hidden under a faded army cap. She stamped Beth's passport with a red star.

"Four pockets in her jacket," said the curio man as they moved to customs. "That's how you tell an officer. The others get two."

The woman at customs also had four pockets. She waved the curio man through, but stopped Beth and gestured for her to open her suitcase and handbag. "I'll look for a cab," the curio man said.

The customs officer was middle-aged and tired. She wore the same severe eyeglass frames favored by Jiang Qing, Mao's last wife and leader of the Gang of Four. Her thin hands rummaged through Beth's things. In the bottom of the handbag, they found the ivory figurine. The woman glanced at it and almost dropped it back in the bag; then she looked more closely. Behind the thick, scratched lenses, her eyes narrowed. Then she brandished the figurine at Beth and spoke sharply in Chinese.

"I'm sorry. I don't understand."

The woman raised her voice and tried again.

"I don't speak Chinese."

Without taking her eyes off Beth, the woman knocked on a plywood door behind her. A man in a blue uniform came out, yawning and rubbing his eyes. The woman handed him the figurine and pointed to Beth. He studied it for a moment, then looked at her.

"Coming this way, please," he said, taking Beth's passport from the customs woman. His voice was polite, his eyes expressionless.

Beth looked around for the curio man, but he had already disappeared through the door leading into the main part of the terminal. The customs woman tugged at her sleeve.

"Let go," Beth said, trying to shake free. Anger rose in her throat: anger at the customs woman, at the curio man, and at herself for acting as carelessly as someone who hadn't been through what she had since the morning at City Hall.

The customs woman watched her in puzzlement, as though Beth was doing something odd at the dinner table, like pouring sugar in her soup; or maybe it was just the look ugly Americans got. She didn't let go. She was much smaller than Beth, but her grip was strong.

"Coming this way, please," the man in the blue uniform repeated, his voice no less polite, his eyes no more expressive. Beth moved toward him. The woman's hand left her sleeve. The man held the door open and followed her inside.

It was a small room with four unfinished wooden walls, no ceiling but that of the terminal itself, high above, no windows, no decorations, no rugs: just a metal desk, two metal chairs, and a narrow metal bench. A man in a blue uniform was asleep on the bench, hands between his thighs, face to the wall.

The other man sat down behind the desk, opened a drawer, and removed a thick black book. He studied her passport for a moment, then opened the book to the place where the H's would be, if the contents were in alphabetical order and not written in Chinese, which had no alphabet to make order with. Her armpits grew damp. A country that could evade SOSUS with its submarines or train agents like Han Shih probably had the resources to catch her at the border. She could smell her sweat, and wondered if he could too.

The man turned a few pages; his flat brown eyes tracked rapidly up and down as he read. Then he closed the book and replaced it in the drawer. He looked at Beth's photograph, then at Beth.

"Eyes blue," he said. "Hair blonde." He laid the passport on the desk and put the figurine on top of it. He motioned to the other metal chair. Beth sat down, facing him across the desk. She noticed there were only two pockets in his jacket, but perhaps it meant nothing: His uniform was blue, not green. On his cap he wore a red badge with one gold star and four small ones. It was just the Chinese flag, but for the first time in her life she was aware that flags were more than ornaments that looked nice when you waved them.

Beth's gaze moved down to his eyes, and she saw he was studying her as she had studied him—failing, maybe, as she had, to come to hard conclusions. How did a suede jacket, black silk shirt, Levi's, and walking shoes from L.L. Bean add up in his mind?

Their eyes met. "What is the aim of your visit to China?" he asked. The man on the bench groaned in his sleep.

"I've always been interested in China."

He nodded slightly. "Why are you not with a tour?"

"Is it necessary?"

"No. You have an individual visa." He opened the passport and ran a long fingernail over the page it was on. "But how will you make yourself understood?"

"I'm doing all right with you."

"I am begging your pardon?"

"Nothing. You're probably right. If I have trouble, I'll get a guide." She paused. "If you let me in, that is."

He looked at her for a moment before speaking. "It is forbidden to import pornographic materials into China. It is an insult to the Chinese people."

Beth thought of the painting on Y.K. Ling's easel, but said: "I agree. I found that object on the plane. My only purpose was to bring it to the attention of the proper authorities. I'm happy to leave it with you."

The man blushed. "This is not possible."

"Not you personally," Beth said. *Happy* had been the wrong word. "Officially. In case the state requires it as evidence."

"Not the state. The people."

"Of course."

The man looked at the figurine and shook his head. "This, too, is not possible." He reached for the figurine, then quickly drew back his hand. He picked up the phone, dialed a few numbers, and said, "*Wei?*" He listened, said, "*Wei?*" four or five more times, and gave a short command.

A few minutes later an old woman came in carrying a bucket. She had wispy white hair and watery eyes. The man handed her the figurine. She placed it carefully on the floor. Then she took a hammer from the bucket and smashed the figurine into splinters. The man on the bench bolted up in alarm. The old woman swept up the remains and left the room.

The man behind the desk rose. He held out the passport. "You may go."

Beth took the passport. He made a polite little bow, but his eyes showed nothing. As she left, he sat down and began filling out a buff-colored form.

Beth went outside. The night smelled of burning coal. Fields stretched into the shadows. A broad avenue lined with spreading trees and lit here and there with orange streetlights led away from the airport. There was no traffic on the road. There were no cars, buses, or taxis waiting in front of the terminal. And no curio man.

Perhaps it was because she was so tired, perhaps because of what she had done to Baldy and he had tried to do to her, perhaps because she had almost ruined her chances of finding Teddy in her first minutes in China; whatever it was, Beth felt a tremor in her lower lip. It took her by surprise. And with it came the certain knowledge that she was out of her depth. The next moment she was sobbing, all alone on the pavement in front of the airport, suitcase in one hand, handbag in the other. "*I come to China, Ma, to find me man,*" mocked a voice in her head.

"God damn you, Teddy," she called out, and heard the sound, thick and ugly with pain. That stopped her. She wiped her face on her sleeve. It was very quiet. The stars burned coldly in the black sky. Shouldn't they look the same from Shanghai as they did from San Francisco? They didn't. She couldn't find Orion with his sparkling belt, stalking his prey across the universe.

Beth heard a car approaching on the avenue. The sound grew louder and louder, but she didn't see the car itself until it was very near: no lights. It was a small, dusty car without markings of any kind. It stopped in front of her. The driver leaned out his open window and said: "Taxi?"

Beth looked at him. He wore a black shirt with the collar turned up, a silver jacket made of shiny material, and sunglasses.

"Taxi?" he repeated, making driving motions in case she didn't get it.

She shoved her luggage across the back seat and climbed in. Lighting a cigarette, the driver watched her in the rearview mirror. Blue smoke curled around his dark glasses. He said, "Hotel?"

"Peace Hotel."

The driver grunted and turned the key. As the car pulled away, he felt for something on the floor. Plastic clicked plastic. Then something snapped into place and the car filled with the sound of a Chinese woman singing imitation rock music; her voice was cute enough for a cartoon mouse. The driver's fingers began tapping the steering wheel, but soon stopped.

He drove east, toward the city. He didn't put the headlights on. They sped along the avenue in a pocket of vision, abyss all around. Gradually Beth's eyes adjusted to the darkness. Through the trees she saw flooded fields, silvery and still; squat structures she took for farmhouses lay like barges at anchor.

Trees dwindled away. Houses appeared, no bigger than storage sheds. Beth only knew they were houses from the TV aerials on their roofs.

"Does everyone have TV?" she asked. The dark glasses shifted to her in the mirror, but the driver didn't speak. "Television," Beth explained.

"I'm not very clear."

Four- and five-story apartment blocks replaced the storage-shed houses. The smell of coal became stronger. Beth felt pressure behind her left eye, threatening to grow into a headache the way a tropical storm blows up into a hurricane. It wasn't 1956. It was the nineteenth century, in some place like Allentown, Pennsylvania, or Birmingham, England.

A dark shape loomed ahead. The driver honked. It loomed larger. At the last moment he swerved, and they shot past a bus, also driving without lights. Then someone else honked behind them and another darkened bus roared by and cut sharply across their path. The driver flashed his lights at it in retaliation.

In the few moments the yellow beams shone, Beth glimpsed an endless convoy of buses cutting through a sea of bicycles.

Then the lights went out and everything disappeared except the bus in front, the bus behind, and a few cyclists on either side. One wore a surgical mask: a doctor late for an operation, or a citizen who didn't like breathing coal. The clock on the dashboard said six A.M.

Beth stared out the window. She'd had a half-Chinese baby in her womb, she'd made love to a Chinese man, been in Chinese homes like the Lings', but the shadowy world she saw outside the window—China—was unreal. Was it a world where she could do things, have an effect, or could she only watch and not understand? Maybe she hadn't known Teddy, either. Maybe they hadn't haggled enough over money.

"Wait," she said to the driver. It would soon be day. She wouldn't find the answer to her question sleeping in a room at Noel Coward's favorite hotel. "I don't want to go to the Peace Hotel. Not right away. Take me to three sixteen Xicangzhonglu."

The driver made a sharp little questioning sound. "No Peace Hotel?"

"No. Three sixteen Xicangzhonglu."

The dark glasses shifted in the mirror. The driver made the questioning sound again.

"Three sixteen Xicangzhonglu." Beth still had the curio man's guidebook. Holding it close to her eyes, she found the section of numbers. Three one six. *San yi liu.* "*San yi liu.*"

"*San yi liu?*"

"Yes. *San yi liu* Xicangzhonglu."

He made the questioning sound. Beth tried *Xicangzhonglu* several ways, pronouncing the *x* like *s, ch, z.*

"I'm not very clear," said the driver.

"Jesus Christ," Beth said, realizing the answer to her question was obvious if she couldn't even get a taxi driver to take her where she wanted. Then she remembered the Chinese name of the church. "*Mu En Tang.*"

"*Mu En Tang?*" The driver's voice rose in pitch.

"Yes."

"Is closed."

"No. It's open."

He shook his head. "No go there."

"Please. *Mu En Tang.*" Beth looked up the word for *please.* "*Ching. Mu En Tang. Ching.*"

"Is closed."

Beth reached into her handbag. She'd bought ten yuan from

the stewardess. She held them out, a little more than four dollars, and said, *"Mu En Tang."*

The driver glanced around. When he saw the money, he made an angry sound and knocked it away. The bills fell on the floor. Beth sat back. She felt blood rushing to her cheeks. She had a lot to learn about haggling over money in China.

The taxi picked up speed. The driver jerked it around several corners and braked abruptly to a stop. Beth looked out. They were on a narrow, darkened side street.

"Where are we?"

The driver waved his hand impatiently. *"Mu En Tang."*

On the opposite side of the street stood a structure very different from a storage-shed house or a concrete apartment block: a massive stone building that would not have looked out of place in Edinburgh or Oxford. It had two huge wings, separated by a narrow courtyard. A single light shone from a mullioned window on the top floor of one of them. The only entrance was a steel door in the surrounding high stone wall.

"Mu En Tang," the driver repeated, louder than before, and motioned for Beth to get out.

"What do I owe you?"

"Go," he said. *"Mu En Tang.* Go."

Leaving the money on the floor, Beth got out. He drove quickly away.

Beth crossed the street and stopped in front of the steel door. She'd been to Edinburgh and Oxford; maybe it was a building she could deal with.

There was no buzzer to press or telephone to speak into. She knocked. Silence. The yellow light still shone in the mullioned window, but the rest of *Mu En Tang* remained dark. She knocked again, harder. *Mu En Tang* was silent.

"Hello," she called, and banged on the door until her fist hurt. A light went on in an apartment block across the street. Beth remembered Han Shih's talk of street committees. She raised her hand to try once more. Without a sound, the steel door swung open.

A young Chinese man with rumpled hair looked out. He wore white pajama bottoms and a sleeveless undershirt. His face was pale, and paled more when he saw Beth.

"I'm very sorry to trouble you," Beth said, "but I've got to talk to the reverend."

The pale young man closed the door in her face.

24

Beth listened for the pale young man's retreating footsteps, but heard nothing. That didn't mean he was poised on the other side of the steel door: She hadn't heard his approach, either.

She stepped back onto the pavement and looked around. The smell of excrement filled the air. A figure came struggling out of the shadows, moving like someone glued to the darkness. It was a man pulling a cart; on the cart lay a big iron barrel. As he turned into a narrow alley a woman leaned out of a low window and emptied a pail into the barrel. The man struggled into the shadows. The smell went away.

Overhead the stars were gone, but the sky was still dark. Beth walked a few yards to the corner of a wide street. The east had caught fire. As she watched, the fire's light spread across the dome, as if a planetarium worker had turned the dial. Dawn. The wide street was filled with people—walking, cycling, jammed on buses. In their baggy pants and drab shirts they overwhelmed her as no crowd in business suits and trench coats ever could. She went back to the steel door and banged on it, not out of hope that the pale young man would return, but because she needed something to bang.

The door opened. The pale young man poked his head out and shouted at her.

"I have to see your minister," Beth said. "I've come a long way."

The pale young man snapped an abrupt phrase at her and started closing the door.

"The hell with that," Beth said, her voice rising. She leaned all her weight against the door. "And stop pretending you don't speak English. I can see it in your eyes." He didn't say anything, but Beth felt less pressure against the door. She lowered her voice. "If you're any kind of a Methodist at all, you speak English. Methodism came from England."

Pinks and reds flushed to the surface of his skin, driving the pallor away. "That may be," he said, spittle flying off his tongue, "but Jesus Christ was Asiatic."

"Let's argue the fine points inside." Beth squeezed past him and ran into the courtyard.

"This is not permitted," the pale young man said, but he shut the door. Just before it closed, Beth saw a woman watching from a window in the apartment block across the street.

"What do you want?" the pale young man asked furiously.

"I told you. To talk to the reverend. You have a reverend here, don't you?"

"Oh yes, we have a reverend. We are very advanced." He spun away from her, crossed the courtyard, and opened a low wooden door. His thin shoulder blade jerked beneath his undershirt as he turned the knob. Beth followed him, knowing she was as ugly an American as the golfer who wanted to lose balls in the Chinese rough.

The pale young man hurried up a steep, narrow staircase that smelled of dust and moldy books, then walked quickly to the end of a dark, bare hall. The musty smell grew stronger.

He knocked on a door. An old, reedy voice called from the other side. The pale young man opened the door. They went in.

The room was small and lined with books. There was a cot, a desk, a chair, a naked yellow bulb in the ceiling, and a mullioned window. A man sat at the desk, bent over a book. He was bald except for tufts of white hair above his ears. His face was lined. A pearly cataract obscured one of his eyes; the other was keen and alert. Seeing Beth, he rose from his chair, but remained bent forward; his back was curved like the end of a parenthesis.

The young man spoke to him in a complaining voice, jabbing his thumb once or twice at Beth. The old man's good eye watched him; then it shifted to her.

"I am the reverend here," he said. His voice was weak, and dry as desert sand. "There is no public service today. What is it you want?"

"I want to talk to you. I've come a long way."

"So Winston says. Where have you come from?"

''San Francisco.'' When the reverend said nothing, Beth added, ''In the United States.''

''I know San Francisco.''

''You've been there?''

''In my reading, yes.''

She scanned the bookshelves. ''You have a fine library.''

''It is not mine. It is the church's. The people's, that is.'' Beth heard no irony in his tone. ''What did you want to see me about? Is it a religious matter?''

''No. I need your help.''

''Mine?''

''Maybe not yours specifically. I need someone active in the Protestant church, old enough to recall events in this area during the forties.''

''Why is that?''

''A man has disappeared,'' Beth said, unable to think of any innocuous cover story that would account for banging on his door at six in the morning. ''I'm trying to find him.''

The reverend looked up at her. Even without his deformity, he would not have been big; as it was he stood less than five feet tall.

''Are you employed by the American government?'' he asked.

''No.''

He ran his good eye over her from head to foot. ''What do you do?''

''I teach history.''

''At what level?''

''University.''

''Which one?''

''University of California.''

''What campus?''

''Berkeley.''

''Ah.''

His good eye studied her again, perhaps looking for something it had missed initially. Beth wondered whether she'd just been put through a credentials test similar to the one she gave Robert Means through her door at home, and was amazed that the reverend had the knowledge to do it.

He went back to his desk and sat down. ''And what, may I ask, is your period?''

"The Inquisition."

He glanced down at the book he'd been reading. Beth couldn't see the title, but she recognized the cover. He held it up. *Montaillou: Village Occitan de 1294 à 1324*, par Emmanuel Le Roy Ladurie. "Then you know this book?"

"Yes. In fact, I contributed an article to the *Annales* last year."

"Did you? Unfortunately I am not a subscriber. Research materials are scarce in China. I am lucky to have my books. So many were lost during the Cultural Revolution."

"Why weren't yours?"

A tiny spark shot up in the old man's eye. "I buried them."

The pale young man blurted something at the reverend. The reverend replied calmly, shaking his head. The pale young man opened his mouth to argue, then turned and left the room.

"Now, Miss—"

"Beth Hunter."

He bowed politely. "I am Reverend Huang. Please sit down, Miss Hunter," he said, indicating the cot. She sat on the end of it. The cot was hard and unyielding, but a wave of fatigue swept through her the moment she touched it, leaving her body numb.

"I am interested to know your analysis of the Inquisition."

"My analysis?" she said, thinking of all the silly papers she had marked. "That's not really my approach. I've been using Inquisition records as a sort of tool for a demographic study of manpower in the sixteenth-century Spanish shipping trade."

Reverend Huang looked at her for a few moments before speaking. "You use the Inquisition as a tool?" He closed the book on his desk and put it aside. "I myself have only begun a serious study of it in the last few years. Since . . ." He stopped himself. For a moment the light faded from his good eye. "I find it illuminating," he continued. "The Inquisitorial cast of mind is not bound to any one society or era. It has a past, a present, a future." There was a silence. Then Reverend Huang leaned toward her across the desk. "Do you agree, Miss Hunter?"

"I don't know." She sighed. She hadn't come so far to be trapped in the kind of conversation she would have gone to some length to avoid at home. "I'm not sure such a pervasive system of spiritual repression could be instituted as successfully in moder—"

"You're not?" Reverend Huang interrupted. His good eye was filled with astonishment; the other eye reflected the gray light coming through the mullioned window. After a while the astonishment faded from the good eye, and watchfulness took its place. The glazed one stayed the way it was. "A man has disappeared," Reverend Haung said at last.

"Yes."

"What man?"

Beth told him about Teddy and the letter from Shanghai.

"So you think he is here?"

"Not necessarily in Shanghai. But somewhere in China."

"Somewhere in China," Reverend Huang repeated in a neutral tone. "And your government thinks he has defected."

"Yes, but—"

"And that would involve my government."

"Yes."

When Reverend Huang spoke again, the coldness that had disappeared from his tone during their talk on the Inquisition returned. "So what is it you want me to do? Many people have disappeared in China, Miss Hunter. I myself disappeared."

"What do you mean?"

"It is not important."

"But you're here now."

"In a manner of speaking."

The door opened. The pale young man came in with a teapot and two glasses. "Thank you, Winston," said Reverend Huang. Without looking at him or Beth, Winston filled the glasses and went away. Beth took a sip of tea. It tasted soapy.

She put her glass on the desk. "This is why I think you can help me, Reverend Huang: My . . . Dr. Wu was born in China. He was brought to the United States as a baby, through the services of a Protestant church in Shanghai. Three months ago he began making inquiries into those events. I believe his disappearance is somehow connected with his early life in China, or the manner of his going to the U.S."

Even as she spoke, she wondered: *Is that my belief? What about Mordell's conjecture? What about the* Timoshenko? She didn't share her doubts with Reverend Huang.

"Do you know the name of the Protestant church?" he asked.

"The Pacific Church of the Holy Spirit."

Reverend Huang went very still, like a figure in a tableau. "I can't help you," he said.

"Do you mean you're unfamiliar with that church, Reverend Huang?"

"Perhaps you had better go, Miss Hunter."

"Something was wrong with the Pacific Church of the Holy Spirit, wasn't it, Reverend Huang? Tell me."

Reverend Huang's voice rose—not very much, but it was so thin it broke after a few words—and he finished in a hoarse whisper: "I didn't say there was anything wrong with it."

"You didn't have to."

Anger flared for a second or two in his eye. After it passed he rubbed the bad one roughly with his index finger. "I won't have my church threatened," he said in a quiet but firm tone.

"I don't understand."

"How can a historian not understand? Surely you know Christianity has had a difficult time in China since the Revolution."

"Yes."

"Then you can understand my wish to spare the church further hardship." Reverend Huang rose and walked stiffly to the mullioned window, head drawn back to compensate for his crooked torso. He looked out. "*Mu En Tang* has always been self-supporting, self-governing, self-propagating." He turned to her. "That is to say, Chinese. Others did not make this effort. And so were seen as agents of a foreign church. And foreign governments."

Rex Heidemann got involved with evil men, Helen Brock had said. Jimmy Han had been one of them. But they were only following orders. Government orders. What government? Beth was too tired to remember Helen's exact words. "And the Pacific Church of the Holy Spirit was one of those?"

Reverend Huang was silent for so long she thought her question would go unanswered. Then he said: "Yes."

"But how can they still make trouble for you? So many years have passed."

"You had better go, Miss Hunter."

"Please, Reverend Huang. Just a few more minutes."

"I'm sorry. I have nothing more to say."

He began walking toward the door. Beth jumped up from the cot, grabbed Helen Brock's album from her suitcase, and ran after him. She reached him as he stepped into the hallway, and shoved the album in front of his face, opened at the photograph labeled "Rex and Me, April 8, 1948."

Reverend Huang grunted in irritation, but he looked at the

picture. "That is the man," he said reluctantly. "An American. I don't remember his name."

"Rex Heidemann."

He nodded. Before he could take another step, Beth had flipped the pages to "Rex, Me, and J. Han, Lake Tai, 1948." "Do you know him?" she asked, pointed to J. Han.

"No."

Reverend Huang moved away. Beth hurried in front of him, holding up her last picture: "The Children, Shanghai, Spring 1949."

"That was their church," Reverend Huang said, indicating the building in the background. "It's a textile mill now." He kept walking.

Beth backpedaled before him, hunched over to bring the picture to his eye level. "Never mind the background," she said, pointing to the crying Chinese baby in the foreground. "That's the little boy."

Reverend Huang stopped. His good eye moved closer to the photograph. "The one who disappeared?" he asked at last.

"Yes."

She felt his latent forward motion ebb away. He turned and walked slowly back into his study. Beth followed, closing the door behind her. He sat behind the desk and watched her as she laid the open album on it and sat on the cot.

"Well?" he said.

Beth leaned forward. "He had an amah. I'm pretty sure he was trying to locate her. Her name was Pei Ming. I don't know anything about her, except she saved his life. At a place called the lake house."

"Was this house at Taihu?"

"Taihu?"

"Lake Tai. *Hu* is *lake*. Taihu—Lake Tai." Impatience sharpened his tone.

"I don't know. I'm counting on it."

"Lake Tai is very big."

He waited for Beth to say something. She said: "I'm hoping she's still there."

"Hoping," Reverend Huang said. "Excuse me for saying so, but you don't seem to speak a word of Chinese, or know anything of China. How will you find her?"

Beth felt her face growing hot, but she kept her voice under control. "Pei Ming saved Teddy's life at the lake house, and put him in the hands of the Pacific Church of the Holy Spirit. The Heidemanns spent time at Lake Tai. Maybe it was their lake house. In any case, some people there must remember the Americans and the house. Old people. Especially ones who still have connections with Christianity."

There was a long pause. Then the corners of Reverend Huang's mouth turned up in a brief smile, and he said: "So it is a religious matter, after all."

"If you want to look at it that way."

"Do you?"

Beth didn't answer immediately. She wondered what sort of price he would ask her to pay: Would his next question concern the immortal life of the soul? Finally she said, "I love him, Reverend Huang."

Reverend Huang studied her face. Then he opened his mouth and laughed—a merry laugh that reminded Beth of her grandmother. "Then we're agreed: It is a religious matter. On that basis, it is my duty to help you."

Gratitude swept through Beth. She'd made a connection in China; maybe she wasn't out of her depth. Tears filled her eyes. She wanted to thank him, but before she could say the words he had walked out and closed the door.

Beth sat back on the cot. She looked up and examined the books. The titles blurred. She put her feet up. She let her head fall back on the hard canvas. Irresistible gravity tugged her eyelids shut.

A damp hand pressed her arm. She opened her eyes. The room was dark. Outside the mullioned window, night had fallen; the earth had spun through another day while she slept.

The pale young man was looking down at her. Winston. "Are you awake?"

"Yes."

The air was hot and smelled of burning coal. She felt it dry the damp patch on her arm.

"Then come. Reverend Huang has found someone to take you to Wuxi."

"Wuxi?"

Winston's eyebrows shot up in surprise, as though she hadn't heard of Chicago. "The city on Taihu."

Beth sat up, trying to remember who had mentioned Wuxi before. Her mouth was dry. She found the glass of tea on the desk where she'd left it. It still tasted soapy; now it was cold as well. She drank it anyway.

"Is there time for a quick shower?"

"Shower?"

"Or a bath?"

"There is no bath here. Only a washbasin."

Beth rose. "Should I take my suitcase, or will I be coming back?"

"Take your suitcase."

Beth followed Winston down the hall. The suitcase had grown heavier during the day, or her muscles had softened. "I'd like to say good-bye to Reverend Huang."

Winston didn't answer. They came to a door by the stairs. "The washbasin is in there," he said.

Beth went in and found the light. The room was no bigger than a closet. It contained a cast-iron sink with one tap, a mirror, and a plastic pail half full of urine. Beth looked at herself in the mirror. Her face was thinner, the two thought lines between her eyes deeper, the patches under them darker. She splashed cool water on her face and behind her neck. Her eyes surprised her. They weren't tired and scared, the way she felt, but very hard, and cold as Arctic sky. Not her eyes at all; her eyes were supposed to look like Giorgione's distant mountains.

Winston was waiting for her in the courtyard, alone. She looked around for some sign of Reverend Huang. No lights shone in any of the windows of *Mu En Tang*. Winston unlocked the steel door and they went out.

They walked to the corner and turned into the wide street. A long line of people waited at a bus stop. They joined it. Everyone was staring at a display window with nothing in it but a white refrigerator, about the size of the one she'd had on *Pop-up*. They couldn't take their eyes off it.

A bus pulled up, trailing black fumes. It was full. The doors opened anyway. Everyone got on. The bus heaved forward. Beth lost her balance, but there was nowhere to fall. Human flesh caught her and held her firmly on her feet. Human heat made the pores open in her armpits and down her spine. Human lungs sucked the oxygen out of the air. No one spoke. A few people stared at her, but didn't keep it up for long. Everyone was too busy enduring.

The bus stopped. "Here," said Winston. Bodies squeezed against her. She stumbled out the door and onto the sidewalk. "Where is your suitcase?" he asked.

"Christ."

Winston blushed. The bus pulled away. The suitcase dropped out of the open doorway and bounced on the pavement. Beth grabbed it before the next bus ran it over.

"It is wrong to take His name in vain," Winston said.

"I wasn't. That was just the vocal part of a silent prayer. It was answered."

Winston knew she was making a joke, one he didn't understand but which made her blaspheming worse. "I leave you here," he said coldly.

"Where?"

"That," Winston said, pointing with his chin at a building across the street, "is the Peace Hotel."

The Peace Hotel was fourteen grimy stone stories with a row of tall arched windows along its base. Except for the green and red cupola on the roof, it could have fit comfortably in any second-rate European city.

Winston followed her gaze, and maybe her line of thought as well. "It used to be called the Cathay. In the old days."

"Is that when Noel Coward stayed there?"

"The name is not familiar to me."

They crossed the street. There was no doorman. The lobby looked dimly lit and empty. "Good-bye," Winston said.

"Aren't you coming in?"

Winston glanced abruptly over his shoulder, as though he had felt someone watching. But no one was. That didn't stop his feet from tapping nervously on the sidewalk; they couldn't wait for him to get it over with. "No," Winston told her. "Go into the coffee shop. You will be met."

"By whom?"

"Just go in." He turned to leave; maybe his feet did it by themselves.

"Wait."

He paused. "What?"

"Thank you. And thank Reverend Huang."

"Reverend Huang is a very foolish man." He walked quickly away.

25

A boat horn blew a bass note that wobbled in the night. Beth turned. The street she stood on intersected a wide boulevard— she knew it must be the Bund. Beyond it a passenger ferry, five decks of shining light, slid across dark water.

Beth entered the Peace Hotel. The lobby had a marble floor that needed washing, a souvenir stand with no customers, and a yawning clerk behind the counter. From the mezzanine above came Australian voices and the sound of colliding billiard balls. She didn't feel she was in a second-rate European city; she wasn't sure she was in China, either.

Beth crossed the lobby to a door marked COFFEE SHOP. A sign said, *This coffee room provides services for foreigners and overseas Chinese only. Cooperation is expected.* The coffee shop was quarantined to Winston even if he'd wanted to accompany her. But the door wasn't soundproof: "Muskrat Ramble" leaked seditiously through.

Beth went in. The coffee shop was a brightly lit, rectangular room with a low ceiling and forty or fifty tables. Arabs sat with Arabs, Africans with Africans, Japanese with Japanese, Westerners with Westerners. There were also a few Chinese who must have been from overseas: They wore silk suits and the kind of watches needed for swimming underwater through several time zones.

Beth found an empty table near the back, partly hidden by a pillar. She sat down. A band was playing jazz. A middle-aged woman was on piano; all the other instruments—drums, bass, trumpet, sax, violin—were played by old men. They weren't wearing silk suits. They were dressed like the people on the bus.

The violinist was the oldest of all. He had wispy hair and

snowy overhanging eyebrows that caught the light from his music stand. He took a rapid solo that rose to a double-stopped wail and led the band into the closing chorus of "Muskrat Ramble." When it was over he grinned hugely, revealing a mouthful of brown teeth. Wild applause came from one of the Arab tables, muted reaction from the rest of the room.

The musicians had a chat, hummed snatches of a few tunes, flipped through their song sheets, and swung into "Satin Doll." A shadow fell across Beth's table. A voice said: "We meet again." Beth looked up into the red eyes of the curio man.

Her first thought was that Reverend Huang had sent him. It was an absurd thought, and she dismissed it almost at once, but the resulting silence unsettled the curio man. His red eyes blinked. "Remember me?"

"Of course. You didn't wait very long at the airport."

"So sorry. I'll make it up to you, if you know what I mean."

"I don't."

He leaned on her table, a little unsteadily. "Women's liberation," he said. "The best thing since free beer. I mean it. And you look like a liberated lady. So I'll respect that by coming right out with it." But he didn't. Instead he gave her a long red stare that was meant to be seductive. Then he said huskily: "Let's go up to my room."

"No thanks."

He wavered slightly from side to side. "You mean I have to go through all the chitchat and drink buying first? That's not liberated."

"Just go."

He looked hurt. Then annoyed. "Maybe you're not as liberated as you think."

"Good night."

"If that's the way you want to play it." He leaned across the table. His breath reeked. "But that figurine turned you on, sweetheart. Why not admit it? Loosen up a little. Get in touch with your feelings."

"You're drunk."

"I can hold my liquor," he slurred with pride. The red eyes went into their mesmerizing routine. Then they just went dull. The curio man turned and walked out of the coffee shop without banging into anything.

Beth looked around. No one had noticed their little scene, except one man who was watching from a table by the door. He was Chinese, but wasn't sporting a silk suit or a fancy watch. Instead he wore a faded blue Mao jacket and matching pants, with no watch at all. Neither did he have the prosperous beefiness of the overseas Chinese. His cheeks were hollow, his forehead high, his fingers long and tapering, like the ones El Greco's saints gestured meekly with on their way to martyrdom. But his eyes, meeting Beth's for a brief moment, belonged to the other school of sainthood, the fiery one, seldom painted by the masters. He was smoking a cigarette. The hollow cheeks sucked in, growing hollower on smoky nourishment.

A waiter came. Beth ordered coffee. It was weak and tepid. She swallowed a sip or two. When she looked again at the table by the door, the hollow-faced man was gone.

At eleven o'clock, the band finished playing "We Ain't Got a Barrel of Money" and packed up their instruments. The tables were cleared. The customers left. The waiter removed Beth's cup and saucer. "Close now."

There was no one left in the coffee shop but the waiters and the violinist, who was softly whistling "Do You Know What It Means to Miss New Orleans?" while rubbing rosin on his bow. He put it in the case, snapped it shut, stepped lightly off the riser, and came to Beth's table.

"How is the Reverend?" he asked.

Beth hesitated.

That made him laugh. Beth saw an orange candy cradled on his tongue. "Surprise," he said. "Yes?"

"Yes."

The violinist sat down. *"Shi fu,"* he called. A waiter ambled toward them. "Master of a trade," the violinist explained to Beth in a stage whisper. "That's what they like to be called now. Before, it was always *tong chi. Tong chi* this and *tong chi* that."

"Tong chi?"

"Comrade."

The violinist ordered tea. "I am Mr. An," he said after he'd had his first sip. "My work unit has given me permission to travel to Wuxi tomorrow to visit my sick brother. Would you like to come?" He watched her expectantly, as if waiting to see whether she got some joke.

"Yes."

He clapped his hands. "Very good." He laughed again. Beth

wondered whether he wasn't a bit mad. "I will meet you at the railway station at six A.M."

"Should I spend the night here?"

"Why not? It is the best hotel in Shanghai."

Beth remembered that the curio man held the same opinion. "I'll bet it has the best jazz in Shanghai, too."

Mr. An's smile faded. "It has the only jazz in Shanghai. The only jazz in China." He gulped the rest of his tea. "Good night." Mr. An walked away, battered violin case in hand. He left behind the smell of honey and oranges.

Beth went into the lobby. It was very quiet. No noises, billiard or Australian, floated down from the mezzanine. The clerk was slumped on the counter, his head in his arms. Beth woke him and took a room for the night.

Maybe it had once been the kind of room Noel Coward liked. But now the overstuffed chintz chairs were stained, the floral carpet was thin and faded, the mattress sagged on the four-poster bed. There was a chipped lacquer desk he hadn't carved *N.C.* on, and a telephone that would have made a good prop in one of his plays. All that had been added was a color TV; all that had been removed was the Gideon Bible.

Beth bathed in the claw-footed tub and climbed into bed. The room was hot. It grew hotter. A bedspring squeaked in the room above. It squeaked again. Maybe someone fat and red-eyed was having trouble sleeping. Beth rose and opened the window. Across the street a narrow park ran along the riverbank. A couple embraced in the shadow of a tree. Beyond them a string of dark barges glided toward the sea. The boat horn blew its wobbly bass note, now far away. Beth went back to bed. She listened to the plumbing. And the squeaky bedspring. "Do You Know What It Means to Miss New Orleans?" ran around in her mind and wouldn't stop. At last her eyes began to close.

Too late. Outside the night was turning gray. Someone started shouting. Beth got up and went to the window. There was a commotion on the sidewalk below. Two Chinese men in proletarian blue were tugging a third man toward a steel-gray car. He didn't want to go. He was bigger than they were, but not very strong. In the struggle, his short terrycloth robe came undone; flabby whiteness spilled out. It was the curio man. They shoved him into the back seat and got in on either side. The engine was already running. The car sped away, but not before Beth caught a glimpse of the passenger in the front seat: an incomplete, shadowy view. The only clear detail was the saintlike hand, resting on the base of the open window.

Beth backed away. Her first thought was that the curio man had been arrested by an antipornography squad of plainclothes police. Her second was that the first might be wrong. It made her throw on her clothes, grab her suitcase, and go to the door. She stood there. Her heart began to pound. She put her hand on the knob and slowly turned it. The door opened noiselessly. She looked out. There was no one in the hall.

Beth hurried out, past the elevator and down the stairs. Instead of going all the way to the lobby, she stepped out on the mezzanine, walked by the billiard table, and looked over the edge.

A man in a blue jacket and baggy blue pants sat in a chair facing the elevator. Another man, similarly dressed, stood near the door to the street. Beth ducked out of sight.

She went back to the stairs. She thought of returning to her room and telephoning for help. But who? The hotel manager? Reverend Huang? The U.S. consul? None of the choices seemed promising.

Beth didn't return to her room. She continued down the stairs, past the lobby door, and down another flight.

It ended in a damp, unlit stairwell that smelled of sewage. Beth brushed a spider web from her face and waited for her eyes to adjust to the darkness. After a minute or two she could make out a flimsy door set crookedly in the earthen wall. It opened on a dusty staircase leading up. She climbed it.

There was another door at the top. She tried the handle. It wouldn't open. As she felt for a lock, something scratched the top of her foot. She looked down and saw a huge rat moving through the shadows. Beth had never been afraid of rats before. Now she kicked out wildly, and drove her shoulder against the door. It gave. She burst outside, into a narrow street.

A taxi was parked on the other side. The driver was polishing the headlights and humming to himself. Beth approached him. "Take me to the airport" was what she intended to say. But maybe the men in the lobby had nothing to do with her. What did she know of China? In a few hours she could be at Lake Tai, where Pei Ming saved Teddy's life. So she said: "The railroad station, please."

The driver replied in Chinese.

"The train," Beth said. "Take me to the train."

He shrugged and turned back to his headlights.

"Jesus Christ," Beth said. "The fucking train—*chug-chug-chug, woo woo!*"

He swung around to look at her, startled. Then he began laughing. *"Huochezhan,"* he said. *"Huochezhan."* He tossed Beth's suitcase into the front seat, held the rear door open for her, and jumped behind the wheel, still chuckling. Beth looked back. No one followed.

But as the taxi approached the station, Beth saw crowd-control barriers blocking the entrance. In the narrow gateway soldiers examined the papers of everyone filing through.

"Wait," Beth said, gripping the top of his seat to pull herself forward. "Stop. Stop here. I don't want to go to the railroad station. Take me to the airport."

Half turning to her, the driver nodded. *"Woo-woo,"* he said.

"No!" Beth shouted. "The airport, God damn it!"

He laughed. *"Woo woo, woo woo."* He drove straight to the nearest barrier and honked. A soldier came to the car. Beth reached for the door handle on the other side, but before she could open it, the soldier poked his head in the driver's window. The driver pointed his thumb at Beth, struggling with the handle. The soldier nodded and pulled the barrier aside. The taxi rolled through and parked by the station entrance. *"Woo woo,"* said the driver as Beth got out, almost bumping into a man walking by with a gutted pig on his shoulders. Reverend Huang was right: She knew nothing of China.

"Good morning," said someone behind her. Beth spun around. It was Mr. An. He was dressed exactly as he had been the night before—an old cardigan with all the buttons buttoned, dark-gray pants that stopped above his ankles, scuffed brown leather shoes—but now he carried a Japan Air Lines flight bag instead of his violin case.

He checked his watch. "On the dot," he said, peering up at her through his snowy eyebrows. "Very Chinese."

"Punctuality is the courtesy of kings," Beth responded without thinking. It was a family favorite because long ago Sam Goldwyn had spent an evening getting her father to explain it to him.

"Is that a saying?"

"Yes."

"Not Chinese."

"I don't think so."

"Not at all Chinese." Mr. An looked thoughtful. "But I like it."

They bought soft-class seats on the 6:27 to Wuxi. The soft-class car had cracked sunflower-seed shells on the floor, thinly padded leather seats, martial music on the loudspeaker. Beth and Mr. An shared a fold-out table covered with a stained cloth. An attendant with dirty fingernails plunked two mugs of hot water on it. Beth waited for teabags. They never came.

No one else was in the car. At 6:27 sharp the train started rolling. Mr. An looked at his watch. "On the dot," he said again. "We get to work on time. We don't do much when we're there, but we're never late." He laughed, a little too long and a little too loudly. The smell of oranges and honey filled the air. Beth wondered again if he was slightly mad, but she found herself sitting close to him.

Mr. An tucked his flight bag under the seat and said, "Did you sleep well?"

"Not really."

Mr. An was surprised. "But it's a good hotel. Noel Coward used to stay there." He waited for an explanation. When it didn't come, he rested his head against the antimacassar and closed his eyes. "Do you like his work?"

"Not very much."

"No?"

"Do you?" Beth asked, wondering what Mr. An knew of it. Time passed. She looked at him. He was asleep.

Beth sipped her hot water. A cloud of red specks hung suspended near the bottom of the mug. She stopped drinking when she got near them.

The train rumbled through nineteenth-century Allentown, on a bad day. The sky was gray, although there wasn't a cloud in it. Here and there, tiny patches of green vegetables clung to margins between the concrete and the steel tracks.

Gradually the green spread and the gray shrank. Then they were in the country. The sky turned blue. The land, flat and treeless, turned green. By the edge of the tracks Beth saw soft new rice shoots. Sometimes clusters of low buildings went by; sometimes Beth looked down canals that ran straight as brown prairie roads to the horizon. Once she saw a man in a broad-brimmed hat poling a sampan; a goat stood watch in the bow. Later she saw a lone woman doing tai chi in a field. Except for the martial music, it was so peaceful she almost forgot about the curio man.

The train stopped at a small station. There was a sign, but it was in Chinese only. Two soldiers boarded the soft-class car. Adrenaline shot through Beth's limbs; she shifted her weight to the balls of her feet. But the soldiers paid no attention to her. One of them sat down. The other went to the end of the car and flicked a switch on the wall. The martial music stopped.

Mr. An woke up. He reached into his flight bag and took out a ball of wrapping paper. Inside were hard orange candies. He offered them to Beth and popped one in his mouth.

"Is your brother in Wuxi very sick?" Beth asked.

Mr. An smiled. "Not at all. And he doesn't live in Wuxi." He leaned closer. "But the secretary of my *danwei* has a sister in Wuxi. A sister who has an old bicycle she doesn't need anymore. A bicycle just the right size for the secretary's son. And I'm going to bring it back." He paused, the expectant expression again on his face.

"After you've seen your sick brother."

"Exactly." Mr. An laughed and clapped his hands. "Now you understand China." The soldiers glanced at him. He didn't notice.

As the train left the station the attendant took away the mugs and switched the martial music back on. They went by a long line of men and women digging a ditch beside the tracks. It was a deep ditch and they dug on two levels. Diggers on the bottom shoveled earth onto a bamboo platform; diggers on the platform heaved it up to the bank. The dirt got shoveled twice. There wasn't a machine in sight.

Mr. An wasn't interested. He sucked candy. His eyes began to close.

"Who are you taking me to see?" Beth asked.

"I don't know him. Some friend of the Reverend—a Christian."

One of the soldiers rose and switched off the music. "Are you a Christian, Mr. An?"

"No. The crucifix makes me feel guilty."

The train picked up speed, then settled into a steady rhythm.

Mr. An's eyes closed. Beth thought he was asleep. Then, without opening them, he said: "I am a jazzman."

"I found that out last night."

Mr. An opened his eyes and smiled. "I'll show you something." He took a worn leather billfold from his jacket pocket and removed a yellowed newspaper clipping. *"Satchmo à la Boîte Rouge"* read the headline. There was a photograph of Louis Armstrong—a very young and sassy Louis Armstrong. He was laughing: not the famous bug-eyed laugh, but an unambiguous one he might have lost later along the way. In one hand he held a trumpet; his other arm was wrapped around the shoulders of an even younger man, no more than a teenager. The second man had a violin in his hand. He was Chinese.

"You played with Louis Armstrong?"

Mr. An nodded. "One summer in Paris. And later in Berlin." His eyes moistened. He brushed them with his sleeve. "I haven't seen him since nineteen thirty-two. I would like to see him again." He stared at the clipping.

Beth watched him. "Do you know he's dead?" she asked at last.

Mr. An looked up. "Who killed him?"

"Nobody. He just died."

"When?"

"I don't remember. Ten or twelve years ago."

"You don't remember?"

"Not exactly. I'm surprised it wasn't reported in the Chinese press."

"I'm sure it was," Mr. An said. He tucked the clipping away. "I was absent during that period."

"Out of the country? Performing?"

Mr. An smiled, but it wasn't the smile she'd seen before. It was just a grimace that showed his teeth. "Out of the world," he said between them.

"What do you mean?"

"I was in Qinghai Province."

"Where is that?"

He looked at her in surprise. "Qinghai Province is bigger than France," he said. Then he laughed. "But not as famous, you are right. It is in western China. North of Tibet. There were many labor camps in Qinghai. Maybe there still are. The Red Guards sent me to one of them."

"Why?"

"Because I was a jazzman." He showed his teeth again, brown and rotting.

"What kind of labor did you do?"

"Road work. Four years. Not a long sentence. The Reverend was there for ten."

"Reverend Huang?"

"That's how I know him."

"Was he there because he's a minister?"

Mr. An nodded. "For two years they kept him in a cell too small to stand in. Or to lie flat down. That's why he's crooked."

Outside the window another double line of diggers flashed by. "It is better now," Mr. An said. "I didn't have a violin in my hands for twenty years. Now I am playing again." He smiled the smile that wasn't merely showing teeth and popped an orange candy in his mouth.

Outside there were buildings. They grew bigger and closer together. The train glided into a station. "Wuxi," said Mr. An, rising.

"How far is it to Lake Tai?"

"Not so far. We take the number eleven bus." Beth followed him to the door. She glanced at the soldiers. They didn't seem to be getting off. The attendant walked through the car cracking sunflower seeds between her teeth. She switched on the martial music. The soldiers glared at her back but they didn't move. They knew when they were beaten.

But not Reverend Huang, Beth thought. *Not Mr. An. And not me.*

26

Four posters were stuck to the sooty wall behind the number 11 bus stop. The first showed a photograph of an unsmiling middle-aged man. Number two: currency-exchange slips and a stack of Hong Kong dollars. Number three: a drawerful of watches. Number four: the unsmiling middle-aged man, head now shaven, kneeling on stadium turf, a placard covered with Chinese writing around his neck. A soldier stood behind him; spectators watched from stands in the background.

Mr. An said, "Is it clear to you, without the captions?" There was no irony in his tone, only curiosity.

Beth said, "The man illegally purchased Hong Kong dollars. He used them to buy watches, probably to sell on the black market."

Mr. An clapped his hands with delight. "Very good. Very, very good." For a moment Beth thought he was going to slap her on the back.

"And then what happened, Mr. An?"

He looked surprised, and a little disappointed, as though he'd overestimated her IQ. "Do you mean in number four?"

"Yes."

"The soldier shot him, of course. Don't you see the gun on his belt?"

"I thought it might have been the trial, or something."

"It was. First trial. Then execution." He giggled.

The bus came. The ticket seller was a beautiful girl with hair like raw black silk. Her eyes examined everything Beth was wearing.

The bus turned onto a four-lane road and crossed an arched

foot bridge. Murky water ran beneath it. "The Grand Canal," said Mr. An. A soldier on the bridge emptied his nostrils into it.

The road led out of town and followed the shore of a blue lake. Beth saw oyster nets and, farther out, a junk with a square brown sail, tacking slowly away. The other side of the lake lay beyond the horizon.

The bus stopped at a gate. Beyond it a bridge, not more than three or four yards long, linked the shore to a rounded green island. Sloping tile roofs glinted in the sun. Beth turned to Mr. An. He was asleep.

"Mr. An."

His eyes opened. They were full of dark clouds. He blinked twice and the clouds were gone. "Turtle Head Island," he said.

"Turtle Head Island?" The name reminded her of something.

Mr. An showed her his surprised look. Her IQ was falling again. "Don't you see the likeness?"

They got off the bus and walked to the gate. Tickets cost one jiaow apiece, a tenth of a yuan: five cents. They went through. The first thing they saw was a graceful pavilion overlooking the lake. It was stocked with gifts and souvenirs.

"I suppose you like cloisonné?" Mr. An asked, suddenly gloomy. His French accent was as good as Yves Montand's.

"Not much."

They passed the souvenir shop, crossed one tiny arched footbridge, then another. There were plum trees in blossom, rock gardens, dainty pavilions, paths that curved when they didn't have to, junks on the lake. Turtle Head Island was a Taoist Disneyland.

The path led to a little pink lighthouse with a pagoda roof, standing by the water's edge. At its base, an old man with a bamboo-handled broom was sweeping plum blossoms into a wicker basket.

"That must be him," Mr. An said. "Wait here."

He walked ahead and spoke to the man. The man listened, glancing from time to time at Beth. Because of the shadow cast by his conical straw hat, Beth couldn't see the expression in his eyes. He said something high-pitched. Mr. An replied in a voice too low to hear. The man was silent. Mr. An waved Beth forward.

"This is Mr. Lao," he said. Mr. Lao stood no higher than

her shoulder. She noticed his hands immediately: thick and swollen with muscle; the rest of his body was lean enough for an anatomy demonstration. Under the shade of the straw hat, his eyes flickered over her.

"Do you speak English, Mr. Lao?" she asked.

"A little." His accent was so thick that at first she didn't understand what he'd said.

"Do you know the amah Pei Ming?"

His eyes shifted. "Sorry."

"What do you mean?"

"Sorry."

"He doesn't understand," Mr. An explained. He said a few words to Mr. Lao, of which Beth distinguished two: *Pei Ming*.

Mr. Lao nodded reluctantly.

"He knows her," Mr. An said.

Beth moved closer to the little man, as though carried by a wave. "Where is she? Can I see her?"

Mr. Lao backed away, watching her carefully as he listened to Mr. An's translation. He was shaking his head before it ended.

"Why not?"

Mr. An asked Mr. Lao. Mr. Lao replied. Mr. An asked another question. Mr. Lao answered that too. The conversation expanded and took on a freer form. Mr. Lao rummaged in his pocket for cigarettes. The package had a panda on the cover. He offered a cigarette to Mr. An and helped himself. Mr. An lit them and tossed the match into the lake. Beth watched their eyes, listened to every nuance of their voices, noted the pauses and the way they held their bodies, and understood nothing.

Finally Mr. An turned to her and said: "The woman went away."

"Where?"

"He doesn't know."

"When?"

"Fifteen years ago. More or less. It was during the Cultural Revolution. She was accused of associating with bad elements."

"You mean she was arrested?"

"She was taken away."

"Did she leave any family around here?"

Mr. An turned to relay the question, but before he'd uttered a sound Mr. Lao shook his head. He knew the word *family*. Then he said something to Mr. An, who translated: "The whole family was accused of associating with bad elements."

Beth gazed out at the lake, trying to think of the next question. Three big junks with high square sterns and dark battened sails were angling across the water. Beth felt the eyes of the men on her. "Was Mr. Lao arrested during the Cultural Revolution?"

Mr. An asked him. Mr. Lao's eyes narrowed. He shook his head.

"Why not, if he's a Christian?"

Mr. An stared at her for a moment before laughing —a short, barking laugh. "They couldn't arrest everybody. That's the most important thing to know about China. We are one billion."

Ten or twelve white people came over a footbridge, following a guide. They looked at Beth. She had a crazy desire to run over and talk to them—about baseball, apartment-hunting, anything. Then they saw the junks. "Hey. Real Chinese junks."

They straggled past the lighthouse.

"A Chinese lighthouse."

They went around a rockery and out of sight. Behind them came an old woman with a broom, sweeping up. She had a drooping wen on her forehead, almost covering one eye. When she saw Mr. Lao, Mr. An, and Beth, she stopped and spoke angrily.

Mr. Lao replied. Whatever he said made her angrier. She came forward and shook the broom in his face, her voice rising. Mr. An stepped between them and spoke soothingly. Beth heard the word *Huang*.

The woman fell silent. She looked again at Beth. Then she hawked, spat, and walked toward the rockery, stooping for a discarded candy wrapper, which she smoothed and put in her pocket.

"What was that about?" Beth asked Mr. An.

"She is Mr. Lao's wife," he said simply.

"But why was she so angry?"

Mr. An looked embarrassed. "There is a restaurant here. Perhaps you would like some lunch. Then we could return to the town. There is a train to Shanghai at three." He paused. "I am sorry this trip has not been more successful."

He'd put it into words, gentle but undeniable: She wasn't going to find Pei Ming. The first step would require access to records of arrests during the Cultural Revolution—if they existed. Access, she realized suddenly, that an important defector might be granted. She felt a sickening in her stomach as she asked: "Has anyone else been here looking for Pei Ming?"

Mr. An asked Mr. Lao. "No."

The feeling in her stomach went away, leaving her numb. She stood motionless, waiting for an idea, or just the energy to start moving.

Mr. An glanced at his watch. "Well, then . . ."

"Just one more thing." Beth took a photograph from her pocket—Rex Heidemann, Helen Brock, and J. Han, Lake Tai, 1948—and showed it to Mr. Lao.

"Ask if he knew any of these people." The words weren't out before she saw the answer in Mr. Lao' eyes. He jabbed his finger at the picture, and began talking excitedly. The three of them moved closer together.

"He remembers the foreigners very well," Mr. An said. "Especially the man. He was a missionary. Mr. Lao often went to his services. He was also his gardener."

"Where?"

"Here. At Taihu. The foreigners had a summer house here."

Beth asked the question she should have started with: "Did he know Pei Ming in those days?"

Mr. An asked him. "Yes. Pei Ming worked in another summer house, nearby."

Mr. Lao spoke to Mr. An, not taking his eyes off the picture for a second. Maybe it reminded him of his youth: maybe he hadn't seen many photographs before.

"He asks if you know the foreigners."

"I do." Something inside her rewoke and drove the numbness away. "They gave me the photograph, and asked me to pass on greetings to any of their old friends I met."

Mr. An translated. Mr. Lao, hanging on every word, beamed when he heard the message. Pointing beyond the rockery, he spoke to Mr. An.

"He says the foreigners' house is no longer standing, but he can show you the house where Pei Ming worked, if you like."

"I would like that very much. Is it far?"

"Not far. The house is here on Turtle Head Island. In those days, this was a place where rich people came in the summers."

Mr. Lao led them around the rockery and up a hill. He still had the photograph in his hand.

"Ask him if he knew the Chinese man."

Mr. An relayed the question. Frowning, Mr. Lao replied.

"He saw him once, " Mr. An said.

"Is it his old house we're going to see? Is that where Pei Ming worked?"

Mr. An translated. Mr. Lao stopped and looked at Beth for a moment before speaking. "He says no. He asks why you want to know all these things."

Beth looked into Mr. Lao's eyes, half hidden in the shadow of his hat. "Tell him I am doing a favor for Reverend Huang."

Mr. An glanced at Beth; then he spoke to Mr. Lao. Mr. Lao replied quietly.

"What did he say?"

"That Reverend Huang is a great man," Mr. An answered, watching her. She said nothing.

They reached the crest of the hill. On the other side was a little bay, framed by two spits of land jutting into the lake. On the far spit stood a big yellow house with a pointed green-tile roof. A foot path connected the two spits, passing through a plum orchard and bridging a narrow stream. On the near spit was a red pavilion.

Mr. Lao pointed at the yellow house. "That is where the amah worked," Mr. An said. He scanned the shoreline. "A happy combination of elements. In Chinese terms."

Beth walked down the hill to the red pavilion. It had an upswept red-tile roof, supported by thin red columns; a high latticed balustrade enclosed it. Beth opened the half-door in the balustrade and went in.

Dried leaves were scattered on the wooden floor. In its center was a trapdoor with a rusted latch. Beth bent down and tried it. The latch snapped off in her hand.

She left the pavilion. The two old men were watching her from the top of the hill. She climbed it and said: "I'd like to hear about the time Mr. Lao saw the Chinese man in the photograph."

Mr. Lao studied the picture for a few moments before he began to talk. He talked for a long time. Once he pointed up the stream and made running motions with his hypertrophied fingers. When he finished, Mr. An asked him something in a sharp tone. Mr. Lao grunted. Mr. An grunted.

He turned to Beth. "Mr. Lao saw the man once, as he said before. It was in the spring of nineteen forty-nine. He doesn't remember the exact date, but it would be easy to determine because it was the day before the liberation of Wuxi.

"There were two houses then—the yellow house with the pavilion, and the foreigners' house by the stream, just behind those small trees. I don't know their name in English."

"Palmettos."

"Palmettos. Thank you. One never comes to the end of learning English. Chinese is the same." He thought for a moment. "The difference is that all Chinese words sound Chinese. So many English ones sound like something else. Palmettos." Mr. An laughed, the laugh that was slightly too loud and slightly too long. Then he slipped back into thought. A silver fish jumped from the water and fell back with a splash. That broke the spell he was under.

"The house of the foreigners. It was empty at that time. The foreigners had not yet come up from Shanghai. Mr. Lao had been readying the garden for their arrival. That night he went to bed early, not long after sunset. He slept in the tool shed, a short distance from the house.

"During the night, something woke him. He saw lights in the house. He was afraid because he thought some of Chiang Kaishek's soldiers might be inside. Or bandits. He stayed where he was. Then he began to worry that if any damage was done, he would lose his job. So he got up and crawled to the house.

"He looked through the window. Inside he saw many men—a dozen, maybe more. Rough-looking types. Then something happened that confused him. Two more men came into view. One was the foreign missionary who owned the house." Mr. An pointed to Rex Heidemann in the photograph. "The other was him." He pointed to the big Chinese man. "Mr. Lao didn't know what to think—he was a member of the white man's church, but the others looked like bandits. So Mr. Lao went back to the tool shed. But he couldn't sleep. Just before dawn he heard men running down toward the lake.

"He stayed in the tool shed until noon. Then he went back to the house. It was empty. He never saw any of the men again."

"Not even the foreigner?"

"No. The People's Army took Wuxi that day. The foreigner never returned."

"What about Pei Ming?"

"Mr. Lao says he walked down to the yellow house in the

afternoon. It too was deserted, although he knew the people had been there the day before. And the door was broken. Mr. Lao waited for the police to come, but they never did.

"After the war, he was sent north for reeducation, due to his involvement with missionaries. Three years later, he was allowed to return to Turtle Head, and assigned to a farming commune. That's when he saw Pei Ming again—she was also a member of the commune. After the Cultural Revolution, the commune was disbanded and Mr. Lao was given his present job as caretaker of this park."

"And the people Pei Ming worked for in the yellow house— did he see them again too?"

Mr. An asked Mr. Lao. "No."

"Who were they?"

Mr. An passed on Mr. Lao's answer: "A rich family from Shanghai. A man, his wife, and a baby cared for by the amah."

"What was their name?"

Mr. An translated the question.

"Wu," said Mr. Lao.

A charge went through Beth, as though a circuit had been completed. "Ask him what else he knows about them."

Mr. An did. Mr. Lao replied impatiently. "Nothing, he says."

"Nothing? But when he and Pei Ming were together on the commune, didn't he discuss what happened on the day everyone disappeared?"

Mr. Lao snorted when he heard the translation.

"What does that mean?"

"Talking about the past was not usually a good idea."

Mr. Lao glanced around. Reverend Huang's name was losing its magic.

"Who lives in the yellow house now?"

"High-ranking cadres come in the summer. No one is there now."

Beth looked at the yellow house where Wu Tun-li had lived, saw it again reflected upside down in the calm waters of the lake. Then she turned to Mr. Lao and held out her hand.

Mr. Lao took it reluctantly. His hand was hard, rough, inanimate. It enfolded hers for an instant, then let go. He turned and started back the way they had come, walking in the shadow of his big hat.

Beth and Mr. An descended the hill and followed another path to the parking lot. The tourists were taking pictures of themselves in front of their bus.

"Cheese!"

The number 11 bus wasn't there. "I hope it comes soon," Mr. An said.

They waited. Two small black cars entered the lot and parked by the gate. A man got out of one of them. He was tall and wore a Western suit. A woman moved out from behind the ticket booth to talk to him. Mr. Lao's wife.

The number 11 bus drove up. Beth and Mr. An boarded it. The bus, empty except for the driver and the ticket seller, wheeled around and turned onto the road to Wuxi.

Dappled sunlight shone through poplars by the road. They passed a man and a woman riding bicycles, side by side. He had his arm around her. Beth closed her eyes.

"Excuse me for asking," said Mr. An, "but why are you looking for this woman Pei Ming?"

"Reverend Huang didn't tell you?"

"No." He paused. "People form careful habits."

Why not tell him? Wasn't she going home anyway? What more could she do in China? She had completed a circuit, and although she didn't have much to show for it, at least she didn't feel at a dead end. For one thing, she knew that Teddy hadn't come to Lake Tai. For another, she wanted a second talk with Rex Heidemann.

Mr. An was watching her closely. And Beth would have explained everything, if his remark about careful habits hadn't been fresh in her mind. Instead she said: "You've been very good to me, Mr. An. Please don't take this as an insult, but is there anything I could send you from the States?"

There was a long silence. Then he said, "I would love a Walkman."

Beth laughed and put her hand on his knee. He shifted away. A worried look came into his eyes. "Perhaps it is not a good idea. The package would be opened, of course."

"I know someone who works at a radio station that plays jazz. I'll send it from there, without my name. As a sort of cultural exchange."

Mr. An sighed. "No. It is definitely not a good idea."

Beth wondered if he would accept an offer of money instead. She was still thinking about it when two small black cars overtook them. The driver of the second car stuck out his hand and made a signal. The bus pulled over to the side of the road.

"What's going on?" Beth asked.

The black cars stopped in the middle of the road. The man in the Western suit stepped out of one and came toward the bus. Two men got out of the other and followed him. They wore blue uniforms and had short-barreled automatic rifles in their hands.

"Gong An Ju," said Mr. An, so softly she could hardly hear him.

"What?"

"Public Security Bureau." Mr. An had gone very still, watching the man in the Western suit approach the bus. He barely seemed to breathe. The man in the Western suit boarded the bus and spoke to Mr. An: one word of one syllable. Mr. An rose like an automaton and walked toward him.

"Mr. An!"

He made no sign of hearing her. The man in the Western suit looked at her. He gestured for her to come. Beth glanced around. The driver and the ticket seller avoided her eyes. He gestured again. She got up and followed Mr. An off the bus.

The man in the suit was waiting at the bottom of the steps. He had a thin face and a long thin nose, with a prominent bridge for a Chinese. He motioned them toward the cars.

Mr. An was no longer watching him. He was looking up at the sunlight shining through the trees. All at once he began to run—across the road, between the poplars, and into a field that stretched toward the lake. He ran like the old man he was, with stiff little strides that didn't eat up much ground.

One of the armed men ran after him. "No!" Beth said, moving forward. "Leave him alone! He hasn't done anything." The other armed man stepped in front of her, rifle raised across his chest.

The first armed man was gaining ground. Mr. An must have heard him coming, but he never looked back. He kept running. He wasn't fast, but he wasn't tiring either. He was almost halfway to the lake when the armed man caught up with him, raised his rifle, and brought the butt down on Mr. An's head. Mr. An fell forward, onto his hands and knees. He started crawling, frantically, still not looking back. The armed man let him crawl a few yards before he hit him again. Mr. An went all the way down, lost from sight in the knee-high grass. The armed man stood over him.

Beth turned to the man in the Western suit and shouted: ''What are you doing to him? He's an old man.''

The man in the Western suit ignored her. He gestured to the bus driver, who started his engine and drove off, eyes straight ahead. Then he motioned for Beth to get into one of the cars.

''I don't have to go anywhere with you.''

The armed man raised his rifle a little higher. The man in the Western suit motioned again.

The bus rounded a curve and disappeared. It was very quiet. They were all by themselves on the dappled road—Beth, the man in the suit, the man with the gun. The air was full of spring. Anything could happen. No one would ever know.

Beth walked to the car. The armed man opened the door. She got in. The door closed.

27

It was about as simple as a room can be. Four cement walls, cement floor, cement ceiling. No paint, no whitewash, no furniture, no lights. One window, overlooking a brick wall. One door. But it wasn't the room's simplicity that made it objectionable. What made it objectionable were the bars on the window and the fact that the door was locked from the outside.

No one had charged Beth with a crime. No one had read her her rights. No one had brought her food. All they had done was put her in the room and lock the door.

All she could see was the brick wall. All she could hear was the sound of traffic, not far away, and once a loud voice saying, "Cheese."

No one came when she pounded the door. In one corner was a pitcher of water, now almost empty. The other corner she had finally had to use as a toilet.

At night she slept on the floor. In the daytime she walked back and forth, or leaned against the bars of the window, hoping for a breeze. But the brick wall blocked any breeze, and whatever air there was smelled of burning coal.

Panic came when she woke in the middle of the night. It came with a jolt that made her heart pump crazily. She tried to calm herself with talk: "What's wrong with you? No one's beating you; no one's giving you electric shocks. You're not even tired anymore. Just a little hungry, that's all. You spent a night in cold water. This is nothing. Just waiting. So wait."

But the sound of her voice failed to calm her. She paced. She stared at the brick wall. She sat with her arms around her knees. She lay down with her hands tucked between her thighs. She felt like one part per billion.

The door opened on the morning of the fourth day. The man in the Western suit came in, the same suit he'd been wearing before: brown polyester with a button missing from one of the sleeves.

Beth got up from the floor. He looked at her. His long nose wrinkled.

He opened a cardboard folder and took out a sheaf of papers. Before he closed the folder, Beth glimpsed her file—the one containing Helen Brock's photographs, the *Chronicle* clipping, Teddy's passport, and the letter from Shanghai.

"Investigation finish," he said, handing her the papers. "Tomorrow trial."

Beth leafed through the papers: columns of Chinese characters, a red seal at the bottom of every page. "What are the charges?"

"Tomorrow trial," the man repeated. "Now confession." He took out a ballpoint pen and made writing motions at the papers in her hand. "Signing confession," he said.

"What confession? I haven't even been questioned yet."

Her words came too quickly, pouring meaninglessly into his ears. "Signing confession," he said again, brandishing the pen in her face.

She took it. He came closer, pointing at the line for her signature. He wrinkled his nose.

"If I stink it's your fucking fault." Beth threw the pen against the cement wall.

Tendons stuck out in his neck. "Spy!" he shouted.

"Bullshit! And if you've been through my file, you know it." Beth snatched the cardboard folder and took out her file. Her fingers fumbled for Teddy's letter. "You've got Teddy. You kidnapped him. Now you've kidnapped me. That's my confession!"

The man in the suit made a grab for the folder, the file, Teddy's letter. Everything, including the unsigned confession, fell between them; papers glided across the room. He chased after them, stooping and plucking like a field laborer in a harvesting contest. The door was open, but Beth stood there, watching him scoop up the papers. Once or twice he glanced at her furiously. When he'd gathered the papers, he tucked them under his left arm, stepped forward, and punched her in the face. Beth fell down. The man in the suit backed out the door, hooking it shut with his foot.

After a while she got up and went to the door. It wasn't locked. She listened. Silence.

She opened the door. Outside was a long corridor that ended in a patch of gray-blue. Beth started running.

She got halfway down the corridor. Then a door opened in front of her. A man in a blue uniform came out, zipping up his pants. He shouted when he saw Beth, and drew a gun. Beth heard it click. She stopped running and raised her hands. The man prodded her chest with the barrel, hard. She backed into the wall.

More men came. They marched Beth back to the cement room. They laid her facedown on the floor and shackled her wrists and ankles. She could feel the urge to beat her in their hands. They were waiting for an excuse. She didn't give them one. They went out. The door closed.

Beth couldn't stand or sit. She could roll over. She rolled over a few times. It wasn't easy and it hurt her shoulders. She stopped doing it. Outside the window, the brick wall began to lose its color. Then it turned from solid into haze. And finally disappeared.

She didn't sleep. She thought about Mr. An. "Tomorrow trial," the man in the suit had said. "First trial," Mr. An had told her. "Then execution."

Night. Traffic sounds died away. Wuxi was very quiet for a city of—what? She no longer had the curio man's guidebook. She didn't have her file, her handbag, her passport. She didn't have Teddy. Or freedom. She'd lost it in less than two days in China. She'd accomplished nothing, other than one negative accomplishment: the death of Albert Ling.

The long-haired boy in Berkeley had died, too. And they had tried to kill her: first at sea, then in the Hotel Dolores; tomorrow or the next day in some drab building run by the Gong An Ju.

Much later, the brick wall separated itself from the night, like a TV image coming slowly into focus. First it was a gray shadow, then a solid. Colors came—brown, yellow, and finally red. For a while the wall was as interesting as the facade of Rouen Cathedral had been to Monet. Then it was just a wall.

The shackles made her body ache. She tried lying on her right side, her left, her back. None were any good, and all got worse. But it could be much worse; she knew that already. They could leave her in shackles until she was as bent as Reverend Huang. She tried not to think about that. It was the kind of thinking they wanted her to do.

The door opened. Beth, prone, twisted her head and saw a woman come in. The woman carried a mop and a pail. Without looking at Beth, she cleaned up the mess in the corner and left.

In a few minutes the woman returned with a food tray: teapot, cup, bowl of rice, chopsticks. She laid it on the cement floor, beside the almost-empty water jug, and went out.

Rice smell filled the room. It overwhelmed burning-coal smell, human-waste smell, her own smell. Was she expected to roll over to the rice bowl and sink her face in it? Was it meant to be torture?

But it was only disorganization. The door opened again. The old woman entered, rattling keys. All at once the pressure of the shackles was gone. The door closed.

Beth moved her arms and legs. Feeling returned. It returned as pain. She stood up. She saw white. White spun. She sat down.

A few minutes later, Beth tried again. She walked shakily to the corner and picked up the water jug. The water tasted tepid and dusty. She drank all that was left.

She looked at the rice: soggy, with stringy gray chunks that might have been fish mixed in. She didn't touch it.

Beth poured tea. It was still hot enough to warm the chipped cup. She sat against the wall, cradling it in her hands, sipping now and then. Tea flowed into her bloodstream like a soothing drug.

The door opened. The man in the suit came in. Same suit, same button missing. Same man, same nose—so bony for a Chinese nose; almost a deformity. He had a big anxious smile on his face. The smile looked like a deformity, too.

"Tea all right?" he asked. "Tea all right?" He saw the rice bowl. "Rice no like?" He bustled over to it, took up the chopsticks, and mimed shoveling rice into his mouth. "Rice good. Yes?" He was like a big brother who'd bullied little sis all day, in the moments before Mom and Dad came home. Beth wondered if the judge, assuming there was a judge, would examine her for signs of maltreatment. It didn't jibe with anything Mr. An had told her.

The man in the suit laid the chopsticks down. "Tea all right?" he asked again, with less enthusiasm in his tone and more anxiety in his smile. That was fine with Beth. She put the teacup on the tray. He looked at it unhappily, his eyes, his body full of persuading and cajoling he couldn't translate into English.

He teetered in front of her for a few more seconds. Then he pulled up the sleeve with the missing button and showed her his watch. Hers had been taken with the rest of her things. It was ten minutes to eight. "Go now," he said.

"To the trial?"

He laughed as though she'd cracked a good joke. "No no no," he said. "Peking."

"Beijing?"

This one was even funnier. "Beijing: Yes, yes. Come."

"Is the trial in Beijing?"

"Ha ha. Sorry, sorry."

They went down the corridor, and out into gray-blue. A jeep was waiting. A driver and a uniformed man sat in front. Beth and the man in the suit climbed in back. Her suitcase and hand-bag lay on the floor.

She glanced back at the building where she'd just spent four days. It was a plain four-story cement structure with a flat roof and a flat facade—a normal PRC building. A few soldiers lounged by the entrance. They might have been on duty; they might have been waiting for the bus.

The street was a normal PRC street. People went by on foot, on bicycles, in buses. No one was interested in the plain cement building. An old man limped past, carrying a white bird in a bamboo cage. A man in torn sneakers pulled a heavy cart loaded with rags. No one was interested in them, either.

The driver honked and drove into the street. Beth saw two Western women walking on the sidewalk. They wore padded silk jackets embroided with red phoenixes. The jackets looked Chinese, but no Chinese women were wearing them—they must have been far too expensive. The Western women noticed Beth riding in the back of the jeep. She thought of calling out to them for help, just shouting her name and nationality; she was still thinking about it when an oncoming steel-gray car swerved in front of them and braked to a noisy stop in front of the Gong An Ju building. No one in the jeep seemed to mind, or even notice, except Beth, who saw a man get out of the car and hurry into the building. He had a high forehead and a hollow face; a cigarette burned between his long, saintlike fingers.

Beth's pulse drummed in her ears, drowning out the street sounds, but the Gong An Ju men seemed unaware of any change in her. The jeep kept going, and was soon rolling through the countryside southwest of the city. Lake Tai sparkled between the trees. After a while the road veered away from the lake and cut through a flatland of paddies lush with spring rice. Beth kept looking back. The road was empty. Here and there egrets stood motionless like white exclamation marks in a green story.

The jeep mounted a treeless rise. On the far side lay a small airstrip: a red wind sock, two jet fighters with red stars on the wings, a squat old propeller plane. The driver parked beside the old plane.

The man in the suit took Beth's suitcase and handbag and led her onto the plane. The uniformed man closed the door from the outside. There were three rows of unpadded steel seats in the cabin, two seats to a row; the rest of the cabin was empty. The man in the suit sat in the first row. Beth sat in the last, as far from him as possible. He didn't object.

Shaking like a palsy victim, the plane strained down the runway and bumped into the air. It struggled up into the blue and leveled off. Beth looked out the window. The plane wasn't yet at high altitude; she could easily distinguish the thin strip of pavement cutting through the rice fields between Wuxi and the airfield. There was a little traffic near Wuxi; at the other end she saw only one car, a tiny steel-gray rectangle advancing slowly toward the airfield.

The plane rose higher. The gray rectangle disappeared, and then the road. Soon there was nothing but engine noise, airlessness, and a hard, cold seat. Beth let herself fall asleep.

Thump.

She opened her eyes and looked out. The plane was twenty feet off the ground, drifting in a high arc. Up to the top of the arc, and down.

Thump.

The pilot bounced the old plane a few more times and let it roll to a stop like a tired basketball. The door opened. The man in the suit led Beth outside.

They were at the end of a long runway. A terminal building rose in the distance. The land was flat. A strong, dusty wind blew across it from the north.

A black car was waiting. It was bigger than any car Beth had seen in China, and looked brand-new. Perhaps it was meant to be a top-of-the-line limousine. It might have been taken for one in 1948.

A man got out of the back. He wore a black tunic, made of silk, and black pants. He had thick black hair and skin like a baby's, without wrinkle or blemish. The only clue to his age was his mustache, white as the egrets in the rice paddies. He came closer. He was looking at her avidly, as though she were a famous painting he'd read about but never seen. He had the knowing eyes of an emperor in a Chinese opera.

Beth glanced at the man in the suit. He was rapt, like one of the Disciples. It didn't do him any good. The man in black didn't see him. He only saw Beth.

He held out his hand. "Miss Hunter?" he said in perfect English. "How do you do? I am General Ma."

"Are you the judge?"

"Judge?"

"For my trial."

He looked at the man in the suit. The man in the suit looked at the ground. "There will be no trial," General Ma said. "You are here as my guest."

She took his hand. It was warm and dry, and knowing as his eyes.

28

"Perhaps we could go for a little drive," General Ma said.

"Do I have a choice?" Beth asked.

"Certainly. You are free to go at any time." An airliner glided down from the eastern sky and banked toward the terminal.

"Where?"

"Wherever you wish," said General Ma. "Home, if you like."

"Tell that to your bullyboy."

"My bullyboy?"

Beth looked at the man in the suit.

"Oh," said General Ma. "The gentleman from Public Security." The man in the suit was watching closely, hanging on every half-understood word. "He's not exactly my bullyboy. I represent another department."

"The army, you mean?"

General Ma smiled. He had a toothy smile, but its effect was more like the Mona Lisa's than Carol Channing's: There was nothing simple about it. "Not exactly," he said.

"Then what department?"

"The actual name defies translation. Shall we just say it is a more flexible organization than the Gong An Ju?"

Beth looked at the big car and its driver. He wasn't wearing a uniform, or a short-barreled gun. "Let's go for a ride," she said.

General Ma showed her his smile again. "I love the way American women speak English," he said. "Just like the cinema."

They got in the car. The man in the suit stood outside, his hand resting lightly on the shiny bodywork. With a modest surge, the car accelerated away from him and sped through a gate at the end of the runway.

The back seat was padded in red plush. There was more of it on the two jump seats and in the front. The shock absorbers were plush, too: Beth didn't feel a bump as they rolled north on a highway that was full of them. There were no other cars, only a few people walking and a man on a horse-drawn cart. General Ma saw her looking at them.

"This Red Flag automobile doesn't belong to me personally, of course. It belongs to the people."

"I'll bear that in mind."

General Ma smiled again. This time it was just showing teeth. "Communism doesn't oppose material things. It simply demands they be shared equally."

"I know the theory," Beth said.

"Do you? We must discuss it someday."

Beth searched his eyes for a clue as to what he meant by *someday;* there was plenty in them, but no meanings she could find. Moments went by—Beth didn't know how many—before she realized they were staring into each other's eyes. She looked away.

"Would you like to see the Great Wall, Miss Hunter? That way we'll have a destination."

"It depends."

That brought the smile. "In two words, precisely how I feel about the Great Wall. And all the leftovers from old China—the Forbidden City, the Summer Palace, the temples, the pagodas. It depends." He paused. "Do you know Shelley's *Ozymandias?*"

"Yes."

"Then you know what I'm talking about."

"Not really."

"No?" His eyes probed as though teleporting the connection from his brain to hers. "Well, it doesn't matter. What matters is that the Great Wall is a wonderful place for a picnic. Do you know I hadn't been on a picnic in my life, until last year? I only knew of them from English novels. And now we've had three. This will be the fourth."

"Who is we?"

"My nephew and I," said General Ma, pointing his chin at the back of the driver's head.

"Just the two of you?"

"Yes. We've found the perfect spot—a part of the Wall not open to the public."

Beth thought about that. The thought led to another. Her heart beat faster. "Will Teddy be there? Is that what you're saying?"

"Teddy?"

"Theodore Wu. Are you taking me to him? Is that what this is all about?"

General Ma didn't answer at first. He opened a briefcase that had been lying on the floor, and took out a blue file. Her file. She hadn't seen the man in the Western suit pass it along; that meant General Ma already had it—it must have been sent to Beijing.

He turned to her. "Dr. Wu, the mathematician, is not in China, Miss Hunter."

"I don't believe you. He sent me a letter from Shanghai."

General Ma opened the blue file. "Yes. The letter from Shanghai." He took out the Xerox. "The postmark looks authentic. The handwriting may be as well—we would need a genuine sample to make a verification. But letters can be written anywhere and posted from anywhere, by anyone. What we do know is that the content of the letter is completely false. Dr. Wu has not defected."

"I know that. You kidnapped him."

A fire flared deep in his eyes, and was quickly extinguished. "We did not, Miss Hunter. We did not even know of Dr. Wu's existence until Washington began acting strangely."

"How can you say that? I was there. I saw the submarine."

His fingers, rummaging through the file, went still. "Submarine?"

"Yes. The one that picked up Teddy off the California coast." General Ma was watching her eyes, waiting. "What kind of ports does a Han-class submarine have, square or round?"

"Round," he replied immediately.

"Do you have any submarines with square ports?"

"Perhaps. But no Chinese submarine, Han class or otherwise, has ever been near California."

"The U.S. government disagrees."

"But?"

"What do you mean—'but'?"

"I heard 'but.' "

Beth sat silently for a few moments. Then she nodded. "You're right." She tried to think of reasons for withholding information from General Ma, and couldn't. If he was lying, she had no way to force the truth out of him. If he wasn't, she had nothing to lose. So she told him about the sub pictures, the *Timoshenko*, and what she'd seen in the fog off San Francisco.

General Ma didn't speak for a long time. They passed a man and a woman arguing by the roadside. The woman struck the man across the face with a straw bag as they flashed by.

General Ma turned to her. "Are you interested in history, Miss Hunter?"

"Yes," she replied, thinking that if China had been involved in Teddy's disappearance, he would have known the answer to that question.

"Then you might recognize that this is the type of incident that can unleash huge international forces—the way the assassination of Archduke Ferdinand led to World War One. In that case, the result was not foreseen. But I can't help thinking that this incident was intended from the beginning to set those forces in motion."

"What forces?"

"Surely, you—" He stopped himself, folded his hands neatly on the file, and went on: "China is in the middle of a power struggle. We have been in it constantly since nineteen forty-nine. It is between those who put ideology first and those who put ideology second. Second. Not fourth, tenth, or ninety-ninth, as Westerners who think we're on the way to becoming a giant Hong Kong like to imagine. Those, like me, who put ideology second, believe the development of China must have priority. We've been in power since the fall of the Gang of Four. But the struggle hasn't ended. It still goes on. It goes on in my own office, Miss Hunter. And what is happening now plays into the hands of those who put ideology first, who want to return to the old ways. Dr. Wu's disappearance has set off a series of actions and reactions. It has made Washington turn very hostile toward us—quite naturally, since they think we've stolen their cryptological secrets. Then our leftists say, 'You see? The Americans cannot be trusted. We know nothing of this Dr. Wu. Therefore it's some sort of dangerous trick.' The effect is to drive the two countries apart. And in the long run, without economic interaction with the U.S., the modernization of China will fail."

Outside, China went by in a green and brown blur. Beth glided through it in her plush capsule. All physical sensation was gone, except in her stomach: It felt like a basket of snakes.

She took a deep breath to make them go away. "Are you saying that the leftists in your government kidnapped Teddy on their own?"

General Ma looked at her—into her eyes: a look that once again went deeper and lasted longer than she'd expected, without making her uncomfortable. "You're a very intelligent person, Miss Hunter. That is the question I've been asking myself since I learned of Dr. Wu's disappearance. I don't know the answer."

"But if they didn't take him, who did?"

"I can't answer that question, either. Not yet. But with your help I may be able to."

"With my help?"

"Yes. And the help of my regular guide."

"Who is that?"

"Cui bono."

For a second, Beth mistook it for Chinese. Then she smiled. "What can I do?"

General Ma opened the blue file. "Tell me everything: why you are searching for this woman Pei Ming, who these people are in the photos, all you know about Dr. Wu's disappearance. And why you're interested in our touring chefs."

"All right. But before I do, what is going to happen to Mr. An?"

"Who is Mr. An?"

Beth explained, without mentioning Reverend Huang.

General Ma thought for a moment. He didn't ask how she'd met Mr. An, but he said, "That coffee shop is not a good idea."

"What does that mean?"

"Nothing. Your Mr. An will be released, of course." General Ma spoke briefly to his nephew, who took a radiophone from under the dashboard and spoke into it.

"I thought that wasn't your department." Beth said.

"We cooperate." Like Lathrop, Beth remembered, who cooperated with the Coast Guard. General Ma handed her the file. "Now tell me what you know."

Beth told him. She told him about Pei Ming, Rex Heidemann, and Helen Brock. She told him about Han Shih. The Taipei Social Club and Baldy. The long-haired man with the green snake on his wrist. The Lings. Lathrop and the Colonel.

General Ma listened quietly. He asked one question: "What is the Colonel's name?"

"I don't know."

He took the file and went through it slowly by himself. Beth looked out the window. The car climbed into green hills and turned onto a slightly wider road that followed a stony ridge; below ran a fast-flowing stream. Women washed clothes in it. Men fished with hand-held lines. Children splashed. Low stone houses were scattered like geological outcrops on the hillsides.

General Ma saw her looking at them. "*Pingfang,*" he said. "Flat-houses. All those were built with stones from the Great Wall. Now do you understand what I mean about *Ozymandias?*"

"Not exactly." She waited for an explanation; none came.

The winding road filled with tour buses, climbing noisily up, coasting too quickly down. General Ma's nephew kept his hand on the horn. It had an unusually deep tone, like some enormous woodwind. The buses gave way. White faces peered out as the Red Flag went by. Some were curious; some were bored; some had Instamatics thrust upon them.

The big car crested a hill taller than the rest. In the distance, Beth saw the Wall—"snaking," as the curio man's guidebook had put it, from hill to hill as far as the eye could see. Snaking toward it was the long line of tour buses. The two snakes met in a sea of bobbing reds, blues, greens, and yellows, like dots spilled from a color TV.

They were halfway there when General Ma's nephew turned abruptly onto an overgrown dirt track that was almost invisible from the road. The car bumped up a steep slope and down the other side. At the bottom, a *pingfang* stood by a narrow stream. General Ma's nephew parked and went in through the heavy wooden door.

General Ma got out of the car. "Come," he said. Beth followed him. He unlocked the trunk. Inside was a finely made picnic hamper.

Beth admired it. "Does it come from Beijing?"

"Fauchon."

General Ma hoisted the hamper out of the trunk. Although he was no taller than Beth and it looked heavy, he did it without

effort. His nephew came out of the house with a thermos. Beth
had her first good look at him. He was tall and well built, with
the longest hair she had seen on a man in China. He wore jeans
that said *Calvin Klein* at the back, a shirt with a polo player on
front, and a thick black mustache. She could have bumped into
him at any of the smart fern bars on Nob Hill, if she ever went
to one.

General Ma took the thermos. "Tea," he said, putting it in
the hamper. His nephew went back inside.

General Ma slipped off his shoes and socks and rolled his
pants above the knee. "It's not deep," he said, lifting the hamper on his shoulder and heading toward the stream. His calves
were strong and sinewy.

Beth took off her shoes and socks, rolled up her jeans, and
waded in after him. The water was clear and cold. She splashed
some on her face. She splashed more behind her neck and in her
hair. She drenched her head. She washed away four nights in the
cement room in Wuxi.

General Ma was watching from the other side. "That's the
beauty of picnics," he said. "Nature."

They walked through tall grass. Little flowers, blue and yellow, bent aside as they went by. They climbed another rise and
there, on the far side, stood the Wall: crumbling brown and gray
stone, eroded battlements, ragged slots for the bowmen. Grass
grew through holes in the rock.

"My favorite part," said General Ma. "It hasn't been restored."

Broken steps led to the top of the Wall. The stones slid under
Beth's feet as she followed him up.

The top was like a Roman road after an earthquake: Enough
remained to prove it had once been a miracle of construction.
General Ma opened the hamper, took out a thick red blanket,
and began spreading it. Beth looked over the parapet to the north.
A dusty plain stretched into the distance.

"It's like that all the way to the Gobi Desert," said General
Ma. "That's where the barbarians always came from."

"And now they come on seven forty-sevens."

General Ma laughed. The laugh came from deep in his chest.
It gurgled in his throat like a brook before it came out. It was as
complicated as his smile.

"Do you like wine?" he asked, holding up a bottle. "Or does it depend?"

"I like wine."

General Ma sank the tip of the corkscrew into the cork. Then he paused and looked up. "No matter what happens, I want you to know how much you've helped me."

"How have I helped you?"

He twisted the corkscrew into the soft wood. "You've put my mind at ease."

"How?"

"By demonstrating that the leftists had nothing to do with it. The submarine was obviously Russian, and the leftists would never cooperate with them. They hate the Russians more than they hate us. And they would never risk attaching an agent to an official tour. Besides, the Green Snakes, the baroque touches like the severed head and the roomful of flowers—none of that fits their usual—"

"Modus operandi?"

General Ma smiled. "Exactly. That doesn't mean they won't try to take advantage—they already are. It just means that China had no involvement in Dr. Wu's disappearance, although great effort has been spent to make it look like we did."

"By whom?"

"I don't know. But I'm going to do everything I can to help you find him."

"Why?"

"Because it is in the interest of my party and my country." *And other reasons*, said his eyes. "You and I are victims of the same crime. We've been approaching its solution from opposite directions." He paused. "Our meeting makes this a lucky day."

"I'm lucky to be alive."

General Ma smiled again. "True."

Beth studied his smiling face. He didn't look like a victim. "Exactly what do you do, General Ma?"

"Foreign relations."

"Does that mean intelligence? Like the CIA?"

"It's liaison work, mostly," he said, drawing the cork. "I hope you like Burgundy."

Beth noticed the label. *Romanée-Conti, 1962.* "Where did you get that?"

"We have Maxim's in Beijing now."

"And Fauchon?"

"Not yet. I bought the basket in Paris."

"Do you go there often?"

"Sometimes."

General Ma set food on the red blanket: Brie, *chèvre*, two *baguettes*, ham, roast beef, Dijon mustard, green apples, red grapes. He poured the wine into ordinary drinking glasses. The smell of France overpowered her: She was intoxicated before she'd tasted a drop.

"Do you think it's had enough time to breathe?" asked the General.

"I don't care."

Beth drank. The wine rippled through her like fresh warm blood.

They sat cross-legged on the red blanket. General Ma was good at sitting cross-legged. His sinewy calves slowly darkened under the sun. They drank. Warm breezes patted floral scents through the air. A bird with a blue body and a black tail landed on the parapet, sang a few notes, and soared away. They ate the ham, the beef, the Brie, the *chèvre*, the grapes, the apples. Beth ate until she could eat no more. She drank until the wine was gone.

General Ma put his hand on her knee. She didn't take it away.

They lay amid the leftovers of the Western picnic. Despite his knowing eyes and his knowing hands, he was as simple and straightforward as an adolescent. It was what she needed. The sun shone down.

Later, he said, "We in China are reputed to be puritanical. And yet there are so many of us. Isn't that a contradiction?"

Beth had been thinking: At home, a woman and a man sometimes went to bed together without knowing each other's surnames; here, when the same thing happened, it was surnames only. So she said, "It depends."

General Ma laughed.

Overhead a single-engine plane flew lazily by.

29

Only a few hours had passed since the picnic, but General Ma was hungry. His chopsticks pinched chunks of glistening meat and swept them to his mouth in swift, mechanical motions. "Peking duck," he said between mouthfuls, "do you know it was invented in this restaurant?" Then he noticed Beth wasn't eating. "You don't like it?"

"I do, but I'm not very hungry."

"No?"

The waiter stood by the sideboard, carving the plump bird into paper-thin strips. General Ma spoke to him, and he hurried to the table with a bowl of black bean sauce. "Dip it in this," said General Ma.

Beth dipped a piece in the sauce and put it in her mouth. She had no desire to do any more with it and had to force herself to chew.

"You handle chopsticks very well," said General Ma. "Most of the tourists don't"

"I had a lot of cheap dates in high school."

"Dates?"

"Nothing."

Beth felt herself sagging in the chair at the round table for eight, or maybe a dozen, where she sat alone with General Ma. He'd been given a private upstairs dining room. It wasn't a big room and it wasn't cheerful; the walls were lima-bean green, nothing hung on them, and the sole light, a ceiling fixture, was too bright.

"Good?" asked General Ma when she finished chewing. "Now wrap a piece in some of this green onion. It's even better."

She did what he said.

"Am I right?"

"Yes."

"What about something to drink? Chinese wine—which I don't recommend—or beer?"

"Beer."

"Pijiu," he said to the waiter, who returned with two bottles of Qingdao beer.

General Ma ate and drank heartily. Beth sensed that the whole multistoried building was eating and drinking heartily. Chopsticks clicked behind thin walls. Glasses clinked. Smells wafted up from below, smells Beth knew were delicious, but which didn't arouse her appetite. The General's big teeth mashed the juicy shreds of duck. Beth watched that for a while; then she slumped forward on the table, her head in her arms.

Silence. The waiter's knife stopped carving; the General's teeth stopped chewing. "What's wrong?" he asked. "Are you ill?"

"No."

"Not . . . weeping?"

"No." All the internal apparatus was in the weeping mode, but no tears came. "I just thought I'd find him, or some trace of him, in China, that's all."

General Ma touched her shoulder, but quickly took his hand away. "Cheer up," he said. "You've made a lot of progress."

Beth sat up. "How so?"

General Ma spoke briefly to the waiter, who hurried out of the room. "You've discovered that there are two trails in this case, a false one and a real one. All the signposts on the false trail point to Dr. Wu's being in China; these we can now ignore. Then what remains is to identify the tracks on the real trail and see where they lead."

"What are they?"

General Ma popped a roll of fatty duck skin in his mouth and replied, "The submarine, for one. No one was meant to see that. So it must be part of the real trail."

"But I've never been positive about my identification. The visibility was bad; it was all over in a few—"

"You didn't make a mistake," General Ma said. "We know it wasn't Chinese, so it's a certainty that the one tracked by your intelligence people was the right one."

"Then why do they insist it wasn't? Why do they insist it was Chinese?"

"Because everything else has been arranged to make it look Chinese. And because that interpretation accords with the leanings of certain people in Washington."

"Are you saying that some sort of right-wing American conspiracy kidnapped Teddy and set the whole thing up?"

He smiled. "Americans are always so suspicious of their own government. I very much doubt it was anything like that. Heavyweights like the U.S. government don't need to use long levers to move things around. This is a case of a lighter weight—a smart one—and a long lever."

"How can you say that if the sub was Russian?"

"I say it. We don't have all the facts yet."

"When will we?"

"Never. We won't need them. We only need to reach a critical mass; from there the answers come in an intuitive leap."

Beth remembered Y.K. Ling's Taoist MO. Was this the same method? "Do you just let the facts flow around you, is that it?"

"No," the General laughed. "I'm not a mystic." He stopped laughing and put down his chopsticks. "I'm a psychologist. I put myself in the minds of all the participants, and then I assume the basest motives." He smiled. A shred of duck skin was caught between his front teeth.

The waiter returned. Following him was a plump man in a stained white apron. The plump man didn't look happy. He approached the table warily, face shiny with sweat or kitchen grease or both.

"Do you recognize this man?" General Ma asked Beth.

The plump man's eyes shifted nervously to her. "No," she said.

"That surprises me." General Ma put the blue file on the table and took something from it. Beth leaned closer to see it. Their heads touched. They both drew back.

It was the *Chronicle* photograph of the touring chefs. There was Han Shih, once more looking her in the eye. That look dissipated the surface tension General Ma's nearness had caused. Beth studied the photograph. In the second row stood the plump man, looking much more at ease than he did now.

"The eight cooks have been located," said General Ma, "and

interviewed this afternoon. Five do not remember the woman you call Han Shih. Apparently this one does.''

General Ma turned to him, but said nothing. After ten or fifteen seconds of silence, the plump man blurted a high-pitched question, and pointed at the duck on the sideboard. General Ma waved his question aside. The plump man's face grew shinier.

''A skittish fellow,'' said General Ma. ''Too unreliable, I would have thought, for such a tour.'' He beckoned the plump man, who reluctantly came closer. General Ma showed him the photograph, and pointed out Han Shih. While the plump man looked at the picture, General Ma watched his face, glistening now like the duck on the sideboard. The plump man straightened. ''What should we ask him?'' General Ma said to Beth.

''What he remembers about her, I suppose. You're the expert.''

General Ma glanced quickly at her before questioning the plump man. The plump man replied. It was a long reply. General Ma listened carefully. So did Beth. She caught one word: *pijiu.*

General Ma translated: ''He says they were staying at a hotel. He doesn't remember the name. The bed was too soft. After lunch, they assembled for a photograph. The photographer was a young American woman—he says she looked something like you. She arranged the cooks in two rows. Then, just as she was about to take the picture, a Chinese woman slipped into the back row. The picture was taken. The woman went away.''

''Did she say anything?''

''No.''

''Did anyone question her?''

''No.''

''Why not?''

General Ma asked the plump man.

''I thinking there is reason,'' he said in English.

''What reason?''

The plump man had no answer.

''What about the photographer?'' Beth asked. ''She must have seen Han Shih in her viewfinder.'' The plump man had no answer to that, either. He shrugged his soft shoulders.

''The photographer, too, must have thought there was a reason,'' General Ma said to Beth. He looked at the cook in a dissatisfied sort of way that basted his face a little more and said to Beth: "Is there anything more you would like to ask?"

"What did he say about beer?"

"Beer?"

"*Pijiu.*"

General Ma laughed. "It was not germane. Or very gracious."

"I can take it."

"He said American beer was served at lunch. He thought it tasted like cat urine."

The cook left. The waiter came with tea. Beth and General Ma drank it. "You have a long face today," he said. "I wish you'd make a circle face."

"I don't feel like making a circle face."

General Ma fastened the top button of his black tunic. "I see," he said. He refilled their cups. They drank some more—General Ma sitting very straight at the table, feet together on the floor like a model pupil in a one-room schoolhouse, Beth slumped in her chair.

There was a long silence. Then General Ma said: "I was born during the Long March. Did you know that?"

"No."

"It's true. There were women on the Long March. I was born two days before the crossing of the Tatu River bridge. My mother carried me over." He stared into his teacup. "I've always thought Mao liked me because of that."

"Were you friends?"

General Ma seemed not to hear. He went on gazing into the cup. "Once he said to me, 'If the gods had feelings, heaven too would grow old.'" He looked up, into her eyes, the way he had looked into them in the plush back seat of the Red Flag.

Beth looked back. The Long March ended in 1935, but the only sign of General Ma's age was his white mustache. "How did he work that into the conversation?" she asked.

That struck a spark of anger in his eyes. It smoldered there while he smiled and said, "Some people forget Mao was a poet as well as a great revolutionary. This is something that you, coming from a land of professional politicians, cannot understand. There were times when it was like being ruled by T.S. Eliot."

"That bit about the gods sounds more like Rod McKuen to me."

"Excuse me. I am not familiar with his work."

Beth felt ashamed. She was full of zing, but it was all misdirected. "It was just a joke."

His eyes caught fire. "There is a time for joking and a time for not joking," he said; his tone was harsh, the undertone hectoring.

That was something Teddy would never say. The differences between the two men began to crystallize in her mind. Teddy was as smart as General Ma, but he never pontificated; not that he kept his opinions to himself, in the sense of playing close to the vest, or being canny. Teddy was uncanny. He was the uncanniest person she knew. Beth had never loved him more than at that moment. Maybe it was the comparison that did it. She felt a pulse in her groin, as though her conscience had relocated there.

"I'm sorry," she told the general. "You're right."

He nodded. "We have no time to waste." The fire in his eyes went out. "More tea?"

"Thank you."

He poured. They drank. "Good tea," he said.

"It is."

General Ma emptied his cup and put it through a series of maneuvers on the table before saying, "Did you enjoy our picnic?"

"I did."

"Perhaps we could do it again someday."

"I don't think so."

"No." General Ma stopped pushing his cup. "No," he repeated quietly. "Of course not."

General Ma's nephew came into the room, wearing a suede jacket and pleated trousers. He handed the general a sheet of paper, thick with Chinese writing. General Ma's eyes flickered over it: down and up, down and up. Then he lit a match and held it to one corner of the paper. It went yellow, the lines of the characters bent, smoke puffed up, then fire. General Ma dropped the burning paper on his plate. It turned to ashes.

"What was that?" Beth asked.

"A report from an old friend. A mathematician. One of the best we have. I asked him to look into Dr. Wu's work on Mordell's conjecture. Specifically, I wanted his evaluation on how useful knowledge of Dr. Wu's secret finding would be to us.''

"Why, if there's no chance he's in China?''

General Ma looked at her for a long moment and went on: "My friend says that Dr. Wu is a very great mathematician. Even before the work on Mordell's conjecture, my friend considered him one of the top two number theorists in the U.S. And now—''

"Who is the other one?''

General Ma glanced at the ashes on his plate. But only for a moment: He had a good memory. "A Dr. Kesselman, also at Berkeley.''

"Marty? I didn't know that.''

"You know Dr. Kesselman?''

"Yes.''

General Ma's nephew looked at his watch and said something in Chinese. The general nodded. "The main point my friend makes is that Dr. Wu's new findings, while interesting theoretically, would be of no practical use to us. Not for many years. We lack the equipment to set up a comprehensive intercepting network, and we lack the know-how to manufacture the kinds of decoding machines that would make use of Dr. Wu's discoveries.''

But hadn't Marty said the Chinese would want Teddy's findings—even more than the Russians?

"Is something wrong, Miss Hunter?

"No. I was trying to think who would want them.''

General Ma smiled. "Cui bono?''

"Cui bono.''

"There is only one answer to that.''

"But if Teddy's in Russia, why didn't he get off the *Timoshenko* in Petropavlovsk?''

"I don't know. I told you we need more facts. Now, if we're quick, we may be able to discover a few.'' He rose.

"Where are we going?''

"To test one of your ideas. We're going to meet Pei Ming.''

"You've found her?'' Beth was on her feet.

"Oh yes.''

"Where is she?''

"Somewhere safe.''

On the way out, General Ma's nephew swept the ashes off the plate and put them in his pocket.

"Why did you burn the report?" Beth asked.

General Ma sighed. "I told you the mathematician is an old friend. I value friendship."

His gnomishness made her impatient. "What do you mean. Are you in some kind of danger?"

General Ma's tone sharpened. "Are you being deliberately obtuse? Did I not mention we are engaged in a struggle for power?" He waited for a reply. Beth said nothing. "Perhaps not," he said, and went on more gently. "This struggle is intensifying because of Dr. Wu. Unless he is found it will soon reach a critical stage. Then my ability to use the power of my office will be threatened." A muscle jumped under the smooth skin of his cheek; Beth sensed the tension he was controlling. "And the leftists do not want him found. It would disturb them to think there was even a possibility of his being found. There is also a faction in your country that does not want him found, and possibly one in Russia as well. And surely in Taiwan."

All at once Beth knew the distance between their two worlds: not so much the difference between China and America, although that was part of it, but between his life and hers.

As they got into the Red Flag, she said: "Do your . . . rivals know I'm here?"

"Now you're back to your acute self." A fleeting smile crossed his face. "My answer is that there is no evidence they even know of your existence."

"But what's to stop them from finding out? You found out."

"I have access to the information apparatus of the state. And a good man in the Gong An Ju."

"Not that good. I was in that room for four days."

General Ma smiled again. This time it lingered on his face a little longer. "China is a Third World country. Don't expect the same ruthless efficiency you enjoy at home."

Beth smiled back. The emperor eyes glowed.

In the only Chinese opera Beth had seen, the emperor was poisoned in the last act.

30

West. She was always moving west, like a barque at the mercy of the trade winds. Looking for Teddy meant going west: first twenty miles offshore, then across the ocean, now farther still. But she never found him. One could keep going west all the way around the world, back to San Francisco. An empty apartment was waiting.

Now she had General Ma to help her. But she'd had a helper before. Albert Ling. She was hard on the help.

And maybe General Ma wouldn't be able to help, after all. In that case, she would need another plan. Sitting in the airplane, Beth had nothing to do but think of one. She thought.

The plane glided west over a sea of puffy gold. It was the same kind of plane that had taken her from Wuxi to Beijing: old and boxy, with a few rows of seats and empty cargo space behind. Beth was the only passenger. General Ma had gone up to the cockpit to sit with the pilot. Perhaps he wanted to use the radio, or to play aviator. Perhaps they had run out of talk.

Beth closed her eyes but didn't sleep. Hours went by. She thought of writing a postcard to her mother, with a picture of a panda, or the Forbidden City. Or the Great Wall. "Dear Mother, Love Beth." The rest wouldn't come. Some people could dash them off. Teddy, for example. She remembered his postcard from Washington, all about Giorgione and the color of her eyes. Then she recalled there'd been a panda on the front. One of the pandas at the Washington Zoo, of course. A perfectly natural choice. But it unsettled her. It made her think of Marty Kessel-man saying, "Did Teddy slip you the chloral hydrate?"

She opened her eyes. General Ma was watching her from the cockpit door. "Thirty minutes," he said, and went back inside.

The engines changed pitch. The plane's nose dipped and sank into the clouds, filling the cabin with gilded, hazy light: Giorgione's never-never-land light. Gravity pulled the plane down.

It broke through the clouds into a lead sky. Below lay a barren world: dirt-brown hills, twisting olive-brown valleys, bleak depressions dusted with salt. Qinghai Province, where Mr. An had met Reverend Huang: the never-never land of the labor camps.

The plane flew over a brown-and-gray town and landed on a dirt strip. Beth and General Ma got out. A dusty wind blew in their faces. "It gets very hot in summer and very cold in winter," General Ma shouted into it. "This is the best time of year."

"If you have to be here at all." Talking made her breathless. The air was very thin.

General Ma heard her but said nothing. It must have been the wrong time for joking.

An open jeep drove up, rusty and dented. The driver was a teenager in army green. He spoke deferentially to General Ma. The general climbed into the jeep beside him. Beth sat in back. The seat was torn and covered with dust. A jerry can cramped her feet. Shifting it, she caught the boy glancing at her in the rearview mirror.

General Ma saw it too. He said something to the boy, just three or four quiet syllables. The boy bowed over the steering wheel and started the motor. A blue vein jumped in the back of his hand.

The boy drove them across country untouched by any of the colors of the rainbow. Dust swirled round like a moving cocoon as they followed a bumpy dirt track west from the town.

After an hour, the track climbed a range of jagged, stony hills and slanted down the other side. The deepest pockets between the hills sheltered patches that might have looked green under a sunny sky.

"Springtime," said General Ma, squinting at Beth through the dust. He had a sprinkling of it on his mustache.

Groups of men were bent over whatever was growing, worrying at it with hoes. They weren't Chinese, but slighter and wirier, with skin the colors of Havana cigars. Some wore ragged turbans; a few had skullcaps embroidered in mosaic patterns. They looked up as the jeep passed by, and stopped everything when they saw Beth.

A brown plain lay ahead. Seen from the hills, it could have been a land of rivers and sparkling lakes. But as they rode across it the lakes turned to dry salt beds, the rivers lines of polished stones. An animal like a groundhog twitched its nose as the jeep went by.

A black needle quivered in the distance. Slowly it grew, assuming bulk and finally form: a man on horseback, also moving west. Soon Beth could make out a second man following on foot, hands behind his back like a philosopher on a long walk.

The jeep overtook them and stopped. Rider, horse, and walker were shrouded in dust. The rider wore a green uniform like the boy's but he looked older and tougher. He had a machine gun slung over one shoulder. The horse had been overheated not long before: Lines of caked salt scarred its flanks. The philosopher was barefoot and in tatters. He had steel cuffs around his wrists. Blood had trickled from one of his ears, but it was dry now, a spidery brown blot on the side of his neck.

The rider spoke to the boy, who dug out a canteen from under the seat and handed it to him. The rider tilted his head back and drank; his throat bobbed like a pump. He gave the canteen to the boy. The philosopher watched it go back and forth.

They drove on. "Sometimes they run away," said General Ma. "But there is nowhere to go in Qinghai." Beth looked back. The three figures were already shadows in a cloud of dust.

"General Ma?"

"Yes."

"Something happened in Shanghai I think I should tell you about."

He turned. "What?"

Beth told him about the arrest of the curio man.

"Don't worry. It had nothing to do with you."

"But I saw him again in Wuxi."

"Who?" he asked impatiently.

Beth described the man with the saintly hands. Impatience faded from the General's face. An aggressive look replaced it.

"Why didn't you tell me this before?"

"I didn't know what to make of it."

"All the more reason to tell me."

"What's wrong? Do you know him?"

"Of course I know him."

Beth waited for him to continue. When he didn't, she asked: "Who is he?"

"The assistant director of my department." General Ma paused. "He was the director in Mao's time."

"Who is the director now?"

"I am."

"I don't understand. Is he working with you on this?"

General Ma's voice rose. "Against me. How often must I explain? The man you saw is one of the leading leftists in the party." General Ma turned away from her and stared into the distance.

"What's his name?"

"It would mean nothing to you."

Beth bit back an angry phrase. Instead she said: "If you're the director, can't you get rid of him?"

General Ma barked a bitter laugh but didn't reply.

After a while, low hills appeared on the horizon. The sky grew darker. Beth looked at her watch: almost eleven P.M. "What time is it?"

"Ten fifty-three."

"Not Beijing time. I mean here."

"Ten fifty-three. The whole country is on Beijing time." His back stiffened, perhaps in anticipation of another joke. But Beth wasn't in a joking mood.

It was not quite fully dark when they reached the hills. Rows of mud buildings stood at their base, extending in both directions as far as Beth could see. So did the barbed wire: two fences of it, and more between the fences, coiled like snakes.

The boy drove to a gate. A big truck was ahead of them. It had high sides but no top, and was packed with standing people, mostly men, with no room to move. They were coal-black, except for the whites of their eyes. A guard stood in a tower by the gate, counting them. He waved the truck through. It drove inside. Another truck drove out. It too had high sides and a full load of people. The only difference was that they weren't black.

"Miners," said General Ma. "Changing shift."

The jeep entered the compound and parked before a mud building somewhat taller then the rest. General Ma went inside. Beth watched the blackened miners file by. They were all very thin. Their twisted hands hung like heavy burdens at their sides. One or two saw Beth; their eyes registered nothing.

General Ma came out of the mud building with a soldier at his side. He didn't seem to notice the miners straggling past, a few yards away. Beth realized she was glaring at him. He didn't seem to notice that, either.

He climbed into the jeep. The soldier hung on the side and directed the driver to a mud hut with a crude corrugated-steel chimney.

The miners were shuffling past the open door, each holding a tin bowl. A woman in a faded blue jacket stood in the doorway, behind a trestle table. On the table were two big black pots. One contained rice; the other, a thin brown liquid. The woman ladled one helping of rice and one of the brown liquid into each tin bowl. She didn't look at the miners; her eyes went from one bowl to the next.

The miners didn't have chopsticks. They didn't have chairs. They raised the bowls to their faces and ate where they stood. Then they moved off down the long row of barracks, empty bowls in their hands. One or two looked back at the big black pots.

When the last miner had gone away, the woman dragged the trestle table inside. She emerged a moment later with a bamboo-handled broom and swept at the dirt in front of the hut. Mr. Lao had a broom just like it.

The soldier tilted his chin at the serving woman. "Pei Ming," he said to General Ma.

The General turned to Beth. "I heard him," she said before he could speak.

General Ma spoke to the driver. The boy nodded. "Come," General Ma said to Beth. They got out of the jeep. It drove away. They walked toward the woman. She looked up.

Pei Ming was short and squat. She had a thick trunk, thick limbs, and a thick face. She was built for resisting change. But, drawing closer, Beth saw that change had had its way with her anyway. Pei Ming's hair was white and stringy, with patches of skull showing through. She had swollen eyelids and watery eyes, and a rough white scar on her neck. She hunched behind her broom, waiting for trouble.

"Pei Ming?" said General Ma.

The woman answered in a guttural, querulous voice. Her teeth were soft brown stumps.

General Ma spoke to her. Beth caught nothing but two names: Taihu and Wu Tun-li.

With a harsh cry, Pei Ming fell to her knees and clutched the hem of General Ma's black tunic. Her hands were twisted grappling tools, like the miners'. General Ma tried to back away, but she held on, crawling after him like a performer in a sick dance, peering up at his disgusted face through watery eyes.

"What's wrong?"

General Ma tore himself free. Pei Ming uttered a raspy wail and pounded her head in the dirt. "She thinks she's going to be tried again."

Pei Ming thumped her head on the ground once more. Beth knelt and put her hand on Pei Ming's back. She felt bone and knots of flesh; Pei Ming didn't appear to feel her at all. Beth took her hand away.

General Ma spoke. He sounded annoyed. Pei Ming made a questioning noise. The General said something. Pei Ming responded, quiet, incredulous. Clumsily, she got to her feet. She looked at General Ma and at Beth, and then at the sky.

Beth looked up too. Night had fallen. The cloud bank had broken up. Hard white stars blinked down, reminding people of their insignificance. Pei Ming probably couldn't see them, but it didn't matter: She didn't need the stars to tell her that.

They entered the hut. It was dark inside. Beth stayed in the doorway. She heard Pei Ming shuffling across the dirt floor. A match was struck, an oil lamp lit. Flickering light drove the darkness into the corners, illuminating the little room: blackened stove, trestle table, stool, and a raised board covered with a blanket for sleeping.

Pei Ming, General Ma, and Beth stood around the oil lamp. General Ma reached into his tunic and took out a packet of tea. He handed it to Pei Ming. She held it to her nose and sniffed deeply before going to the stove. She filled a pot with water from a bucket on the floor and began heating it. When it boiled she dropped in three pinches of tea, carefully closed the packet, and tucked it away. She poured the tea into three tin cups, which she put on the trestle table. Wisps of steam rose, and for a few moments the smell of tea overcame the other smells in the hut: oily smoke, burnt rice, dried sweat.

Pei Ming waited for General Ma to reach for his cup. Then

she picked up hers, raised it to her lips, and sipped. She sighed, and cradled the cup against her breast like a baby.

Beth drank. The tea was weak, the cup very hot. She put it on the table. Pei Ming didn't seem to feel the hot metal. Neither did General Ma.

He emptied his cup. Pei Ming refilled it, but he didn't pick it up. Instead he looked at her across the trestle table and said: "Wu Tun-li."

Pei Ming cradled her cup and said nothing. "Wu Tun-li," General Ma repeated in a sharper tone.

The cup began to shake in Pei Ming's hands. Tea overlapped the edge and spilled down the front of her jacket. "Wu Tun-li," she said, so softly the name could hardly be heard. General Ma leaned forward, into the yellow lamplight. It shone on his emperor eyes. He waited for more.

But no more came. There wasn't a sound in the room; no sound anywhere in the camp. It was as quiet as the most peaceful spot on earth.

Beth took the pot and walked around the table. Pei Ming shrank away. Beth reached out and refilled her cup. The watery eyes looked up at her. Something shifted in them, deep down, like fish below the surface.

"Tell us about Wu Tun-li," Beth said quietly. "Wu Tun-li and Taihu."

Pei Ming's mouth opened. Beth was listening so hard she could hear the wick burning in the lamp. But instead of words, a croaking sob bubbled out of Pei Ming's throat. And then more: hacking sobs ripped loose from deep inside. Other sounds followed; these might have been words.

"What is she saying?"

General Ma had backed away. On his face was the look he'd had when Pei Ming clutched his tunic. "She says she didn't mean to kill him."

"But she didn't kill him." Then Beth had a thought that drove a shaft of ice down her spine. "Was he here? Did they kill him in the mines?" She moved toward General Ma, barely stopping herself from grabbing his tunic.

He backed up another step. "Control yourself. She is talking about long ago."

Pei Ming's sobs subsided. Then words came, gushing out as though a long-blocked passage had been cleared. General Ma's eyes locked on Pei Ming's face. They sucked the golden light from the lamp and glowed with it.

After a few minutes, the words ceased. Pei Ming rubbed her sleeve across her gummy eyes. General Ma turned to Beth. ''The woman is confused.''

''What did she say?''

''It hardly bears repeating.''

''What did she say?''

''She says she didn't mean to kill him. She seems to be talking about her intentions, not actual events. The actual events aren't clear. She keeps saying that the gods did not believe her. They believed she meant to smother him under a red pavilion. She thinks that's why she's here—it's the punishment of the gods. She is a very ignorant woman.''

Pei Ming had been listening to him. Now, her dim eyes shifting to Beth, she spoke. Her voice was low and thick.

''She says she never killed anyone. Not the baby. Not the others.''

''What others?''

''Who knows? These are just ravings.''

''Ask her.''

General Ma looked at Beth coldly, but he asked.

''*Shan-chu*,'' Pei Ming murmured.

Abruptly all emotion drained from General Ma's eyes; they became pure instruments of sight. ''The Master of the Mountain,'' he translated for Beth. He was murmuring too.

One of Pei Ming's misshapen hands strayed to her shoulder and rubbed it as though it pained her. She added a few words.

''And his wife,'' General Ma said. ''They were both killed at the lake house.''

''What does she mean by the Master of the Mountain?''

General Ma stared at the burning wick. ''It is a secret-society title. The Master of the Mountain is the chief.''

''A secret society like the Brotherhood of the Green Snake?''

The general nodded. Then he sank into stillness, eyes fixed unblinkingly on the burning wick.

Beth was thinking too. She thought about Teddy's father. Somehow she had no trouble believing he'd been leader of the Brotherhood of the Green Snake. In Pei Ming's shadowy hut in the mud prison camp it was easy to believe anything. It was easy to believe that Rex Heidemann and Jimmy Han had murdered the Master of the Mountain. It was easy to believe that Pei Ming had brought the orphaned baby to Helen Brock, and that Helen had taken him to the States. Much harder to believe was what she'd seen with her own eyes: the hungry miners clutching the little rice bowls in their maimed and blackened hands.

General Ma was looking at her. "It's time to go."

"Go? But there's much more to find out."

"For example?"

"Why they were killed, for one thing."

General Ma smiled. His smile didn't look complicated in the oil lamp's flickering light. It looked savage: a savage smile in a civilized face. "That is certainly the question," he said. "But this woman will not know the answer."

"Ask her anyway."

General Ma stopped smiling. He spoke to Pei Ming. She replied. Whatever she said seemed to puzzle him.

"Did the gardener Lao mention seeing a woman on the day of the killings?"

"No. Just Rex Heidemann, Jimmy Han, and some other men. Why?"

"She says the Master of the Mountain and his wife were killed by the Master's concubine. The concubine hated the Master's wife."

"Concubine?"

"She says he had a concubine in Shanghai."

"What was her name?"

But Pei Ming didn't know. She didn't remember what the concubine looked like. She wasn't even sure the concubine had been at the lake house on the day of the killings.

"Then how can she say the concubine killed them?"

"I don't know," General Ma said. "But it probably doesn't matter. At least now I have something to work with." He moved closer to the lamp so Pei Ming could see him better, and spoke to her. The old woman nodded vigorously. Then he turned to Beth, said, "Come," and walked out the door.

Pei Ming's head continued to nod slightly. Beth extended her hand across the table. At first, Pei Ming didn't know what to do with it; she stared at it, cradling her tin cup. Then, very slowly, she reached out and took Beth's hand, lightly and only for a moment. Pei Ming's hand felt like a grindstone.

"Good-bye," Beth said.

Pei Ming said nothing. She took up her bamboo-handled broom and started sweeping. Beth went outside.

The moon had risen, a full moon that had the look of a face still developing in a darkroom tray. General Ma was gazing at it.

"What did you say to her?" Beth asked.

"I insured the privacy of our conversation."

"How did you do that?"

General Ma said nothing. He watched the moon.

"Mr. Lao informed on Mr. An and me, didn't he?"

"It was his wife, actually. I thought you knew."

"How would I have known?"

"Wasn't it obvious?"

"Maybe to you."

General Ma kept looking at the moon. "It seems to be a habit with her, actually. According to the records, it was she who denounced Pei Ming, during the Cultural Revolution."

Beth felt breathless. She inhaled deeply. The air was full of dust. "On what grounds?"

"Something about association with bad elements. The records aren't clear." He stopped gazing at the moon and turned his eyes on her. "We're not sufficiently computerized yet. In any case, her sentence ended several years ago."

"Then what's she still doing here?"

"Many ex-prisoners remain as paid employees."

"By choice?"

"Choice?" The jeep drove up. "She has been here too long to live anywhere else."

They got in the jeep and drove out of the camp. No lights shone anywhere. There was only silvery moonlight, falling on mud barracks and sparkling on barbed wire.

"What sort of machinery is used in the mines?" Beth asked.

"Machines are still scarce in China. We cannot allocate large quantities to reform-through-labor camps."

We. The word chilled her. She shivered. General Ma shivered too.

They drove across the plain. The wind was strong and cold. Beth huddled in the back seat, but after about fifteen minutes she sat up and raised her voice above the wind. "Stop. I want to go back."

"Back?"

"I want to describe Han Shih to her and see what she says." General Ma thought. "All right."

They drove back, past the barbed wire, through the gate, along the row of mud huts. The boy parked in front of the one with the corrugated-steel chimney. Beth and General Ma got out. She knocked on the flimsy door. There was no answer. General Ma pushed it open and they went inside.

The oil lamp was no longer burning. General Ma lit a match. In its dim light they saw Pei Ming lying on the sleeping platform, dressed as she's been before they left. It was cold in the hut, but she hadn't bothered to cover herself with the blanket; it lay crumpled on the floor.

General Ma called to her. Her eyes remained closed. He called again, more loudly, but Pei Ming didn't wake up. They went closer. General Ma tapped her shoulder. Then, suddenly, he bent forward and turned her over.

The back of Pei Ming's head was crushed.

"Quick," he shouted, and began running toward the door. The hut went black. Beth didn't move. She was staring at the patch of darkness where Pei Ming's bloody head was. General Ma grabbed her arm and pulled her, stumbling, through the door. She saw a gun in his free hand, felt him push her into the jeep, heard him yell at the boy.

The jeep shot away. Beth lay on the floor. Above her General Ma kneeled over the seat, the gun in his hands, his eyes sweeping the darkness.

The wind howled. Dust blocked the moon and the stars. The jeep raced across the plain. Beth couldn't stop shivering.

They came to the airstrip. The plane was waiting. General Ma ran up the staircase, pulling her along. The plane started rolling before they were in their seats.

Beth shivered all the way back to Beijing.

31

As the plane descended on Beijing, General Ma came back into the cabin. He'd spent the whole flight in the cockpit, talking on the radio. At first he spoke in sharp bursts that sounded like questions, then in calmer, declarative rhythms, and finally in terse statements that might have been commands.

"Did you sleep?" he asked Beth.

"No."

"A good soldier sleeps whenever he can."

Beth said nothing. General Ma looked out the window; it was a methodical look, as though the airport were marked in a grid pattern and his eyes were scanners.

"What are you looking for?"

"Nothing in particular." But he kept looking until the wheels touched the ground.

Beijing was warmer than Qinghai province. The sun filtered down through dusty haze, bringing a very faint reminder of spring. But still Beth couldn't stop shivering.

The Red Flag was waiting at the end of a runway. General Ma's nephew was wearing penny loafers, gray flannels, and a button-down shirt with a sleeveless sweater, but the button-down buttons weren't fastened and he was biting his lip. He handed the General a bundle of files. Beth sank into red plush. It didn't make her any warmer. The General sat beside her, flipping through the files as the car moved off.

"What are those?" Beth asked.

General Ma pulled out a pink sheet covered with Chinese writing and studied it. He didn't answer her question. He finished with the pink sheet, examined a blue one and then another

264

pink one. ''What exactly was Rex Heidemann's reaction when you questioned him?'' he asked without looking up.

''At first he was annoyed, I guess. He didn't think any good could come of digging up the past. But then he told me about his conversation with Teddy. Teddy said he wanted to trace his roots. Heidemann told him all the children they had brought over were orphans with no relatives they'd been able to find, so that tracing his roots would be impossible.''

''He didn't get angry? Or threaten you?''

''No. Why? What's in the files?''

''Dr. Wu's roots. He has very interesting roots, in a political sense.''

''Tell me.''

''Not now. There is still research to do, and I only have until two-thirty.''

''What happens at two-thirty?''

''I meet with the Premier.''

''But do you know where Teddy is? Just tell me that.''

''Not yet, but I'm closer to knowing. I need more documents.''

''Do you know where to find them?''

''Oh yes. If they haven't been destroyed.''

They came to an intersection of two broad streets. A traffic cop held up his hand, but General Ma's nephew sounded the horn and drove through. ''Is that why Pei Ming was killed?'' Beth asked. ''Destruction of evidence?''

General Ma looked up from a file. ''Of course. But I was one step ahead.''

Beth felt colder than she ever had in her life, except for the night in the water. Her hand began to hurt.

They dropped her off in the center of the city, at Tiananmen Square. ''Don't worry,'' said General Ma. ''See the sights. My nephew will come for you at three.''

Beth hesitated.

''There are lots of tourists here. You'll be safe. By three we will all be safe.''

Beth got out. The General began closing the door, but she grabbed the handle. ''Has Mr. An been released yet?''

''Mr. An?'' he said impatiently.

''The violin player.''

General Ma's nephew spoke from the front seat.

"He has not yet been located," said General Ma.

"How can that be?"

"I have no time to discuss it. Three o'clock. Here by the gate." He closed the door. His nephew stepped on the gas, buttoning his button-down collar as the car sped away.

General Ma was right: There were lots of tourists in Tiananmen Square. But they didn't make her feel safe. The vast space scaled them down to nomad bands wandering the Sahara. Beth wandered too. She crossed the square once or twice. No one seemed interested in her. She stared at the huge government buildings surrounding the square. One of them, she knew, was called the Great Hall of the People, but that didn't fool her. Tiananmen Square was a demonstration in concrete and stone of the relative proportions of citizen and state.

For a while Beth followed one tour group or another, but she couldn't keep her mind on what the guides were saying. She walked to the southern end of the square, past a fleet of tour buses, and onto a busy street. A woman was selling bottled drinks from a cart by the side of the road. Beth was approaching her when a Red Flag limousine passed by, escorted by motorcycles. She looked to see if General Ma was in it. He wasn't. Two men were in the back. One was the Premier of China. The other was a hollow-faced man, inhaling a cigarette. He held it to his lips in long, El Greco fingers.

He was gazing out the window. He took in the drinks cart, the seller, Beth. For an instant his eyes met hers. Then the car flashed by. It was fifty or sixty yards beyond her when his head whipped around for a second look.

Beth turned away and barely stopped herself from running. She bent over the cart, pretending to select a drink. The woman waited for her to make a choice. Beth looked around. The Red Flag was out of sight. She walked quickly back to the square, feeling the eyes of the drinks seller on her back.

Beth found a big tour and fell in with it. "On your left," said the guide, "is the Monument to the People's Heroes. The obelisk is thirty-six meters high. The cornerstone was laid by Chairman Mao himself, and this inscription is written in his own calligraphy."

"What's it say?" someone called.

"I'm sorry?"

"The inscription. What's it say?"

"It says, 'The heroes of the People are immortal.' "

"Oh."

Beth looked at her watch. 2:20. General Ma was supposed to meet the Premier of China in ten minutes. But the Premier was riding in a limousine with the hollow-faced man.

The tourists began moving toward a bus. Beth moved with them and sat on a bench. The tourists got on. The bus went away, leaving a wide gap in front of her. She could see right across the square.

A group of soldiers was walking across it. They were big men, northern Chinese, with deep chests and strong limbs. Beth felt the vibrations their boots made on the stones as they came closer. They passed right by her, not marching, but not strolling either, their eyes straight ahead. An envelope dropped in her lap.

She opened it. Inside was a sheet of paper with four words on it, printed in blue ink: *Go to the pingfang.* Beth looked up. The soldiers were moving off down the street.

General Ma had told her that a *pingfang* was a traditional Chinese flat-house. There was only one she knew specifically. She looked at her watch. 2:33. There was no signature on the note, nothing to indicate its sender, other than the message itself. She decided to wait.

She waited. She saw tourists, guides, soldiers. No one seemed to be watching her, but she felt watched all the same. At 2:55 she went to the gate. A Red Flag went by; a soldier was driving and no one was in the back. 3:00. 3:05. 3:10. At 3:15 she started looking for a taxi. There were none.

She left the square and began walking down a street. It was busy, with buses, cyclists, trucks, a few private cars, pedestrians. But no taxi. She walked for two blocks, two long blocks, before she came to a huge building, or rather three huge buildings joined together. BEIJING HOTEL, said the sign. It had three entrances. She took the middle one.

Inside was a lobby, carpeted in stained purple. Dozens of Africans were lost in one corner, drinking beer. Beth crossed the lobby and spoke to the clerk behind the desk.

"I want a taxi."

"Yes. To go where?"

"The Great Wall."

The clerk consulted his watch. He double-checked with the

clock on the wall. It was definitely 3:58. "But it is not possible," he said.

"Why not?"

He pursed his lips. "Soon it will be very late." He showed her the dial of his watch. "Night," he went on. "Too dark to see anything. It's much better to go in the morning. And there is a bus. Not so expensive."

"But I've always wanted to see the Great Wall at sunset."

The clerk blinked.

"And I've come all this way."

He let a little sigh escape his nostrils. "I will try." He picked up a phone. "Wei," he said into it. "Wei, wei, wei." Then he added something else. He listened, put down the phone, and shook his head. "He says it is not possible."

"Who?"

"The man from the taxi-drivers' *danwei*."

Beth considered asking to speak to the man directly and repeating her performance. But he might not speak English, and even if he did, she sensed her chances would be poor. So she said, "Thank you," and went outside.

Five or six taxis were lined up by the entrance. Beth returned to the desk, where she'd seen a stack of brochures. The clerk gave her an encouraging smile. She found a brochure with a picture of the Great Wall on the front and took it outside.

She showed it to the taxi drivers. The first three looked at her incredulously and shook their heads. The fourth was sleeping. Beth tapped on his windshield. He woke up. She pointed to the brochure and made driving motions.

"The Great Wall?" he said. "Very expensive."

"How much?"

"Thirty-two yuan."

Beth found the money in her handbag and gave it to him. He filled out a receipt and handed it to her. She got into the cab. He turned the key and sped into traffic. Cyclists rang their bells angrily.

"Your English is very good," Beth said.

"Yes, yes," the driver answered. But he didn't feel like using it.

The taxi followed the road north from Beijing. After a while it climbed into green hills and ran along a stony ridge. In the valley below, Beth saw the fast-flowing stream; now, with the sun sinking in the sky, it was cast in shadow. Shadowy women washed clothes in it. Shadowy men fished with hand-held lines. The flat-houses built with stones scavenged from the Great Wall threw slaloming black versions of themselves across the hillsides.

The sun dropped out of sight. In the interregnum between day and night, the sky went crazy with color. Down below, the land grew darker. Beth worried she would miss the overgrown dirt track. "Slow down a little," she said to the driver. He didn't seem to hear. "Slow down."

"Yes, yes." But he didn't.

The taxi mounted a steep hill. From the top, Beth could just see the Wall. The last rays of the sun made red sawteeth of the tops of the battlements. Beth rolled down her window and squinted at the roadside.

"Stop!"

He kept driving.

"Stop here!" The second time she spoke loudly enough to make him pull over and turn round to look at her.

"Something is wrong?"

"I have to get out. Wait here for me."

"I'm not very clear."

"Toilet. I have to use the toilet."

"Ah."

Taking her handbag, Beth got out and walked toward the dirt track. She looked back. The taxi was already merging with the darkened earth and the driver was a faint silhouette inside. But she could tell from his posture he was watching her. She followed the track up the slope and started down the other side.

Beth heard the narrow stream flowing over its stony bed. Then the *pingfang* came in sight, a blur at the bottom of the hill, darker than the surrounding shrubs. No lights showed. Again she looked back. There was nothing to see but the dark mass of the hill rising behind her.

She walked down to the *pingfang*. Grass rustled under her feet. Outside the heavy door she stopped and listened. All she could hear was water rubbing stones. She knocked lightly.

The door opened. A tall man stood in the shadows on the other side. For one moment, Beth thought he was Teddy. Then she recognized him: General Ma's nephew.

He had changed. His hair was cut short, his mustache shaved

off, and he wore baggy work clothes instead of his button-down shirt and gray flannels. He looked past her, into the falling night.

"Did anyone follow you?" His voice was high and thin.

"I don't think so. What's wrong?"

"How did you get here?"

"Taxi."

"Where is the taxi?"

"Waiting by the road. Why? What's happened?"

"My uncle . . ."

"Yes?"

"He's been arrested." The word shook his voice. "If only you had come earlier."

"I got here as soon as I could."

"Not tonight. If only you had come to China earlier." His voice was so pinched the words barely squeezed out.

"Who arrested him?"

"I don't understand your question."

"Why was he arrested, then?"

"He needed more time."

"That's not—" She stopped herself. "Is there something I can do?"

The nephew made a sharp, squeaky sound. She didn't know what it meant. "No," he said. "There is nothing you can do. He told me to give you this." He thrust an envelope into her hand.

Beth started ripping the envelope open. "Is there a light?"

"Not now, " he said. "There is no time. You must leave China."

"When?"

"Now. Tonight. There is a midnight flight to Hong Kong. Go directly to the airport."

"Is the car here? My suitcase is in it."

"Suitcase?" The word flew into the darkness like a scared bird. "The car is gone," he continued in a harsh whisper. "Seized." He thought for a minute. "Is your passport in the suitcase?" His voice was full of fear. She caught it from him.

"No, I've got it. But won't they be waiting for me at the airport?"

"Not yet." But the fear in his voice spoke louder than the words.

"What about you?"

He was silent.

"Are you going to hide here?"

Again she heard the squeak in his throat. "There is nowhere to hide in China." He closed the door.

Beth stood outside. She put her hand on the door, took it away. She started walking back to the road.

The moon was up now, a little less than full, as though slowly averting its face. High cumulus clouds blew across it; their shadows swooped over the earth like huge rays at the bottom of the sea. Beth's walk became a stumbling run—up the slope and down to the road.

The taxi was gone.

32

The night was quiet. Beth heard nothing but her own breathing. Inhaling was a sucking through the nostrils, exhaling a puffing through the mouth. She looked in every direction. Nothing moved except the rays, racing uphill and down.

She was an hour and a half from Beijing. By car. And she didn't know the way.

She ran back to the *pingfang* and knocked on the door. No answer. She knocked a few more times, then tried the handle. The door opened.

"Hello?" she whispered.

No reply.

She went in. It was black as a mine. "Hello?" She stared into the darkness, listening. It wasn't the kind of room where some-one was sleeping. It was the kind of room someone had left.

Beth felt her way inside it. She found a table, chairs, a gas burner with an unlit pilot light, dishes on a shelf, and a sleeping platform in one corner. But she didn't find a light, or anything to make one with. She was on her way outside when something brushed her face. A cord. She pulled it, and a ceiling light came on.

General Ma's *pingfang* looked like a summer cottage. It had a wooden floor, woven rugs, and dust balls in the corner. Beth sat on the sleeping platform and opened the envelope.

Inside she found a letter and a black-and-white photograph. The photograph was an aerial view of a man and a woman. They were lying naked on a blanket spread on top of a wide stone wall in hilly country. It was better than a satellite photograph. The faces weren't merely identifiable by race—one yellow, one white—but as individuals as well. The woman was smiling.

272

Beth remembered the little plane flying slowly overhead. Someone had seen her land on the outlying runway at Beijing Airport, and followed General Ma's Red Flag to the Great Wall. But how had anyone known she'd come on the plane from Wuxi? There was only one answer: It came to her mind in the image of a steel-gray car.

Don't expect ruthless efficiency, General Ma had said. But the hollow-faced man had demonstrated it. She recognized the links—the smashed figurine, the buff-colored immigration form, the curio man—that had led him to her. Mr. Lao's wife had saved her by calling the Gong An Ju. Even so, the hollow-faced man almost caught her in Wuxi. Now he had the field to himself.

A little unsteadily, she unfolded the letter. It was neatly handwritten in black ink, and bore no date or salutation.

If this is in your hands you are in danger. Leave at once.

The enclosed came anonymously, an hour ago. It is an invitation to suicide. In other words, it was sent by a friend, who knew it will be taken as irrefutable evidence of collusion with an American spy.

I don't have time to give you all the facts, but you must

The light went out.

Beth sat very still on the sleeping platform, General Ma's letter in her hand. She heard nothing but metallic ticks from the cooling filament.

The bulb might have burned out. It might have been a power failure. Perhaps the generator was shut off every night. They were all possibilities. But Beth stood up and walked quietly to the door.

She heard the sound of running water and nothing more. She went outside. The night was still. She walked down to the stream, took off her shoes, and waded across. Before, the water had been cold; now she didn't feel it at all. She moved through the knee-high grass on the other side and climbed the steep rise. Beyond lay General Ma's favorite section of the Wall. The night hid its decrepitude; it might still have been in use. Beth turned her back on it and lay prone in the hilltop grass.

From there, she could look down at the stream, shimmering in the moonlight, the low bulk of the *pingfang*, and beyond it the dirt track leading to the road.

Beth lay in the tall grass. The moon slipped down the dome of the sky. The land darkened. Once or twice her eyes began to close.

The moon had almost sunk behind the hills when Beth heard the sound of a distant motor. She squirmed down into the ground and watched the opposite hilltop.

The engine noises came closer. Beth sorted out the beats of its rhythm and decided there might be more than one car. In the next instant four yellow beams probed up at the sky. Then they arced quickly down and shone in her eyes: two sets of headlights cresting the rise.

Beth huddled into the earth. She felt her heart beating against it. The lights bobbed down the slope, leaving her in darkness. First one set of beams found the *pingfang*, then the other. Then they stopped bobbing, illuminating the house in their steady glare.

Metal doors opened and closed. Armed silhouettes moved toward the *pingfang*. The wooden door crashed open. The silhouettes disappeared. Hard boots trod the floor. Silence. Then the silhouettes returned, crisscrossing in the lights. Beth heard low voices. The lights were switched off. Little beams flashed on in their place.

The little beams poked light around the *pingfang*. One moved toward the stream. It shone on the flowing water and slid across, through the knee-high grass and up the hill, zigzagging methodically toward Beth. It lit a bush a few feet from her head, rested on it, then zigzagged back down.

The little lights moved together like clustering stars. They went out. The headlights came on. They turned away and pointed up the far slope. The beams bounced up to the top and disappeared. The sound of the motors died away.

Beth stayed where she was. The sky began to lose its blackness. For a few moments there was no sky at all. It came back purple, streaked with yellow and green and banded with fire in the east. Then the sun came up and restored order.

Beth waited. Dew coated the grass she lay in, dampening her clothes. She sat up and looked around. The door of the *pingfang* hung open. A big crow batted its way across the sky. Nothing else moved.

She heard a motor. It drew nearer. But nothing came over the opposite slope. The sound faded into a silence that was soon

broken by another motor, then another, later a chorus of them:
tour buses on the way to the Great Wall.

Beth opened General Ma's letter.

you must go to Taiwan. I am certain that Dr. Wu is there.

The files I've examined contain information on two
events—Dr. Wu's emigration from China as a baby and his
disappearance from the U.S. As you have already surmised,
these events cannot be unconnected.

The Brotherhood of the Green Snake dates from the early
nineteenth century, when it was not wholly criminal, as it is
now. In the 1920s it became a supporter of the Kuomintang.
The Party infiltrated it about the same time, so we have de-
tailed records of its activities prior to Liberation.

The Brotherhood backed the Kuomintang almost to the end
of the fighting. But in December 1948, the head of the Brotherhood—the Master of the Mountain—secretly approached the
Party with an offer to switch its support to us, in return for
certain concessions after our victory. His proposal was accepted, as were all like proposals at the time. The secret societies were dealt with after Liberation.

Before allegiance was formally changed, however, the head
of the Brotherhood disappeared. His second-in-command assumed leadership. The agreement was abrogated. The head
of the Brotherhood was named Wu, as you know. The second-in-command was named Han Jimin.

There is no mention of Rex Heidemann in reports filed by
our agent within the Brotherhood during that period. But his
name appears in another file, dating from the winter of 1947.
It is labeled "Known or Suspected Agents of Foreign Powers."

Han Jimin is still head of the Brotherhood, but passes as a
legitimate businessman in Taipei. The Brotherhood is based
in Taiwan, and has prospered despite its illegality, which in-
dicates it has maintained its ties to the Kuomintang.

Dr. Wu's inquiries threatened to expose this information.
But he wasn't simply killed. He was used—to foster strife between China and the U.S. This plan depended on American
belief that he was in China. What bothers me is that the proof
of his being in China does not seem substantial enough. I can-

not help but think more definitive proof will be offered. That is why I am sure he is alive, but in what state, I do not know.

Cui bono? Taiwan, of course, but Russia too. Even if you hadn't seen the submarine, we could have deduced it was Russian. Russia benefits from any split between China and the U.S. They also have a use for Dr. Wu's mathematical discoveries. But Dr. Wu was not on the submarine when it reached Russia. We can conclude that he must have been taken elsewhere, perhaps first transferred to another craft at sea. Elsewhere can only be Taiwan.

How can Russia and Taiwan be partners? My enemy's enemy is my friend.

Han Jimin has his business headquarters in the Han Corporation Building on Nanking Road in Taipei. Across the street is a restaurant called the Little Pearl. Go there at noon on Friday. You will be met. If you are not, go again at noon on Saturday. Do not approach your own government. There are people in Washington, like their counterparts here, who are content with the situation as it is.

Do not attempt anything on your own. It would be foolhardy, and worse, useless.

There was no signature.

Beth reread one phrase: *but in what state, I do not know.* Then she stood up. General Ma expected her to be in Taipei by Friday noon. Today was Friday. That was Problem One. Problem Two was her memory of Lathrop saying the *Timoshenko* had been submerged from the moment they began tracking it until its arrival in Petropavlovsk. That raised two questions she would have liked to ask General Ma. Could the submarine have transferred Teddy at sea without surfacing? And if not, how could he be in Taiwan?

She walked down the hill and waded into the stream. Halfway across, she stopped, shredded the letter and the photograph, and tossed them in the water. Then she followed the dirt track over the slope to the road and started walking north, toward the section of the Wall where the tourists went.

She hadn't gone very far before a girl went by, carrying two buckets of water on a yoke. She smiled. Beth tried to smile back, but the muscles in her face were too tight. The girl walked on.

Beth began moving faster. She was foreign. She wasn't with

a tour. Someone, even the smiling water-girl, could tell some-one else. If there was nowhere in China for General Ma's nephew to hide, where was there for her? By the time she reached the parking lot by the Wall, she was running as hard as she could.

Five or six tour buses were parked by a souvenir store. As Beth ran up, tourists came filing out of the store and straggled toward a bright-blue bus. There were a lot of them—twenty or thirty. They were carrying Great Wall T-shirts, Great Wall tow-els, Great Wall ballpoint pens, Great Wall ashtrays.

Beth stopped running. She walked across the parking lot at what she thought was normal speed and fell in with the tourists. They seemed slow, or half-alive, as though they'd all been drugged. The sound of her breathing was harsh and loud. She fought to control it.

The tourists climbed onto the bus. It took forever. Beth got on with them. The Chinese driver was reading a comic book. He didn't look up. Beth found an aisle seat halfway back.

The guide, a big plain woman with thick glasses, got on the bus and said, "Is everyone here?"

"Yo," said a voice at the back.

"I hope you all enjoyed the Great Wall?"

"Yo."

"Good. Next—lunch."

"Where?"

"The hotel."

"Not again."

The guide blushed.

The driver rolled up his comic book and turned the ignition key. The bus began to move.

Beth's companion was a plump woman of about her own age, with tight blonde curls and a supply of Toblerone chocolate bars in her purse.

She split one with Beth. "Good, huh?"

"Very."

"You've got some grass in your hair."

"Thanks." Beth brushed it off.

"What did you think of the Great Wall?"

"Interesting."

"Yeah? Just between you and me, I've seen enough of the sights. When are they going to take us shopping? I love that cloisonné."

The bus climbed the hill, went by the dirt track leading to General Ma's *pingfang*, passed the stream where women washed clothes and men fished with hand-held lines. Beth and her companion split two more Toblerones. Beth was chewing her last bite when the bus began to lose speed. She looked up and saw two jeeps blocking the road a few hundred feet ahead.

The bus stopped. Men in blue Mao jackets climbed out of the jeeps and came forward. All but one carried guns. The unarmed man had a hollow face and El Greco fingers. He motioned with one of them. The driver and the guide got off the bus at once and stood before him. The finger moved again. They produced their papers. The hollow-faced man glanced through them. Then he turned toward the bus.

The passengers were all watching him through the windows. Beth rose and went to the lavatory at the back. Her legs wanted to run again; this time she didn't let them.

She closed the door and locked it. The room was the size of a closet. It contained a sink and a toilet. And a mirror: Her eyes were huge and wild.

Footsteps in the aisle. There wasn't even a trash bin to hide behind. The guide said: ''Please get out your passports. This is just a routine inspection.'' Her tone indicated it was nothing of the kind, but none of the passengers seemed to notice. Beth heard them obediently opening purses and leather folders. It was all part of the fun.

The footsteps came slowly nearer. Plastic curtains hung in the window of the lavatory. Beth opened them an inch and looked out. She saw a ditch, and beyond it a field sloping into the distance, but no armed men. They were all on the other side of the bus.

Quickly she unlocked the door and slid the window open. She climbed out, leaving the window open but closing the curtains after her. Then she crawled under the bus and lay still.

Booted feet stood near the door, more of them around the front of the bus. Someone was walking overhead. The lavatory door opened. Pause. Another footstep. Then the plastic curtains parted with a rustling sound. Another pause, longer than the first.

It was very quiet. A bird sang, far away. And then the rustling sound came again. Footstep. The lavatory door closed. The footsteps began going the other way. Two feet shod in plain black leather stepped down from the bus. They moved off. The booted feet followed.

An engine fired. And another. Then the bus shuddered above her. She crawled out and pulled herself through the lavatory window. The bus started rolling.

Beth waited a few minutes before opening the door. No one noticed her. The driver's eyes were on the road. The guide sat in the front looking straight ahead, hands folded in her lap. Beth returned to her seat.

"How was it?" asked the plump woman.

"What?"

"The can. You know. Is it gross?"

"No."

"It's not a squatter, is it? I hate those squatters—I always lose my balance."

"It's a regular toilet."

"Good." The plump woman rose. "My back teeth are floating. It's all the tea they keep feeding us." She squeezed by Beth and moved toward the back.

Her purse lay open on the seat. A Toblerone bar stuck out the top. And her passport. Beth thought about the midnight flight to Hong Kong. General Ma's nephew had said she could board it safely. But he hadn't sounded sure. It was much less sure now.

Beth slipped the plump woman's passport out of her purse and opened it. Nancy Johnson. She was thinner in her photograph—taken a number of Toblerones ago—and her hair was straight. That still didn't make them twins, but it would have to do: Nancy Johnson's passport had already survived inspection. Beth dropped it in her handbag.

"Excuse me," said Nancy Johnson, standing in the aisle. Beth stood up to let her by. Nancy Johnson pushed her purse out of the way and thumped into the seat. "That feels better," she said. "How about one more Toby? For the road."

"No thanks."

But Nancy Johnson's chubby hand was already burrowing in the purse. It came out with another chocolate bar. "Then I'll just have to manage all by myself," she said with a giggle. "I'm so bad."

The bus entered Beijing. It parked in front of the Beijing Hotel. "Lunch," said the guide. "We meet back here at one-thirty."

"What's on tap this afternoon?"

"The Temple of Heaven."

Someone groaned. The guide blushed again.

"I never thought I'd say this," said Nancy Johnson, "but I'm sick of Chinese food. I'd kill for a BLT. With fries." Everyone got off the bus. "How about a quick beer?" asked Nancy Johnson.

"I'll meet you inside," Beth told her.

She waited until Nancy Johnson had gone into the hotel. Then she went to the cab rank. She looked inside the first taxi, made sure that the driver wasn't the one who'd taken her to the Great Wall, and said: "Airport?"

"Airport," the driver repeated happily. Beth got in. The taxi shot away.

The terminal at Beijing Airport was like the one in Shanghai: small and quiet. There was a flight to Hong Kong in an hour.

Beth went to the ticket counter. She stood there, watching the clerk write tickets for three Japanese men. Then she stepped forward and asked for a seat on the Hong Kong flight.

The clerk's eyes narrowed. "Don't you already have a return ticket?"

Beth cleared her throat. "Yes, but one of my children is sick. I have to go home right away. And I can't change the booking—it's a charter."

The clerk looked at her for a moment or two. Then he said, "Passport, please."

Beth handed him Nancy Johnson's passport. Her fingers left a wet patch on the blue cover.

The clerk didn't bother to see whether she looked like Nancy Johnson. He just copied Nancy Johnson's name onto a blank ticket and gave the passport back.

The immigration officer looked at the ticket and the passport, but not at Beth. He checked the thick black book full of names. Nancy Johnson wasn't one of them. He let her go: China was a Third World country.

An hour later Beth was in the air.

33

China was beautiful. At least, the part of it outside the window of his room in the white house was beautiful. He could see a plum tree in blossom and beyond it a high white wall with the texture of a movie screen. On the far side of the wall a green hill sloped sharply up to the sky. The sky was blue; the sun was warm. It hurled up colors every morning when it rose over the hill.

Some mornings a peasant in a wide straw hat came and swept up the plum blossoms with a bamboo-handled broom and carried them away in a wicker basket.

Where? What did they do with the plum blossoms? How nice it would be to have that basket of plum blossoms, top it off with purple plums and a bottle of wine, and give it to her!

His vision blurred. It always did when he thought of her. And sometimes when he thought of nothing. That was probably because he was weak and hungry. Maybe his weakness and his hunger made China seem so beautiful.

"Where in China are we?" he'd asked Jimmy.

"The south. It's the nicest part."

"But where in the south?"

"Near a little village. The name would mean nothing to you."

"I need solid food, Jimmy."

"We have needs too."

"I can't get the numbers right if you drug me. I told you that. My head has to be clear."

"No one is drugging you. Except for pain."

"I'm not in pain."

"Only because we're drugging you."

He lay on his bamboo bed—too weak to get up, and anyway

281

he was attached to the IV—and daydreamed about the basket of plum blossoms. Maybe he would toss in red plums along with the purple. And what about the wine? He tried to remember the wines she liked, but all the French names eluded him. His memory was very bad. He wondered whether he really would be able to get the numbers right if they stopped drugging him. He thought for a while. The equations came back, strung like jewels on a perfect necklace—a necklace locked in a strongbox in his mind.

He had thought he was being very clever with the equations, the way he'd been clever with the letter. The letter had fooled them. But the equations hadn't. It had amazed him how quickly his alterations had been spotted —not all of them, but most. Was there anyone in China that good? No. Certainly not Han Shih. All her questions were prepared. He could see his answers meant nothing to her. Who was evaluating them?

He made a mental short list of everyone he knew who might be capable of evaluating them. There were two Russian names on it, three or four American, one British, perhaps a Finn and an Egyptian. But no Chinese names.

Then he thought of the blue eye he had seen through the butterfly hole in the door on his first day in China.

A bubble of nausea popped up in his stomach and swelled like a balloon. Soon he was heaving and retching again, but nothing came out. It never did.

He felt weaker. He lay on his back, breathing heavily. The IV bag hung over his head, half-full of clear liquid. They never gave him needles now, so the drug must be in the bag. He reached up for the tube and tried to pull it down.

He wasn't strong enough. Not nearly. He examined his arm. Skin, tendon, bone. The muscle was gone.

The butterfly door opened. Jimmy came in. The room shrank. He was wearing a gray Mao jacket and roomy gray pants: very proletarian, except for the gold watch. Han Shih was with him. There was nothing proletarian about her: She had black silk on her body and diamonds in her ears. Her eyes seemed harder than the diamonds, until she saw he was looking at her. Then they went as soft as Leslie Howard's.

"Feeling better today?" she asked.

He didn't reply.

Jimmy broke the silence. "Your mother and I have talked to the doctor."

"She's not my mother."

"Of course she is."

"My mother wouldn't treat me like this."

"Don't say that. You hurt her very much."

Leslie Howard's eyes filled with tears. So did his own. Jimmy loomed up through the blur. His eyes and mouth seemed very big, especially his mouth. "The doctor thinks you should be back on solid food." Jimmy's mouth formed a huge black smile. "What do you think of that?"

"Are you going to sprinkle drugs on it?"

"Of course not. We want you to be strong and healthy. How is your head?"

"Fine." That was true, It had stopped hurting.

"Good. Then maybe your memory of Mordell's conjecture will be more accurate."

"When will I see my father?"

Han Shih made a clicking noise with her tongue. Jimmy sighed. "I've told you so many times. Your father is angry with you. Very angry. He will not come until he is satisfied with our mathematical discussions."

He shouted at Han Shih: "I want to see him! You said he'd be on the fucking submarine!" They watched him silently. He lowered his voice. "Where is he?"

"In the capital," Jimmy said.

"Peking?"

"Yes."

"Beijing," Han Shih said.

"Who is he?"

"Someone very important."

"I don't believe you."

Jimmy came closer. "No?" He reached down and laid a hand on his forehead as if feeling his temperature. But he wasn't feeling his temperature. His hand was pressing too hard for that. It was a massive hand, hot and damp.

"No? Do you think we'd have been so patient with you if he wasn't important?"

He didn't reply. He just felt the hand. It pressed harder. He wanted badly to see his real father. Finally he said, "No."

The hand went away. "There are other methods," Jimmy

said. "Your father is a kind man, but he is a patriot first. He knows how important those equations are to the homeland. Your homeland."

"I tried to give them to you. But my head hurt. And the drugs confused me."

"Drugs?"

"You know."

"The only drugs you've had are painkillers."

There was a long silence. He tried to understand why the other methods hadn't been used. Maybe Han Shih was his mother and he did have a powerful father protecting him from the capital. Or they might have feared that obvious brutality would antagonize him into falsifying the equations. But he had done that anyway. And they had caught him. Maybe they really believed his weakness and the drugs were responsible for the mistakes.

"I'll do my best," he said to Jimmy.

"Good. You will have a wonderful life here."

"Will I have a passport and freedom to travel?"

"Of course."

But how could that be true? What difference would the accuracy or inaccuracy of the equations make to his future? He thought about his future.

It depended on the existence of his father. Or, but surely it was a pipe dream now, it depended on the letter. Either way, he had only one thing to do: play for time.

Time. "We don't have much time," Han Shih had whispered in the dining room. "Your father is on the submarine. He wants to see you."

And so he'd gone out on *Pop-Up*.

The balloon swelled in his stomach. He retched and heaved, then lay panting in a cold sweat on his bamboo bed.

Later, the IV was disconnected. Han Shih brought him tea and a bowl of rice. "I'll need a fork," he said. She took the chopsticks away and brought him one. She helped him sit up. He ate and drank very slowly. A sleepy warmth spread through his body.

Han Shih stood at the foot of the bed, watching. "How do you feel?" she asked when he finished.

"Better."

"Well enough to go over the equations?"

"Not yet, please."

"When?"

"Soon."

"Tomorrow?"

"I don't know. I'm very tired." Their eyes met. "Prove you're my mother."

"No mother should have to do that. You're very cruel."

His eyes blurred. Then he saw she wasn't bothering with the Leslie Howard effect and the blur went away.

Han Shih leaned over him, brushed her cool lips against his forehead. "You'll feel better very soon," she said. "Your doctor is a brilliant man. Did you know that?"

"No. Will I meet him?"

Han Shih gazed out at the plum tree, the high white wall, and the last red rays of the sun shining on the hill. "Perhaps," she said. "He is a brain surgeon."

The sun set. Red and green flared across the sky.

34

The Han Corporation Building was a mirror, thirty or forty stories high. Taipei flickered across its facets like a movie in multiscreen projection, the kind of big-budget production unknown in China. It featured a man in an L.A. Dodgers jacket riffling through blue money like a teller or a bagman as he went quickly by. Two strolling policemen in tailored black uniforms and white helmets didn't bother to look at him—they were too busy clenching their jaw muscles. Brightly colored cars and taxis pulsed by like brush strokes in a Klee painting. The backgrounds were authentic-looking late twentieth-century display windows, full of jewels, watches, perfume, cognac, cassette players, cameras, furs, silk, crystal. The credit role named names like Piaget, Dior, Mercedes-Benz, Courvoisier. The message was their usual message. It was a blockbuster in Taiwan.

Beth sat in a booth by the front window of the Little Pearl Restaurant. She was in the movie, too. Through breaks in the traffic, she could see her face reflected in the lower left-hand corner of the Han Corporation Building across the street: a white blur behind smoked glass.

Saturday. The fallback day for her rendezvous with General Ma's representative. Lunchtime. Beth drank tea and ate a sautéed fish that looked like pompano. People came in. Some of them noticed her, some didn't. They ate. They left. None of them tried to talk to her. The waiters mopped the floor. Then they divided their tips and went home, leaving Beth alone with the woman behind the cash register. She paid her bill and walked out.

General Ma had failed. And any attempt she made on her own would be foolhardy. But what would making no attempt be?

Beth crossed the street. Her image grew on the face of the Han Corporation Building. For a moment, she didn't recognize it as her own; the body was so thin, the face so hard. She climbed marble steps, opened a tall glass door, and walked in.

The lobby had a green-marble floor with a black-marble fountain in the middle. Two armed guards stood by it. Fat goldfish swam in the pool at the bottom. It wasn't the kind of pool people threw money into for luck—or else the guards fished it out when no one was looking.

Beth crossed the lobby to the elevators. On the wall above them were digital clocks flashing the time in all the world's important capitals except Beijing. There was also an office directory. The executive offices were on the top floor. Beth pressed the UP button. While she waited she studied the directory. The Han Corporation had many divisions. One of them was the Gladd Group.

The elevator doors slid open. Two men got out. One was Chinese, with thick glasses on his face and a medical bag in his hand. His hair needed washing. The other man was white. Once he might have been handsome; now his even features were buried in fat. It was Rex Heidemann. He and the Chinese man walked right by without looking at her.

Perhaps her face showed nothing; perhaps she looked like anyone else waiting for an elevator. But inside, the blood drained from her and the colors bleached out of her vision.

The two men were already outside, going down the marble stairs, when Beth recovered. She ran after them. A green Rolls-Royce pulled into the curb below. Rex Heidemann opened the rear door and started to get in.

"Where should we meet?" the Chinese man asked him in English.

"Here. In an hour."

"That's not much time." There was a whine in the Chinese man's voice.

"There isn't much time." There was a snap in Heidemann's.

That didn't stop the other man from complaining. "It took so long."

"So what? He cracked, didn't he?" Heidemann slammed the

door. The car shot into traffic, rounded a corner, and disappeared.

The Chinese man sighed and started walking the other way, down Nanking Road. Beth followed. She didn't try to be subtle about it; all she wanted to do was to stay with him.

The man with the medical bag walked a few blocks, then turned into a narrow street. He went by a pet store and entered a windowless black-painted building. HOT CLUB, said the sign over the door.

Beth hesitated outside. She heard a scraping sound. A monkey was gnawing at the steel bars of his cage in front of the pet store. It stopped when it saw her watching and looked at her with liquid brown eyes that seemed full of meaning.

Glass cases the size of small aquariums were piled on top of the monkey's cage. Thick snakes were curled inside them: brown, red, green. Beth pushed open the door of the Hot Club and went in.

It was dark. She paused in the doorway, letting her eyes adjust. The room was long and narrow with a bar on one side and a row of booths on the other. A beaded lantern hanging from the ceiling cast a pool of weak yellow light, just enough to illuminate the only two people in the Hot Club: a woman behind the bar, in a tight dress slit to the waist, and the man with the black bag, seated on a stool. She was filling a brandy glass for him; he was watching her do it. The moment she finished he grabbed the glass and drained it. The woman filled it again.

Beth walked in and sat on the next stool.

The man looked at her in surprise, then turned away. He started to gulp it down again, but this time settled for half, before looking at Beth out of the corner of his eye. The woman behind the bar was watching her, too. Behind stage sets of mascara, blue shadow, and false lashes waited flat bored eyes that couldn't be shocked by anything money-making; the only question in them was who would make it.

"I'll have a brandy too," Beth said.

That was a promising start. The woman reached back and selected the fanciest-looking bottle on the shelf: She splashed brown liquid in a cheap snifter and slid it across to Beth. It looked and smelled like any brandy.

"Four hundred dollars," said the woman. The ratio was forty Taiwan to one U.S.

Beth paid. Then she moved closer to the man. It was time for hocus-pocus; extravagant and baroque, but it scares some people. She picked up the glass, careful that her middle finger was touching the bottom and her thumb and forefinger were wrapped around the edge—the way Y.K. Ling had shown her.

"Cheers," she said, and hoisted the glass in his face so he couldn't miss the way she held it.

He saw. His eyes widened. "What is it? Has something gone wrong?"

Beth nodded.

He opened his mouth as if to speak, then glanced at the barwoman and poured the rest of his drink into it instead. He winced. "Let's go over there," he said, and led her to a booth at the back.

She sat opposite him. His thick glasses reflected the lantern light. She couldn't see beyond them, even when he hunched toward her over the sticky table, bent like a question mark.

"What's happened?" he said in a hoarse whisper. He had no trace of Chinese accent; his voice was American.

"You tell me."

Fright pitched his voice higher. "What do you mean? I said I'd do it. I'm flying out tonight. Doesn't he know yet? Didn't Heidemann call him?"

"Who are you talking about?"

He sat back a little. "Jimmy, of course." He leaned farther back, into the shadows. All Beth could see were tiny yellow lanterns where his eyes should have been. "Haven't you just come from him?"

"Not directly. Where is he?"

Silence. The tiny lanterns were still. "Let me see your wrist."

"Let me see yours." Beth reached across the table, but he was up and gone before she could touch him.

Beth ran after him, out of the Hot Club and into the bright street. He raced away, heading for Nanking Road. The medical bag, swinging at his side, struck one of the glass cases stacked on the monkey's cage. All the cases toppled off, shattering on the pavement. Snakes writhed in broken glass. One of them whipped its head through the bars of the cage and sank its fangs into the monkey's thigh. The monkey howled. Beth darted around the snakes and ran toward Nanking Road.

The man with the medical bag was climbing into a taxi in the

far lane. Beth cut across the traffic. Horns honked. The taxi
swerved out of her reach and sped away. She chased it for a few
steps, then halted. People stared at her in astonishment. Beth
hardly saw them. She hailed the first empty taxi that came by.

"Hertz."

"Hertz?"

"Rent-a-car, God damn it. Rent-a-car."

"Oh," said the driver. "Budget."

Five minutes later she was renting a car. It meant using her
own passport in Jimmy Han's territory, but there was no choice:
She hadn't stolen Nancy Johnson's credit card.

Beth found her way back to Nanking Road and parked in front
of the Little Pearl Restaurant. She looked at her watch. Almost
time.

After a few minutes, the green Rolls-Royce drew up in front
of the Han Corporation Building. Rex Heidemann sat in the
back. He looked around in annoyance. Beth turned away.

A taxi double-parked beside the green Rolls. The man with
the medical bag got out; now he carried a matching suitcase as
well. The chauffeur lifted it into the trunk. The man with the
medical bag got into the car, beside Heidemann. They both
started talking at once. The chauffeur took his place behind the
wheel and turned into traffic.

Beth followed. She could see Heidemann and the Chinese
man through the rear window. They didn't look back. They were
too busy yelling at each other.

The green Rolls left Nanking Road for an expressway lined
with enormous movie billboards. Traffic flowed thick and fast.
Beth hunched over the wheel. Other cars tried to cut her off.
Chinese movie stars flashed by, kissing and killing in garish
colors. Beth stuck to the back of the green car.

It exited onto a divided highway: the airport road. But it didn't
go to the airport. After only a few minutes, it turned onto a narrow road that dipped through a tunnel before climbing toward
higher ground northeast of the city. There was much less traffic.
Beth stepped off the pedal and allowed the green car to gain.

The road wound steeply up through lush green hills, some terraced with rice paddies. Fat water buffalo lolled in the lower
pools. The air cooled. Sometimes Beth glimpsed Taipei down
below in its damp, crowded basin overhung with brown air. The
hills were where to live.

And a few lucky people lived there. Their big houses clung to the hillsides. They had plenty of living space; there were two or three houses to a hill. Beth could see the topmost hill in the distance. There was only one house on it: a sprawling white structure surrounded by a white wall. It glared in the sunlight.

The road climbed toward the big hill, twisting back and forth across the green slopes. All Beth saw of the Rolls-Royce were brief flashes of its taillights as it rounded another corner. She hoped that meant they couldn't see her at all.

As the road curved up the big hill, the vegetation thickened: a dark-green undergrowth decorated with blue and yellow flowers and topped with spreading palms. Beth lost sight of the green car. Then, suddenly, she went right by it: parked in front of a barred gate in the high white wall. The chauffeur was walking toward the gate, a key in his hand. Beyond the gate a long drive led to the big white house.

Beth drove on without slowing down. Around the next bend, she pulled over and eased the car as far as she could into the bushes, parking so that it was pointing back down the way she'd come. Then she crossed the road and began climbing the hill on the other side.

It was late afternoon, but still warm enough to make Beth sweat as she made her way up through the shoulder-high bushes. There was no sound but her feet squishing in the moist earth and nettles tearing at her clothes. She tried not to think of snakes.

She came to an overgrown path and followed it to a small clearing two-thirds of the way to the top. Through the waxy leaves of a palmetto at the edge of the clearing, she peered down the hill.

She was on the back side of the white house, and well above it. The house had a green dragon-tail roof and two long wings, projecting into the hillside. The high white wall, topped with shards of broken glass that glinted in the sun, completely surrounded it. Blossoming fruit trees grew on the mown lawn between the back of the house and the wall: apple or plum, she couldn't be sure from the distance. It was a quiet, isolated house, the kind of house where a man could be hidden away and no one would ever know. Beth crouched behind the palmetto and waited for dark.

The hill blocked the lowering sun. Its shadow flowed slowly

toward the house like a black tide. But it was not yet nearly dark when something happened that forced Beth to change her plan.

First the sound of a closing door rose up the hill. Then the chauffeur appeared in the drive on the far side of the house, carrying suitcases. He put them in the trunk of the car and held the door open. Rex Heidemann and the man with the medical bag got in. The car rolled down the drive, onto the Taipei road, and out of sight.

Beth ran down the hill, tearing through bushes and ferns. When she came to the wall, she pulled off her jeans and flipped them over the top; the denim caught and held on the sharp glass. Then she found a rock and put it in her jacket pocket.

Beth backed a little way up the hill to make the jump easier. Then she took a few running steps and leaped as high as she could. Her fingers touched the denim and gripped it. As she swung in, her left hand started to lose its hold, but she dug her toe into the wall and pushed herself onto the top. A jagged edge of glass pressed through the jeans into her breast. She took the rock from her pocket and pounded the cloth. Glass crumbled beneath it. She swept the debris away, pulled herself over the wall, dropped into the compound, and put her jeans back on.

The house was silent. Beth moved through the fruit trees—apple, she saw now—to the nearest wing. The end room had a sliding glass door. On the other side was a storage room, half-filled with lawn furniture. Beth tried the door. It slid open.

She went inside. A distant clinking sound that might have come from a household machine reminded her of something, but she couldn't remember what. There was no other sound. The house felt deserted. Teddy had to be there, but she knew in her heart that he wasn't. Not alive. She started searching anyway.

The storage room opened onto a long, thickly carpeted hall. There were many doors off it. She opened each one with dread, and saw nothing but empty rooms with bare mattresses on the beds.

The hall led to the core of the house. The living room was two stories high and echoed every sound she made. Half a dozen old Chinese rugs were scattered on the marble floor; there were or-molu coffee tables, end tables, and display cases, and enough heavy floral furniture to fill a showroom.

The paintings on the wall were floral also, except for two above the stone hearth. They were oil portraits, painted in West-

ern style: a man and a woman. The man had a big, powerful
body, a broad face, and thick graying hair. He'd been looking
directly at the artist, the same way he had looked into the camera
at Lake Tai in 1948. J. Han. Han Jimin. Jimmy Han. He was
ten or fifteen years older in the painting. The added years helped
Beth bridge a gap, and then she knew she had once seen the man
himself, not merely the image: a big man with thick, silvery hair,
who had come out of the office of Berryessa Wines with Rex
Heidemann and driven away in a big black car—a Rolls-Royce,
she remembered. And Berryessa Wines was owned by the Gladd
Group, which was owned by the Han Corporation.

Beth knew the woman, too. Han Shih. A woman of the Han
family. In the portrait, she was much younger and very beautiful. There was such a strong, open expression of sensuality on
her face that Beth was surprised the painting was on display. Her
mind made a jump back to the mud hut in Qinghai, where Pei
Ming had said that the Master's concubine had been responsible
for the killings at Lake Tai: She had hated the Master's wife.

Had Han Shih been the concubine of Teddy's father—hating
the Master's wife, and perhaps the wife's baby boy as well? Beth
didn't know, but she did know why Han Shih had been unable
to take her eyes off the pictures of Teddy and her hanging over
the fireplace on Telegraph Hill.

Beth stood before the portraits while bits of knowledge rear-
ranged themselves in her head. There was no need to search the
rest of Jimmy Han's house. And no time. The sub had come up
empty. Teddy wasn't in Russia. He wasn't in Taiwan. General
Ma was right: He must have been transferred at sea. But what
General Ma hadn't realized was that the transfer had taken place
before Lathrop began tracking the sub—while it was still near
the California coast.

That made it time to get in the rented car and catch up to
Heidemann and the medical man. They had a head start, but she
knew where they were going.

As Beth turned to leave, she was suddenly aware that the
clinking sound had stopped. Clinking. Like a giant rattling
change.

The next moment she was running toward the hall, but after
no more than a few strides she heard soft footfalls coming the
other way. She froze.

A man wearing nothing but damp sweatpants came into the

room. He had a massive torso, marred only by a raw red scar on one shoulder. Recognition dawned on his face, and slowly gave way to the look of a man whose wildest dream has come true. It was Baldy.

Beth whirled and ran across the room. She bumped into a table. Something smashed on the floor. She spun into the hall of the other wing and sprinted down it. She heard Baldy's footsteps scuttling behind her. And gaining.

The hall ended in another room with a sliding glass door, full of weight-lifting equipment. The door was open. Beth raced through and onto the mown grass, fleeing toward the high wall. Baldy was right behind her. A whimper escaped her throat. It made Baldy growl like a Doberman. Beth ran harder.

As she went through the apple trees the sound of his footsteps seemed to diminish. Beth glanced back. He had slowed down a little, but not because he was tiring. His face was shining with the knowledge that she was trapped.

Without thinking or even looking at the wall, Beth headed straight for the spot she'd cleared of glass. She jumped up, gained hold, scrambled over, and slipped down the other side. Protected for a moment by the wall, Beth felt her mind suddenly clear of panic, leaving only the realization that lay behind it: She could never outrun Baldy over rough country. So she didn't start running but crouched in the shadow of the wall.

Baldy drew up on the other side. He paused, then grunted. His palms smacked the top of the wall. He swung smoothly over and dropped toward the ground, feet apart for a solid landing. He didn't even see Beth. She straightened her legs and drove her fist into his groin with all her might.

The blow knocked air from Baldy's lungs; it came out with a harsh, tearing sound. He fell on Beth. They tumbled on the ground and came to rest with Baldy on top. His body was inert but very heavy. Before she could struggle free he grabbed a handful of her hair. She bit him in the fleshy part of his palm. The fingers of his other hand clamped on her nose and twisted. Something snapped. Blood gushed out and ran down her face. She bit harder and tasted his blood too. His hand smothered her face and pressed her head into the ground. Beth felt the power flowing back into his body.

She scratched at his fingers, tried with all her strength to bend them back, but couldn't budge them. Her fist pounded wildly at the unyielding mass weighing on her. One of her blows struck his shoulder. For a moment his grip relaxed. Then he pressed even harder, as though he would crush her face. Beth's hand clawed sightlessly against his bare chest until it found the rough, raised wound. She dug her fingernails into it and ripped.

Baldy roared, so loudly she was stunned by the sound and didn't notice at first that his hand was no longer on her face. She squirmed out from under him and started running.

Beth tore across the hillside, found the path, crashed down toward the road. She didn't hear him coming, but she didn't look back to see. She jumped in the rented car, turned the key, and pressed the pedal to the floor.

The car screamed around the bend. Ahead she saw the entrance to Jimmy Han's drive. She hadn't been quick enough. Baldy was coming through the gate with a pistol in his hand.

He planted himself in the middle of the road and aimed it at her. His eyes were wide and mad. Metal ripped metal. Beth ducked her head below the top of the dashboard and drove blindly. Metal ripped metal again. The windshield shattered around her head. The she felt a hard bump. The steering wheel twisted in her hands.

She raised her head. Baldy was crawling up the hood, one hand grasping the windshield wiper. His other hand, empty now, reached through the space where the windshield had been and grabbed her around the neck. His fingers met on the other side. He squeezed.

The world divided into points of light. Beth gasped for breath. Baldy squeezed harder. The light began to fade. Beth tried to turn the wheel sharply, but Baldy jerked it back. His face was so close she could feel his hot breath and see the red veins swelling in the whites of his eyes. Then her vision blurred. Baldy growled again.

Beth tried to scream at him, but no sound came. In desperation she pressed the accelerator to the floor. The car, which had been rolling to a stop, surged forward. Baldy's hand tightened like a garrote. Beth took her foot off the gas, found the brake, and stepped on it as hard as she could.

Her forehead smashed into the steering wheel. The next moment the pressure on her neck was gone. The car swerved through undergrowth, glanced off a tree, spun around, and came to rest by the side of the road.

Beth looked back. Baldy lay twitching on the pavement.

Then he was still. Beth's ears filled with unbearable roaring. After a while it passed. She became aware of blood dripping from her nose. She wiped it on her sleeve and eased the car onto the road.

Beth drove down out of hill country. Numb, almost unconscious of what she was doing, she went through the tunnel and onto the divided highway. She knew she should hurry, but the wind blowing in her face kept her from going very fast. Then the numbness went away, and she had to grip the wheel with all her strength to stop the shaking that replaced it.

She took the exit marked *Chiang Kai-shek Airport*, and was almost at the terminal when she saw the green Rolls-Royce coming the other way. The chauffeur was alone.

Beth parked her car in front of the first entrance she saw, jumped out, and ran inside. She scanned the list of departures on a monitor. Three planes had taken off in the past hour: to Hong Kong, Sydney, and Bangkok. China Airlines had a flight leaving in five minutes—direct to San Francisco.

She ran to the China Airlines counter. There was a long line. The people in it turned as one to look at her. They gave way without a word.

Beth confronted the clerk. "San Francisco," she said. Her voice was harsh and urgent.

He backed away. "Our next flight to San Francisco is tomorrow afternoon."

"No. I want the plane that's leaving now."

"That flight is closed."

"There's still five minutes."

"It is also full."

"There must be a seat."

"I'm sorry.

Beth banged her fist on the counter. "Get me on that goddamned plane."

"It is too late." He looked past her.

Beth turned. Through smoked glass she saw the green and white 747 taxiing down the runway. It rose into the sky and shrank to nothing.

Beth walked away. Behind her, people started talking.

Singapore Airlines had a flight to San Francisco two hours later. Beth went into a bathroom and cleaned herself as well as she could before buying a ticket in Nancy Johnson's name. Then she went into a phone booth and got Y.K. Ling's number in San Francisco from the international operator.

The phone was answered before the first ring finished. A scratchy voice said, "Yes?" The sound was as weak as a recording played a million times.

"It's Beth Hunter. Can you hear me?"

The voice on the other end responded, but Beth couldn't understand what it said. "Can you hear me? Can you hear me?" A Chinese woman passing by the booth turned to look. Her gaze fastened on Beth's nose.

"What?" said the faint voice on the other end.

"It's Beth Hunter," Beth shouted at the top of her lungs. "Can you hear me?"

Suddenly the line went very clear. "You don't have to shout," said Y.K. Ling. "Why are you bothering me at six in the morning?" He might have been in the next booth.

"I've just killed a man," she blurted. It wasn't what she'd meant to say at all.

"Who?"

"The man who killed Albert."

"I'm listening." Not a trace of annoyance remained in his tone.

"Albert was on the right track after all."

"Go on."

"You told me you had some dynamite."

"That's right."

"Have you still got it?"

"Yes."

"Do you want to do something about Albert?"

"Don't ask stupid questions."

"Could you make a big bang? It doesn't need to do a lot of damage. It's the noise that's important."

"More of a diversion?" He was back in form.

"Exactly."

"I can make a big bang. Where and when?"

She told him. Her plan had seemed better untold. She wondered how it struck the old man.

But he wasn't telling. "Wear dark clothes," was all he said.

Beth went through immigration. Immigration stared at her nose and punched Nancy Johnson into a computer. The computer didn't react. It wasn't looking for Nancy Johnson. It might not be looking for Beth Hunter either, but she didn't want to test its memory.

She boarded the plane. Outside, the night was warm and humid; inside it was cold and dry. Beth covered herself with a blanket and put a pillow behind her head. She had to sleep.

But her eyes wouldn't stay closed. They didn't want to look at Baldy twitching in the road.

A copy of *Newsweek* stuck out of the seat pocket. Beth leafed through it. There was an article on China. The Maoists were coming back into power, it said. Moderates were being purged. Some of their leaders hadn't been seen for a while. There had been executions.

The story was illustrated with a picture of a Chinese crowd looking at an execution notice pinned to a wall—the kind of notice Beth had seen in Wuxi. Inset was a photograph of two men being executed. They knelt, placards around their necks in the usual way. A soldier with a gun stood behind them.

Newsweek didn't identify the men—they were only there to give the story some visual punch—but Beth knew who they were. Reverend Huang was bent over, his eyes on the ground. Mr. An gazed at something far away.

The stewardess came round with hot towels.

35

Buzz buzz.

He opened his eyes.

Han Shih and Jimmy were standing over him. She had a cord-less shaver in her hand.

"Time for a shave," Jimmy said. "You can't go anywhere looking like that."

"Where am I going?"

"Home."

"Home?"

Jimmy showed his big white teeth. "The equations were perfect this time. You're going home."

"Perfect?"

Jimmy nodded. "The medication must have confused you the first time." He sat on the edge of the bed. It sagged under his weight. "But we were reluctant to take you off it. We were worried about your head injury."

"My head's fine."

"I hope so. We want to send you back in mint condition."

"When am I going?"

"Very soon."

"Will I see my father first?"

Jimmy's eyes met Han Shih's. A thought passed between them. The speed and intimacy of their communication forced a realization on him.

"If she's my mother you're my father."

Jimmy and Han Shih exchanged another look. "You're very clever," Jimmy said, standing up.

"Wait, I want to talk to you." He reached for Jimmy, but his movements were slow and his grasp feeble. Jimmy slipped away.

"Later," he said. "Now it's time for your shave." The door closed.

Han Shih bent forward. The shaver buzzed.

"But are you my mother?"

Vibrating steel mesh touched him behind the ear.

"What are you doing?"

"Shaving you."

"But that's not my face. It's my head." He raised his hand to stop her. She pushed it away. He tried again. She took both his wrists in her free hand and pressed them down against his chest. She shaved his head.

Their faces were very close. In her eyes he could see she was thinking of something else. Her movements were methodical; not gentle, not rough. She might have been clipping the hedge-row. It wasn't the way a mother groomed her boy.

Han Shih finished and went away. His shorn hair lay on the pillow around his head. He brushed it off. That took a long time and made him tired. He rested. After a while, he reached up and felt the top of his head. That stirred up the nausea that never quite disappeared from his stomach. He vomited undigested rice.

"I'm a fool," he said, and began to cry.

He closed his eyes and tried to sleep, but the smell wouldn't let him. His sense of smell had become very strong; the rest of him was very weak. The law of conservation of strength. He opened his eyes and looked out the window: the plum tree, green now with its first dewy leaves, the high white wall, the green hill beyond. A dog barked, not far away.

He pushed himself up to a sitting position, then inched his legs to the edge of the bed and lowered his feet to the floor. He stood up.

The room spun around him: bamboo bed, scroll paintings, goldfish, butterfly door. He leaned against the wall and waited. It was a peaceful room, when it stayed still.

After a minute or two, he started walking toward the door. His steps were short and shuffling. He was afraid to lift his feet— he might float up to the ceiling, he was so light.

He tried the door. Locked. He pushed and pulled at the carved butterflies. One of them had opened once. A blue eye had looked through.

But the butterflies wouldn't open for him.

He recrossed the room and examined the window. The frame was divided into vertical halves, like French doors. There was a brass latch at the bottom. He lifted it and pushed. The window wouldn't open. He looked up. There was another latch at the top, out of reach.

He glanced around the room. The bed. Too heavy. The bamboo chair. Light enough, but not very firm. It would have to do. He dragged it to the window and gauged the height. If he could stand on it, he could reach the latch. They'd been careless about the window. When he was hooked to the IV it was far beyond his range. But he wasn't hooked to the IV now.

Leaning on the windowsill for balance, he got one knee onto the chair and then the other. He drew his feet up underneath him, crouched, and rose shakily, steadying himself against the window. The chair trembled. He reached up and raised the latch. The chair began slipping out from under his feet. He pushed the window. As it opened he lost his balance and fell outside.

He landed facedown in soft green grass. He felt no pain, but didn't try to rise. He was breathing too hard. Each lungful overwhelmed him with the smell of mown grass.

Something rough and wet rubbed his cheek. He opened his eyes and saw a moist mongrel nose and a long pink tongue.

"Hello, Trotsky."

The dog wagged its tail and trotted off to the shade of the plum tree.

He stood up and swayed in the sunlight. It dazzled his eyes. He squinted at the world through his eyelashes. It wobbled in the glare.

He took a few baby steps toward the plum tree, careful not to float up into the blue. The plum tree was far away, the high wall much farther. And much too high, even if he could drag the bamboo chair all that way. He turned and shuffled to the side of the house.

A broad green valley spread out toward a distant ridge. In the middle of the valley, a few low hills sheltered a group of buildings. He must be on a commune. He couldn't tell what they were growing, but whatever it was had been planted in long neat rows, like vines. A tractor moved up and down the rows, spraying pink clouds.

So they had tractors in China, despite the surplus manpower.

Maybe communal life wasn't so bad. They had swimming pools too. There was one by the side of the house: an in-ground pool that wouldn't have been out of place in Beverly Hills or Bel-Air.

But there was no water in it. Instead, a mixing cylinder from a cement truck lay on the bottom, propped on wooden skids. It was a big mixer; at the widest part of its circumference, it rose higher than the side of the pool. It was the only cement mixer he'd ever seen with a hatch cut into it. A wooden catwalk led to the hatch from the side of the pool.

Step. Pause. Step. Pause. He made his way across the catwalk to the mixer and bent over the hatch cover. It was very heavy. He tugged it open an inch or two, wedged his toe inside, tugged some more, and finally swung it back on its hinges. Steel struck steel with an echoing clang. He looked around. No one came running.

A stepladder led into the mixer. He climbed down. On one side of the stairwell was the hole where the finished cement slid out; light entered through it. On the other side was a steel door. It looked thick and heavy, but at his first touch swung open with a hydraulic sigh.

He peered into the shadows beyond. Enough light came through the cement hole to illuminate a switch on the doorframe. He flicked it. Harsh white light drove the shadows away. He saw a narrow steel chamber. It had a high bunk on one side. Above the bunk hung a bag made of loosely woven plastic string. The bag was full of moldy oranges.

There was another switch on the wall. He tried it, too. The bag of oranges began to sway, to and fro. The steel walls hummed. He closed both switches, climbed the ladder, shut the hatch, and crossed the catwalk.

Ideas whirled through his brain. But there was no time to sort them out. A car was approaching from the other side of the house. He ran toward the window of his room.

The sun dazzled him. The earth wobbled. He fell. And couldn't get up. He crawled. The sun didn't stop dazzling him, the earth didn't stop wobbling, but he kept crawling. His life depended on it.

He crawled around to the back of the house, put his hands on the windowsill, and pulled himself up. It took all his strength to wiggle over. He tumbled into the room.

He picked himself up, closed the window, and tottered toward the bed. He was almost there when his foot struck the leg of the desk. There was a loud crash. He fell on the bed.

He heard voices outside. The two goldfish flipped around in a puddle on the floor. There was nothing he could do about them.

The door opened. Jimmy and Han Shih came in with a man he'd never seen before: a man with dirty hair, carrying a medical bag.

Jimmy's eyes moved to the fish on the floor, then quickly to the window. ''Up and about?''

There was nothing to say.

Jimmy flicked the goldfish under the desk with the toe of his shoe. ''You're going home,'' he said.

''How?''

''On the submarine. It's waiting right now at the naval base.''

''What naval base?''

''What do you mean? Shanghai, of course.''

''That's good.''

Jimmy looked at him. He started to say something, then changed his mind. ''First we're going to make sure your little head injury is all better.''

''I'm fine.''

''And you'll be even finer. This is your doctor. Trained in America.'' Jimmy turned to the man with the medical bag, who was gazing at the floor. ''He's going to take a tiny piece out of your brain tonight. Just to relieve the pressure.''

He raised himself up on his elbows. ''Are you talking about a lobotomy? Dad?'' He turned to Han Shih. ''So I won't remember any of this, Mom?''

Han Shih's mouth tightened. ''Oh no,'' Jimmy said, ''nothing like that. You'll remember all about your visit to China. You may no longer retain your old proficiency in mathematics, that's all. But you should be able to hold down an accounting job or something of that sort with no difficulty.''

He sat up and tried to get off the bed. Han Shih put a hand on his chest and pushed him back down.

The butterfly door opened. Two Chinese men wheeled an operating table into the room.

36

Eleven hours of blue went by before it vanished in a fog bank. The plane cut through it and landed at San Francisco Airport. Beth rented a car and started driving.

It was late afternoon. The sun shone. The breeze blew gentle and warm. She followed the familiar roads, but it was like returning to the scene of her childhood after a long absence.

She crossed the Bay and drove north. Only the highest parts of San Francisco were visible on her left, sticking out of the fog like the tops of buried ruins. She thought of *Ozymandias*, and tried to understand what General Ma had been saying about China's past. That took her mind off her fatigue, the grittiness in her eyes, and the pain across the bridge of her nose. She didn't let herself look in the mirror.

Rush-hour traffic poured onto the freeway. It was after six when she reached Vallejo, almost seven when she went through Napa. She turned onto Route 121 and began climbing out of the valley.

Traffic thinned. Beth passed a blonde girl on a horse and a pickup full of olive-skinned laborers. She smelled eucalyptus, and later oak and pine. It was the smell of China—not the People's Republic or Taiwan, but the third China, where Teddy was. In that China, Baldy had spent a night driving back and forth, as though on a long journey. That's what anyone blindfolded in the back of the van would have thought.

The shadows of even the shortest trees lay fully across the road by the time Beth came to Wooden Valley. She parked in front of Reno's Bar. BUD ON DRAUGHT, the sign still read, but the price had risen to sixty cents.

Reno's had sawdust on the floor and a blackened bar where

three dusty men in straw cowboy hats were drinking beer. They watched Beth come in; their eyes went up and down.

Y.K. Ling and his granddaughter Jade were sitting at the lone table in Reno's and looking out of place: the old man with his straggly beard, dark-blue suit, and plain black tie; the girl with earphones, bomber jacket, and mirror sunglasses. Beth wanted to embrace them. Instead she shook hands with the old man, smiled at Jade and sat down.

Y.K. Ling pressed a button on his wheelchair and came closer. His eyes swept over her. "It doesn't look like travel agrees with you."

"Don't be rude, Grandpa," Jade said.

"What do you mean, rude? Look at her nose."

Jade's eyes went vacant instead. She cracked her gum.

The bartender, an indoorsy man with purple veins on his face, called: "What'll it be?"

There was a Coke in front of Jade; the old man had water. "Coffee," Beth said.

"Coffee," repeated the bartender gloomily. He brought it, weak and tepid. When he'd returned to his post behind the bar, Beth lowered her voice and asked: "Is everything set?"

"Set," Y.K. Ling answered loudly. "That's the word for it all right." He laughed to himself.

Beth glanced at the bar. No one had turned to look at them. "You're in a good mood," she said to the old man.

"I like touring wineries. It's very educational. Too bad I had to miss some of it when I went to the men's room. That kind of thing takes time when you're in one of these." He patted the arm of the wheelchair. His eyes gleamed. "And I had to go twice. The guide was very understanding. I offered him a tip, but they're not allowed to accept them."

"Twice?"

He nodded. "They've got two men's rooms. One off the tasting room. The other in the cellars. I went down in an elevator. It's very modern."

Beth looked at him closely. His eyelids drooped like veils, but not enough to hide the gleam. She thought about old Chinese men—Y.K. Ling, Reverend Huang, Mr. An, Mr. Lao—still on the front lines of a war that had been over for thirty-five years. "All I want is a big bang."

"I know what you want," said Y.K. Ling in the soft, murderous tone she'd heard once before, at Albert's funeral.

"I want Teddy. That's all."

Y.K. Ling gazed at her for a moment without speaking. Then he looked at his watch and said: 'It's getting late. You'd better set your watch to mine. I have twenty minutes to eight. That leaves you exactly one hour and twenty minutes."

Beth adjusted her watch. It took several attempts because her fingers were trembling. Y.K. Ling looked away politely.

They went outside. "Better take this," Y.K. Ling said, handing her a map drawn on a paper napkin.

Jade helped the old man slide onto the passenger seat of a station wagon, before getting behind the wheel. Beth wouldn't have thought her old enough to drive. Jade leaned out the window and touched Beth's arm.

"Don't go near the winery."

"I don't intend to."

"Not anywhere close."

Jade started the car and wheeled far too quickly out of the parking lot. Perhaps speedy music was playing in her earphones. The station wagon roared down the road toward Napa.

Then it was very quiet outside Reno's. The first dim star showed in the purple sky. Beth got into her car and drove the other way.

The road ran along the ridge. Barbed wire appeared on her right. An arrow pointed to Berryessa Wines. Beth didn't turn onto the narrow road that led over the ridge—the watchman was waiting on the other side with his barking dog. Instead she stayed on Route 121 until she came to the top of a rise. There she stopped and looked at the valley.

She saw the gate and the guardhouse; the winery and the office, sheltered by the low hills; and, fading from view in the dying light, the little milky patch at the foot of the higher hills across the valley. "Barracks," Rex Heidemann had said, used only during the harvest.

She remembered then General Ma's question about Rex Heidemann: "What exactly was Rex Heidemann's reaction when you questioned him?" General Ma had seemed surprised when she told him Heidemann hadn't been angry or threatening. Now she saw that her reply had been honest, but not true: Heidemann had tried to kill her at the winery.

First he'd determined that Beth was alone in looking for a link between Teddy's disappearance and his past, alone in her knowledge that Teddy had talked to him. Then he'd led her through the olive grove, where she'd found the corkscrew, and into the vineyard.

There he'd shot the rabbit. But now she knew he'd drawn the gun to shoot her. The picnicking woman, returning for her corkscrew, must have seen it in his hand. So the rabbit had died instead: a legitimate target. The corkscrew had saved her life.

Heidemann had been forthcoming with information. He'd even told her about Teddy's honeymoon plans. Why not? She wouldn't have lived to use the knowledge. Of course he could simply have killed her without saying a word. It was a cruel touch but, more than that, unnecessary, extravagant—what word had General Ma used? *Baroque. Hocus-pocus*, Y.K. Ling had said. The bright red glads, *fu lu shou* on the florist's card, secret recognition signals, severed heads, the Death of a Thousand Cuts: the MO of the Brotherhood of the Green Snake.

Beth drove on. After a few miles, she reached the end of the barbed wire and slowed down. Mesquite and chaparral grew thickly by the road. Several hundred yards went by. She was beginning to think Y.K. Ling's map was wrong when she spotted a break in the shrubbery. She turned into it and bumped along a rough track.

It crossed the valley and climbed the ridge on the other side. Beth parked under a pine tree and walked south.

The sky darkened. More stars came out, first in twos and threes, then in huge clouds. The moon rose, three-quarters full and very white. The stars that made up Orion's belt lined up in their usual places.

Yellow lights shone in the valley below. The lights in the middle came from the winery, now partly hidden by the low hills; other lights, much closer, came from the barracks. Beth walked steadily across the hills on the eastern side of the valley. The earth was hard and dry under her feet; scrub grew in scattered clumps.

It was 8:25 when she reached the top of the hill behind the barracks. The building below didn't look like a barracks—it looked like a mandarin's country retreat: a small white house with a pagoda roof, a fruit tree, and a pool, surrounded by a high white wall. It might have been designed by Jimmy Han's ar-

chitect. And why not? He owned the whole valley, through the
Gladd Group. Lights glowed in a window. Beth made her way
down the hillside.

The wall wasn't as high as the one around Jimmy Han's
house, and it wasn't topped with broken glass. Beth climbed it
and dropped softly on the grass.

She listened. No sounds came from the house, but a shadow
moved across the window. Beth crouched behind the fruit tree—
too small to be apple, more likely plum. The shadow disappeared.

Twenty-three minutes to nine. Beth moved toward the side of
the house, planting each footstep quietly in the grass. She went
around a swimming pool filled with an enormous metal cylinder
and came to the front of the house. It had an ornate door, decorated with carved butterflies. A black Rolls-Royce was parked
in the courtyard. At the end of the drive stood a white stone arch.
Beth walked through it. A paved road led across the valley floor
to the winery. She could see its silhouette rising on the side of
the low hills.

As she went back through the arch, Beth saw that it bore two
Chinese characters, inscribed in gold or silver, and a picture of
Mao Zedong. Above rose a three-tiered pagoda roof, held on the
heads of gargoyles. It would have been a big tourist attraction
in China.

Beth circled round to the back of the house and approached
the window. The sill was waist-high. The window had two vertical halves, like French doors. Beth crawled the last few yards
to the house and slowly raised her head above the sill.

She saw what looked like a small operating theater. A powerful white light hung from the ceiling. Under it was an operating table. A man and a woman stood on opposite sides of the
table, wearing surgical masks and greens. Beth had last seen the
man leaving Jimmy Han's house in Taipei with his black bag.
Now he was attaching a tube to a plastic bag labeled *Pentothal*.

The woman was Han Shih. She was arranging scalpels on a
medical tray. A big man with thick silvery hair stood watching
by the door. Jimmy Han.

And strapped to the table was a naked man—a man whose
body was wasted, whose head had been shaved, whose face
dripped with sweat. Teddy.

Her hands clung to the sill as though the earth were capsizing.
Definitive proof was going to be offered.

Beth heard a car. The engine died. The door at Jimmy Han's
back opened. Rex Heidemann came in. Jimmy Han turned and
waved him away. Heidemann backed out the door. Teddy tried
to see who had entered but could barely raise his head off the
table. A killing rage swept through Beth.

Blow, you goddamned dynamite, blow!

Jimmy Han looked suddenly toward the window. Beth
ducked. Nothing happened. She looked at her watch. Eight minutes to nine.

Beth peered over the sill. The doctor had finished connecting
the tube to the plastic bag. The other end of the tube was attached to a long needle. Holding it, the doctor bent over Teddy,
examining the veins in the crook of his arm. Teddy tried to
squirm away, but he couldn't move.

Blow.

But it wouldn't blow.

Wires, Beth thought. *Where are the wires?* She stepped back
from the window. No wires. That meant they were underground. She raced around the house.

There. She saw a small box attached to the foundation at
ground level. It was padlocked. She yanked at the lock. It didn't
give. Instead an alarm went off inside the box. Beth jumped
back.

"Hey!" Heidemann called from the front of the house.
"What's going on?" Then came Chinese voices.

Then *boom*.

Not very loud: more like the noon gun at the ceremonial fort.
But the alarm stopped ringing. And the lights in the house went
out.

Heidemann shouted, "Christ! What was that?" People hurried outside. "Christ!" They got into a car. It roared away.

Beth ran around to the front of the house. The Rolls-Royce
was gone. She could see its taillights, already halfway to the winery. Above the winery, flames waved like pennants in the night
sky.

She turned to the door. They had left it open. A figure stood
in the doorway. Han Shih. She was still wearing a surgical mask.
Their eyes met. Han Shih's shone with firelight.

"Get out of my way," Beth said.

A weak call came from the darkened room. ''Beth?''

Maybe Han Shih hadn't recognized her until that moment. Now she whirled and ran into the house. Something glinted in her hand. Beth sprang after her, reached her, brought her down. They crashed against the operating table and rolled on the floor. Beth struggled to get on top. Then she realized she was the only one struggling.

She turned Han Shih over. Her eyes were open, but they no longer shone. Only the steel scalpel stuck in her chest was shining now, in the moonlight that streamed through the door.

Beth rose, bumping the operating table. Her fingers brushed warm skin.

''Beth. Is it you?''

''Yes. Oh yes.''

She hugged him close. Their hearts pounded together.

''It's you.''

''Yes, Teddy.''

She unfastened the straps binding him to the table. ''Can you walk?''

''I think so.''

But he couldn't even sit up. Beth put one arm under his shoulders, the other under his knees, and lifted him off the table. He was so light she wanted to cry.

She carried him outside. The taillights of the Rolls-Royce were very near the burning winery. ''We don't have much time.''

But Beth was wrong. The next moment the earth quivered under her feet. The Rolls-Royce rose high in the air, silhouetted against shooting flames. Then the noise of the explosion washed across the valley. When it passed there was a great stillness.

''Is it war?'' Teddy asked.

''No.'' It was a father's revenge.

Teddy twisted his head to see better. ''We're not in China, are we?''

''No. We're close to home.''

He looked into her eyes and smiled. ''Good.''

Flashing red lights appeared on the far ridge. Beth walked toward them with Teddy in her arms.

Epilogue

"Cui bono?" Lathrop said. "What's that?"

Beth told him.

He took out a notebook and wrote it down. "Cui bono—I like that. What else can you tell me about General Ma?"

"What do you want to know?"

"Anything you remember. We're always updating our profiles of their top intelligence people."

"I don't have solid information. And he may be dead by now."

"We don't expect a professional critique. What about a physical description? His full name? Fluency in English? That sort of thing."

"His profile must be pretty thin."

"It never hurts to verify details we already know." He looked at Beth, waiting.

"I'll have to think about it," she said.

"I see," Lathrop said, trying hard to hide his irritation. His eyes went to the notebook. "Cui bono." He arranged his face in an affable smile. "It explains a lot. The Russians wanted the equations of course, but they also love any trouble between the Chinese and us. So, with minimal risk, because Han did most of the work, they get the equations while the Chinese get the blame."

He turned to Teddy. "That's why they went to such lengths to make it look like you were in China. But the subtlest part wasn't fooling us—it was fooling you. Much smarter than just killing you off. The Chinese could have denied their involvement till doomsday, but who'd have believed them? Because there you'd be, half-lobotomized but still able to remember all

311

kinds of details about your capivity in China. Walking proof of Chinese barbarity.''

"And you'd have swallowed it," Beth said.

Lathrop looked unhappy. "Those decisions come from on high.''

"Sure."

"Would they have bothered with a real sub at the end?" Teddy asked.

"No. They had to use one the first time. It was their best prop, especially with a few of Han's men dressed as sailors so you never saw a Russian face. Then, with you unconscious, they rendezvoused with another boat—we've impounded a fifty-foot Bertram registered in Heidemann's name—and sent you to the backyard sub. You probably weren't on the *Timoshenko* for more than an hour.''

"You mean I was back on land while Beth was still in the water?"

"I hadn't thought of that. I guess so.''

"That was the first hitch in their plans, wasn't it?" Teddy said. "Even if its import wasn't widely recognized at the time.''

"I'm not following," Lathrop said.

"I'm talking about Beth seeing the submarine. And identifying it.''

"Oh. I suppose you could say that. She must have come within a few minutes of actually seeing you." Lathrop cleared his throat. "In any case, on the way back they'd just have driven you around in the van for a while, put you back in the cement mixer, and drugged you. You'd have come to in a dinghy a mile or two offshore.''

"And all of that just because I wanted to trace my parents?"

"That started it. When you contacted Heidemann he panicked. He was afraid that once in China, someone like you would be able to get enough official help to discover his involvement in the murder of your parents, as well as the fact that he's been an employee of a criminal organization for thirty-five years. A criminal organization with ties to the Kuomintang. The Chinese government still has an obsession with the Kuomintang, so Heidemann's fears weren't groundless. He contacted Han. Han saw the threat, both to Heidemann and himself, but he didn't get to where he was by panicking easily. He saw a way of exploiting the situation, politically and financially. I say financially because the Russians must have paid him a fortune. All he had to do was drug you and play on your interest in your parents while covering up any trace of that interest over here, because he couldn't risk suspicion in that area.''

"Beth proved that.''

Lathrop made a vaguely affirmative sound.

"Was Heidemann also covering up the fact that the U.S. government was behind the murder of Teddy's parents?'' Beth asked.

Lathrop's eyes narrowed. Beth knew that in a minute they could be yelling at each other again. "Rex Heidemann was not an employee of the U.S. government.''

"As of what date?''

"That is classified information.''

"I'll bet it is. What kind of deal did the U.S. government make with Jimmy Han in nineteen forty-nine?''

"I'm unaware of any deal.'' Lathrop struggled to keep an even tone.

"Was the Taiwanese government involved?'' Teddy asked.

"We have no evidence of that.'' Lathrop glanced up at Beth from under his eyebrows, as though expecting a blow. "No hard evidence.''

Beth and Teddy rose to leave. Lathrop hurried around his desk and opened the door. He could hardly wait till they were gone.

But Beth had one more question. "What's being done about the Russians?''

"We're working on that. It won't be easy. All the evidence is inferential—don't forget the *Timoshenko* came up empty. But they must have had an agent close by—they were so quick to evaluate the equations. We'll let you know as soon as we've got something. Don't worry.''

"I'm not worried.''

She and Teddy were far ahead of Lathrop.

They already knew that the Russians had an agent close by: someone who knew a lot about number theory, but had told Beth he didn't; someone who'd tried to learn whether the long-haired man had said anything before he died; someone who'd known their wedding date, and passed the information on to Jimmy Han; someone who had helped her analyze the drugged teabags because it cast suspicion on the Chinese and away from him.

They drove across the bridge to Berkeley and parked in front of the tall terraced house on Shasta Road. Trotsky was by the front door, shut in the kind of cage used for taking dogs on airplanes. The door wasn't locked. They walked in.

Marty Kesselman wasn't in his psychedelic basement, and he wasn't wearing running gear. They found him in the living room, wearing a suit and tie. He was packing a suitcase.

"Going on a trip, Marty?" Teddy asked.

Marty didn't look up. "I was thinking about it."

"Where?" Beth asked. Marty kept packing. "Someplace with a fat bank account waiting in your name?"

Marty picked up his jogging shoes and started wedging them into the sides of the suitcase.

"Those equations were wrong, Marty," Teddy said, "from beginning to end."

Marty's hands stopped moving.

"Your friends will find out eventually," Beth said. "If they don't know already. They won't be happy."

Beth and Teddy left Marty squatting by his suitcase.

They went home and stood on the balcony. "There's one thing I never liked about you," Teddy said.

"What's that?"

"Your nose. It was too perfect. Now it's got character." He gave it a kiss.

"Enjoy it while you can. I'm having it fixed."

Sailboats raced across the Bay. One put up a spinnaker. It puffed out like a plump breast.

"Let's get married," Teddy said.

"Let's get pregnant first."

He put his arms around her. "Would now be too soon?"

There was a knock at the door.

Teddy answered it. A messenger handed him a package, addressed to Beth.

There was no note inside. Just a bottle Of Romanée-Conti, 1962.

"Romanée-Conti, nineteen sixty-two!"

"Open it up," Beth said. "I'll tell you later."